LIFE ON EARTH

Nigel lay quietly as the machines sniffed and poked at him. Then Ted Landon came in and Nigel smiled wanly as he went through the customary hospital-visiting remarks. Ted was nervous. To deflect him, Nigel asked about research.

"Oh, we're pretty much sure that idea of yours was right," Ted said. "The EMs must've tinkered with their genes to come up with that semiconductor and electrical storage system. Their radio is natural. The Watchers seem to be hunting down technology. Ergo, natural radio is safe."

"Could be. We'll have to study them more to be sure, but it seems—"

"'Fraid not," Ted stated flatly. "We're moving on."

"What?" Nigel spat out.

"Just got a long squirt from Earth. We have a new target star. A long trip."

"Why?"

"Things have changed back there. New life-forms." Ted looked at him bleakly. "Somebody's seeded our oceans. Using starships..."

Bantam Spectra Books by Gregory Benford
Ask your bookseller for the titles you have missed

ACROSS THE SEA OF SUNS
HEART OF THE COMET
(with David Brin)
IN THE OCEAN OF NIGHT

ACROSS THE SEA OF SUNS

GREGORY BENFORD

BANTAM BOOKS
TORONTO · NEW YORK · LONDON · SYDNEY · AUCKLAND

*This low-priced Bantam Book
has been completely reset in a type face
designed for easy reading, and was printed
from new plates. It contains the complete
text of the original hard-cover edition.*
NOT ONE WORD HAS BEEN OMITTED.

ACROSS THE SEA OF SUNS

*A Bantam Book / published by arrangement with
the author*

PRINTING HISTORY

*Simon & Schuster edition published April 1983
Bantam edition / August 1987*

*Bantam Books are published by Bantam Books, Inc. Its trade-
mark, consisting of the words "Bantam Books" and the por-
trayal of a rooster, is Registered in U.S. Patent and Trademark
Office and in other countries. Marca Registrada. Bantam
Books, Inc., 666 Fifth Avenue, New York, New York 10103.*

PRINTED IN THE UNITED STATES OF AMERICA

KR   0 9 8 7 6 5 4 3 2 1

To DAVID HARTWELL

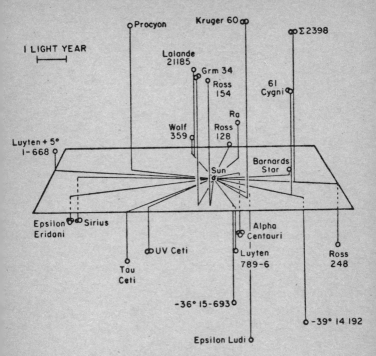

THE NEARBY STARS

After the final no there comes a yes
And on that yes the future world depends.
No was the night. Yes is this present sun.

Wallace Stevens

ONE

Fire boils aft, pushing the ship close to the knife edge of light speed. Its magnetic throats dimple the smooth dipolar field.

—An arrow scratching across the black—

—blue-white exhaust plume of fizzing hydrogen—

—a granite-gray asteroid riding the roaring blowtorch—

It sucks in the interstellar dust. Mixes a caldron of iostopes. And spews them out the back, an ultraviolet flare in the swallowing abyss.

Inside, Nigel Walmsley was eating oysters.

The last of the wine, he thought moodily, peering into his cup. And it was. As nearly as ship's rumor had it, nobody else had brought more than a bottle or so, and that had been well exhausted in the last two years.

He swirled the cup and swallowed the final chilled mouthful. The Pinot Chardonnay cut the faintly metallic taste of the oysters and left only the sea flavor and the succulent texture, a memory of Earth. He drank the last cold liquid from the shells and savored it. Eight light-years from Earth, the echo of the Gulf Stream faded.

"That's the lot," Nigel murmured.

"Uh . . . what?"

He realized he had been neglecting his guest. Ted had arrived unannounced, after all, and dead on the supper hour, as well. "I doubt I'll be able to replace California Chardonnay, and certainly not oysters."

"Oh. No, I suppose not. Are . . . are you sure the oysters were still okay?" Ted Landon shifted awkwardly.

"Considering they've been vac-stored for years, you mean?" Nigel shrugged. "We'll see." He lounged back on the tatami mat, nearly elbowing a lacquered lamp into oblivion.

1

His nudity clearly bothered Ted. The man moved again, adjusting his cross-legged sitting position. Well, so be it; Nigel hadn't had time yet to run out some chairs in the wood shop.

Ted's tobacco pouch appeared. "Mind?" Nigel shook his head. During meals, he did, yes, but Ted probably knew that already. He knew everything. They had a personality profile on Nigel a yard long, even in ferrite storage. He'd seen it himself.

A slow, profound stuffing of the pipe. "Y'know, when I heard you were carving an apartment in the Low Amenity Area, I thought you'd be living pretty raw. But this looks great."

Nigel nodded and studied the living room, trying to see it with Ted's eyes.

—crimson vase, pale yellow flower sprouting, tray cupping single flake of smoldering incense, teakwood box, gossamer paper walls, oblique blades of yellow light drawing motes upward in the fanned air—wait until Ted had to excrete and found the loo, a hole lined with porcelain straight from Korea, closed with a wooden cover, on either side stepping-stones in the shape of feet for the slow learners: squat and deliver, why put a mask on a valuable moment of the day—

"What gives?" Nigel asked, lapsing into transatlantic shorthand.

Ted looked at him flatly, still slightly edgy. "I'm reorganizing staff."

Aha. "You're the new Works Manager."

"That's not the term, but—look, Nigel, there are some hard choices."

"Indeed."

Ted gave a smile, reassuring and broad but capable of vanishing, along with the flicker of one eyelid, as suddenly as it had come.

"You've been an ExOp so far."

"Gridded, yes." Nigel was too old to do the work directly, with his own muscle power. But his coordination and reflexes, enhanced by constant medservice, were still good. So they linked him by grid into servo'd robots that operated outside the ship.

"Well, y'see, there's a big waiting list for that job classification. And you're . . ."

"Too old," Nigel said bluntly.

"Well, a lot of people think so. When the community vote came in—the vote on who'll do what in Isis space—you got a lot of red flags."

"Not surprising."

"So I'm here to ask you to resign. Drop out of ExOp."

"No."

"What?"

Surely it couldn't have been that difficult to follow. "No."

"But community votes are pretty near binding."

"No, they're merely indicative. My fellow crewmen can't give me the sack, *zip*, like that. *You're* the command structure, Ted. Surely you know you can overrule anything short of an absolute majority in the community."

"Well—"

"And with 1266 voting, I doubt a majority wanted me out of my slot. Most don't know my work, or care."

Ted had a small habit. He braced his jaw a bit and tightened his mouth, so slightly that Nigel could scarcely see the pressure whiten the red of his lips. Then he touched his front teeth together and rubbed them carefully back and forth, as though he were methodically sharpening them against each other. His jaw muscles rippled.

"Technically, Nigel, you're right."

"Fine, then."

"But your sense of community must lead you to see that active opposition by a significant minority is, well, contrary to the long-term interests of our mission and—"

"Bloody hell!"

Again Ted made his teeth-sharpening motion, jaw muscles flexing. "The alternative job I think you'll find quite attractive."

"What is it?"

"Heavy foundry work."

Fusing the asteroid rock, prestressing struts, using laser cutters and e-beams. "Socketed?"

"Uh, yes, of course."

They hooked you into the big machines, connected you at hip and knee and elbow and wrist, the delicate electronic interface matching directly to your nerves. And you sensed the machine, you felt the machine, you worked the machine, you served the machine, you were the machine. "No."

"You've been using that word a lot lately, Nigel."

"It's terribly economical."

Ted sighed—spontaneous, or calculated? Hard to tell—and clapped his big hands to his knees. The zazen position was uncomfortable for him, even with his shoes off. For some reason most guests adopted that position, even though Nigel usually sprawled on the cushions. Perhaps they felt the rectangular simplicity of this Oriental room suggested a spine-straightening discipline to its inhabitants. To Nigel it suggested just the opposite.

"Nigel, I know you won't like leaving external operations, but I think after you made the switch to foundry work, you'd feel—"

"Like a canceled stamp."

Ted's face reddened suddenly. "Damn it, I expect sacrifice from everyone on board! When I ask you to change jobs, elementary—"

Nigel waved him to silence. He had found that a particularly abrupt gesture, ending in a thrust forefinger, nearly always stopped Ted's rapid-fire attacks. A valuable trick. "And if I don't comply? The Slowslots?"

This had the intended effect. Dragging the Slowslots suddenly to stage center raised the stakes. This in turn disturbed the controlled way administrators liked to negotiate, and also brought floating to Ted's mind the fact that Nigel had helped develop the Slowslots as a volunteer guinea pig; he had already paid dues that were more than metaphorical.

"Nigel . . ." Ted drawled, shaking his head soberly. "I'm surprised you would think in those terms. No one in the *Lancer* community wants to stick you into a sleep box. Your friends are simply trying to tell you that perhaps it is time to step aside from the tasks that require reflexes, skill, and stamina which—let's face the facts—you're gradually losing. We all—"

"Right. In other words, they've always seen my appointment to a real, working exo job as a political fish thrown to a 3-D-elevated seal."

"Harsh words, Nigel. And of course completely untrue."

Nigel smiled and laced his hands behind his neck, leaning back with elbows high, easing the quiet chorus of strain in his lower back muscles. "Not so far from the mark as you might think," he said almost dreamily. "Not so far . . ." His mind flitted over old pictures: the alien incursion into the solar system, the pearly sphere of the *Snark*, an exploratory vessel he had met for only moments, beyond the Moon; the *Mare Marginis* wreck, a crushed eggshell that had fallen from the stars a million years ago; the webbed logic of the *Marginis* alien computer that had taught them how to build *Lancer*. He had been there, he had seen it, but now the pictures were faded.

Ted said solemnly, "I had hoped to impress you with the weight of opinion behind this vote. We'll be in Isis space within months. The surface teams must begin practicing in earnest. I cannot in all good—"

"I'll go on fallback status," Nigel said casually.

"What?"

"Put me in the reserve exploration unit. There'll be dead times when we're on the surface, surely. Times when most of the crew is asleep or working on something else. You won't want those servo'd modules standing idle on the surface, will you? I'll simply hold down the position, keep watch until the real working crew comes back on control."

"Ummmm. Well, it's not exactly what I had—"

"I don't give a ruddy toss for your plans, if you must know the truth. I'm offering a compromise."

"Backup isn't a full-time position."

"I'll do scutwork, then."

"Well . . ."

"Hydro jobs. Agri, perhaps. Yes, I'd like that."

He watched Ted savor this new possibility. The man treated the idea like a small quick animal, probably no threat but unpredictable, as likely to sink fangs into his thumb as it was to suddenly dart off in unexpected directions. Nigel was neither snake nor sturgeon, though, and Ted disliked things without labels. Behind *Lancer*'s cosmetic groupgov policy lurked these traditional top-down managers, with instincts as old as Tyre.

Ted's smile suddenly reappeared. "Good. Good. Nigel, I'm happy you were able to see it our way."

"Indeed."

"Nigel."

A weighty silence. "There's something more, Ted."

"Yes, there is. I think you ought to realize that you are

kind of... distant... from your fellow crew members. That might have influenced this vote."

"Different generation."

Ted looked around at the flat, mute surfaces of the room. Most interiors in *Lancer* covered every wall with a crisp image of forest or ocean or mountains. Here there were severe angles and no ersatz exteriors. Ted seemed to find it unsettling. Nigel watched him shift his sitting again and tried to read what the man was thinking. It was becoming harder for Nigel to understand people like Ted without committing himself to the draining process of letting himself go into them completely. Then, too, Ted was an American. Nigel had lived in the United States a great portion of his life but he retained his English habits of mind. Many of the senior positions on *Lancer* were held by the affable American managerial types like Ted, and more than age differences separated Nigel from them.

"Look," Ted began again, his voice resolute and factual, "we all know you're... well, your neural activity was somehow maximized by the *Marginis* computer. So your sensory input, your processing, your data correlation—it can all occur on a lot of levels. Simultaneously. With clarity."

"Uh-huh."

"You're going to seem a little odd, sure." He smiled winningly. "But do you have to be so standoffish? I mean, if you even gave some sign of trying to get through to us about what it's *like*, even, I think—"

"Tanaka and Xiaoping and Klein and Mauscher..." Nigel gave the names a drum-roll cadence. Those men had come after him and experimented with the alien *Marginis* computer net. They had all been altered, all thought differently, all reported seeing the world with an oblique intensity.

"Yes, I know their work," Ted broke in. "Still—"

"You've read their descriptions. Seen the tapes."

"Sure, but—"

"If it's any help. I can't make much out of that stuff, myself."

"Really? I'd guess that you would all have a lot in common."

"We do. For example, none of us talks very well about it."

"Why not?"

"What's the point? That's scarcely the way to go."

"The 3-D that Xiaoping made, that means a lot to us. If you—"

"But it doesn't to *me*. And that fact itself is more important than anything else I can tell you."

"If you'd just—"

"Very well. Look, there are four states of consciousness. There's *Aha!* and *Yum-yum* and *Oy vey!* But most of the time there's *Ho-hum*." Nigel grinned madly.

"Okay, okay. I should know better." Ted smiled wanly. He sipped the dregs of his tea. Nigel shifted position, taking less of his weight on the knobby end of his spine. This apartment was farther out from *Lancer*'s spin axis, so the local centrifugal tug was stronger than at his old digs in the dome. As he moved his skin crinkled and folded like a bag used too long. He was still sinewy, but he knew better than anyone how his muscles were tightening, growing stringy and uncertain. He looked at the blotchy red freckles on his hands and allowed himself a sigh. Ted would misinterpret the sound, but what the hell.

Ted chuckled. "I'll have to remember that. Hu-hum, yes. Hey, look," he said brightly, preparing to leave, "your response on this job thing was first-class. Glad it worked out. Glad we stopped the problem before it got, well, harder."

Nigel smiled, knowing they hadn't stopped anything at all.

TWO

"What do you think Ted really means?" Nikka said.

They strolled along a path that wrapped all the way around the inside of the dome. The best part was a hundred-meter patch of forest, dense with pines and oaks and leafy bushes. It may have been his imagination, but the air seemed better there, less stale.

"Probably no more than he says. For now."

"Do you think they'll do the same to me?"

A fine mist drifted over the treetops, obscuring the fields which hung directly over their heads. In the distance, along the axis, Nigel could make out the other side of the dome. Cottonball clouds accumulated along the zero-g axis of the dome, and through them he could see a distant green carpet, so far away only the Euclidean scratches of the planting rows were apparent: a garden zone.

"He said nothing about it." Nigel turned to her, spreading his hands. "And at any rate, whatever for?"

"Next to you, I'm the oldest crew member."

"But, blast it!—you're not *old*."

"Nigel, we're two decades ahead of anybody else in the crew."

He shrugged. "My work requires motor skills. And they're dead right, I'm getting stiff and awkward. But you're a general handy type. There's no—"

"Your years in the Slowslots retarded all that."

"Some. Not a lot."

Nikka walked faster, her vexed energy coming out in a particular irked way she had of swinging her hips into her stride. She was still in marvelous condition, he thought. Her straight black hair was drawn back in a Spartan sheath above her lidded, open face. It joined a natural cascade at the crown, to become a jaunty black torrent down half her back. Nigel forced himself to look at her as though she were a stranger, trying for Ted's perspective. With age her skin had stretched tight over her high cheekbones. She didn't have her full strength any longer, granted, or the gloss of early middle age she'd once had. But she was a fine, slim edifice that showed no signs of sinking squat and Earthward.

She breathed in the air with obvious relish. It was better here, near the plants and algae vats. If you closed your eyes you could very nearly think you were in a genuine forest. You could blot out the muted bass rumble of the unending fusion flame.

"Nigel, it seems so *long*," she said suddenly, plaintively.

He nodded. Twelve years since *Lancer* fired its dropaway accelerators and boosted achingly up to light speed. He took her hand and squeezed. They had all passed the vast tracts of time with their work, with study, with experiments like the Slowslots, with astronomical observations. But the years had weight and presence.

* * *

Lancer was a rush job.

In 2021 a giant radio net, laced across the far side of the Moon, picked up an odd signal. It was a weak, shifting pattern, amplitude-modulated. It came in sharp at 120 megahertz, smack in the middle of the commercial radio band. Originally, the farside radio grid had been strung to carry out astrophysical studies in the low-frequency range, down to the 10 kilohertz region. The designers at Goldstone, Bonn and Beijing had only recently installed gear to take the system up into the megahertz range, because the jammed commercial bands were so noisy now that sensitive astrophysical work was impossible from Earth's surface. The Moon made an effective shield.

The emission pattern had, as the jargon went, significant nonrandom elements. Patterns would rise out of the galactic background radio noise and then, before the sequence of amplitude modulations could form a coherent pattern, the dim electromagnetic tremor faded.

The most likely explanation was some intermittent natural process, perhaps resembling Jupiter's decametric sputtering. That radiation came from electron swarms in Jupiter's magnetic belts. Waves passing through the belts made the electrons bunch together, so that they radiated like a natural antenna. Jupiter's emissions had wavelengths hundreds of meters long, well below the megahertz range. To explain these new emissions, astronomers invoked a gas giant planet with much stronger magnetic fields, or higher electron densities.

When they pinpointed the source, this model made sense. It was BD +36°2147, a dim red star 8.1 light-years away, and it seemed to have a large planet. This was somewhat embarrassing.

The funding agency, ISA, wondered why a star that close had not been checked routinely for unusual emissions. An obvious explanation was that the action and the grants were in high-energy, spectacular objects—pulsars, quasars, radio jets. Also, the small, red stars were boring. They were hard to see and they led dull lives. BD +36°2147 had never been named. The scramble of letters and numbers simply meant that the star had appeared first in the Bonner Durchmeisterung catalog in the nineteenth century. The declination angle was

+36 degrees and 2147 was a serial number in the catalog, related to the star's other coordinate, Right Ascension.

From the star's slight wobble, one could deduce that something large and dark was revolving around it. That was a perfectly logical candidate for the superJovian. Orbital optical telescopes had by this time found hundreds of dark companions around nearby stars, proving that planetary systems were fairly common, and ending a centuries-old argument.

The first unsettling fact came to light when ISA poked around in the old survey reports from Earth-based radio telescopes. It turned out that BD +36°2147 *had* been observed, repeatedly. There had been no detectable emission. The present radio waves must have started sometime in the last three years.

The second surprise came along a few months later. For one rare two-minute interval, a strong wave pattern got through. The amplitude-modulated signal was a carrier wave, just like commericial AM radio. Filtered and speeded up and fed to an audio output, it quite clearly said the word "and." Nothing more. A week later, another three minute portion said "Nile." The big radio ear was now cupped continuously at BD +36°2147. Seven months later it picked up "after."

The words came through with aching slowness. Some radio astronomers argued that this might be an odd way of cost cutting. As the signal faded in and out, a listener missing a piece of a long sound could still recognize the word. But this theory did not explain why the signal blurred and shifted so frustratingly. It was as though the distant station started transmitting one word and then changed to another before the first was finished.

The signals continued, occasionally coughing forth a fragment, a word, a syllable—but never enough for a clear message. Still, they had to be artificial. That killed the superJovian magnetosphere theory. They kept to a fairly sharp frequency, though, and this proved useful.

Eight months of careful observations picked up a Doppler shift in the frequency. The shift repeated every twenty-nine days. The logical explanation was that the scattered pulses came from a planet, and that planet moved alternately toward and away from Earth as it orbited the red dwarf star. Optical observations fixed the star's luminosity, and reliable theory then could give the star's probable mass. It was 0.32 solar masses, an M2 star. Given the twenty-nine-day "year" of the planet, and the dwarf's mass, Newton's laws said the planet was nine times closer to its cool star than Earth was to the sun.

That was as far as observations from near-Earth could go. The radio teams spent years trying to see a Doppler shift from the revolution of the planet itself. It wasn't there, but nobody expected it to be. A planet that close to its star would be locked with one face eternally sunward, due to the tidal tug between them. Earth's Moon and the Galilean satellites of Jupiter were tide-locked to their planets, after all. Mercury would be locked toward the sun, but for the competing pull from the other planets.

But tide-locked worlds were deadly. Everybody knew that. One side would be seared and the other frozen. Who could survive such a place and erect a radio transmitter? Did they only live in the twilight band?

The only way to find out was to go and see. In 2029, ISA launched small relativistic probes on near-recon missions to BD +36°2147. One failed in a burst of gamma rays 136 light-years from Earth. The inboard diagnostics told a lot about the flare-up in the fusion burn, before the ship disintegrated. ISA adjusted the burn in the second probe and it survived, to dive past the BD +36°2147 system at 0.99 light speed.

It spotted a gas giant in the right place to cause the star's wobble, as seen from Earth. But the radio mumble came from an Earth-sized world nearer the star. The probe had been programmed to pass near the gas giant, since its orbit could be deduced from BD +36°2147's slight rhythm. The other planet was exactly on the other side of the red dwarf star when the probe shot through, so the automatic devices, in a mad scramble to readjust, did not get much data.

Small, fast probes were cheap. The International Space Agency favored them. But they couldn't respond flexibly, and game theory proved they were a bad strategic choice, in the face of unknown risks.

The best posture, the conflict metricians calculated, was reconnaissance in force: *Lancer*. So the three superpowers used their muscle and appropriated the just-finished Libration Colony project. ISA took the life zone inside the spinning asteroid world, tunneled more rooms in the rock, and added duralith thrust chambers that could bottle a fusion burn. The design was a copy of the *Mare Marginis* wreck and it worked well. They stirred the soils, planted crops, burrowed hallways, sliced rock, and fine-tuned a miniature ecology inside the hollowed-out ellipsoidal dome.

All this, to fly at velocities a hairline below light. Toward the red beacon of BD $+36°2147$, now renamed Ra. The word "Nile" in the transmission, while seemingly irrelevant and possibly a mistake—the error bars in the decoding were significant—became a pretext for invoking Egyptian mythology. The transmitting world was named Isis for the goddess of fertility. The outer gas giant was named for her son, Horus. The astronomical community took two years to decide all this, there were letters discussing the matter in the London *Times*. The engineers, of course, didn't give a damn.

As they walked on through the fields grain rustled, and the dry rasping was like Kansas on a ripe fall day. Nigel shielded his eyes against the hard glare of the phosphors. The huge squares were regularly spaced in the curving floor of the dome, illuminating the fields on the opposite side, powering the ecology of *Lancer*. Wraparound lighting. The fusion burn in *Lancer*'s throat gave ample electricity for the phosphor panels, but to Nigel it still seemed like a wasteful squandering of photons.

Nikka interrupted his thoughts with, "What do you think is our best tactic?"

"Um?"

"We have to keep down criticism of us. Of our . . ."

"Decaying physical abilities."

"Yes."

"Right, then—we should work in modest jobs. Low profile."

"Until we reach Isis."

"Then—well, we maneuver ourselves into interesting work."

"Don't let them argue us into a desk job."

"Right. Maybe we'll have to be content with merely controlling robots or something, but—"

"No paper pushing."

"Just so. Meanwhile—"

"Stave off the bastards."

She smiled and repeated with some relish, "Stave off the bastards."

Months before, *Lancer* had dropped a self-constructing radio net, letting it tumble away in the wake. Riding inside a cocoon of shock-ionized plasma, they could not make high-resolution radio maps.

The net uncurled and deployed. Alex controlled the servo'd antennas by remote, painstakingly assembling aperture synthesis maps of the Ra system. The star itself flared violently, sending tongues high into its corona. Detailed mapping of their target, Isis, took much longer.

Nikka prodded Nigel awake when their apartment Sec chimed. "Let me be," he growled.

"Stop doing your croc-in-the-sun impersonation. It's the Assembly review of the first Isis map. You wanted to see it."

"Ah. I'd fancy that."

Nikka tapped her wrist and the wall screen clicked on. She silenced Alex's voice-over explanations and enlarged the map. Nigel peered at the round image. The Isis disk was a spaghetti scramble of contour lines.

"Planetary acne," he said.

Nikka said, "Looks like a river valley system, there."

"Couldn't be. Trick of the eye, probably. This isn't radar, remember. They're picking up the Isis transmissions."

"How can it come from all over the planet?"

He squinted. "It *can't*. The simple, efficient way to send across interstellar distances is with one fixed antenna."

"Yes . . ." She combed back her sleek black hair with her fingers. "Or so we think."

"Electromagnetic waves are culture-independent. Makes no sense to use lots of antennas."

He tapped into the interactive-mode discussion, still lying in bed. No interesting ideas surfaced. "Wait'll we're closer," he said.

Nikka dialed the map to max scale. "I *still* say it looks like a river valley."

THREE

Isis was a red world. *Mars-tinged*, Nigel thought, staring down at it. But rich with air, cloud-choked.

One warm face forever pinned toward Ra, the other staring blank and frozen into the eternal cold: tide-locked. In the immemorial night the land groaned beneath vast blue glaciers. Half a planet, capped in ice.

Winds from the twilight fed the great, slumbering, white-crusted mountains, bringing breaths of fresh moisture. At the eternal dawn line where dim pink light licked, icebergs calved into a red ocean. The sea circled Isis, pole to pole, separating ice and land. It was pink and glinting, scratched by winds, dotted with orange-yellow clouds.

More sunward still, broad fans of waves battered at the base of steep, flinty chasms. The sea clawed at the rising ramparts of the one vast stained brown continent.

Fingers of water thrust inland, toward Ra. River valleys carved the gray granite, as if clutching the world's face, to force it toward the fire. Fingers: poking at the Eye.

Channel #11: "Yeah, that pattern, what'd I say, fits the theory. Perfect stress pattern there, you can see the normal faulting and graben at the poles—"

Channel #20: "Jess a sec, theh ah no poles at all, an' if I unnerstan your calc, your equilibrium is wrong from step one—"

Channel #5: "—Jeezus, check the chem inventory down there, I'd—"

Channel #11: "No, I've got a whole continuum of theoretical equilibria I can use and this case fits in; it all works if we assume Isis formed rotating, with a bulge at the equator, and then when Ra spun it down that released the centrifugal energy, so Isis tried to readjust its surface to get rid of that pot belly, and you get fracturing in a global pattern—"

Channel #5: "—too much absorption in those oceans, an' some odd lines, lookit those spikes around 5480 angstroms, that's not—"

Channel #18: "Funny, the lakes in those highlands, partway out from the Eye, they're blue, but the ocean is *pink*. I guess whatever—"

Channel #5: "That's fresh rainfall up there in the mountain passes, melted snow, it *should* look blue—"

Channel #11: "—that leaves the equator free, see, so thrust faults split the dome pattern, and the energy got released toward the rim—"

Channel #20: "Okay, no poles, your calc stipped a bound'ry layer an' thahs what makes the calc work out. Those headwalls in the rim gouge pattern, see 'at? I guess they prove some kinda big crust relaxation when it slowed down, started a whole big tectonic process—"

Channel #5: "—the 5480 structure is just backscatter from the hills, must be, Nigel, 'cause that's the iron silicate group clear as day, damn muddy day down there though, an'—"

Channel #11: "—you get these compression networks that give those wrench faults, or lateral faults, I can see them on this IR blowup, here, lots of rifting, a whole morphology set up when the planet spun down—"

Channel #3: "—but then what're those ghastly spikes dead center of the polarization pattern, eh? You're surely not going to ask me to believe a mud flat is giving us those spikes, are you? Scarcely. The *sea* is giving us those, and it has to have iron oxides to do that and give sufficient line strength—"

Channel #18: "Blue lakes means that whatever makes the seas red *doesn't* operate at high altitudes—"

Channel #5: "That's garbage, there can't be a height effect with that kind of gentle gradient, it just won't support a—"

Channel #18: "Okay, then it takes time to make the chemistry go, so by the time the rainfall has run down to the lowlands something's—"

Channel #29: "—he'd got that wrong *twice*, Christ, so I kinda shrug and mutter, nothing wrong with having nothing to say, sure but try not to say it out loud, and the sonabitch went straight to Gulvinch about it then—"

Channel #20: "—intensifahs all 'at till the domed strata— yeah, 'at's the ticket—they can't support the shear stress an' they rupture, all back unner that ice on the other hemisphere too I bet, uh-huh, an' you get lotsa cyclin' in the surface materials, rip open the seams ever' couple hunnert thousan' years, think what that does to the rep rate with the *atmo*sphere when you bake out that iron exposed fresh ever' time—"

Channel #5: "Look, that's one thing we *do* know: look at that spectrum, it would be a reducing atmosphere with all that iron, for sure, except the oxygen levels get pumped up, but even so it's only around the two percent level, two percent O_2, you can see that right here, look, it's just a spike out on that wing, the line strengths are wrong, nothing like Earth, but I bet it's the same damn process, the same way our air converted over from reducing billions of years back, trouble is it's not much O_2 is it? Not damn much if you want to breathe down there."

Channel #6: "It's *both* forms, open your eyes, lay that one over the other and it jumps right out at you—"

Channel #3: "Ah, ferrous and ferric. Both. So there's a lot of oxygen down there, as much as Earth, but it's tied up in the iron."

Channel #29: "—nothing I could say would—"

Channel #20: "—so see this fits what the backscatter boys say, the faultin' rips up the goddamn turf so much the iron gets reprocessed alla time an' the air, it jess can't hold onto its oxygen, the water jess runs off ever' time it rains an' the sea, it's jess this solution a ferrous crap, 'at's where th' O_2 is, man I tell you—"

Channel #56: "That jocko over in P4 has got some crazy idea, lissen to him, thinks it's all iron, but give a gear at this, in the big spot there, see that big volcano, that's sulfur for sure, big spouts of it coming out reg'lar as Maybelle, sulfur volcanoes smack in the middle of the Eye, and if that doesn't tie up a lot of oxy, with those winds, I mean, we measured, gusting velocity from the action-frame zats and they'll mix the whole damn atmosphere in two, maybe three years, so you've got sulfur oxide all down there, that's what the Eye *is*, that's not sand dunes, not silicon dioxide, it's *sulfur* dioxide—"

The picture sharpened as computers edited out random refractions from the clotted air below. Isis swam nearer.

Yellow. A dry, ancient yellow. Smooth sands of it, shimmering, flecked with tan ridges of weathered rock. The Eye peered at Ra, which hung forever directly overhead. Out from the hard-baked center, the subsolar point, swept winds heavy with pungent acid dust. Dunes marched before the winds in ranks a hundred kilometers long. Slowly they swerved as the air currents circled, following a trade-wind pattern, returning to the blistered pupil of the Eye, surging in a timeless cycle.

The Eye's edge faded into russet, then into brown. A hint of moisture; scrub desert. Rumpled red hills built into a concentric ring of mountains: socket of the Eye. Snow dotted the peaks white. High valleys cupped cold air over the steel-blue sheen of lakes.

The steady rub of the Eye winds had smoothed the land. The breeze stirred up pink dust, thick sheets that poured over the high mountain slopes and down, outward from the Eye, filling the valleys with a roiling haze. Only in the shifting spots where neither clods nor dust lay upon the land could the distant telescopes see the dry plains and carved valleys of Isis.

The single, immense, concentric mountain range was intricate and fault cut. Muddy rivers ran down the broad slopes, away from the Eye, toward the planet-circling sea. Farther from the Eye, scrub desert yielded to matted vegetation. Brown grass. Something like trees. Shades of brown, of pinks and grays and pale orange.

A fine dust hung in the lower air, fuzzing optical images, stealing definition. Only in the infrared was the seeing good enough to distinguish objects in the five-meter scale range. Large flora. Bands of vegetation crowding the snaking rivers.

The IR peered down and picked out detail. Dark beds of plant life in the sea. Grasslands. And then, movement.

"RappleDex, this is Command. You guys got that system up yet, or do we kick ass out there?"

We got good definition in the radio right now, Ted. Give it a—

"I'm looking at it, Alex. What we want is the interferometry—"

"They're point sources, aren't they?"

"Nigel, this is Ted. Get off the comm lines."

"I'm a consultant, remember? Just eavesdropping, anyway."

"Okay, so long as you don't get in the way of—Hey, RD, when can we have—"

He's right, Ted, we still can't resolve the sources. They're damned small. Any really big dish we could see at a range of one AU, so I'd think by now we shoulda picked up—

"Okay, okay, that's interesting. But—"

—and the reason we've never been able to make sense out of the signals, we've got that figured now—

"Oh? What?"

There are these point sources, maybe a million of 'em, but they're not transmitting together. I mean, they're not in synch phase-locked. All the sources are trying to send the same stuff, but they're all a little behind or a little ahead of each other, so it gets muddied up.

"Beats the hell out of me, why somebody'd pick that way for interstellar communication."

"Alex, what is the length over which the signals *are* correlated?"

"Nigel, I asked you—"

"Leave *off* a bit, eh? Alex?"

Well, lemme run this here... Yeah, the spatial correlation length is about thirty klicks, maybe a little more.

"How does it fit in with the topography?"

Here, plug me in on that multichannel, Ted, and—Yeah, there it is.

"Does it follow the valley profiles?"

Uh, yeah. Sort of. Sources are strung out along the valleys. Not many in the mountains.

"The valleys are where the best living is. The water. Over to you, Ted."

"Many thanks, Nigel. It is nice to get a word in now and then. Let me get this straight, Alex. If you scan the interferometer across the valley, you find the signal is coherent. All the point sources are sending together?"

Correct.

"But if you go to the next valley, the sources are sending something slightly ahead or behind of the first valley?"

Yeah. That's what's so goddamn strange. The bit rate is still low, too. And the sources, they're not steady.

"How so?"

Well, every few minutes one of 'em will drop out. A new one comes in every now and then, too, so the number is about constant.

"Huh. Look, Alex, I called to ask about the outflyer dish. You were going to have it on line by 1400 hours, and that's come and gone. We need that bigger base line to get the definition we need, and we damn well need it *now*."

"Give it a rest, Ted."

"Nigel, I thought you—"

"Merely kibitzing, if you please. I'm sure Alex will have matters cleared up at his end if you cease ragging him about it. I wanted to take a moment to review all this, Ted. You've got the optical and IR profiles right in front of you, I'm sure."

"Yeah, you can come down here to Command and see them if you want."

"Already have. I'm sticking to this console, to use the self-programming capabilities. Anyway, Command is crowded."

"Okay, okay. If you'd wait for the input like the rest of the crew—"

"I was wondering if you'd considered the implications, Ted. No trace of cities. No urban areas. No big straight features, no fields or roads. And the EM transmissions are weak, except for that interstellar signal."

"Yeah. Damn funny. But maybe they're living under-ground, using all the land for agriculture, and they use cables for info transfer. Hell, we do that back on Earth. We wasted power on atmospheric transmissions only in the start-up days of radio and TV."

"Even agriculture has a signature, this close. We could see croplands."

"Maybe so, maybe so."

"I've been cross-correlating Alex's prelim fixes on the radio sources—the EM points, he calls 'em for electromagnetic—with the IR. Anyone in Command done that?"

"Uh, I don't—"

"I'd like to check my work. There are signal-to-noise problems and I've been using the self-programming subsystems to unfold it—"

"No, look, Nigel, we've been too busy to try all that yet. I'd suggest—"

"Point is, some of the EM points and the IR points are the same."

"Which ones?"

"There's the rub. It's the moving IR sources, looks like."

"The ones we got variable fixes on? I don't under—"

"What I'm saying, Ted, is that the radio transmitters give off heat as well. And most important, they're moving."

"Well, I don't—"

Hey, we've got this whole rig up, but you guys got to keep aligned with us or we'll have shit to show for it when—

"Alex, this is Ted, give us an overlay of your mapping. I want to match it—"

With the IR?

"Uh, yes."

Nigel was flimming me about that stuff. Wanted the early results. I just repped and verified the points he asked about. They're variable. Slow, but moving.

"You're sure?"

Yeah. The IR points are pretty weak, almost fuzzed out by the thermal landscape background.

Jenkins told me they were probably small volcanic vents—

"Not bloody likely."

"Since when did you become a geologist? Look, the dust and crap down there, nobody can be sure of that IR."

"Right. We have to go down and see."

"That's a little premature, Nigel. We're standing off at a safe distance. Going to surface mode now would violate our guidelines, and you know it."

"Dead right I know it. But that's what we'll have to do."

FOUR

Ted arrived at Nigel and Nikka's apartment a little late. He carried his usual prop, a clipboard jammed with notes. Nigel steered him first to the bar, then into the deep-cradled cushions of their new couch. Ted eased into it as if uncertain of its reliability; with its slanting legs and oblique joints, it looked rickety. Nigel had designed it for their apartment's low gravity, using the wood he had in his personal mass allotment. He was the only person in *Lancer* with high-quality oak, and he had carefully carved this, polishing it with the oil of his hands.

"Wish you'd come down to Command to talk," Ted began.

"It's a jam down there."

"Yeah, pretty busy. No wonder you stay home, low gravity, plenty of rest—"

Alex knocked; Nigel waved him in. Alex was a heavy, balding man, face dark with fatigue. He sat down on the couch like a man dumping a weight off his back. Muscles rippled in his shoulders as he flexed them, seeking an alert posture in the deep couch. Nigel had designed it to thwart such aims; finally Alex relaxed into it.

"Whoosh!" Alex puffed. "I been worshipin' those consoles like an acolyte."

"Drink?"

"Just make me go to sleep."

"You've brought them, though?" Ted prompted.

"Sure. I piped 'em down to your input here. They're waitin' on your screen."

Nigel said a soft "Thanks," and thumbed on their flat. The screen filled with a grid. Small white dots peppered the green field. "These are your time-stepped maps, Alex?" Nigel prompted.

"Yeah, weeks' worth. I followed 'em one by one. Talk about your low bit rate—"

Ted smiled and put his hands on his knees. "Well, it's first-class work, Alex, all of it. First-class."

Nikka sat zazen beside Nigel, studying the men. "But the message?" she asked. "That's what everyone's waiting for, enough phase-coherent signal to tell—"

"We've got it." The words came out dry and tired.

"You *have*?" Nigel said, surprised.

"Yeah. It's not all that hard, once you unnerstan' that there are maybe one, two million, sources on at once. Each winks on and off, but what they're doin' is trying to boost the signal up by, well, ever'body chippin' in."

Ted said carefully, "We haven't released the information yet because it's well, disturbing. But Alex has cracked it, that we're sure of. Until—"

Alex said wearily, emphatically, "It's a 1956 Arthur Godfrey show."

"What?" Nikka said. "You mean . . . literally?"

"Yeah. It's a slow, slow playback of a radio comedy broadcast in 1956."

"Jesus Christ," Nigel said with relish.

Ted began: "We've been trying to place this in a context, to understand—"

"So—we've come—!" Nigel erupted with laughter. The others sat, blinking, stunned. He roared on merrily, tears squeezing from under his eyelids. For a long moment the others were stiffly silent. Then they began to shift position awkwardly, looking at one another. Nikka slowly smiled. At last Nigel descended to a chuckle, gasped for breath, and seemed to notice them again.

"The Bracewell hypothesis!"

Ted nodded. "Some of us have ventured that explanation, but I feel it's too early—"

"Christ, it's obvious! Those poor sods down there are intelligent, no mistake about that."

Nikka interjected, "But no more so than Dr. Bracewell."

"Right," Nigel said, "because they've hit upon his same idea." He spread his hands, palms up, open and obvious. "They picked up weak radio signals from us. Mulled them over. To get our attention, they figured the smartest strategy was, send back the same thing. Not some clever mathematical code or TV picture—hell, they can't pick up TV, much less 3-D."

"Well..." Ted shifted among the pillows. "We've checked with our entertainment discs—an enormous file. The voice profile matches that of Arthur Godfrey, the most popular entertainer of the 1950s in the USA."

"Dead on," Nigel said. "A crummy, old, fleebag radio show. Scandalously banal. Something we'd recognize." He laughed again. "Ah, old Bracewell, would that thou could be with us now...."

Alex growled. "Depressing, you ask me. Come all this way, find out we're listening to ourselves."

Ted patted Alex's thick shoulder. "Look, this is a fantastic discovery. You're just tired."

"Yeah. Maybe." Alex sighed.

"You've got something more, then, Alex?" Nigel said lightly.

Alex brightened. "Uh, yeah, I had to track individual sources of the radio to get a phase fix. I figured, hell, might as well get 'em all. Just a rep-rate problem, following all those emitters on a time-sharing basis."

"Here." Ted tapped his own wrist comm and the flat screen stirred to life. The white dots began to move, some winking on and off. "These EMs are also hefty infrared sources. From their body heat, I guess. They're alive, and apparently each carries a transmitter."

"Perhaps a nomad culture?" Nikka said softly.

"Well, we're thought about that. they don't have fixed transmitters, that's for sure, but as for why—"

"Naw," Alex put in. "I got a few that don't move."

"Oh?" Ted asked, puzzled. "Is your resolution good enough to be—"

"Yeah, look, see that?" Alex lurched to his feet and walked to the flat. He pointed to a cluster of dots that did not join in the slow snowflake swirl. "These aren't goin' any-where. I can tell for sure 'cause they've got little individual signatures in the radio spectrum, if you look close. Li'l shifts in the phase and amplitude, stuff like that."

Nikka studied the dots as they moved in jagged little jumps. "A few remain still. Perhaps they are old? They no longer take part in the nomadic cycle?"

"Doesn't look nomadic to me," Nigel said. "They aren't moving all together. Look how well spaced they are. They don't cluster."

Ted nodded. "Correct. They move through the valley systems, Alex thinks. Sometimes they follow the dust clouds, sometimes not."

"Any optical fix yet?" Nigel asked.

Ted shook his head. "Dust, clouds, damn dim sunlight in the first place . . ."

"What is the next step, then? We cannot stand out here in the dark forever," Nikka declared firmly.

Ted said, "Well, our resolution is—"

"About as good as it's gonna get," Alex said.

Nikka said mildly, "Then perhaps it is time for the surface probes?"

The vessels fell, crisp and clean. Winds scorched them; billowy parachutes eased their fall. The slumbering world below was mottled and cloud-shrouded. In some lacing val-leys the dryness of the sulfur dust prevailed. There, brackish ponds greeted the first flyback probe.

In the wetter valleys the dust rolled over damper air beneath. Mud fell from the sky. The sluggish rivers were clogged with it. Twisted yellow weeds sprouted on the banks and curious, small creatures scuttled for safety when the second probe popped and murmured and thrust forth a jerking, ratcheting scoop.

Green greeted the third probe, where water had won a permanent victory. The roiling dust blew in nearby mountain passes, but did not eddy and fall here. For this spherical, inquisitive probe the feast of life was more rich. And richer still was the land toward the seas.

The flyback strategy was smash-and-grab. They were

instructed to boost at the first sign of anything large. Thus the fifth probe took only one lingering view of the approaching EM creature which had been drawn by its *whooshing* crash. But the image was clear: a huge thing, leathery, unclothed. Three thin arms rode above the tangle of stiff legs. An awesome head.

It carried nothing. No tools. No radio transmitter.

It had no eyes.

Instead, there was a chunky, rectangular slot in the huge head, a meter across. It turned toward the probe, just as the boosters fired to fling the black cylinder skyward. The probe radio registered a burst of noise, a crisp sputter. Then the landscape dwindled below and the thick pink clouds of Isis consumed the EM creature.

But the spiky rattle in the radio spectrum had come from the creature itself. That much was sure.

FIVE

Preliminary exploration inched on. Nigel tried to hasten matters, but he had long ago learned the uselessness of trying to put body English on the universe.

Instead, he worked in the fields and tanks, making the fat vegetables swell under ultraviolet phosphors. Rubbery plants stretched tall, driven not by nature's cruel competition but by well-runed DNA, stepchild of laboratories. Amid these cathedral trees of 99 percent usable, man-centered life, he walked with a slow shuffle, hoarding his energy. The other men and women on the agri team did their work with a quick, efficient energy, but they flagged at the end of the shift, more from boredom than fatigue. Nigel did it slowly because he liked the musk and raw damp of the soil, the click of the hoe, the lofting high into the air of a bundle of rattling dry stalks.

The aliens had given him that. The ability, the oddly tilted sensitivity, had been in him—was in everybody—and the blinding moments in direct contact with the *Mare Marginis*

computer, in the splintered alien ship, had set it loose. In the
first years afterward, the stink of enlightenment had followed
him everywhere. Before, the dripping of water from a thick-
lipped stonework urn had been a restful, pretty sight, nothing more. Then, after the *Mare Marginis* ship, the same
dripping had become a wonderful thing, packed with meaning. Now, at last, it was a dripping into a thick-lipped urn
again.

He had talked about that, occasionally, and the words
had been distorted and ramified and defined into oblivion.
He knew, but others didn't, that he really could not speak for
anyone else, could not penetrate to the experience so that
others felt it. Things happened to you and you learned from
them, but the pretense of a common interior landscape which
one could cart—nonsense. Nothing captured it. He had seen
the usual menu of savants, with their crystallized formulas,
but they seemed no different. He listened to those Tao and
Buddha and Zen phrases, like great blue-white blocks of
luminous granite through which pale blades of light seeped,
cool and from a distant place, eternally true and forever,
immutable and as useful as alabaster statues in a town square.

So he had been grateful when others finally left him
alone. He had worked and he did the Slotsleep job, submit-
ting himself to the trial runs with the calm of a domesticated
animal. But the alphabet jumble of organizations—ISA, then
UNDSA, then ANDP—they were machines, not people. And
machines have no need to forget. So to them he was an odd
bird with a certain fame and fading glory. He had been in the
space program since his early twenties. He had taken part in
the series of discoveries that led to the bleak *Mare Marginis*
plain and to the encounter with the alien computer. That
made his name useful to the ISA.

It also meant they had to let him go on *Lancer*. He had
put in years of developing Slotsleep, trimming seventeen
years from his span. He had done it for the value of research,
yes, to bring the stars within range of the extended human
life-span. But he had also spent the years floating in the milky
rich fluids to keep his own effective age down, so the alphabet
agencies could not use age alone as a weapon against him.

The flaw in the logic, he saw, was that after launch, the
Lancer crew could do whatever they liked about task assignments. Now he had to maneuver.

He knew what he was and that they should not make a ceramic saint out of him . . . but still, the illusion had its uses. They gave him more privacy than the usual crew member, let him and Nikka carve a fresh apartment for themselves in *Lancer*'s rock. And the privacy gave him time to think.

Nigel straightened up from his gardening. He felt a twinge in his back and then a sudden lacing pain. The shock of it made him drop three tomatoes he had plucked. He winced and grimaced and then, before anyone saw the look, made his face go blank. The pain ebbed. He bent carefully to pick up the dusty tomatoes. Traitor muscles along his spine stretched and protested. He let the pain come flooding in, feeling it fully and so disarming it. Enough for today. A legend should not display back problems if he could help it.

PART TWO 2061 EARTH

ONE

Warren watched the *Manamix* going down. The ocean was in her and would smother the engines soon, swamping her into silence. Her lights still glowed in the mist and rain.

She lay on her port side, down by the head, and the swell took her solidly with a dull hammering. The strands that the Swarmers cast had laced across her decks and wrapped around the gun emplacements and over the men who had tended them.

The long green-and-yellow strands still licked up the sides and over the deck, seeking and sticking, spun out from the swollen belly pouches of the Swarmers. Their green bodies clustered in the dark water at the bows.

A long finger of tropical lightning cracked. It lit the wedge of space between the hovering black storm clouds and the rain-pocked, wrinkled skin of the sea. The big aliens glistened in the glare.

Warren treaded water and floated, trying to make no noise. A strand floated nearby and a wave brushed him against it but there was no sting. The Swarmer it came from was probably dead and drifting down now. But there were many more in the crashing surf near the ship and he could hear screams from the other crewmen who had gone over the side with him.

The port davits on the top deck dangled, trailing ropes, and the lifeboats hung from them unevenly, useless. Warren had tried to get one down, but the winch and cabling fouled and finally he had gone over the side like the rest.

Her running lights winked and then came on steady again. The strands made a tangled net over the decks now. Once they stunned a man the sticky yellow nerve sap stopped coming and they lost their sting. As he watched, bobbing in the waves, one of the big aliens amidships rolled and brought in its strand and pulled a body over the railing. The man was dead and when a body hit the water there was a frothing rush after it.

Wisps of steam curled from the engine room hatch. He thought he could hear the whine of the diesels. Her port screw was clear and spinning like a metal flower. In the hull plates he could see the ragged holes punched by the packs of Swarmers. She was filling fast now.

Warren knew the jets the Filipinos had promised the captain would never get out this far. It was a driving, splintering storm, and to drop the canisters of poison that would kill the Swarmers would take low and dangerous flying. The Filipinos would not risk it.

She went without warning. The swell came over her bows and the funnel slanted down fast. The black water poured into her and into the high hoods of her ventilators and the running lights started to go out. The dark gully of her forward promenade and bay filled and steam came gushing up from the hatches like a giant thing exhaling.

He braced himself for it, thinking the engine he had tended, and the sudden deep booming came as the sea reached in. She slid in fast. Lightning crackled and was reflected in a thousand shattered mirrors of the sea. The waters accepted her and the last he saw was a huge rush of steam as great chords boomed in her hull.

In the quiet afterward, calls and then screams came to him, carried on the gusts. There had been so many men going off the aft deck the Swarmers had missed him. Now they had coiled their strands back in and would find him soon. He began to kick, floating on his back, trying not to splash

Something brushed his leg. He went limp.

It came again.

He pressed the fear back, far away from him. The thing was down there in the blackness, seeing only by its phosphorescent stripes along the jawline. If it caught some movement—

A wave rolled him over. He floated facedown and did nothing about it. A wave rocked him and then another and his face came out for an instant and he took a gasp of air. Slowly he let the current turn him to the left until a slit of his mouth broke clear and he could suck in small gulps of air.

The cool touch came at a foot. A hip. He waited. He let the air bubble out of him slowly when his chest started to burn so that he would have empty lungs when he broke surface. A slick skin rubbed against him. His throat began to go tight. His head went under again and he felt himself in the black without weight and saw a dim glimmering, a wash of silvery light like stars—and he realized he was staring at the Swarmer's grinning phosphorescent jaw.

The fire in his throat and chest was steady and he struggled to keep them from going into spasm. The grin of gray light came close. Something cold touched his chest, nuzzled him, pushed—

A wave broke hard over him and he tumbled and was in the open, face up, gasping, ears ringing. The wave was deep and he took two quick breaths before the water closed over him again.

He opened his eyes in the dark water. Nothing. No light anywhere. He could not risk a kick to take him to the air. He waited to bob up again, and did, and this time saw something riding down the wave near him. A lifeboat.

He made a slow, easy stroke toward it. Nothing touched him. If the Swarmer had already eaten, it might have just been curious. Maybe it was not making its turn and coming back.

A wave, a stroke, a wave—He stretched and caught the trailing aft line. He wrenched himself up and sprawled aboard, rattling the oars in the gunwale. Quietly he paddled toward the weakening shouts. Then the current took him to starboard. He did not use the oars in the locks because they would clank and the sound would carry. He pulled toward the sounds but they faded. A fog came behind the rain.

There was a foot of water in the boat and the planking was splintered where a Swarmer tried to stove it in. A case of supplies was still clamped in the gunwale.

Awhile later he sighted a smudge of yellow. It was the woman, Rosa, clinging to a life jacket she had got on wrong. He had been staying down in the boat to keep hidden from the Swarmers but without thinking about it he pulled her aboard.

She was a journalist he had seen before on the *Manamix*. She was covering the voyage for Brazilian TV and wanted to take this fast run down from Taiwan to Manila. She had said she wanted to see a Swarm beaten off and her camera crew was on deck all day bothering the ship's crew.

She sat aft and huddled down and then after a time started to talk. He covered her mouth. Her eyes rolled from side to side, searching the water. Warren paddled slowly. He wore jeans and a long-sleeve shirt, and even soaked they kept off the night chill. The fog was thick. They heard some distant splashes and once a rifle shot. The fog blotted out the sounds.

They ate some of the provisions when it got light enough to see. Warren felt the planking for seepage and he could tell it was getting worse.

A warm dawn broke over them. Wreckage drifted nearby. There were uprooted trees, probably carried out to sea by the storm. The rain had started just as the first packs struck the bows. That had made it harder to hit them with the automatic rifles on deck and Warren was pretty sure the Swarmers knew that.

There was smashed planking from other boats near them, an empty box, some thin twine, life jackets, bottles. No one had ever seen Swarmers show interest in debris in the water, only prey. The things had no tools. Certainly they had not made the ships that dropped into the atmosphere and seeded the ocean. Those craft would have been worth looking at, but they had broken up on the seas and sunk before anyone could get to them.

The wreckage would not attract Swarmers but they might be following the current to find survivors. Warren knew no school of Swarmers was nearby because they always broke surface while in a Swarm and you could see the mass of them from a long way off. There were always the lone Swarmers that some people thought were scouts, though. Nobody really knew what they did but they were just as dangerous as the others.

He could not steer well enough to pick up wreckage. The boat was taking more water and he did not think they had much time. They needed the drifting wood and he had to swim for it. Five times he went into the water and each time he had to push the fear away from him and swim as smoothly and quietly as he could until finally the fear came strongly and he could not do it anymore.

He skinned the bark from two big logs, using the knife from the provisions case, and made lashings. The boat was shipping water now as it rolled in the swell. He and Rosa cut and lashed and built. When they had a frame of logs they broke up the boat and used some of the planks for decking. The boat sank before they could save most of it, but they got the case onto the raft.

He pried nails out of some of the driftwood. But now his vision was blurring in the bright sunlight and he was clumsy. They cleared a space in the frame to lie on and Rosa fell asleep while he was pounding in the last board. Each task he had now was at the end of a tunnel and he peered through it at his hands doing the job and they were numb and thick as though he were wearing gloves. He secured the case and other loose pieces and hooked his right arm over a limb to keep from falling overboard. He fell asleep facedown.

TWO

The next day as he got more driftwood and lashed it into the raft there was a slow, burning, pointless kind of anger in him. He could have stayed on land and lived off the dole. He had known the risks when he signed on as engineer.

It had been six years since the first signs of the aliens. With each year more ships had gone down, hulled in deep water and beyond protection from the air. The small craft, fishermen and the like, had been first to go. That did not change things much. Then the Swarmers multiplied and cargo vessels started going down. Trade across open seas was impossible.

The oceanographers and biologists said they were starting to understand the Swarmer mating and attack modes by that time. It was slow work. Studying them on the open water was dangerous. When they were captured they hammered themselves against the walls of their containers until the jutting bone of their foreheads shattered and drove splinters into their brains.

Then the Swarmers began taking bigger ships. They found a way to mass together and hull even the big supertankers.

By then the oceanographers were dying, too, in their reinforced-hull research ships. The Swarmers could sink anything then and no one could explain how they had learned to modify their tactics. The things did not have particularly large brains.

There were reports of strange-looking Swarmers, of strays from the schools, of massed Swarmers who could take a ship down in minutes. Then came photographs of a totally new form, the Skimmers, who leaped and dived deep and were smaller than the Swarmers. The specimens had been killed by probots at depths below two hundred fathoms, where Swarmers had never been seen.

The automatic stations and hunters were the only way men could study the Swarmers by that time. Large cargo vessels could not sail safely. Oil did not move from the Antarctic or China or the Americas. Wheat stayed in the farm nations. The intricate world economy ground down.

Warren had been out of work and stranded in the chaos of Tokyo. His wife had left him years before so he had no particular place to go. When the *Manamix* advertised that it had special plates in her hull and deck defenses he signed into a berth. The pay was good and there was no other sea work anyway. He could have run on the skimships that raced across the Taiwan Straits or to Korea, but those craft did not need engineers. If their engines ever went out they were finished before any repair could get done because the loud motors always drew the Swarmers in their wake.

Warren was an engineer and he wanted to stick to what he knew. He had worked hard for the rating. The heavy plates in the fore- and aftholds had looked strong to him. But they had buckled inside of half an hour.

Rosa held up well at first. They never saw any other survivors of the *Manamix*. They snagged more wreckage and logs and lashed it together. Floating with the wood they found a coil of wire and an aluminum railing. He pounded the railing into nails and they made a lean-to for protection from the sun.

They were drifting northwest at first. Then the current shifted and took them east. He wondered if a search pattern could allow for that and find them.

One night he took Rosa with a power and confidence he had not felt since years before, with his wife. It surprised him.

They ate the cans of provisions. He used some scraps for bait and caught a few fish, but they were small. She knew a way to make the twine tight and springy. He used it to make a bow and arrow and it was accurate enough to shoot fish if they came close.

Their water began to run out. Rosa kept their stores under the lean-to and at seven days Warren found the water was almost gone. She had been drinking more than her share.

"I had to," she said, backing away from him at a crouch. "I can't stand it, I . . . I get so bad. And the sun, it's too hot, I just . . ."

He wanted to stop but he could not and he hit her several times. There was no satisfaction in it.

Through the afternoon Rosa cringed at a corner of the raft and Warren lay under the lean-to, and thought. In the cool, orderly limits of the problem he found a kind of rest. He squatted on a plank and rocked with the swell, and inside, where he had come to live more and more these past years, the world was not just the gurgle and rush of waves and the bleaching raw edge of salt and sun. Inside there were the books and the diagrams and things he had known. He struggled to put them together.

Chemistry. He cut a small slit in the rubber stopper of a water can and lowered it into the sea on a long fishing line.

The deeper water was cold. He pulled the can up and put in inside a bigger can. It steamed like a champagne bucket. Water beaded on the outside of the small can. The big can held the drops. The drops were free of salt but there was not much.

Nine days out the water was gone. Rosa cried. Warren tried to find a way to make the condensing better but they did not have many cans. The yield was no more than a mouthful a day.

In the late afternoon of that day Rosa suddenly hit him and started shouting filthy names. She said he was a sailor and should get them water and get them to land and when they finally did get picked up she would tell everybody how bad a sailor he was and how they had nearly died because he did not know how to find the land.

He let her run down and stayed away from her. If she scratched him with her long fingernails the wound would heal badly and there was no point in taking a risk. They had not taken any fish on the lines for a long time now and they were getting weaker. The effort of hauling up the cans from below made his arms tremble.

The next day the sea ran high. The raft groaned, rising sluggishly and plunging hard. Waves washed them again and again so it was impossible to sleep or even rest. At dusk Warren discovered jelly sea horses as big as a thumbnail riding in the foam that lapped over the raft. He stared at them and tried to remember what he had learned of biology.

If they started drinking anything with a high salt content the end would come fast. But they had to have something. He put a few on his tongue, tentatively, and waited until they melted. They were salty and fishy but seemed less salty than seawater. The cool moisture seemed right and his throat welcomed it. He spoke to Rosa and showed her and they gathered handfuls of the sea horses until nightfall.

On the eleventh day there were no sea horses and the sun pounded at them. Rosa had made hats for them, using cloth from the wreckage. That helped with the worst of the day, but to get through the hours Warren had to sit with closed eyes under the lean-to, carefully working through the clear hallways of his mind.

The temptation to drink seawater was festering in him, flooding the clean places inside him where he had withdrawn. He kept before him the chain of things to keep himself intact.

If he drank seawater he would take in a quantity of dissolved salt. The body did not need much salt, so it had to get rid of most of what he took in. The kidneys would sponge up the salt from his blood and secrete it. But doing that took pure water, at least a pint a day.

The waves churned before him and he felt the rocking of the deck and he made it into a chant.

Drink a pint of seawater a day. The body turns it into about twenty cubic centimeters of pure water.

But the kidneys need more than that to process the salt. They react. They take water from the body tissues.

The body dries out. The tongue turns black. Nausea. Fever. Death.

He sat there for hours, reciting it, polishing it down to a few key words, making it perfect. He told it to Rosa and she did not understand but that was all right.

In the long afternoon he squinted against the glare and the world became one of sounds. The rattling of their cans came to him against the murmur of the sea and the hollow slap of waves against the underside of the raft. Then there was a deep thump. He peered to starboard. A rippling in the water. Rosa sat up. He gestured for silence. The planks and logs creaked and worked against each other and the thump came again.

He had heard dolphins knocking under the raft before and this was not their playful string of taps. Warren crawled out from the lean-to and into the yellow sunlight and a big green form broke surface and rolled belly-over, goggling at them with a bulging eye. Its mouth was like a slash in the blunt face. The teeth were narrow and sharp.

Rosa cried in terror and the Swarmer seemed to hear her. It circled the raft, following her awkward scuttling. She screamed and moved faster but the big thing flicked its tail and kept alongside her.

Warren's concentration narrowed to an absolute problem that took in the Swarmer and its circling and the closed geometry of the raft. If they let it come in when it chose, it would lunge against the raft and catch them off-balance and have a good chance of tumbling them into the water or breaking up the raft.

The green form turned and dived deep under the raft.

"Rosa!" He tore off his shirt. "Here! Wave it in the water on the side." He dipped the shirt, crouching at the edge. "Like this."

She hung back. "I . . . but . . . no, I . . ."

"Damn it! I'll stop it before it gets to you."

She gaped at him and the Swarmer broke water on the far side of the raft. It rolled ponderously, as if it were having trouble understanding how to attack a thing so much smaller than a ship, and attacking it alone.

Rosa took the shirt hesitantly. He encouraged her and she bent over and swished a tip of it in the surf. "Good."

Warren brought out the crude arrow he had made with a centimeter-thick slat from the *Manamix* lifeboat. He had tapered it down and driven a nail in the head. He tucked the arrow into the rubber strip of his bow and tested it. The arrow had a line on it and did not fly very straight. Not much good for fish.

He slitted his eyes against the glare and looked out at the shallow troughs. The sea warped and rippled where the thing had just disappeared. Warren sensed that it had judged them now and was gliding back in the blue shadows under the raft, coming around for its final pass. It would not see the shirt until it turned and that would bring it up and near the corner where Warren now stood, between its path and Rosa. He drew the arrow back in a smooth motion, sighting, straining, sighting—

Rosa saw the dim shape first. She flicked the rag out of the water with a jerk. Warren saw something dart up, seeming to come up out of the floor of the ocean itself, catching the refracted bands of light from the waves.

Rosa screamed and stepped back. The snout broke water and the mouth like a cut was leering at them and Warren let go the arrow *thunk* and followed it forward, scrabbling on all fours. The thing had the arrow in under the gills and the big flaps of green flesh bulged and flared open in spasms as it rolled to the side.

Warren snatched at the arrow line and missed. "Grab the end!" he called. The arrow was enough to stun the Swarmer but that was all. The thing was stunned with the nail driven deep in it, but Warren wanted more of it now, more than just the killing of it, and he splashed partway off the raft to reach the snout and drag it in. He got a slippery grip on a big blue ventral fin. The mouth snapped. It thrashed and Warren used the motion to haul it toward the raft. He swung himself, the wood cutting into his hip, and levered the body partway onto the deck. Rosa took a fin and pulled. He used the pitch of the deck and his weight to flip the thing over on its side. It arched its back, twisting to gain leverage to thrash back over the side. Warren had his knife out and as the thing slid away from him he drove the blade in, slipping it through soft tissue at the side and riding up against the spine. Warren slashed down the body, feeling the Swarmer convulse in agony. Then it straightened and seemed to get smaller.

The two stood back and looked at the scaly green body, three meters long. Its weight made the raft dip and turn in the swell.

Something sticky was beginning to drain from the long cut. Warren fetched a can and scooped up the stuff. It was a thin, pale yellow fluid. He did not hear Rosa's whimpering, stumbling approach as he lifted the can to his lips.

He caught the cool, slightly acrid taste of it for an instant. He opened his mouth wider to take it in. She struck the can from his hands. It clattered on the deck.

His punch drove her to her knees. "Why?" he yelled. "What do you care—"

"Wrong," she sputtered out. "Ugly. They're not . . . not *normal* . . . to . . . to eat."

"You want to drink? Want to live?"

She shook her head, blinking. "Na . . . ah, yeah, but . . . not that. Maybe . . ."

He looked at her coldly and she moved away. The carcass was dripping. He wedged it against a log and propped cans under it. He drank the first filled can, and the second.

The dorsal and ventral fins sagged in death. In the water he had seen them spread wide as wings. The bulging braincase and the goggle eyes seemed out of place, even in the strange face with its squeezed look. The rest of the body was sleek like the large fish. He had heard somebody say that evolution forced the same slim contours on any fast thing that lived in an ocean, even on submarines.

The Swarmer had scaly patches around the forefins and at each ventral fin. The skin looked as though it were getting thick and hard. Warren did not remember seeing that in the photographs of dead ones, but then the articles and movies had not said anything about the Swarmer scouts either until a year ago. They kept changing.

Rosa crouched under the lean-to. Once, when he drank, she spat out some word he could not understand.

The third can he set down on the boards halfway between them. He cut into the body and found the soft pulpy places where it was vulnerable to an arrow. He learned the veins and arteries and ropes of muscle. There were big spaces in the head that had something to do with hearing. In the belly pouch the strand was shriveled and laced with a kind of blue muscle. Around the fins where the skin became scaly there were little bones and cartilage and gristle that did not seem to have any use.

Rosa edged closer as he worked. The heat weighed on her. She licked her lips until they were raw and finally she drank.

THREE

He kept track of the days by making a cut each morning in a tree limb. The ritual sawing became crucial, part of the struggle. The itching salt spray and the hammering of the sun blurred distinctions. In the simple counting he found there was some order, the beauty of number that existed outside the steady rub of the sea's green sameness.

Between the two of them they made the killing of the Swarmers a ritual as well. The scouts came at random intervals now, with never more than three days of waiting until the next thumping probes at the planking. Then Rosa would stoop and wave the shirt in the water. The thing would make a pass to look and then turn to strike, coming by the jutting corner, and Warren would drive the arrow into soft place.

Rosa would crouch under the shelter then and mumble to herself and wait for him to gut it and bleed the watery pouches of fin fluid and finally take the sour syrup from behind the eyes.

With each fresh kill he learned more. They cut up some cloth and made small bags to hold the richer parts of the carcass and then chewed it for each drop. Sometimes it made them sick. After that he twisted chunks of the flesh in a cloth bag and let the drops air in the sun. That was not so bad. They ate the big slabs of flesh but it was the fluid they needed most.

With each kill Rosa became more distant. She sat dreamily swaying at the center of their plank island, humming and singing to herself, coiling inward. Warren worked and thought.

On the twenty-first day of drifting she woke him. He came up reluctantly from the vague, shifting sleep. She was shouting.

Darting away into the bleak dawn was something lean and blue. It leaped into the air and plunged with a shower of foam and then almost in the same instant was flying out of the steep wall of a wave, turning in the gleaming fresh sun. "A Skimmer," he murmured. It was the first he had ever seen.

Rosa cried out.

Warren stared out into the hills and valleys of moving water, blinking, following her finger. A gray cylinder the size of his hand floated ten meters away.

He picked up the tree limb they used for marking the days. His hands were puffed up now from the constant damp, and the bark of the limb scraped them. No green shapes moved below. He rocked with the swell, waiting at the edge of the raft for a random current to bring the gray thing closer.

A long time passed. It bobbed sluggishly and came no closer. Warren leaned against the pitch of the deck and stretched for it. The limb was short at least a meter.

He swayed back, relaxing, letting the clenching in his muscles ease away. His arms trembled. He could swim to it in a few quick strokes, turn and get back in a few—

No. If he let go he would be sucked into the same endless caverns that Rosa was wandering. He had to hold on. And take no risks.

He stepped back. The thing to do was wait and see if—

White spray exploded in front of him. The lean form shot up into the air and Warren rolled back away from it. He came up with the knife held close to him.

But the Skimmer arced away from the raft. It cut back into a wave and was gone for an instant and then burst up and caught the cylinder in it slanting mouth. In the air it rolled and snapped its head. The cylinder clunked onto the raft. The Skimmer leaped again, blue-white, and was gone into the endlessly shifting faces of green marble.

Rosa was huddled in the shelter. Warren picked up the cylinder carefully. It was smooth and regular but something about it told him it had not been made with tools. There were small flaws in the soft, foamy gray, like the blotches on a tomato. At one end it puckered as though a tassel had fallen away.

He rubbed it, pulled at it, turned the ends—It split with a moist pop. Inside there curled a thick sheet of the same softly resistant gray stuff. He unrolled it.

SECHTON XMENAPU DE AN LANSDORFKOPPEN SW BY W
ABLE SAGON MXIL VESSE L ANSAGEN MANLATS WIR
UNS? FTH ASDLENGS ERTY EARTHN PROFUILEN CO
NISHI NAGARE KALLEN KOPFT EARTHN UMI

He studied the combinations and tried to fit them together so there was some logic to it. It was no code, he guessed. Some of the words were German and there was some English and Japanese but most of it was either meaningless or no language he knew. VESSE L might be *vessel*. ANSÀGEN—to say? He wished he remembered more of the German he had picked up in the merchant marine.

The words were in a clear typeface like a newspaper and were burned into the sheet.

He could make no more of it. Rosa did not want to look at the sheet. When he made her she shook her head, no, she could not pick out any new words.

A Swarmer came later that day. Rosa did not back away fast enough and the big shape shot up out of the water. It bit down hard on the shirt as Warren's arrow took it and the impact made the blunt head snap back. Rosa was not ready for it and she stumbled forward and into the sea. The Swarmer tried to flip away. Warren caught her as she went into the water. The alien lunged at her but Warren heaved her back onto the deck. He had dropped the bow. The Swarmer rolled and the bow washed overboard and then the tail fins caught the edge of the raft and it twisted and came tumbling aboard. Warren hit it with the tree limb.

It kept thrashing but the blows stunned it. He waited for the right angle and then slipped the knife in deep, away from the snapping jaws, and the thing went still.

Rosa helped with the cutting up. She started talking suddenly while he looked for the bow. He was intent on seeing if it was floating nearby and at first did not notice that she was not just muttering. He spotted the bow and managed to fetch it in. Rosa was discussing the Swarmers, calmly and in a matter-of-fact voice he had not heard from her before.

"The important thing is to not let one get away," she concluded.

"Guess so," Warren said.

"They know about the raft, the Swarm comes."

"If they can find us, yeah."

"They send out these scouts. The pack, it will follow where the long ones tell it."

"We'll get 'em."

"Forever? No. Only solution is land."

"None I've seen. We're drifting west, could be—"

"I thought you are sailor."

"Was."

"Then sail us to land."

"Not that easy," Warren said, and went on to tell her how hard it was to get any control of a raft, and anyway he didn't know where they were, what the landfalls were out here. She sniffed contemptuously at this news. "Find an island," she repeated several times. Warren argued, not because he had any clear reason, but because he knew how to survive here and a vague fear came when he thought about the land. Rosa was speaking freely and easily now and she thought fast, sure of herself. Finally he broke off and set to work storing away the slabs of Swarmer meat. The talk confused him.

The next day a Skimmer came and leaped near the raft and there was another cylinder. It swam away, a blur of silvery motion. He read the sheet.

GEFAHRLICH GROSS HIRO ADFIN SOLID MNX 8 SHIO
NISHI. KURO NAGARE. ANAXLE UNS NORMEN 286 W
SCATTER PORTLINE ZERO NAGARE. NISHI.

He could make no sense of it. Rosa worked on it, not much interested, and shrugged. He tried to scratch marks on the sheets, thinking that he could send them something, ask questions. The sheet would not take an impression.

A Swarmer surfaced to the west the next day. Rosa shrieked. It circled them twice and came in fast toward Rosa's lure. Warren shot at it and hit too far back. The tip buried itself uselessly in a spot where he knew there was only fatty tissue. The Swarmer lunged at Rosa. She was ready, though, falling back from the edge, and it missed. Warren yanked on the line and freed the arrow. The Swarmer flinched as the arrow came out and rolled off the raft. The Swarmer sank and was gone.

"Don't let it get away!" Rosa cried.

"It's not coming up."

"You hit it in the wrong place."

"Went in pretty deep, though. Might die before it can get back to the pack."

"You think so?"

Warren didn't but he said, "Might."

"You, you have *got* to find us an island. *Now.*"

"I still think we're safe here."

"Incredible! You are no kind of sailor at all and you are

afraid to admit it. Afraid to say you don't know how to find land."

"Bullshit. I—" But she interrupted him with a flood of words he couldn't keep up with. He heard her out, nodding finally, not knowing himself why he wanted to stay on the raft, on the sea. It just *felt* better, was all, and he did not know how to tell her that.

When the argument was finally over he went back to thinking about the second message. Some of it was German and he knew a little of that, but not those particular words. He had never learned any Japanese even though he had lived in Tokyo.

The next morning at dawn he woke suddenly and knew there was something near the raft. The swell was smooth and orange as the sun caught it. On the glassy horizon he saw nothing. He was very hungry and he remembered the Swarmer from yesterday. He had used the meat from the first kills to bait their lines but nothing bit. He wondered if that was because the fish would not take Swarmer meat or if there were no fish down there to have. The aliens had been changing the food chain in the oceans, he had read about that.

Then he saw the gray dot floating far away. The raft was drifting toward it and in a few minutes he snagged it. The message said

CONSQUE KPOF AMN SOLID. DIAØLEN MACHEN SMALL
YOUTH SCHLECT UNS. DERINGER CHANGE DA. UNS B
WSW. SAGEN ARBEIT BEI MOUTH. SHIMA CIRCLE STEIN
NONGO NONGO UMI DRASVITCH YOU.

He peered at the words . . . and squatted on the deck and felt the long dragging minutes go by. If he could—

"Warren! Wa—Warren!" Rosa called. He followed her gesture.

A blur on the horizon. It dipped and rose among the ragged waves. Warren breathed deeply. "Land."

Rosa's eyes swelled and she barked out a sharp cackling laughter. Her lips went white with the laughing and she cried, "Yeah! Yeah! Land!" and shook her fists in the air.

Warren blinked and measured with his eyes the current

and the angle the brown smudge ahead made with their course. They would not reach it by drifting.

He worked quickly.

He took the tree limb and knocked away the supports of the lean-to. In the center of the raft he knelt and measured out the distances with hands and fingers and worked a hole in between two planks. He could wedge the limb into it. He made a collar out of strips of bark. The limb was crooked but it made a vertical beam.

He took the plywood sheet of the lean-to and lashed it to the limb. With the knife he dug stays in the plywood. The wire that held the logs in place in the deck would have been good to use but he could not risk unlashing them. He used the last of their twine instead, passing it through the stays in the plywood and making them into trailing lines. The plywood was standing up now like a sail catching the wind, and by pulling the twine he could tack. The raft took the waves badly but by turning the plywood sheet he could take the strain off the weak places where the logs and boards met.

The wind backed into the east in late morning. They could not make much headway and the land was still a dark strip on the horizon. Warren broke off a big piece of wood at the raft corner. He hacked at it with the knife. A Swarmer surfaced nearby and Rosa started her screeching. He hit her and watched the Swarmer, but he never stopped whittling at the wood in his lap. The Swarmer circled once and then turned and swam away to the south.

He finished with the wood. He made a housing for it with the rest of the bark strips. It sat badly at the end of the raft but the broad part dug into the water and by leaning against the top of it he could hold the angle. He got Rosa to hold two blocks of wood against the shaft for leverage and that way the thing worked something like a rudder. The raft turned to the south, toward the land.

Noon passed. Warren fought the wind and the rudder and tried to estimate the distance and the time left. If dark came before they reached the land the current would take them past it and they would never be able to beat back against the wind to find it again. He had been so long away from firm ground that he felt a need for it that was worse than his hunger. The pitch of the deck took the energy out of you day and night, you could not sleep for holding onto the deck when the sea got high, and you would do anything for something solid under you, for just—

Solid.

The message had said *solid*. Did that mean land?

Gefahrlich gross something something *solid*.

Gefahrlich had some kind of feel to it, something about bad or dangerous, he thought. *Gross* was *big*. Dangerous big blank blank land? Then some Japanese and other things and then *scatter portline zero*. *Scatter*. Make to go away?

Warren sweated and thought. Rosa brought him an old piece of Swarmer but he could not eat it. He thought about the words and saw there was some key to them, some beauty in them.

The rudder creaked against the wooden chocks. The land was a speck of brown now and he was pretty sure it was an island. The wind picked up. It was coming on to late afternoon.

Rosa moved around the raft when he did not need her, humming to herself, the Swarmers forgotten, eating from the pieces of meat still left. He did not try to stop her. She was eating out of turn but he needed all his thought now for the problem.

They were coming in on the northern shore. He would bring them in at a graze, to have a look before beaching. The current fought against them, but the plywood was enough to sweep them to the south.

South? What was there about...

WSW. West southwest?

UNS B WSW.

Uns was *we* in German, he was pretty sure of that. We be WSW? On the WSW part of the land? The island? Or WSW of the island? We—the Skimmers.

He noticed Rosa squatting in the bow of the raft, eager, her weight dipping the boards with the blue-green swell and bringing hissing foam over the planks. It slowed them but she did not seem to see that. He opened his mouth to yell at her and then closed it. If they went slow, he would have more time.

The Skimmers were all he had out here and they had tried to tell him...

Portline. *Port* was left. A line to the left?

They were coming in from the northeast as near as he could judge. Veering left would take them around and to the southwest. Or WSW.

The island seemed to grow fast now as the sun set behind it. Warren squinted against the glare on the waves. There was something between them and the island. At the top of a wave he strained to see and could make out a darker line against pale sand. White rolls of surf broke on it.

A reef. The island was going to be harder to reach. He would have to bring the raft in easy and search for a passage. Either that or smash up on it and swim the lagoon, if there was no way through the circle of coral around—

Circle stein nongo. He did not know what *stein* was, something to drink out of or something, but the rest might say *don't go in the circle.*

Warren slammed the tiller over full. It groaned and the collar nearly buckled but he held it, throwing his shoulder into it.

Rosa grunted and glared at him. The raft tacked to port. He pulled the twine and brought the plywood farther into the wind.

Small youth schlect uns. The Swarmers were bigger than the Skimmers, but they might mean smaller in some other way. Smaller development? Smaller brain? *Schlect uns.* Something about *us* and the Swarmers. If they were younger than the Skimmers, maybe their development was still to come. Something told him that *schlect* was a word like *gefahrlich,* but what the difference was he did not know. *Swarmers dangerous us?* There was nothing in the words to show action, to show who *us* was. Did *us* include Warren?

Rosa stumbled toward him. The swell was coming abaft now and she clutched at him for support. "Wha'? Land! Go!"

He rubbed his eyes and focused on her face but it looked different in the waning light. He saw that in all the days they had been together he had never known her. The face was just a face. There had never been enough words between them to make the face into something else. He...

The wind shifted and he shrugged away the distraction and worked the twine. He studied the dark green mass ahead. It was thickly wooded and there were bare patches and a beach. The white curves of breaking surf were clear now. The thick brown reef—

Things moved on the beach.

At first he thought they were driftwood, logs swept in by a storm. Then he saw one move and then another and they were green bodies in the sand. They crawled inland. A few had made it to the line of trees.

Small youth. Young ones who were still developing.

He numbly watched the island draw near. Dimly he felt Rosa pounding on his chest and shoulder. "Steer us in! You hear me? Make this thing—"

"Wha—what?"

"You afraid of the rocks, that it?" She spit out something in Spanish or Portuguese, something angry and full of scorn. Her eyes bulged unnaturally. "No *man* would—"

"Shut up." His lips felt thick. They were rushing by the island now, drawn by the fast currents.

"You fool, we're going to *miss.*"

"Look . . . look at it. The Skimmers, they're telling us not to go there. You'll see. . . ."

"See what?"

"The things. On the beach."

She followed his pointing. She peered at it, shook her head, and said fiercely, "So? Nothing there but logs."

Warren squinted and saw logs covered with green moss. The surf broke over some of them and they rolled in the swell, looking like they were crawling.

"I . . . I don't . . ." he began.

Rosa shook her head impatiently. "Huh!" She bent down and found a large board that was working loose. Grunting, she pried it up. Warren peered at the beach and saw stubs on the logs, stubs where there had once been fins. They began to work against the sand again. The logs stirred.

"You can stay here and die," Rosa said clearly. "Me, *no.*" The reef swept by only meters away. Waves slapped and muttered against its flanks. The gray shelves of coral dipped beneath the water. Its shadowy mass below thinned and a clear sandy spot appeared. A passage. Shallow, but maybe enough . . .

"Wait . . ." Warren looked toward the beach again. *If he was wrong . . .* The logs had fleshy stubs now that pushed at the sand, crawling up the beach. What he had seen as knotholes were something else. Sores? He strained to see—

Rosa dived into the break in the reef. She hit cleanly and wallowed onto the board. Resolutely she stroked through the water, battling the swells of waves refracted into the opening.

"Wait! I think the Swarmers are—" She could not hear him over the slopping of waves on the reef.

He remembered distantly the long days... the Skimmers ... "Wait!" he called. Rosa was through the passage and into the calm beyond. "Wait!" She went on.

Where he had seen logs he now saw something bloated and grotesque, sick. He shook his head. His vision cleared— *or did it?* he wondered—and now he could not tell what waited for Rosa on the glimmering sand.

He lost sight of her as the raft followed deflected currents around the island. The trade wind was coming fresh. He felt it on his skin like a reminder, and the sunset sat hard and bright in the west. Automatically he tacked out free of the reef and turned WSW. When he looked back in the soft twilight it was hard to see the forms struggling like huge lungfish up onto their new home. Under the slanted light the wind broke the sea into oily facets that became a field of mirrors reflecting shattered images of the burnt-orange sky and the raft. He peered at the mirrors.

The logs on the beach... He felt the tug of the twine and made a change in heading to steady a yaw.

He gathered speed. When the thin scream came out of the dusk behind him he did not turn around.

PART THREE 2056 RA

ONE

Nigel watched Nikka carefully arrange her kimono. It was brocaded in brown and blue and, as tradition dictated, was extravagant by more than ten centimeters. Nikka drew it up until the hem was just level with her heels, once, twice—at the fifth try he stopped counting and fondly watched her turn this way and that before the polished-steel mirror. She arranged a red silk cord at her waist and smoothed down the slack of the kimono. Then came the obi: a broad, stiff sash, fully five meters long. She wrapped it around herself at breast level, frowned, wrapped it again. Each time he watched this ceremony it seemed more subtle, revealed more of her shifting mind. He murmured a detailed compliment and a knot of indecision in her dissolved; she firmly fastened the two small cords that secured the obi. This layering and sure smoothing done, she tried a brass front buckle. Pursed her lips. Changed it to an onyx clasp. Turned, studied the effect. Plunged an ivory comb into her butterfly *chocho mage* crown of hair. Then a pale, waxy comb. Next, a brilliant yellow one. Then back to the ivory. He loved these pensive, hovering moments when she revealed the light and childlike core of herself. *Lancer* tended to iron out the graceful, momentary interludes, he thought, and replace them with clear, sharp decisive certainties.

"You must have the largest wardrobe on board."

"Some things are worth the trouble," she said, fitting on zori of worn, woven stalks. And smiled, knowing he too sensed how important such age-honored moments were to her.

A knock at the door. He went for it, knowing that Bob Millard and Carlotta Nava would be there, coming a bit early.

The shipscene multifass began in ten minutes: time-bracketed communality.

Lancer was organized in the now-accepted mode. Whenever possible, decisions about work were made at the lowest level, involving the most workers possible. The intricately structured weave of social and political forces was a sophisticated descendant of an old cry—*ownership of the means of production by the workers!*—without the authoritarian knee jerks Marx left in the original model. It was flexible; it allowed Nigel to work on whatever odd bit of astronomical data caught his eye, as long as he also pitched into overall drudge jobs as they came up. The details were worked out by small labor cells.

To break down the ever-forming rigidities of hierarchy, the Shipwide Multifaceted Social Exchange blended all workers together, Mixmastering them into a classless puree. There were a minimum of classlike distinctions. Ship command officers ate the same boring commissary food and griped about it in the same sour, hopeless way. They wore the same blue jump suits and had no privileges. Nigel had some perks because of his age, not his rank; within the limits of efficiency, there were no ranks. Ted Landon headed the shipwide assembly, but his vote weighed the same as an obscure techtype's.

Nigel liked it: smorgasbord socialism, without a true profit motive, since *Lancer* had only to return to Earth to be a success. This simplified the sociometric analysis; consensus communities, as the jargon had it, were notably stable. Nigel ignored most of the earnest entreaties that he participate more. He liked the community well enough, while distrusting its bland surface, its solicitous sensitivity. But the swelling exuberance of the multifass could sweep him along, drown his reserve. Bright, young people had an undeniable momentum.

"Hi."

Carlotta kissed him. "Had another face smoothing, I see."

"No, I decided to skip that and go straight to embalming. How's it look?"

"It's *you*, dahling. Are those laugh lines or an irrigation project?"

Bob shook hands in his good-ole-boy persona. "You figure there's much on fer tonight?"

Nigel fetched drinks. "The free-form sex is down the hall, second left."

"Don't look for *him* there," Carlotta said. "Nigel gets all tired out just struggling with temptation."

Nigel handed her a drink. "Hot-blooded kid. I suppose you'll be playing hopscotch tonight with real Scotch?"

"Sí. You're so much wittier after I've had a few drinks."

"You two!" Nikka shook her head. "One could never guess you had spent the night together."

"Mating rituals of the higher primates," Carlotta said, taking a long pull. She stroked Nikka's kimono. "*Madre!* It's so attractive on you."

Nigel wondered why women spoke that way when presumably it was men who were best qualified to judge attraction; yet men seldom used the term. Curious. Though of course in this case his generalization fell on its face. In their first hand touch they reestablished a lazy, familiar sensuality.

He watched Carlotta approach Nikka, speaking rapidly and approvingly, and then move away, and then return, an unconscious push-pull to draw Nikka out. Carlotta's heavy, springy hair flowed with these movements. In marked contrast, her large brown eyes did not share this social gavotte. He liked the rigor of those eyes and the unashamed way they locked on whatever interested her, holding it for rapt attention.

Her intensity was too much for Nikka's mood, so soon after the reflective dressing in the kimono. Nikka escaped into the kitchen for hors d'oeuvres. Carlotta reached out a hand as if to delay her and then drew back, seeing that she had stirred up some unintended current. She turned, her long scarlet skirt flowing, and studied a sunsomi triptich nearby. Nigel watched her eyes narrow from some inner effort. There was some reservoir of emotion she was tapping that eluded him. Something deep, another fulcrum for her personality. Which proved that merely sleeping with a woman did not open her to you fully, no matter how you might try.

Bob started in about shipboard work policy and Nigel joined in, glad of the diversion. A musical theme chimed: multifass.

"Ummm," Carlotta murmured and turned to Nikka to

try again. "What are you doing under the new job rotation?"
A relatively neutral subject.

"Odd jobs here and there." Nikka retreated behind a
blank mildness. He recognized this as an old habit, common
to Japanese, though Nikka had returned to it only in the last
few years, as a day-to-day shield aboard *Lancer*. In this case,
she was uncomfortable because a small deception was involved. He and Nikka had agreed to collaborate, without
appearing to do so, filling in each other's weak areas. That
would help keep their labor ratings above minimum. It
seemed a prudent tactic for the oldest members of the crew.
"And you?"

"Well, systems analysis of the microbio inventory, of
course, from the first flyback probe."

Nigel said, "Until you're finished, we don't go down?"

Carlotta laughed, her eyes now moving with liquid ease.
"Bob has been after us for a week, panting for the green light.
We've got lots of results—"

"More'n plenty," Bob grunted.

Carlotta frowned. Friction between departments about
setting a date for touchdown? "Anyway, we've got so much
biochem to interrelate, I don't see how we can understand it
all in terms of relationships to Earthside processes, when
we've had only a few weeks to—"

Another knock. Nigel went to answer. Yes, he should
now leave the door dilated. It still struck him as odd, but
precisely such policy decisions as the touchdown date could
be dealt with and a consensus reached, in the middle of a
multifass. And all with a disarming casualness. The analysts
had discovered that most matters were in fact settled this
way. The formal apparatus only confirmed what was already
worked out. Electronic democracy with your shirt unbut-
toned. A disarming notion, for those reared in the days of
management pyramids.

Here at the door were three people he scarcely knew,
bubbling with good spirits and ready to add to the steadily
rising murmur that he could hear welling up in the corridor,
more coming, the eternal primate chatter and bark, the
voices of the ship—

Toke on this, Nebraska Red, high, angular momentum
stuff—

Those microbes, never *seen* anythin' like 'em. **Dust huggers**. Little fellas, no bigger'n paramecia.

He said if she didn't like it what the hell she could change her whole jawline, he didn't care. She lost it when that lug bolt fractured, you remember that god-awful malf down C Bay, killed Jake Sutherland and her, it clean blew away her bone right up to the eye, they got the frags out of the cornea—

—they're the same chem patterns repeated thousands of times over in the Isis biosphere, just like our left- and right-handedness in the sugars and long chains, y'know. I mean, you've got only so many atoms to work with in the whole universe anyway, right? So shouldn't be a big surprise that the basic Isis chem combos—a five-carbon sugar, with one more phosphate in the carrier, whereas we get by with only three in ATP—are similar, I mean, no big shock there. Got a base tacked on, too. Obvious, simple alteration from our scheme, damn near Earthlike but you can spot the differences.

Christ I thought she'd wet herself when the A4 rating didn't come through from the cell, she screamed bloody murder at the next confab but shit we weren't havin' any you can't put one past us so she's back on the autolathes. Hates it. Ruby's got the A4 and *good* says I 'cause that bitch was—

—that stuff clutches onto the dust in the air like it was free lunch. Dust eaters. Backbone of the ecology. The flagella dig in and *zip* they take the sulfates straight out of the mineral state. No fluid solution needed!

So much for that life-needs-water crap.

Yeah, why should it when a martini doesn't?

So these fellas, they go their whole *lives* without a drink. There's water, sure, but not near the Eye. So the biosphere's tapped this way to get energy out of the sulfates, poor bastards, livin' on *dust*—

Li'l suckers got to hump like bejeezus to make an erg.

—in the wash of technical talk he steps back and studies Carlotta, sees pinched lines at her eyes and wishes he could unblock it. Easier, much easier, if the three of them could collapse into a comfortable, old-shoe life, each satisfied by a dimming echo of the initial passion they all had felt. She turns, visibly collecting words for a burst of talk—eyebrows

knit, mouth purses, blunt tip of her nose dips a millimeter—
and Nikka approaches, quicksilver changes ripple across
Carlotta's face, they touch casually, and Nigel remembers
how they had been instinctively close from the beginning,
sharing jobs, living together while Nigel was in the Sleepslots.
They exchange a word, Carlotta glances at him, she makes
the familiar stretching motion, the one she taught him to ease
knotted muscles, and Nigel feels in her liquid grace why he
has through the years narrowed his ability to see into others.
It is simply too hard now, too involving. For Nikka and
Carlotta, yes, but the thought of reaching this way into Ted or
Alex or others—it is too dense and wearying. He had gotten
it from the Marginis wreck and used it to get through the ISA
Byzantium: chatting up power brokers, sensing what *Lancer*
engineers meant as opposed to what they said, giving them
the appearance of seasoned astronaut that they wanted. And
he had liked it, been good at it. For years afterward he had
remembered each welding inspector's beaming mug. But
now— He feels the reserves ebbing for this; he cannot muster
it for a multifass or even a seminar. Insight comes only in
flashes now anyway, and the sensitivity hurts when he rubs
against the abrasive mysteries people carry inside. Carlotta
pats Nikka on the arm absentmindedly, her attention caught
again by a passing spate of jargon, and Nikka comes toward
him—

Carlotta was awfully tart
when she arrived.

Miffed at something per-
haps.

There's nothing develop-
ing between her and Bob
if that's what you're
thinking.

I'm not thinking at all
actually.

I don't think she knows
herself what's bothering
her; she can't talk about
it, but look at that forced
way she's laughing over

there and how she keeps
glancing over at us.

        Well look at it her way,
        we two've been together
        since the Pleistocene
        and she's always going
        to be the last in, the odd
        number

Funny, it's easier to talk
about her here than when
we're alone

        Ye olde multifass, every-
        thing comes out here—

And you always mixing
around, it looks like aimless walking—

        Walking yes, aimless no

Eavesdropping?

        I, I like the mix—

Thing is, they're going such a long way around in biochem terms, using what they can get after the sunlight scatters around in all that dust. No UV gets through down at the surface to speak of. That poor li'l biosphere, they stack photons on top of each other somehow to get enough energy, then grab onto water near the ocean, split off the oxy, God what a lotta work

Petrowski calcs that the biosphere's older than our solar system, *really* old, been perkin' along over *five* billion years, think 'bout that, figured it from the heavy element abundance—

—dust transfers the energy to the bigger life-forms, uses mostly sulfide electron donors, quite a trick when you consider—

—riding those winds, eating the goddamn dust, little bitsy microbes on their way from the Eye to the sea—

—still think you've got the most beautiful ass honey of any guy who wears those maintenance overalls—

Seems to me you people got a purty good handle on the biosphere, can't see why you don't pass on the touchdown option an' let us get on with it.

Bob it's not that simple

Lissen we let the specialists chip away at the thing

ferever we're gonna turn gray up here 'fore we ever get down
and *movin'*

Squeeze it a li'l an' see what you get

Tough ecology, man, I mean *tough*. This place'd be dead
as Mars with just a little less sunlight and atmosphere. Bio's
creamin' their jeans to see what else's under that dust

Too early to tell; we can't see well enough to estimate the
extent of the life pyramid

Shit this all there is to drink gotta be sumpin' better
down at Nguyen's

Look at him makes you wonder how a multifass can work
with people getting carried away, drink and even drugs on a
ship no less

Him? They're self-canceling, doncha see? Keeps things
loose but when votin' time rolls around they're too fuzzed to
care—

> You look at paramecia or
> your own sperm cells
> even they have this little
> whip,
>
> No thanks not my kind
> of thing
>
> flagella down there is
> your justly famous balls,
> my good man
>
> wigglin' upstream like
> salmon. Story of my life
>
> and if this grack will let
> me finish, there are nine
> fibers on the outside of
> that whip to every one
> fiber on the inside
>
> she's fine y'know won-
> derful but also great at
> takin' the ol' romance out
> of it
>
> and that ratio, that nine
> to one, is the same in
> thousands of organisms
> all over Earth and no-
> body has the slightest
> idea
>
> unoriginal God is the best

explanation. He just got tired

couldn't you mumble a little softer I can still hear what you're saying

okay okay so tell us nine to one

we can't see any obvious selective survival advantage for the nine-to-one ratio but who knows, still the easiest out is that 'way back at the beginning when sex started the nine to ones were just lucky is all and that ratio got locked in early

kiss me quick I'm nine to one

had too much sniffo already eh?

love me love my ratio

well you just keep on holding up that bulkhead it looks like hard work while the adults talk

hark the queen speaketh

so first thing I look for in the dust crawlies from Isis is the flagella, and sure enough—oh thanks, I'm having that rum stuff —sure enough I squint into the electron mike and there are the little whips going like mad, only when I splice some down it's a seven to one, not our nine to one. So question is, what's magic about odd ratios?

only two cases hell honey not statistically meaningful

still sounds suspicious to
me

could be that an odd ra-
tio gives 'em edges to
hold onto?

so what's the compara-
tive advantage?

more leverage with an
odd ratio? maybe that
way it's easier to make
your point even if the
lady's not interested

talk about anthropocen-
tric

must be they need a good
grip right Nigel?

I never speculate on
extraterrestrial pornography

Well they use something
to hold onto those dust
motes while they're rid-
ing the winds out from
the Eye, up those moun-
tains and down to the
sea, chomping away on
those sulfide electron
donors

then when the Eye winds
turn near the seas the
big cyclone pattern that's
when the dust falls

Remarkable how fast
his head clears I could
almost follow that

But do we need to de-
cide basic mechanisms
like that before a manned
landing?

There's lots of biochem

to study we can spend a
year easy   Not me
                   Come now we've been in
                   orbit for months already
                   bloody long enough

                              Much as we all love
                              good, old Bob-boy I'd
                              rather rely on Nigel's
                              judgment
                   Thanks but isn't that what
                   this multifass is about?

Goddamn dust if we
could only *see* more.
That third flyback probe,
it found lots of dust eaters
dropping off near the seas
but you know I keep
thinking
                              Yeah, seems like those
                              li'l buggers are a planet-
                              wide feeding system for
                              the bigger life-forms, so
                              we ought to look at who
                              benefits
Their function is carry-
ing chemical energy you
mean, that's all?   Sure, they've sopped up
                              photons at the Eye and
                              made the right carbo-oxy
                              compounds
                   —which get dumped into
                   the mountain valleys
                   where those EMs are—
                              right
Strange kind of energy
vector, moving biochem
energy out from the Eye.
Hard to see how a whole
biosphere like that could

evolve   This isn't New Jersey
                                m'love
I've noticed.

                    Damnably low-grade pro-
                    cess though, with that
                    skimpy energy budget the
                    deck's stacked against the
                    whole biosphere

                            God's ingenious
                    Well he had longer to
                    work on this one.

Five-billion-year-old biosphere makes you won-
der what could happen
                    You two might talk to Bob
                    over there about the ex-
                    ploration if you've the
                    time—
Sure come on soul mate

                    Damn that sniffo's some
                    stuff isn't it? Whattad I
                    say?
Just let me do the talking
        Nigel, Nigel, lemme tell you, I figure you can
    do somethin', man I was so *mad* I felt like runnin'
    over a toad with a power mower—
                    Ted's more the man to
                    complain to, precious lit-
                    tle I can do
Sure but the right word in, y'know
                    Can't promise anything
                    but if it's a friendly ear
                    you're after
C'mon you could have his job anytime we'd all vote
for you.

                    Nonsense, step over this
                    way the noise is dreadful
                    now what was the—

He values the cascade of impressions more than anything. He drifts down carved rock corridors, in and out of rooms, never lingering long—

—yes, I know him, he's from GHQ, works with Ted, kind of nice but homely as hell—

—uh-huh, ugliness like that is nature's contraceptive, I figure. Forget it. You got anybody else in mind, though, the night is young even if I'm not—

—She came over to me and positively whispered all of it to me in one gush which was a kind of tribute when you think about it, coming from a woman who obviously hasn't found much in the world it was necessary to whisper about—

—Evolution goes all sorts of ways, that's why I don't think we'll puzzle out the radio sources just by peeking at the basic biochem, not when we got such lousy resolution through all that damned dust. I mean, all kinds of things are selected for, right? You and me are myopic because the nearsighted males couldn't hunt so good, so they stayed home while the bruisers went out running down meat. Just hanging around the caves and painting the walls and gettin' a little on the side in the heat of the day. Never mind all that strong pair-bonding stuff they always tell you; fact is, you never know who the father is and that's why a male strategy of spreading it around as much as you can pays off. So it gets selected for. Hell, it *feels* good—that's the sure sign; evolution doesn't read *our* rule books, she's got her own—

—think you've had enough? That rum isn't rum, it's spidmeer and you're starting to look like a lobster—

—we need more recon down there skip this biochem piffle—

—yeah, right, way I see it is, we got a surplus a genius an' a shortage of guts aroun' 'ere—

—an oxidation-reduction cycle, 's what it is, down there in that dust they're playin' the same ol' game we are, only not so profitable. Higher up the chain from those dust eaters there's gotta be starch production using that crummy low-cal sunlight. Leaves oxy as leftovers, an' that's what the EMs gotta breathe, but damned if I know how anything could live off that—

—I don't see why she has to bite my head off just over a spilled *sample* container—

—You get us contami-

nated with those Isis
spores I'll vac you so
fast—

—well I *didn't* why
should I look I don't think
you can say that just like
that—

—Could be wrong but
*some*body left off the
seals.

—then don't look at *me* when you—

—call this a multifass well, this may shape you up for a vote
but nobody's talking about what *I* want

—part of it's to find out what the goddamn issue *is* if you'd
just listen fer once—

—I was saying, when the smaller animals breathe they have
this little sac, kind of an air trap, and it filters the dust out of
the air before they hit the inward stroke to suck in a
lungful—

—Real slow, about two breaths a minute, I've seen it

—No bigger'n your finger, intricate li'l things, damn fine
design for eatin' up those dust-huggin' fellas. Then the ones
fat as your hand, they're lunchin' off the finger-sized guys

—Him? Just a passing thing, yer ol' hump 'n' hustle is all—

—Come on Elinor no civilized woman ever regrets a pleasure
and this is going to be—

—so while you guys are grandstanding it with the survey,
somebody's taking out the garbage, getting meals, agrono-
mists and skiffers, all scutwork, so at least we'd like to be in
on what's comin' out instead of flashin' on it in the weeklies
you squirt Earthside—

—I still say you stack up your shipcred, you can get your tail
upholstered the way he did, just give the usual squeeze to
Dexter in medmon, they'll slip you in, won't be more than a
hairline scar nobody'll notice in the dark

He eased over into the group around Ted Landon and
waited until a break came. It still all came through to him as
overlapping voices, so even his own sounded involuntary,
part of a stream.

—Ted, we've got to go down there and have a look.

—Hold your horses, gosh, this isn't the best place to go over the technical details, Nigel; if you came to the briefings you'd be more up to speed—

—They take too long, never understood why you call them *brief*ings, but I do run through the tapes.

—Glad to hear that, and of course we are doing a study of all the ramifications, looking for a safe way to do it.

—Seems a trifle obvious, actually.

—Well, some are advocating an active recon mode—you know, where we use remote radar sensing to interrogate the internal biochem of the EMs for—

—Sounds bloody awful.

—Ah, there's the alternative, a passive mode which I incidentally favor, which is to station servo'd eyes in well-sheltered spots, and watch the EMs if they pass nearby. We've had good staff review of that proposal.

—Mere eyes? Use walkers. We'll need mobility.

—In the long run, sure. We've got walkers in the ready equipment. Lord, we're prepared for anything Earthside could anticipate. There're even submersibles in storage, in case Isis was an all-ocean planet.

Bob appeared at Ted's elbow and nodded vigorously.

—Walkers? Ah like that better'n sittin' still.

—Ted, I should think it's technically feasible to make a radio-reflecting blanket. One we could throw over a standard walker.

—What about it, Bob?

—Sure. You thinkin' to calibrate them till they reflect the EMs's own signals back?

—Dead on. But scatter their pulses to the side, the same way ordinary rocks do.

—Bettuh than hunckerin' down, waitin' for EMs to come strollin' by.

—Perhaps program the blanket in some way, make its reflectivity change with time? That way the EMs won't register a same-shaped object following them about.

—Mebbe possible. Have to look at the specs.

—Grand. I'll pitch in whatever talents I have.

—Whoa there, Nigel. That's Bob's section. I can't—

—Fine then. Bob, I'm on for the first go.

—Jess a minit now—

—My idea, lads. I should get some fraction of the action, as the slang puts it.

—I dunno about ground team. I mean, assumin' the approach works. Dunno if you're up to physical specs, Nigel.

—Undoubtedly. But most of those walkers are servo'd, true?

—Sure. Havta be. Can't afford to put a big team on the ground. Ted's Operations study showed—

—That's okay, Bob, don't need to bother Nigel about details.

—Must keep surveillance maximized, Ted. Your own study showed that.

—How'd you get to read that part? It isn't due for release until—

—Mere rumor, I assure you.

—Huh. Sounds like we got a big leak somewhere, Bob. Okay, since you got the dope anyway—We'll land enough guys to service the equipment, then have teams from here servo'd to the hardware. Saves logistical problems. Five-hour shifts.

—Good. But there's bound to be dead time there. No one can take a lot of being tied into machines, not on that long a circuit, ship-to-surface. So peg up a short shift, occasional sods like me. We can stand watch, keep an eye for anything odd. Patrol duty.

—Well, I don't know as I like—

—He's got a point, Ted. Long's he's just standin' watch, nothin' special—

—Thanks very much, Bob, I do appreciate it.

—Hey, now, I didn't say definite you could.

—Awfully good of you.

—Nigel, we're out of the rum already and—

—It's not rum, luv, it's spidmeer.

—Hey, now—

—Well, anyway we're out and if you could—

—Certainly. Brilliant interruption. You look as if you're deplorably empty there, Bob, I'll just nip in and get you—

—But hey

—No trouble really, Ted you ought to come have some of the—

—Hey—

TWO

Nigel stirs restlessly, itchy from the encasing probes and pickups attached to him. He is moored to this electroneural net and feels the cramped capsule only dimly.

He waits for Isis to unfurl into him. *There*— it begins. Throughout, he will be trapped in a suffocating machine's clasp, but he is willing to set aside the unpleasant overtones of this in return for the experience it opens to him. *There*—

He shuffles out of the storage and maintenance shed, his suit clanking. Hydraulics wheeze and he steps onto the crusted face of Isis.

It is blurred browns and pinks, the dust whipping by with a lingering gusty ferocity as it slowly ebbs, the cyclone whirl from the Eye losing its force after these three days of lashing storm. Everywhere, a pink cloak. He can see perhaps ten meters in the optical, thirty in IR, in the UV nothing farther than his gloves.

Where are the EMs? Off that way, his pulsing faceplate display says. Beyond the beeping reference tabs the earlier teams have left, lighthouses in the murk. He revectors. The suit swerves with the usual oversteer, huge paws biting into the caked silicates, the sliding ceramic plates at arms and legs rasping in the pressing silence.

Nigel receives split signals from his two worlds. Encased in the hushed module aboard *Lancer,* he feels the subtle clutching flex of servos responding to him, amplifying each movement. Simultaneously, across kiloklicks of space, the feedback exosenses and senceivers give him the rub and clank of the hydrasteel robot, striding over hummocks and stones, two locomotors thrusting forward as two stabilizers seize the crumbly turf. All this spills into the run-on tapes as he gathers data and checks for landmarks—spots now familar to Command but coming fresh and crisp to him, his first time on this storm-worn place.

Rustworld. Grains of iron blow by, licking at his lenses, and sulfur dioxides make white tracers in the ruddy sleet, so much oxygen locked up forever in the land, stirred by the winds. A sudden burst of IR flickers over the ridgeline he is mounting and Nigel thumbs for amplification, the lightpipes gathering in photons and processing them, filtering turbulence in the air and the surges of dust, narrowing the reception cone and the scale, for he knows this opening in the clouds will pass, so he has only moments to grid an overview; he sees the valley he has memorized, checks it against the overlay that flashes on his faceplate and shifts to follow his head turning, the distant scarp looming like a rough-edged knife, the black basalt flow fanning out beneath him, scraggly bushes dotting the gullies where the brown, matlike grass clusters, clinging to heavy topsoil that the winds cannot snatch away. He angles downslope, boots *clank clank* on metal-rich stones, Ra's steady glow making the sky momentarily brim in echo to the strawberry tinge of the soil. The curling smoke to leftward rises from the shank of the mountain. He sees the slumbering heat in the massive shoulder of rock to the east, the oven which can rumble forth with fitful streams of lava and boiling ammonia, steam rising from the caldera, new moisture free at last to wet the winds and stem the tide of dust from the Eye. He crunches forward and suddenly there comes a shift in the insistent singsong that he half listens to, the radio stutter altering. It is a chromatic weave, that much they have learned, not the diatonic tones of Western music, so Nigel cannot seem to feel the scattershot clicks and shifts as music at all, even if he could assemble it in his mind after eliminating the long pauses between each quick darting blip, and yet now something changing in it draws his attention. The buzzing in the radio spectrum—he flashes a time-summed display, watches it evolve—is quickening, new amplitude-modulated pulses adding to the steady pattern.

Where are they? Regional sensos, buried in crevices to elude the EMs's notice, report to him in a flurry of data points. There: a few EMs are active, beaming their labored signal skyward, toward the distant, invisible Earth, which for a few hours now peers around Ra. But most are dormant, their tracers static, though a few show sluggish movement on the 3-D–projected map. Nigel thumbs a flash-forward of his recon path, sees that he will not reach the vicinity of the EM creatures for some hours, and without hesitation stamps down, the suit reinforcing the motion, sending him arcing over a gray boulder and down the opposite face of the blunted ridgeline, gyros keeping him from tumbling at this new surge, and he lands *crump* and is off again, keeping the leaps low to avoid attracting Command's attention, but moving fast, attention riveted to the murk ahead as the dust closes in again, the stubby wire-trees scooting by below. His acoustics pick up the persistent immemorial breath of the Eye winds and higher, a chippering, a rustle of frantic scurryings as small things scatter before him. They run only a few meters and then stop, exhausted and listening, conserving their muscles' reserves as they scavenge the dust-laden air for oxygen. This new sulfur-swollen storm from the Eye has robbed the air of more oxygen than usual and beneath the gale, life becomes torpid, sluggish. Skimming, he runs. Below passes one of the curious cairns, its stones sliced with hacksaw lines, not a representation of anything men can make out, but made by the EMs, they are sure of that. Several of the creatures have lingered near the cairns, rearranging the stones, murmuring in the microwave.

He surges among the rumpled hills, expending power reserves without care, running, rasping, clanking, probing the ruddy murk ahead. The spatterings of radio singsong shift and click. Above, a bright lance of yellow breaks out on the scarp: lava. Its fuming brilliance cuts through a shroud of dust, and Nigel puffs, the exertion building in him now a thin sludge of fatigue, as he trots down a long gully and onto the floor of the ravaged sulfurous valley. A shadow melts and then reforms and Nigel stops dead still, half-hidden by a shank of rock. A strange prickly sensation seeps into him as he watches the shadow behind a veil of dust, a shadow of pale blue that works forward, four legs, yes, the quadrupedal imperative, one of the biomechs aboard had said, and the alien looms, suddenly near, as a gust clears the air. Huge. Silent. Still. Yet a crisp microwave pulse bursts from it as the long rectangular head turns, jerking like a wheel on ratchets, away from Nigel and toward the base of the scarp. Its skin is waxy and rough, cloaking an apparatus of bones so obvious that to Nigel it seems he looks deeply into the radio being, sees the latticework, the boxy ribs, the brittle cage of sticks that encases the abdomen, the stiff long legs that jerk as the thing picks its way among the heat-shattered rocks, stepping tentatively, walking by touch. Nigel lets it recede until it is a mere slight darkening in the rosy haze, and then follows. Above, yellow fingers lace the rock face. His acoustics pick up the frothing bubble of the volcano, a sluggish torrent of lava splashing down a few hundred meters away. Exosense registers rising heat. He follows the EM creature. To Nigel's left a splotch grows suddenly, becomes definite, huge, towers over him in the shifting russet streaming. He squats, shuts down his mechanical murmur, holds his breath—

Nigel, what's the idea bein' off recon path? I jess come on an' run a check on all stations. Ramakristen says everybody's on hold till 'is storm's over, an' I check you—

"Quiet, Bob, I'll rep you later."

What you mean, later? Man, you're three sigmas out from your point.

"In contact mode, Bob. Flag my output for T'ang."
He steps quickly back in the swirling dust haze and the two shadows move off together, stick legs jerking, faster than he has ever seen them on 3-D. The rectangular heads turn and he hears a stuttering, a broadband splash of microwave beats and harmonics.

Christ, you got EMs all round you, Nigel, how'd you get in there and for goddamn sure why?

Nigel calls up the color-coded overview and sees the blips converging, integrated vectors all pointing toward him now—no, no, near him, east a few hundred meters. "Something's happening."

That's jess what's supposed to not; you're there to hold the position, not make—

"What's the radio map say?" Nigel murmurs to deflect the man, and moves cautiously behind the swaying shadows that lumber away, melting in the flowing, clotted air.

I'm gettin' it, Alex is on line, but I got to beep Ted on this Nigel, you've blown the tactical guidelines all to hell.

Nigel stays silent, listening to the howling hollow winds as they sweep over the upthrust crags of split boulders, listening on acoustic channels for anything from the EMs. Nothing comes, and nothing ever has. They appeared to be nonvocal. Yet they are blind as well, and sense each other only with the massive boxy radio emitters in their heads. Their song now lifts, scatters along a diatonic scale. He edges closer. These are among the biggest, over four meters high, and they lurch as they grope for purchase on the rugged gray rocks.

A booming crash rolls through the fine, dust-shrouded eternal days.

Hey, get away from there, I jess picked up—

"It's the volcano, that's all."

But you're smack on top a—

"I can run faster than a lava flow."

What if there's a slide? They're happenin' all time there—

"Quiet."

Fuck, Nigel, you're—

"What's Alex say?" Ahead, more shapes.

Oh, the EMs are all shut down. Went out 'bout a minute ago, all of a—

"Quiet."

The hissing heat of the lava flow is farther away; he picks it up clearly on acoustics. Ahead, the shadows tilt and settle. Seeking heat? It would be useful; they have a low metabolic rate and, while they are not reptiles, they could save valuable reserves by warming up at a convenient though

dangerous source. He shrinks back into a cleft of rock. Six of
them converge on a rough outcropping, where blue-green
mottling dots the broken rock. They move awkwardly, shifting
and canting their hulking bodies, and slowly they settle
downward, the knobby black protrusions that frame their
abdomens thrust forward—a sexual image flits through Nigel's
mind—and down upon the bare rock. He comes closer. No
radio crackle. They might as well be asleep. In the wan rosy
light they could see him if they had eyes, but they do not stir.
Nigel waits. No motion. Then, slowly, their skins begin to
swirl, the pale blue blushing and rippling, quick rainbows of
color washing over them. They are inert, but their shiny,
waxen flesh dances with a gaudy chromatic flourish. The
distant volcano rumbles, flashing yellow. Something is happening, something quiet and important, and if he can catch
the weave of it—

   *Nigel, this is Ted. You're ordered back, right
now. I don't want you—*

   "Certainly."
   In Ted's precise voice there is an edge of anger. Nigel
sees he has pushed the limits of his watch assignment as far as
they will go for this time. Best to retreat. And he is tired,
too, more than he expected to be. There is something intense
here that has drained him in the effort of sense it.
   "Falling back, Ted."
   He edges away. In his servo'd harness he is sweating and
he hopes the tap-ins will not reveal how tired he is. He will
take it slowly on the long walk back. The mere act of
shambling back to the suit storage and maintenance module
will itself be a crisp pleasure. He has learned to savor such
immersion. He scuffs lemony sand and treads backward,
watching the EMs fade from view, and turns into the rushing
howl of wind and the endless streaming of the ancient,
transfixed rustworld.

THREE

Ted stuck his head out of his office doorway as Nigel went by. "Hey, got a sec?"

"Of course." He paused at the open doorway which faced the crescent pit of Command. Consoles and running displays dotted the yawning floor, and tiers of separate subsections rose up from the plain like large trees. People moved everywhere, yet there was only a mild hum of unassignable noise, a blending of typeout machines, human voices, and a steady tremor that seemed everywhere and nowhere, that came from the rock itself. Nigel leaned against the doorframe, a bit tired. Here the slashed rock of *Lancer* was given a cosmetic plastsheen.

"C'mon in."

Ted's office was lined with pseudwood, deep walnut. Nigel wondered once again why the man hadn't simply gotten the real thing; it massed only fractionally more.

"I see you out there in the pit a lot," Ted said conversationally.

Nigel smiled. The preliminary ritual: a touch of how's-the-weather, and then to business. "I like to get round every day. Sometimes takes them awhile to log in new data."

Sage nod. "Yeah. They got this habit of refining the radio maps till they're like Picassos, when all the time guys like you are panting for the raw goods. Difference in styles, I guess."

Nigel nodded. He had long since accepted the mismatch of interests. "You had something new . . . ?" he prompted.

"Give a look." Ted flipped on a meter-sized wall screen, tapped in a command. Isis swam into being. The image swelled, shifted to a narrower focus, and centered on a tiny glint of light. Numbers clicked by in a blur at the lower left hand. The glint moved across the pink face of the Isis highlands.

"A satellite."

73

"Yeah. In a polar orbit, crossing a little to the east of the Eye's center. Here's a closeup."

An irregular rock, pale gray, with a grid of black dots scattered across the face. "Curious," Nigel said. "Those spots, they're not an artifact of the optics?"

"No, that's what everybody thought at first—some bug in the program. But they're there, all right."

"Artificial."

"Yeah. A converted asteroid, I guess. And there's another one."

"Oh?" The images shifted again. A second dot traced out an equatorial orbit as the screen time-stepped. Close-up: Another chunky gray rock, gridded. "Um. In sum, they can survey every square centimeter of Isis. The minimum needed to give full coverage."

"Right. We've run those orbits backward for nearly a million years. They've been stable that long, but if they were put up before that, they've had to make course corrections to stay in place." Ted leaned forward over his desk, fingers laced together. "Got any comments?"

"How is it this wasn't in the dailies?"

"Look, the techs work faster without the whole crew looking over their shoulder."

"Um." Nigel stared at the rough surface of the thing. "Some signs of old cratering, very nearly worn away. Are those scratches there? Perhaps some shock fracturing from old impacts. But the black dots were clearly put in long after that. What's the mag on those?"

"Here." The screen filled with black and then backed off to show some surrounding bright, scuffed rock. "Can't resolve anything. Maybe they're holes."

"Tried active probing?"

"No, not yet, but Alex—"

"Don't."

"Huh? Why not? Alex says he can probably get a good look-see by tonight. his interferometry can give us twenty, maybe thirty pixels in that patch. Then—"

"You're daft to tap on someone's door without knowing who's inside."

"Inside? Good grief, Nigel—"

"I urge caution. This is the first piece of technology we've seen in Isis space."

"Sure, but—"

"Let's study the surface first."

"Dammit, there's nothing *left* down there. The erosion's so fast. And the crater-count expert, Fraser, says there was an era of heavy meteorite bombardment roughly a million years ago, too. That's wiped the slate clean of anything that could've put up those satellites."

"No signs of cities?"

"Not yet. There's damn-all down there, far as the IR and deepscan people can see. That's why seems to me we should look at what's been left in orbit. These two satellites are probably the only old stuff around. Then, when we understand that, maybe those EM creatures will make more sense, and we can start—"

Nigel looked intently at Ted. "The cratering data, I haven't looked at that yet. What's the whole history?"

Ted waved a hand, his mind on something else. "Fraser's still doping out the crater size versus frequency curves. He has to recalc for the fast erosion, and allow for different epochs."

"How many epochs of crater making were there?"

"Oh, Fraser says there was the initial period, just like our solar system, but that was 'way back. He's got that probe data from the moons around the gas giant, and that gives over five billion years ago, when the initial cratering stopped. But then there was this recent epoch, you can see it in the highland terrain on Isis. A lot of junk falling, all over."

"About a million years ago?"

"Yeah. Why?"

"Seems damned strange. After the planets swept their orbits clean of debris, vacuuming up the initial junk from the formation of the whole Ra solar system, there should have been an end to cratering."

"Well, look, Nigel..." Ted leaned back in his net chair and began toying idly with a pen. "Isis has been moving outward from Ra, forced out by tidal forces, so who knows how that's going to change bombardment? I mean, this is a whole new ball game here and the old rules of thumb don't apply."

"Precisely," Nigel said in a clipped, introspective way.

"Meaning what?"

"Why assume the satellites are the last bit of whatever civilization the EMs had? Their orbital age is about the same as the last cratering epoch—but coincidence doesn't mean causality."

"Look, we'll know more when we find some cities."

"One supposes." Nigel shrugged, and got up to leave. "Maybe the EMs never had any."

But there were cities.

Or at least, buildings. Site Team #6 found the circular motif, using IR studies of a particular highland plateau. There was evidence of earlier ages with heavy dust dunes, but now a shift in the Eye winds had uncovered a plain that was, from radioisotope dating, 893,000 years old. Gently curving depressions ringed a central high spot, an ancient weathered hill. Lanes radiated from this point, spokes in a wheel. Excavation found buildings a mere fifteen meters below the dry, wind-scraped terrain. The ancient stones were rectangular and carried faint markings. The anthropologists on *Lancer* deduced little from these scratchings. They could trace the general outline of streets, an irrigation system, and a river valley ecology. There was no trace of fabricated or smelted metals, but then no one had expected any. What the rust did not claim, the winds rubbed away.

FOUR

Nigel watched the blood streaming out of him and yawned. Somehow it always made him sleepy. The first few dozen times it had made him pass out.

"Hey, I didn't ask you wanted ta lay down. Wanna?"

"I'm inclined to it, yes," Nigel said, but the medico didn't smile. She simply lowered his operating chair with a quick, carelessly efficient wrist motion. Nigel watched the tubing carry away pink strands of his plasma into the medmon.

The hulking machine clicked as it moved on to another sampling diagnostic.

"Some skilled job," the medico muttered. Nigel would have nodded sympathetically, except his upper arms, chest and neck were turned off. The medmon had to keep cardiovascular rhythm going despite the drop in pressure, and it was easier if the patient didn't interfere. He could operate his mouth, though. "Let something go wrong and you'd be needed, you know that. Same as a pilot—"

"I only trained for this so, y'know, I could make crew. I was an engineer, best there was, but not the right category for shipwork. Only I noticed this jobclass and I figured it was nothing I couldn't stack in on."

Nigel contorted his lips in a way he hoped conveyed agreement. He peered at the medico's thin, bored face and tried to read the woman's mood accurately. If nothing else, this excercise took his mind off the unpleasant ringing in his ears which always came as the medmon began sucking harder, filtering the plasma out and keeping his red blood cells. The blocky machine mixed in artificial plasma at the same time, but still the ringing came. With the plasma presumably went the damaged blood cells, while new stuff flooded in. Antioxidants to wipe out free radicals. Microenzymes to unlink confused old DNA strands that had gotten tangled. Immunological boosters. Leaching agents to destroy aging cells which had lost the ability to reproduce themselves correctly. The antisenescent cocktail.

"Does seem rather a bore," Nigel said carefully.

"Damn right," she said, surly. "You know, hard to believe, but once doctors used to do this. It was a big deal."

"Really?" Nigel tried to keep some interest in his voice, despite the fact that he could remember when doctors injected one with needles and thought eating meat was bad for you.

"Now a flush job's just, uh . . ."

"Maintenance?"

"Yeah, right. I mean, I like to work with my hands, real on-line stuff, but this jacko—no offense, y'know, I mean I ken you need it, but it's like being a hairdresser or somethin'."

"You were an engineer."

"Fact. Now they got me tracing plasmapheresis and slappin' fixes on hormones and—"

"How'd you like a spate in the drive tubes?"

She came out of her fixed anthology of gripes and looked at him. Until now he had been another anonymous customer, another plug-in for the medmon. "Well, shit, sure I'd tumble to that, only—"

"I believe I might be able to get you on the crew."

"Who says?"

"I do. I'll take it up with Ted Landon."

"You could do that? I mean, it's tough to get—"

"Of course. I can see this is bloody tedious. Must be dreadful, particularly for folk like me, who're just the same old thing, piping it through the medmon."

"You know it." She brightened and her thin face filled with interest. "You could maybe get me workin' with that team? I mean, just cleanin' the tubes would be, you know, interface solid state, lots of fieldwork and some lab stuff, too, I'd—"

"Fine. You seem the sort who should be set free of this." He would have waved an arm in mute demonstration, but he made the attempt and found motor control gone. "Feel like a zombie."

"Here, we're nearly through." She flipped a switch and he could move his right arm.

"Seems a pity I have to use up someone's time to do this—the monitoring, the patching, so on."

"Yeah. You should be able to handle it yourself. How come you're not on self-serve medmon?"

"Ted's being careful. Wants to monitor all the old scruffs like me."

"Jeez. Just makes more work."

"Precisely."

"Frap, if you could get me into engine work—"

"Think you could put me over onto self-serve? I mean, it's a dreadful waste."

"I guess so."

"Good. I'm not going to make a mistake where my own health is concerned, after all."

She looked at him. "Yeah, I guess so."

"Thanks, very."

He relaxed. Relays thumped and sensation returned to his chest and arms. He hated dealing with people the way he had just done, but at times there seemed no way out.

Nigel was in a good mood. He and Carlotta and Nikka had spent the evening playing sambau on a traditional board. He had lost heavily, giving up a month's worth of household chore time to Nikka and some ship credit to Carlotta. Unfazed, he kept up a stream of bad puns and unlikely stories.

"What's got into you?" Carlotta asked. "Been skoffing those disallowed drugs again?"

"Nothing so mundane." he winked and thumped his chest. "You see here a revitalized son of Britain." He paused, weighing whether to go on. Then: "I got on self-serve."

"Oh, good," Nikka said mildly.

Carlotta said, "Translation: now nobody'll know how fast he's falling apart."

"Correct! A man's enzymes are not suitable points for snooping by program directors and similar riffraff."

Carlotta asked, "How'd you do it?"

"Moment of opportunity. Talked the medmon attendant into it."

"Um. The attendant's got the right—decentralized authority and all . . ." Carlotta said, frowning. "But a simple systems review will catch it."

"That's where you come in." Nigel watched her expectantly as she arched an eyebrow. "You've got plenty of comm-systems lackeys. Surely you can exempt me from their small-minded scrutiny."

The two women glanced at each other and laughed. "So *that's*—"

"The old razzmatazz," he said lightly.

"Nigel, you want me to put information into the system that's not *true*."

"Truth is merely an opinion that has survived."

"You mean faking *data*."

"Right, sacred holy data."

"You're presuming on our, our—"

"Oh, come on. We're not English schoolchildren, sitting about eating crumpets and reading *When the Otters Came to Tea*. This is for keeps."

Nikka said softly, "You're asking a lot, Nigel."

"Love survives forever and all that, but vanity is less rugged. I can't sit in this apartment scanning reports and doing nothing."

"If you're not physically capable—"

"Don't you see, that's merely a handy stick to beat me with. Ted—"

"I can't do something dishonest!" Carlotta cried.

"Dishonest? Seems to me it's in what the Americans delightfully call a gray area."

Nikka said slowly to Carlotta, "It would mean a lot to him. Otherwise he'll lose his job."

"Which means what?" she replied. "No more servo work on the surface."

Nikka leaned forward earnestly. "That's very important to him."

"Him! Always him!"

"We have to support each other," Nikka said stiffly.

"*Mierda seca*."

"I believe that means—"

"What *I* mean is, we're both revolving around *him*. Don't you see that?"

Nikka blinked, her face immobile. "There is inevitably some inequality..."

"*Sí*, nobody can balance it all *perfecto*—but we're, we're *competing* for Nigel, and that's wrong."

"Yes," Nigel said, "it is. I don't see this as part of a contest, though. You—"

"*I* see it that way," Carlotta said.

"And I don't," Nikka responded. "I'm simply saying that Nigel needs help."

He said mildly, "I'd like to go down there in person. No chance they'll allow that. So servo'd is the only way I'll see anything of Isis."

Carlotta looked at Nikka and doubt crowded into her face. Nigel watched. It was best to keep well out of things now.

Carlotta had come out of the sun-streaked decaying barrios of Los Angeles, carapaced in executive competence. She skated with womanly grace over the myriad details of a systems-analyst universe.

Her career had involved collisons with managers and bosses, job switches and long hours. The natural drift in a technical career was to loft into contract manager, then program director, then division head, buoyant in the modern managerial morass. She resisted. She wanted to keep close to the work.

In time she got a reputation as a terrific troubleshooter who suffered fools not at all, particularly if they were bosses. She had her own standards and they had made her unapproachable. Until *Lancer* departed Earth orbit and started trials, she had been bottled up inside herself. Nikka had liked her from the start, though, and along with Nigel had slowly developed connections, getting the three of them through the early, uneasy years, and onto a plateau of comfortable intimacy.

But any three-way dynamic was stressed, inevitably, if

only by constant comparison with the conventional two-person model, which looked so bloody easy. How much loyalty did their snug harbor command? Nigel wondered as he watched Carlotta.

"I . . . I suppose I might . . . for a while. Only while we're in Isis space, though."

"Great! Knew you'd see the advantage of an old sod not having to explain every gimpy leg."

He was being falsely jovial, and they all knew it, but it gave the women a chance to sit back and listen to him as he rattled on about the surface work. Nigel studied Carlotta's pensive eyes as he talked. She smiled reflexively at his jokes, but she glanced at Nikka now and then tentatively, as if seeking approval. He saw that she had made this compromise more for Nikka than for him. Very well. He had gone begging and had gotten what he asked. Best not to fret over the reasons.

—*we're competing for him,* she had said. Perhaps so. He had to admit that he rather enjoyed that, had always been open to this sort of arrangement, as far back as California, with Shirley and Alexandria—

He abruptly jerked his head, stopping the thought. The women flicked puzzled looks at him. He made his face become casual, distant.

He didn't like to think of his previous three-way tie, and how it had ended. Letting the past filter into the present that way was a bad idea. He had to try to see Nikka and Carlotta as they were, above a calculus dictated by experience.

Still, he could not ignore the other side of the equation. In counterpoint to competing for him, they in the bargain competed *with* him . . . for each other.

It worked. He kept his own medical records and was able to disguise temporary injuries or stiffness. That kept him on the roster but didn't help him get jobs he wanted. It was weeks before a good servo'd surface mission came along, and Nigel didn't make the squad.

The team went after an EM creature, intact. Alex had tracked thousands of them with the big radio antenna. In a valley system near the Eye, the EM signals had begun to ebb away. Then one winked out.

"Dead?" Nigel asked him.

"Prob'ly. Didn't move for ten days. Then we lost its signal. Weak, for sure."

"Does its body heat show up in the infrared?"

"Did. Doesn't now."

FIVE

It took a week to reach a shipwide consensus, then another to plan the raid. The all-volunteer party dropped down, grabbed the alien, and boosted up—all in less than two hours.

They brought the big polyflex sack into the sterilized bay. The EM creature lay in it like a Tinkertoy monster that had fallen on its side, legs at impossible angles. In the blazing uniform bay light the thing had no shadow. It did not move. The team of sixteen wheeled the specially made cart slowly, carefully, into position among the crowded banks of sensors and diagnostics and gleaming racks of surgical instruments.

Nigel watched intently through the big viewport. He could make out Nikka in a stark white sealsuit. She pulled at the roller platform on the cart and the thing inside slumped into a better position. They were all drilled and sure. They moved quickly to position the instruments around the EM creature. Then they sliced the bag.

As the scalpel went in, the sack exhaled a thin mist. The team drew back for an instant and then, sheepish, watched the dust settle to the deck. The bay air was Isis normal, but without the fine sulfur-rich haze. Nikka sawed away part of the sack and stepped back, handing the polyflex to an assistant behind her. *I hope it doesn't need that wind and dust to live*, she said over General Comm.

This thing's dead already, came from elsewhere in the bay. And the assembled specialists began. For years they had waited to see something like this, and now the waxy skin of the EM lay glistening under the piercing lights. A murmur came from them.

Nigel breathed deeply, not noticing the crowd around him. The air in this corridor was as flat and pure and dead as it was in the bay, BioSci had ordered a clean, positive-pressure balance all around the bay, just in case. He reached up and flicked the comm monitor perched on his ears, and tuned for all channels coming from the work zone.

Careful, careful there, Andreov, peel that back as though it were your daughter's hymen.

thick-skinned isn't the word look at that like shoe leather X rays look good. Complicated bone structure I'd say.

Some kind of tripod spine running down into the underbelly see but what's that big long thing up there, must be in the head

yeah that's parabolic, Jeffreys said that on the boost-up, a longitudinal parabolic antenna fitted into the rectangular frame in the head, so it can pick up microwaves all along the long axis

must be what 'at bone's for, housin' the nerve endings for its radio sight, picks it all up an' 'er's a processor some'ere in 'ere to shape up the input for 'at funny-shaped brain

okay the spectral stuff is coming in on these tissues; nothing big so far pretty stringy stuff really

chem says the flash on that first sample is just plain ole oxy-binding iron hemoglobin wrapped up in a corpuscle blanket, same biochem patent the vertebrate line holds on Earth

this stuff's chromatophores just like I said and McWilliams said was bullshit, remember but lookit it respond see

man look it jumps up like that from smooth to prickly must be papillae in the skin

maybe helps flick off the dust

it's a reflex probably not conscious, just like shivering is for us

you keep ridin' my ass 'bout that I'll oh you think so huh look at that sked we don't get to those incisions for half hour at least, so you can wait for your microspecs until Kovaldy makes his cut

I know we got to move fast can't tell if this thing is clinically dead after all what's it mean we've been through all that before only now looking at the goddamn thing jeezus it's impressive so big the 3D doesn't really make you feel it but still I think we ought to hold back until the superficial team is through we don't know what sort of neural patterns we're going to hit

hey that's some kinda sac you've

sir there's flud over there on team A's incision lots of it they say

caught it fine only can't figure what

look at that pH

like nothing I ever saw it's a metallic salt a whole big bag of it carried up under that

watchat

got the needle okay

standard tissues here high water-storage ability just as we expected

no, nobody touches the head or anything spinal yet didn't you agree on that when we laid out the

hand me the other one I can't cut see this stuff's like leather

flaps are all over the slit there, you can see on the low-E X ray, see sir I think that's a mouth only the flaps are down over it, there are teeth back in there

awful damn sharp but what's it eat

Avery, get those legs braced better no we don't go in yet I don't want it to move is all, tell Kajima we're 'bout ready

clean at up 'fore you

get your lens on this I'm making a cut like so up and across

hold the bowl just in case

Nikka you got a hand I

something tough here I think I

Hey

Jesus

'at's not living tissue at all Sam

little threads of it I thought we'd hit some nerves by this time but this stuff jeez get chemsamp over here

tough innit

grab that

you know what this is it's *silicon*, right, strings of silicon with *boron* in it of all things

I don't get it there are look it's all laced through this living tissue here maybe some intrusion

like cancer maybe?

hey Singh we're getting some weak electroneural noise from the head I think we oughta step down till we

it's gangliated, that silicon, part of the bones maybe?

somethin' like a belly here, let me see that scope shot

yeah it's empty see, just maintaining pressure and notice how it's linked to that tangle of stuff, for sure that's an intestine, all stacked funny how regular they are innit perfect design for getting max digestive surface for the space you want, concentric

yeah, spherical shells instead of the swarm of ropes we've got in our gut

a lot better engineering you ask me

no we must have separate samples of each, I know they're coming fast now freeze-dry or vac-dry them every other one of them if you have to but don't fall behind I told Ladunda we should have had more backup on that but would he of course not well do what you

low metabolic rate they got though listen with that low a blood O_2 you'd be a corpse

this one is already

well sure but not because of that there must've been something else

it stopped movin' jess like the rest in the valley

shit now look just four centimeters away from that boron-silicon string there's that look at the lines that's phosphorus for sure, lots of it, all mixed in with the silicon

I think we oughtta stop right here until we get this straightened out

it must be rotting now already, you want to crack your suit and give it a whiff just go right ahead

come on

we'll have to vac you afterward of course but for science y'know you should be proud

stop gawking Kafafahin and fix that

put a potential drop across it you get funny characteristics see

what are you doing, Jeffreys?

the electrical characteristics of these silicon threads they're damn funny in fact you asked me I'd say it's a transistor, a lot of 'em

yeah that's what makes the thread flexible, see it's made up of little platelets all strung together, just a couple millimeters long max and they have some give in 'em

don't get it

it's a transistorized neural net, that's why you can't find any nerves in those tissues, that's not bone or anything it's a bunch of goddamn chips carrying info back an' forth the blood vessels are so small they sure don't get much oxy to the tissues this way

we're only a few centimeters in don't jump to

platelets I mean platelets of silicon migod 'at's crazy how you going to lay down silicon in a body when

down in the DNA, isn't that obvious there are lots of ways to transfer nucleic acid information into protein structure and build up inorganic structures in parallel if the code is there

sections of each I've got to have sections on each slice get Hendricks he can help, with all this pushing and shoving how'm I supposed to what's that babble over there anyway we're supposed to work not talk when

the opportunity I mean

these are electroplaques for sure, boron for p-type transistors, phosphorus for n-type, stimulated by the adjustments in potential in the tissues themselves, same as our nerves only with more control I'd say, like the difference between a semiconductor transistor and a plain wire, you can do a lot more that way than you can with simple nerves like ours, same as difference between those old vacuum tubes and a microchip at least

hold that steady

shit I'd swear that arm moved

they're pokin' into it, I don't wonder

so it's got both p-type and n-type transistors for different

don't you think we oughta back offa this till we understan' whatinhell is

Hendricks give me that bi-clamp I think there's something else, looks like

here, I'll help you get it

a myelin sheath sort of but thicker, got silicon plating it too here wait hold it there watch your

yeah okay tissues awful dry here

got to cut through hand me that

okay wonder what

something hard here som—

The fierce, dry snap of it jerked heads up all around the huge carcass, as the man shuddered and shook violently, the voltage shooting through him and wrenching open his mouth, a rattle of breath escaping, and his assistant also shared the current for a moment as it surged, rooting him to the floor, and then the assistant's hand, arm went into a spasm and slipped from the clamp he held so the current passed from him and he collapsed to the deck, unnoticed, for the frst man now jerked and shook so violently everyone watched, frozen, and inside him the central pumping chambers of the heart, which had been starting to relax in their cycle, went into ventricular fibrillation, shaking and banging together and stopping the flow of blood, the man's eyes rolling up, the current shooting through his arm to his feet and into the mass of the ship, the crowd around him still unmoving, staring, until at last a woman seized a plastform instrument and hit him, hard, freeing the hand, and the man fell loose upon the deck. Nikka dropped the instrument and knelt beside him. The room burst into babble.

He sees there is nothing he can do of course yes as the man falls, puppet with cut strings, eyes rolled back, Nikka following through with the blow, always stroke through the ball his father had said, and Nigel sees what will happen next, the gasps and quaking thin astonishment around the huge body, the sudden clump of humans forming to get the man out and into a vacced-down and retrosterilized environment, so they can split the skinsuits and treat the charred flesh, probably saving the one man yes but not the other, it will take too long and it must have been high current, the most dangerous kind of discharge, it would have been easier if there had been only high voltage, but no that is—

he blinks, sensing his own slow respiration and the rank scent of the shuffling, muttering, frightened people around him, their sudden bitter sweat fouling the air before they sense it themselves

—that is unlikely, it had to be an electrical discharge appropriate to a biological system, low voltage, high current, stored somewhere perhaps in the electrochemical batteries they carried, the metallic salt fluids in insulated sacs, a very compact way to store energy on an oxy-poor, grim, red dust–smothered world, so the thing on the carry cart—

Nigel steps back, letting the others crowd by him to see the similar milling and pointless released tension dissolve into busy action beyond the viewport, feeling in this nostril-flaring surge the human animal as a tribe—the thing is alive,

alive but muted, it still must feel the prick of the outside but
through a foggy blur of hibernation, a wise, aeon-old tactic, to
let the internal furnace ebb, avoid the mammal's peaks and
excesses of hunger-driven desperation, to wait out the world,
to subside into long watchful inactivity, that is what cool
calculation would teach, not to be of the warm kind like us,
not to be a slave to steady metabolism, not when the grinding
of history is so slow, so fine

   —the crowd now surges back from the port without
thinking, round *Os* of mouths, rasping gasps, a quick heat in
the brittle air as Nigel turns, guessing and sees the humans
scattering away from the carry cart, Nikka well ahead, helping carry the injured men, glancing back now, eyes big
through the helmet bubble, as the EM creature fills the
comm lines with a buzzing rattle, a sighing *chirrup*, and with
aching slowness lifts a leg, struggles, finds a purchase, turns
the great rectangular head—ah yes, the longest axis can
resolve all wavelengths shorter than its length, so to get the
best vision, to sharpen the image, you rotate the head until
the long edge is aligned with the direction you wish to sense,
and by instinct the brain stores the image, clears away the fog
of imprecision, and the head—wobbly, weak, roused only by
a mortal threat, burning now its anaerobic reserves for a final
battle—rotates again, the webbed and waxy skin catching the
light, arms flailing for a grip, legs kicking for a fulcrum to tilt
itself erect, another angry burst of radio noise through the
comm lines

   —but this signal must be only for definition, perception,
to see, Nigel reminds himself—

   it catches the cart's edge, wrenches itself sideways, arms
thrusting, head now tucked down, legs descending to the
deck, heavy, soundless but for the hornet hum in the comm
lines, and surges swiftly erect, towers in the bay

   —Nigel senses what it is like, the metal surfaces everywhere reflecting its pulses back, blinding it with scattered
self as the thing sent out radar pulses to sense its world and at
the same time named itself, the pulse was its signature, so
now the universe so firm underfoot chanted and chattered the
name back to him, the name shattered and unfeeling, not the
way its fellows would return the song, no, but in the clanging,
hard-edged manner of metal flinging the name back in re-
buke and indifferent rejection, no sheltering sky silence

overhead but instead a screaming piling on of echoes, voices and voices all chattering stuttering mindless chaos, hard and hostile, a shouting blankness

It staggered. Eighteen minutes now, and it was still on its feet. The sticklike legs shook. It took a hesitant step, feeling the smooth stone deck for purchase. Slow, achingly slow. The head turned with the soft jerks, tilting this way and that. It was trying to sharpen its definition of this metal-lined world.

"Look at 'ose knees tremble," a man said nearby. Nigel eyed the man and his companions. They wore slick suits and carried heavy packs of equipment.

"It's running out of energy," Nigel said to Ted, who was standing nearby, listening intently to his earplug comm.

Ted nodded once, twice, and clicked off the comm. "That's what we believe," he said.

"It was in some kind of dormant phase," Nigel said. "It had emergency reserves, though, that's obvious. Something—"

"We'll figure it out when we take it apart," Ted said.

"Take it . . . ?"

"Hendricks and Kafafahin are dead. Electrocuted."

"Um."

"Time to stop foolin' aroun'," said the red-haired man.

"I say, you can let the thing run down and simply be more careful next time. There's no reason—"

Ted turned abruptly toward Nigel. "You look yourself. Two men dead, I don't take any more chances. Guidelines are, we fulfill the conventions on alien life-forms—big ones, anyway—*unless* human life is threatened."

"True enough. But—"

"No buts, Nigel. Fritz"—Ted gestured to the red-haired man—"when it falls, give it five minutes before you go in. Then follow that prelim biopsy routine—the one they had as a fallback."

"There's no need to kill it," Nigel said evenly. "I think we can understand what caused that—"

"I'm not risking it," Ted said flatly. One side of his mouth twisted up in a humorless grin. "Keep back from it when you go in," he called to the nearby squad. "No contact."

Nigel stepped between Ted and other men. If he could simply deflect the man's attention from the preparations, slip some thought in on top of the adrenaline—"I believe if you'll allow me to go in, I can sort out what's happened. The thing must have storage points, internal capacitors. From the X rays we can locate them. Then I can short out the remaining—"

"I'm not risking anybody for that thing. Particularly not you, Nigel." A brittle smile.

"If you'll belay that order for a simple blasted ten minutes."

"*No*. Now pipe down and let me think." Ted clenched his jaw and tightened his mouth, touching his teeth together. He rubbed them carefully back and forth, jaw muscles rippling.

Abrupt movement through the port. Nigel watched the EM creature stagger, head wobbling. It kicked over an array of electronics. The arms waved uselessly, clutching at phantom reflected images from the walls, unable to find the key which could unlock this scrambled world.

It fell.

Equipment scattered in all direction. The tall figure toppled slowly, trying to catch itself, hold itself aloft. It could not find the balance. Its hands convulsed and the sharp nails at the end of the six tapered, knobby fingers struck sparks from the stone. Soundless. It kicked once, twice, shattering a biostorage unit.

"Get ready," Ted said, his voice thin and reedy.

Nigel looked at the men and their tight, concentrated faces. He turned and walked away, tired and disgusted.

Nigel thumbed the focus of the phase-contrast microscope. The bio folk had been over the tissue slices a thousand times and he had read their prelim report, but he wanted to see it for himself.

The creature had many organ systems in common with earthly species. A liver, with double-membrane cells, ribosome-studded and intricate. A wrinkled gray brain. And the chunky body used the same economical cradling, bundles of tubes and support rods and swiveled sockets, now fanning out, now joining up.

But evolution's firm hand had brushed aside the inefficient chemical kindling that ran Earthside animals. The EMs stored electrical energy in big cylindrical capacitors and discharged it in bursts when needed. The capacitors were sheets of membrance with fine accordion pleats, all wrapped in a Turkish-towel texture, a pictorial tale of an epic struggle for surface. Each capacitor was a forest of smaller capacitors, all insulated and buffered so that a chance twist of the body could not discharge the precious hoard.

Nigel clicked off the miscroscope. Once you had a glimmer of the idea, it seemed natural. Oxygen was in short supply down on Isis, with all the sulfur belching out to scavenge the air. So nature had used an entirely nonchemical method of making a big, energy-squandering animal. Don't lock up energy in chemical bonds and carry the mass around with the body. Instead, eat whatever food you can find, and then process the chemicals, keeping the energy in separated positive and negative charges. The silicon-platelet "nerves" did some of that, and the odd-looking stomach carried the rest of the job.

No one Earthside had ever anticipated an electrodynamic digestive cycle. Yet once you saw the logic . . .

Nigel scratched his nose, bemused. It was all well and good to know the innards, but how did the EMs actually *live?* How had they got this way? The only clues would lie down there, in the raw, dim landscape.

Bob Millard had set out new exploration-team schedules, in light of the discoveries from the EM death. Nigel had a secondary job in the exploration, teamed with a chap named Daffler. He scratched his nose again. Perhaps an opportunity would arise, he would glimpse some clue. Perhaps.

SIX

Rasping, clanking, clicking, Nigel picks up speed. Behind him Daffler is having trouble getting his left locomotor to rev up. If he can get a lead on the man maybe Daffler will never catch up and Nigel can operate with some freedom, follow his nose—

Hey wait up I said.

"There's something over this way—"

I said wait up and I mean wait up. Look, Nigel, Millard made it pretty plain. You follow my on-site orders or else I shut you down.

Nigel slows. He knew it wouldn't work, but something in him made the attempt worthwhile, something lofting and playful that erupted when he again felt his stabilizers and locomotors bite into the crust of Isis. He senses that this will be his best chance, perhaps his only chance, to see the EMs as they are, not through 3-D or in dry reports, all of which distance him from the real experience and by selecting spectrum, data, site, slivers of information, must always skew the flat facts of perception, and rob him.

I've got this lateral housing secured now. Be with you.

Nigel grins lightly, thinking of the cool stone interior of an English cathedral, the services he had dutifully endured there so long ago, a small boy still awed by rising columns of granite and the heavy solemn weight of the service itself, *and the Lord be with you*, Amen, *and with thy spirit*, the wafer burning his tongue with its bland consuming bond, promising that in the end he would rise up, a blood knot brimming from an eroded body, ready to take in the night, *take, eat, this is my body and blood*, eat everything, swallow a universe of dark that seeps in under doors into the warm orange of the family living room, his father sitting in that bobbing rocker, chewing his lip as he listened, rocking, rocking, stern, his son talking, tones deliberately muted lie the long flat notes coming from the organ as they take up the collection, coins ringing in the plates, granite smooth cool climbing up the air, *rocker* he says will go into rocket, only a *t* for an *r*, Father, Father who art in heaven, Father art in haven now—

Looks like they're vectoring north again

rouses Nigel and he calls up his faceplate web. Red dots. Time sweep shows them drifting up the valley, away from the gusty Eye winds. They are moving quickly. Faster, Alex says, than he has ever seen the EMs travel anywhere, at rates demanding more energy than the low-oxy environment would allow. Alex noticed the activity in this valley over a week ago. But other surface spots had priority, and by the time the big dish had focused on the region a new storm had moved in from the Eye. The valley was pocked with streaming volcanic vents. The dust swirled into the rising columns of heat, into air rich in water and ammonia and carbon dioxide.

Nigel turns his opticals downward, to see his own hydrasteel carapace, where spatterings of brown mar the robot's serial numbers, dribbling off in streaks toward the ground. It is raining mud. The sulfurous dust falls as it strikes the volcanic air. It seems odd that the EMs would prefer this slippery, rumbling valley of murk to the downslope valleys beyond, where the water runs clear and the air carries only the fine mist of Eyedust that survives the moist volcanoes.

> Scoot down to the east, Nigel, I pick up some spiky microwave from there.

He clatters over wet rocks and picks his way down a hillside. The illusion is getting better as the feedback loops lace him into the machine dynamicals better and better, the deft sure movement of the servos coming through to him as the broad feet smack down *clump, clack*, feeling to Nigel like striding over rough terrain in training boots, and even the stabilizers, whose ground grip translates into surges of calf muscles, thighs clenching and relaxing, spine riding on its disks, arms swinging to keep the pace steady, steady, as the hydrasteel clanks through a blurred world, peering at shifting sheets of life-flecked dust, the thick air here a chemical factory driven in the end by the tidal forces that rip the land, thrusting up the Eye mountains, sawing through the caked layers of rock, poking vents into the high mountain valleys, everywhere flinging wet and grime skyward, cloaking the sky forever so the EMs have never known the stars, except perhaps for one night in a thousand years, when the dusts would fall and the silvery points would glimmer in the vastness, but the EMs had no eyes to see.

> Are you picking this up, Nigel? Some sputtering on two hundred megahertz.

"Right, a trifle below sixteen degrees bearing from here."

I make it seventeen point two. Close.

"Lets home on it."

He stamps down. The servos transpond the movement into a leap that takes him/it over a canyon of brown vegetation, bringing him down *crump* on a shoulder of burnished basalt. The feet skid but the robot rights itself in time. Five meters visibility in the optical. Rain fogs his lenses. He leaps again, getting a boost as the back hydraulics come in with a *whoosh*, and he skims over twisted blue-green stumps of plants—slimy, sagging under boughs thick with mud. The radio overlay sputters, orange-tinted vectors pointing dead ahead—not one source, he can see that now, but scattered blotches and patches of radio noise, emitting around two hundred megahertz but not frequency-fixed, some giving off prickly hisses, others booming out long patterns that Nigel's step-down electronics shape into acoustic rattles, the whole bunch sounding like a crowd tromping on broken glass.

Just checked with Alex. There are no EMs within a klick. This must be some other life-form.

"Weak signal. That might explain why Alex can't pick it up. But still..."

Through the dusky swirl a rocky ledge appears. Nigel angles to the left, thumbing to IR. Visibility improves. He can see down a long canyon, dim in the bloodred wash of Ra light. "Rocks here look as though they've been worked." He steps forward gingerly. No life-forms visible. The canyon walls are streaked and carved, long gouges weaving together. He switches back to two hundred megahertz and the snaps and pops leap out at him, coming from the cuts in the rock. "Looks like art, maybe." The seams are lined with odd silvery stuff. Nigel reaches out a maniple, scratches it.

"This stuff is a conductor, an antenna." He turns. He is in a large fenced-in area, like a corral. Through the gloom he sees caves dug back into the rock, caves with oval openings, other blocky and square, some triangular. "It's a village." The popping, chiming radio pulses come from marks near the doorways, *wook wook* for the ovals, *skaah skaah* from the rectangular. Other marks bark and mutter from the bare rock. *Street signs?* Nigel thinks, almost tripping over indentations in the muddy ground, curved patterns that seems to make no sense. He clumps down the canyon, knowing the runon tapes will capture it all and a dozen specialists will have a dozen ideas about it by the time he is out of the servo'd pod.

> *I've found another one, a very similar canyon. I estimate I'm about five hundred meters east. If you—*

"Wait."

Ahead hang woven strands, secured to the canyon walls and stretching across it about six meters above the ground. From the strands hang sheets of the silvery stuff, some of them giving off a chorus of radio sputter, others silent. Nigel approaches. "There something—" and *Ther ing meth rees eesom thingther* comes at him from the sheets, bouncing around the canyon, scrambling. "I think the"—*inkth ti ti thi l kthelith*—"superconduc"—*supduc con sup ducerco perduc*—"superconducting sheets—"

He turns, flees, unwilling to give up his radio spectrum but confused by the mocking wall of echoes. A hundred meters away he stops, sheltered by a jut of stone, and says, "They've got some elaborate, well, rooms, I suppose. A way to get some privacy, I guess—No, that doesn't make sense. Why make them reflecting? No, it must be some kind of amplifier, a way to, well, a public-address system? I don't . . ."

> *Nigel, you're confused. Don't you think you should—*

"Bugger that. Look, get a team down here to go over this, this village."

> *Sure, we will. Just don't get so—*

"It hasn't bothered you yet, Herb?"

> *Huh? What hasn't—*

"Superconductors. How do EMs with no technology left, no cities left standing, make superconductors?"

Oh. Well, there are those satellites. Maybe—

"I got a good look at the sheets. They're tarnished. They have cracks in them. They look as thought they've been folded and refolded many, many times. They're *old*, my good fellow. Old."

The next team is on in, let's see, six running hours. I'll ask for a biodate. But hang on, I want a look at your village, too. I'll be there in—

"Hold. Stay where you are. Or perhaps better, back away."

Why? It's just a—

"The EMs are out milling around, Alex says. We've just stumbled on something that resembles a village, correct? And odds on, the reason we haven't seen one before is that they were always occupied. We didn't want direct contact, so we missed the villages."

Sounds plausible. However, we can't—

"But no one really deserts a village. You leave behind—"
Through the swirling gusts of russet mist a dark shape lurches. Nigel ducks behind a boulder, grimacing, and kills his radio transmissions. You leave behind the weak, the old, perhaps the children—but you don't leave them unprotected.
Nigel tucks his head down, knowing this movement has no analog for the craft he is driving, but does it anyway, aware that to distance himself from the machine in any way now will lessen his effectiveness. To hide, crouch down, avoid the licking radar of the approaching creature, hope the suit reflects like an uninteresting gray stone—
A webbed foot comes down on his foredeck. The EM creature surges up, clumbering over the rocks, head swiveling and tracking, its foot pressing down. Plates buckle on the ribbed foredeck. A motor whines in protest and abruptly goes

silent. Circuits buzz, warning. Nigel feels the blunt pressure turn to a cutting, jarring pain. He fights against his impulse to back away, to scramble out from under.

I've switched to K-band, Nigel, hope you're getting this. Your Mayday beeper just cut in. Should I head into that canyon?

Nigel decides to risk a transmission. If Daffler comes into view, moving, the EM creature will surely catch on, will know there are odd moving rocks in the village. He clicks to K-band and sends "Stop!"

A frozen moment. The EM halts, teetering, two feet on Nigel's groaning deck. Some side band of the K-band wave must have gotten through to it, although the EMs seem to broadcast and receive on a much longer wavelength.

The EM tilts forward hesitantly, feeling its way. A foot lifts. Then the other. It moves off, farther up the canyon. Nigel picks up warbling radio bursts as it echo-locates itself, endlessly sending its "name" and receiving back the reflected and scrambled world-picture painted by the same "name" —the canyon, the metallic scratchings, the superconductor sheets, the sky above which is a blank except for a low mutter from Ra. Nigel wonders, watching its aching slow progress, what effect this way of seeing must have on how the EM thinks—if "think" was the right word at all. To it the world responded eternally with fragments of its own name, like a constant reassuring chorus which both tells the EM what it needs to know and reassures it of its own individuality, its importance in the very act of defining the world. If the EM did not call out its name, the world was a cipher, a silence. Yet if it spoke, the universe itself leapt into being. Only fellow EMs were emitters. Each sends on a slightly different wavelength, so the babble of the community does not blind all. Nigel wonders how a solitary EM had discovered Earth's faint whisper, a voice which appears periodically as a weak dot in the sky not far from Ra's deadening murmur. Perhaps an EM alone, meditating, had seen it, probed it, guessed the existence of other intelligences in the yawning vacancy.

Nigel, Bob wants me to move in on you. I'm

coming up the canyon, bearing north at thirty-eight.
Your subsystems signal damage in—

"Quiet!"

Look, the EM is moving off and Bob's got an
idea that I can check your systems out before we try
to move you or—

"Come on if you bloody well must, but keep quiet."
The EM is gone, swallowed in the sullen red gloom.
Nigel peers about him and sees more of the ruts cut into
rock, lets his eyes be led by the sloping lines down the
canyon. From this angle the design is at once apparent.
Troughs intersect in a downward-tending web, emptying here
and there into small holes near the canyon walls: cisterns.
Farther on, a gust clears the air for a moment and Nigel sees
a spillway, the brown rock that forms it worn and eroded but
still functional, and beyond, a crude catch basin. So the EMs
gathered water here, stored it. But there is no agriculture.

I've got you in the IR, Nigel. Just hold still,
don't try to move.

"I told you, mind the transmissions."

No trouble, I'm sure that—

It comes at them with amazing speed, knees jerking
high. It scrambles over boulders. Daffler emerges from the
veils of dust and does not see the EM bearing in from the
east. Daffler is a hydrasteel walker, like Nigel, and he looks
forward through forward-focused, mag-adjusted optics so he
is blind to the east unless he turns his sensor head; but as he
lumbers forward, now only meters away from Nigel, the dust
falling thick and white-streaked again, the EM lunges and
strikes Daffler from behind. "Roll!" Nigel calls, the word
leaping out of him in his amazement, but Daffler cannot draw
his forward legs up in time and the walker pitches over,
scraping on the rocks, orange sparks scratching the air, and
the EM steps over the tumbling robot that now seems so
weak. Nigel backs away from the towering dark figure, watches

its head dip and turn away from Daffler and toward Nigel, the thing is sure of where he is, must have gotten a fix on him earlier and not given any sign, simply waited them out, Daffler shouting now *got to 'bort out, something hit me* as the huge head sways, Nigel feels Daffler tumble against him, jarring, legs a tangle, and senses a sudden spattering of radio pulses, a highly structured wave form, and then a loud crisp sound like fat frying as the EM lifts Daffler and brings him down on Nigel's deck, crunching, a lancing pain, bright burst of green—

The medmon moved with rectangular urgency, sniffing at him, humming to itself. Nigel lay passively, wanting this to be over. He eyed the ceiling.

"That thing for sure took you and Daffler to the cleaners," Bob Millard said casually.

"It came at us like a bat out of hell. Otherwise, I'm sure—"

"We're sure of nothin', Nigel."

"Well, I *am* sure I don't need this thing"—he thumped the medmon appendage—"nosing about me. Christ, Bob, I was tucked away in the *servo* capsule, not down on Isis. I can't *possibly* be hurt."

Bob shrugged. "This is SOP, according to Medical. Any big accident, we put you through."

"Then why isn't Daffler here?"

"His unit wasn't creamed, 'at's why. We're still getting a carrier and inboard diagnostics from his walker. Yours—zip."

"The EM must've smashed into my outer circuitry. That could precipitate a shutdown in the whole—"

"Could be. Thing is, we can't go back and see right away. Have to wait."

"Why?"

"A whole flock of EMs have moved into that 'village' of yours. Ted 'n' I feel we shouldn't' risk further contact with 'em right now. They'll be waitin'."

"I want to look at those superconductors."

"So does half the crew."

"Then perhaps—"

"No go, Nigel." Bob smiled lazily. "The EMs'll defend that town or whatever it is. Y'know, in all this, you kinda forgot what I sent you down there for."

Nigel saw he was going to have to go through this mild byplay to find out what the tac-strat people thought was the next smart move. "What was?"

"Figure out what's makin' 'em so jumpy."

SEVEN

The spot on Isis lying directly under Ra's glow is bleak and fevered, its dull heat a remorseless engine.

Air drives out of the Eye, cloaking the land with dust, and shadows blur the forms moving on the slopes of the hills. The mountains above mutter like an old man swearing in his sleep.

A shock wave ripples through the carapace of the robot, another shifting of the earth as the churn of the planet cycles and recycles the crust endlessly, quakes and slides and upwellings bringing fresh iron forth to lick the winds and bind up the oxygen. And volcanoes belch forth more water, which in turn is split by random energetic photons into hydrogen and oxygen, elements feeding the ecology that clings to the planetary crust, frail life, suffering the jolts and the million minor deaths and the dry bareness. Gales pour over the mountains with their dust, carrying a howl that never ends in these narrow valleys, hollow and vacant and without hope of change, reedy and distant, as though the air itself is worn out.

He moves on, *clump, crump,* leaden steps carrying him across the silted valley floor toward the hills, ceramic sheaths of his hydraulic rasping, a bitter taste of a stim tab is his mouth. Onward.

Daffler is in the lead and a woman, Biggs, is approaching the clustered EMs from the other flank of the volcano. Orange flash: the mountain mumbles, and the land is for a moment awash in fresh light. The dust thins as the moist volcano breath washes away the sulfur oxide blur from the Eye. Alex has never seen a group of EMs bunched together like this on the radio maps. Something brings them here, away from the "village," so a team now approaches the EMs while a larger team invades the "village" again, to take a look at a superconductor sheet, crawl into the caves, learn what they can. Daffler and Nigel and Biggs are a diversion, an afterthought really, to watch the EMs but do nothing else. If contact is to be made it must come from the specialists, the encoders and analysts who have sat silent and waited, stern and close-lipped, for more input. The biomeds have trapped a myriad of small animals by now, picked them apart, and found nothing that echoes the semiconductor nerves and brain of the EMs. The animal kingdom of Isis is slow, ordinary, run by the grinding inefficient chemical processes of oxidation in an atmosphere where iron and sulfur steal the oxygen at every turn, leaving life to snatch what it can before the oxygen-rich volcanic air is locked up again, for a billion years, in the hungry rocks. Yet it is not oxygen the EMs seek near this volcano; Nigel sees this, watching their shifting specks on his overlay. They do not congregate where the drizzle descends, bringing oxygen.

Sighted one to the south. Headed toward me.
I'm not moving.

"Right." Daffler sounds tight, cautious. As he bloody well might be.

Suggest you bear on it, following an axis through
me. That way it'll see no lateral motion.

"Right."
Nigel plunges on, legs working. Something skitters by him. A small rodentlike thing, running as fast as it can. The animals here have anaerobic reserves, just as Earthside animals, but they are weak and last only a few minutes. After that, they must slow to the rate dictated by the oxygen supply. Nigel peers ahead. Clouds are sweeping in, drawn by the convection call near the volcano, and the ruddy cranberry glow soaking down reminds Nigel of the aura over a distant burning city, the way cities had been devoured since ancient Egypt, the libraries in flames, Alexandria—

It's passed me.

Another small creature, running to the left.
Bob's voice came through clearly:

> Guess you oughta hunker down, Nigel. Don'
> want a repeat a last time.

Nigel obligingly stops all servos, settles to the ground,
tapers off his carrier waves in X- and K- and R-band. A
howling of wind. An orange flash from the crater high above.
Something moving: dog-sized, four legs, matted brown coat,
tongue lolling. Behind it, seventy meters away and closing:
an EM, striding smoothly on the baked sands, negotiating a
narrow wash, coming on as stolidly as a train. But the EM is
tired, too, Nigel sees. The legs waver and the arms are
slumped at its sides. This is a pursuit, and a long one, and in
the space of time the EM takes to make one stride Nigel
pieces together this latest fact, and all the other data on EMs,
and sees that of course they are following a carnivore pattern,
moving steadily over the land but keeping separated so that
each EM has an area to hunt, and between the passing of
each EM there is time for the prey to forget, to grow
careless. No other creature on Isis has the semiconductor
wiring because they have been hunted down, just as man has
no similar land competitor because in the far past he elimi-
nated them. The EM slows now, head lifted, peering to the
north where the doglike thing vanished, and suddenly it
stands erect, stopping, head high and turning east, it seems
to gather itself, and Nigel hears again the fast popping sound,
crisp, bacon frying, louder, louder, louder, until his receiver
circuits overload, and silence washes in.

> Nigel! Goddamn, this animal comes running
> by me, not fifty meters away, and then it just falls
> over. What's—

Nigel studies the EM. It sags to the side, catches itself.
Finally it begins to walk, legs heavy and ponderous.
"It's moving toward you."

> Damn. Wish I could—

"Have a go at that animal. Get a quick look, up close."

Okay.

Pause. Sheets of dust drift in a breeze. The EM fades from sight, moving with thick-jointed weariness.

Well I—this is—

"What?"

It's all black and, and it's, it looks . . . burned.

For a moment Nigel doesn't breathe. Then he nods. "Right. Get straight away from there. The EM hasn't got much energy left, I expect, but there might be enough."

Enough to what?

"Not trample you. Not this time, no. It could fry you, though, friend Daffler. With well-focused radio waves."

Though he cannot see through the rolling mist of fine dust now moving up valley, Nigel watches the EM move on his overlay, and he smiles, thinking of the vast slow creature, exhausted, its capacitors drained and running now an anaerobic stored energy, as it lumbers forward to claim its rightful prey.

Nigel crouches in the shifting murk, watching the finger of orange work its way down the mountain. More lava. The land shrugs and murmurs. He waits.

The EMs are clustered half a klick away and Bob will not allow any closer contact until a larger team comes on duty. There are many other interesting sites scattered around Isis and teams are working them all: digging in the worn old cities; classifying flora and fauna in the downslope passes; dipping into the rust-rich wealth of life beneath the seas; tramping through the arid twilight lands near the terminator.

The entire expedition has now taken on the wide, scattered tone of the fragmented specialties themselves. A busy buzzwork. First they will collect the data, and then they will think. But they do not see that what the data say depends in the end on how you think, and Nigel feels again the strange impatient lust that drives him forward, that always has, that goes through and finally becomes part of the serenity that sits behind his mental darts and dashes, so that he cannot simply gather facts like wheat, he has to inhale this place and see it whole, become the five blind men and the astrophysical elephant, let the greased pig of this world slip through his arms and yet leave behind on each pass a skimmed lesson, so that by accretion he builds it up, hears the EMs that lie beyond the remorseless bark of the data, the clatter of facts.

Hey, they're moving, comes from Daffler.

"Righto," Nigel sends merrily in X-band.

Bob says he's putting a fresh team on in an hour. Sylvano and his guys.

"Hell, Sylvano's a biomech man."

There will be a communications specialist in the team, don't worry about that, Daffler says blandly.

Nigel shrugs, realizing that of course Daffler is the communications man for this miniteam, and thus thinks that's the most important role. The comm people have been riding high lately, sure that understanding EMs rests on knowing how they evolved to see and speak in the radio. Yet they hadn't a clue about the hunting, and the discovery only two hours ago of the EM ability to burn down prey at hundred-meter range has obviously shaken Daffler and Bob and everyone.

So much for the predictive power of science. Yet they should have guessed something of the sort, Nigel muses.

With Ra fixed in the sky, all regions of the planet would have a steady level of illumination. Only the eccentricity of the Isis orbit would make Ra sway slightly through the year, a mild wobble. In the constant pattern of shadow and light, or amid the dust storms and fine mist, the ability to probe, radarlike, would be valuable to a predator. Ordinary eyes—passive, easily blinded by the dust—would be less useful. And in the wan light of the terminator zone, prey with optically sensitive eyes would be nearly blind, even more vulnerable.

But the crucial ability was, as always, killing. So the logic of evolution has pressed the radio eye into service. With oxygen at a premium, chasing down prey could easily exhaust an EM's energy reserves, making it vulnerable. Far better to fry a target and approach it cautiously. The radio eye could probe, identify, and kill—and then probe again, listening for telltale signs that the target's nervous system had gone out of business. All this, without coming close enough to risk the prey's claws or horns or hooves. So with evolution's marvelous economy, the eye did everything: seeing, talking, killing, even cooking. And the mind behind the eye struggled to improve perception, resolution, accuracy. The eye and the mind must have evolved together, perhaps in a bootstrapping loop like the hand/mind link in man.

Nigel, they're drifting your way.

"As I expected," he mutters to himself.

What? What's that? Look, if you have something in mind, Nigel, I would just as soon not have Bob jumping down our throats about—

"Quite. Worry not, friend Daffler. I'm simply here to see what I can see."

There will be plenty of guys down here in an hour. You tell them what to look for and—

"I'm not quite sure myself."

Pebbles rattle against his plates and the land heaves beneath him, an orange flare burst through the shrouding dust, and Nigel sees the descending streams of orange again, bigger now, spilling down the burnished rock faces hundreds of meters above.

Jeez, it's picking up again. That western face might slip down any moment, I'd say.

"Geology's not your department, Daffler. You're the comm man. I'm the jack-of-all-trades."

Well, yes, but simple—

"Nothing down here is simple. Mind the EMs, eh? They're having a go."

What? Oh, I see. They're heading toward you. Straight for that flank of the ridge.

"Right. You can scarcely ask me to maneuver around them, not since Bob's warned us off close contact until the big team arrives."

Uh, yes. But—

"Closing down now, if you don't mind. I want to be sure I'm not seen."

Uh-huh, Daffler grunts suspiciously, but his carrier falls silent.

Nigel is alone in the sleeting amber light as the low murmur of the mountain comes to him through his treads and he listens intently to the muted sputters and chiming beeps that make up the EM conversations and songs and continual probings, the microwave scattering through the canyons and washes of this bleak land. He thumbs on the radio map sent down from *Lancer* and studies the gathering dots that shamble toward him.

A small animal scurries by, frightened, and Nigel marvels that the little thing—eyeless, pea-brained—can sniff the EMs at this range, and know enough to flee.

The EM body itself may serve as a big antenna, the bones acting as low-conductivity pickups, so that to the EM there is a vague sense of smaller beings approaching. Otherwise they would be vulnerable to parasites and ingenious throat-slitters, who could mount them and be invisible. But somehow the whole-body antenna must "see" small predators so the EMs can fry them, step on them, pluck them off. Perhaps under selection pressure the brain had developed some aperture synthesis technique, like the widely separated radio antennas on Earth that have an "eye" the effective size of their separation. And did their spines serve as tuning coils?

Nigel clanks into a narrow gully as the EM specks approach. He wants his performance to be beyond criticism by Bob and the rest, to seem a perfectly responsible pattern in view of the EM movements, and so he draws back into the gully, toward an outcropping of blue-green rock.

A burst of orange throws shadows before him. He pauses at the mottled blue-green place, puzzled, remembering, but the second flash blinds him and then comes a crashing, stones shower him, a rough roar makes him peer upward where the mountain belches clouds and flames, long streams of lava now pouring from the sagging mouth of the fresh crater, huge jets of steam gushing forth into the banks of dust, the moisture clearing the air before it, the sulfur oxides now falling into the valley beyond, where they will feed the scrub plants and weak little animals, the bottom of the food chain which the EMs tap, and have been tapping for a vast long time now, though how long the geologists cannot say, with the crust of Isis always churning and destroying all evidence of the past.

Nigel turns back to the mottling, curious, reaches down— and suddenly sees the EM, sluggish but steady, legs jerking, coming dead toward him. The big head is fixed directly at him and Nigel hopes his radio blanket looks to the EM like a boring, typical rock. He inches backward, shuts down all carrier waves, braces—

But the EM halts, ignoring Nigel, head swiveling, and cants itself, settling downward, thrusting the lumpy black knobs in its abdomen, lowering itself until they make contact with the blue-green veins in the rock.

Its waxy skin ripples, it settles farther, the glazed blue of its skin begins to pulse with other colors, as soft purples seep up from the abdomen, and Nigel reminds himself that in the red Ra light this purple is in a fact a green, a biochem flag of a porphyrin derivative, but the colors wash away the thought as magentas and hard yellows and sprays of red curl across the body of the EM, flowing as *boom* the volcano above rips light through the hovering sheets of fine dust, a stream of lava splits the rock face fifty meters away with a sudden lance of orange, and the EM trembles, trembles, tilts lower, seems to shake with a kind of lust and hunger, not noticing the second and then a third large shape that emerge from the slow, spattering rain that now begins to fall, fat dollops of moist sulfur oxides, drops that streak the approaching, lurching shapes as they lower themselves in turn to the outcropping, ponderous, their mircrowaves filling and merging with a new and stronger weave, the scattershot clicks and barks of radio shifting as the ground surges and a crashing explosion high up the mountain pours light into the gully, the EMs signal now, flowing into song, their boxlike heads tilting, scanning, a steady note emerging now as Nigel recognizes the long, low tone that is from the old Earthside radio show.

They are joining together to point at the sky and send the slow mournful impulse that will wed with the other millions of EMs and stretch across the light-years toward the Earth, a mere dot in the sky that so long ago seemed to speak to these time-weary creatures.

A shower of bright orange blossoms at the abdomen of each EM. Sparks cut the air. Nigel backs away.

A crackling fills his pickups and the EM fugue grows, the huge bodies rocking slightly as the air cracks and snaps with energy, dancing singing joy forever, brimming, flying, the lava crashing over the ridge, prickly heat pours from it, and Nigel sees suddenly how the EMs live for this moment, the single time when they have enough swelling, filling life to burst forth and claw up at the sky that holds a speck of hope and promise, some possibility beyond the smothering sameness of their twilight rusting world.

They seek the volcanoes for *food*, not for warmth. The lava flows down thousands of meters of mountainside, a hot metallic conductor falling in the strong magnetic field of Isis, cutting the magnetic field lines and generating currents, electric fields, a vast circuit that cannot close easily because the rock around the lava is inert, a poor conductor, and so the electrical current builds as the lava flows, cutting across more field lines, gathering energy until it strikes a seam of metal-rich ore and suddenly the circuit can close, it is shorted, the vast currents run through the blue-green rock layers, seeking a return channel to the top of the mountain, to complete the loop, blind current following Faraday's remorseless law.

As the currents find their way through metallic corridors, wandering, the EMs tap into an outcropping of the seam and drink of the rushing river of electrons, sucking in to charge their capacitor banks, feasting, spilling it into radio waves as they celebrate this renewal of themselves. They soak from the land · itself the high-quality energy, without having to undergo the slow and painstaking process of finding chemical foods, digesting them, transferring molecular binding energy into stored electrical potentials.

A joyful strumming life swells and pours into the EMs. Nigel sees in the jagged leaping orange sparks the last link, sees how Isis swings around Ra, the long ellipse taking it now closer, now farther from its star, so that the tidal force first stretches and then compresses Isis, kneading and heating the planetary core like a thick pastry. The energy coming from the orbital angular momentum of the Isis-Ra system, an eternal energy source, endlessly churning the crust of Isis, subducting metals in the soil and then in turn thrusting them, molten, from the mouths of the mountains, the iron-rich rivers snaking and seeking the center of the planet again, driving currents, stripping electrons from the iron, a vast and perpetual generator changing gravitational energy to useful electrical forms, an energy which no other creature than the EMs can tap, giving them the edge they need on this sluggish rustworld, making possible their radio eye and with it a steady survey of the sky, searching for an answering strum of electromagnetic song, a vigil that had gone on now for aeons without machines or computers or the army of mindless servants men have made to help them. Here these creatures had harnessed the grinding workings of the planets themselves, all to survive, all to call a plaintive note into a still and silent sky.

Nigel moves softly away from them, lingering to see the solemn chorusing shapes, singing, bathed in bright sparking bonfires of electrowealth burning through the dusty murk, like rockets straining to lift off, where forever three or more shall gather together a syllable will be cast out into the night, and smiling, Nigel knows that the time has finally come to answer.

EIGHT

Ted Landon was pulling the meeting toward a reluctant conclusion. Nigel watched him, reflecting. Ted called up reports from the exploration teams, from planetary survey, from the subsection on Ra, from inboard systems. A flat wallscreen displayed alternatives; Ted went through the suggested missions, assigning weighted returns-versus-risks factors. Each time a section leader digressed into detail, or shifted the topic, Ted brought him back into line. The staccato cadences by which he disciplined came from his nervous system, immutable.

"Well, the big sweep we tried two days back—following on the Walmsley-Daffler discoveries—doesn't seem to have paid off. Am I right?" Raised eyebrows, inquiring looks around the table. Nods. Nigel nodded, too, for indeed the men and women who swarmed over that volcanic zone had not learned anything more of importance. The EM "villages" were simple shelters and little more. Some of the caves held piles of artfully worked rock; others were bare, with only alcoves clogged with EM droppings to mark their use. In a few, elaborate designs were scratched into the walls and filled with scraps of superconducting stuff. To the EMs these might be art; just as easily, the complex spirals and jagged lines might be history, literature, or graffiti.

Ted segued smoothly into a summary of other missions on Isis surface. They were tracing the outline of a complex ecology, but there were still large holes to fill in. What happened to the ancient EM cities? Why were there no other semiconductor-type nervous systems in the Isis ecology?

"All very interesting," Ted said mildly. "But to many of us"—his eyes swept the length of the table—"the standout puzzle is the two satellites. How did they get there? Are they all that is left of the EM technology? Why—"

"Look," Nigel interrupted, "it's clear where you're headed. You want to pay a visit."

"Well, you're jumping the gun again, Nigel, but yes. We do."

"That's too flaming dangerous."

"They're ancient, Nigel. Spectrophotometry shows the artificial component of those satellites—the metals, anyway—were smelted and formed well over a million years ago."

"Old doesn't mean dead."

"Nigel, I know what you're angling for." Ted smiled sympathetically, his manner becoming milder. Nigel wondered how much of it was a controlled response. "You want first contact. The EMs still don't know we're here, if our tricks have functioned adequately—I'm pretty sure your radio blanket notion has worked out, Bob—and I want to keep it that way. Our directives, as I'm sure I don't need to remind anyone here, are to stay invisible until we fully understand the situation."

"Pretty clear," Bob said laconically.

"Until you inquire into the definition of 'fully understand,' perhaps so," Nigel retorted. "But we've *seen* the EMs. They've tried to catch our attention already. And we don't know bugger all about the satellites."

Ted laced his fingers and turned his palms up, a diffuse gesture Nigel recognized as meaning *What are you trying to say?* with a hint of irritation, a sign all at the table would get, while simultaneously Ted said calmly, completely without any irked tone in his voice, "Surely a well-preserved artifact will tell us more about the high period of this civilization—"

"If it's from here, yes."

Ted's eyes widened theatrically. "You think the Snark came from here? Or the *Marginis* wreck?"

"Of course not. However, in the absence of knowledge—"

"That absence is precisely why I feel—as does the majority of this panel, I take it—that we should keep our distance from the EMs for a while." The section leaders around the table agreed with silent nods.

"They aren't nearly as potentially dangerous to this mission," Nigel said. "And they're native life-forms. We have things in common, we *must*. Any opportunity for our kind of life to communicate—"

"Our kind?"

"The machine civilizations are out here somewhere, too."

"Ummm." Ted made a show of considering the point. "How prevalent do you think life is, Nigel?"

A sticky point. Isis was the sole source of artificial transmissions that astronomers had found in over half a century of cupping an ear to every conceivable part of the electromagnetic spectrum. Nigel paused a moment and then said, "Reasonably."

"Oh? Why the radio silence, then? Except for Isis?"

"Ever been to a cocktail party where the person who's unsure of himself babbles away? And everyone else keeps quiet?"

Ted smiled. "Lord protect me from analogies. The galaxy isn't a cocktail party."

Nigel smiled, too. He had no way of reversing the decision here, but he could show the flag. "Probably. But I think it's not an open house, either."

"Well, let's knock on a door and see," Ted replied.

Nigel found Nikka and Carlotta cooking an elaborate concoction at the apartment. They were peppering slivers of white meat and rolling them in scented oils. There were savories to fold in and each woman worked solemnly, deftly, the myriad small decisions provoking a phrase here, an extended deliberation there, all weaving a bond he knew well. Not the right moment to break in.

He volunteered to chop vegetables. He took out his intensity on onions and carrots and broccoli and had a cup of coffee. The first fruit of the "season" was in so he made a salad, following Carlotta's directions, composing a light, spicy sesame oil for it. The first citrus had come ripe the day before, greeted by a little ritual. Prokofiev's *Love for Three Oranges* had rolled over the witnessing crowd, echoing in the cavern. Someone had salted the clouds that formed on the axis, so that crimson and jade streamers coasted in ghostly straight lines overhead, up the spine of the ship.

Finally, at a lull he said, "I just heard the news."

"Oh," Nikka said, understanding.

"Why didn't you tell me you'd volunteered for the satellite mission?"

"Volunteer? I didn't. I'm on the list for rotating assignments."

"They thought it was better for morale," Carlotta put in, "if we just let the personnel optimization program pick the mission crew. Fairer, too."

"Oh, yes, we must be *fair*, mustn't we? A fabulously stupid idea," he said.

"Everybody's *dying* to get out of the ship," Carlotta said.

"It might well turn out precisely that way," he said sourly.

Nikka said, "I thought it was better if I simply let the news come up as usual. I nearly told you before—"

"Well, then, nearly thank you."

"It's my chance to *do* something!"

"I don't want you risking it."

Nikka said defiantly, "I take my chances, just as you do."

"You'll be on the servo'd equipment, the manifest says."

"Yes. Operating the mobile detectors."

"How close to the satellite?"

"A few kilometers."

"I don't like it. Ted's going ahead with this without thinking it through."

Carlotta put down a whisk beater and said, "You can't run Nikka's life."

He looked steadily at her. "And you cannot expect me not to care."

"*Madre!* You really want to fight over this?" Carlotta asked.

"Diplomacy seems to have broken down."

Nikka said mildly, "This mission is planned, there are backups, every contingency—"

"We're blasted *ignorant*. Too ignorant."

"The satellite rock looks to be about the same age as the last major craters on Isis, correct?" Nikka asked lightly, to soften matters.

"So?"

"It stands to reason they represent the last artifacts of EM technology. The two satellites, the superconductors in the village—that is all that remains."

"Possible," Nigel muttered. "Possible. But to understand Isis we've got to go carefully, start from scratch—"

"We're scratching, that's for sure," Carlotta said.

"I do *not* want you to risk your life on an *assumption*."

Carlotta's face darkened. "God, you push things damned far. Are you *really* going to keep Nikka from doing the job she was *born* to do?"

Nigel opened his mouth to say, *Look, this is a private thing between the two of us*—and saw where that would lead.

"You may be a goddamn living monument," Carlotta said, "but you can't rule by authority. Not with us."

Nigel blinked, thinking, *She's right. So easy to fall into that trap* and

—suddenly saw how it was for Nikka, her mind shifting, restless, clotted with memories, reaching out toward him now with hands still moist from the cooking, the determined cast to the face, the firm lift in the stomach, a tight pull won from endless hours of exercise, keeping the machine ready so that she could still go out, the outstretched hands slick and webbed by age and brown liver spots, narrowing the space between them—

"You cannot fix me in amber," she said.

"Or any of us, damn it," Carlotta added.

To him Nikka's face glowed with associated memories, shone in the spare kitchen with a receptive willingness.

"I . . . suppose you're right."

—It was 2014 again and he comes home in the warm Pasadena evening, putt-putting on a scooter. He clicks the lock open and slams the big oak door to announce himself, bounding up the staircase. In the white living room he calls out to her. Something chimes faintly in his ears. His steps ring on the brown Mexican tiles as he walks into the arched intersection of kitchen and dining nook. A woman's spiked shoe lies on the tile. One shoe. Directly underneath the bedroom arch. He steps forward and the ringing in his ear grows. Into the bedroom. Look to the left. Alexandria lies still, facedown. Hands reaching out, clenched. Arms an ugly swollen red, where the disease was eating at her, would never stop eating—

He knew it then, saw her falling away into nothingness. The ambulance that shrieked through night mists, the antiseptic hospital, the terrible things done to her after—all that was coda to the symphonic life the two of them had shared, had tried to have with Shirley as well, yet the three-body problem had forever remained unsolved—

He saw abruptly that the fear of losing Alexandria had become part of him now. He had never recovered. With age, the fear of change seeped into him and blended with the losing of her. Nikka had now been with him longer than Alexandria had, and a mere hint of danger to her—

Nigel shook his head, letting the old, still-sharp images fade.

"Back with us?" Carlotta asked.

"I expect so," he said unevenly.

Nikka studied him, understanding slowly coming into her face.

He said, "These things take a bit of time."

Carlotta said, "I just *won't* let you push her around." She put her arms protectively around Nikka.

"Why does this conversation keep reminding me of the United Nations?"

"Well, it's *true*."

Nikka said to Carlotta, "Still, we each have some power over the other."

"Not *that* kind."

"All kinds," Nigel said. "Thighs part before me like the Red Sea. Point is, what are the limits?"

"If I don't stand up to you, you'll just run right over her," Carlotta said.

Nikka said mildly, "That depends on the circumstances."

Nigel smiled. "I'm not the ambivalent type. 'Do you always try to look on both sides of an issue, Mr. Walmsley?' 'Well, yes and no.' Not my kind of thing."

"Well, you'd better *make* it—"

"Oh, come on, you two. The crisis is past," Nikka said.

"Indeed. Let's eat. Get back to basics."

Nikka said, "Some Red Sea later?"

"We'll negotiate over dessert."

NINE

The mission team deployed carefully around Satellite A. One-third stayed forty klicks away, with the heavy gear and comm packs. A third scouted the surface. They found nothing special, verified Fraser's dating and cratering count, and reconned the entrance holes. The last third set up the recon machines, tested the dark openings for sensors and trip lines, and finally decided all was well. No murmur of electromagnetic life came from the holes; nothing responded to their elementary probings.

The machines went in, tentatively and quietly. They were blocked by a sealed passageway thirty-three meters inside the rocky crust. The robots were cramped in the passage as it narrowed down and could not find anything to free the seal. Two women went in to eyeball the situation. They attached monitors to the black ceramic seal and listened for acoustic signatures which might reveal a lock.

The crew standing near the edge of the entrance hole

was listening to the two women discuss matters. They felt a slight percussion. At the same instant the two women stopped speaking, forever. Something blue and ice-white came out of the dark hole. A millisecond-stepped scan of the video readback showed only this blue-white fog, and then—next frame—the beginnings of an orange explosion among the three human figures standing nearest the hole. In two more frames the boiling orange had reached the video lens itself and transmission stopped.

The orange moved like a liquid, licking the surface of the satellite clean in seven milliseconds. A tongue of it leaped off the surface, at the point closest to the orbiting mission team. It projected eighteen klicks toward them and then lapped, straining in long fibers, for twenty-two milliseconds. The mission crew had by this time registered only a blur of motion on their monitors. Two-thirds of the crew—all that were on the satellite—were dead.

The orange fibers twisted, coiled, and all but one retracted, fading. One grew, stretched, and struck the mission craft a weakened blow. High-temperature plasma blinded sensors and pitted steel skins. A gigawatt of snapping, snarling death burst over the spider-limbed ships. More died.

The orange thing withdrew, withering and darkening and collapsing down in forty-two milliseconds to a guttering white glow at the entrance hole. The rock of the satellite was now a burnished brown. Within a further fraction of a second, all electromagnetic activity from the satellite ceased. There was no residual radioactivity. The twelve remaining crew members had not yet had time to turn their heads, to see the thing that had come and gone.

> Jesus Christ did you
> is overloaded I can't see anything but ejecta
> they're just gone I said no sign anywhere
> no there's that debris, I'm picking it up now in the IR but
> god-awful, they're all smashed up, all the modules in orbit, like squashed peas
> the camp's smeared all over the surface like something crushed it dammit launch the two now we'll get a booster on and follow
> the people in orbit, I can't see much but ferget

the others, only survivors are gonna be in the modules an' not too blessed many a 'em either I'll bet

Sylvano, I'm getting nothing on insuit for A14 to A36 inclusive, you overlay on that?

are we safe? safe? damn I dunno we're two hunnert thousan' klicks out maybe that's enough distance but what else has that satellite got, answer me that an' I'll say

I never guaranteed pressure seals against whatever that orange was hell Stein measured a three kilo Torr jump in a couple millisec on an interior bulkhead, then all the instrumentation crapped out probably crushed 'em I'm sending the curves over now what you make of that

no, all their antennas are stripped, I can see that much, that's why we can't get

A14, A36 please respond

shit can't pick up anything this range no dish

they're tumbling anyway can't aim the inboard rifle antenna at us even if look Nigel I tell you there's no way I can find that out so get off my band and let me

lookit at here in the IR the whole side of module A burned away looks like see right there as it comes aroun' into the light kind of brown and

Alex here, look I checked those insuit wavelengths and yeah I can tune the big dish for that we're operational in that band if we pull in the lobes a little but you sure the ordinary link is out I mean you know I'm standing by on emergency so

of course it's out cretin their antennas are gone if there's any electronics active in their suits they'll be broadcasting a Mayday with just sodding suit wiring and the only way to pick it up Alex at this range is through you

yeah Reynolds is moving as fast as he can I'd say ETA is four hours plus easy so

yes I well look I know and well fuck off Ted I bloody

look I got hey hold off a minute Nigel one minute I got from Nichols the suit ID and I'm online, reading now you can knock it off look there's we're getting it 2.16 gigahertz right, yeah, hope this right yeah there's lines here, three, four, I count eight, sharpening them a little now, I can read off the IDs maybe straight from the scope face here just a sec

Nikka's A27, Alex, that's 2.39 gigahertz

you say 2.39 yeah Nigel I got that one and 2.41

next to it they're straight Maydays only 2.43 is out

and 2.45 too

how long do you think

Ted we're under boost awready an' 'at was damn fine for the conditions seems to me considerin'

I want to be sure you don't walk into whatever happened to them, so you'll have to take a slow approach, nothing too

okay, putting us there in 2.68 hours, I make it a trajectory with Ra at our backs that'll maybe be some help

reduce our visibility but we'll have to maneuver y'know to reach all that debris it's spreading out fast

Alex says that's not necessary anymore. There are six no eight suits responding to our relayed medical interrogation and they're in two capsules

Jesus eight out of how many was it thirty-six?

Yes, that's why I want extreme caution, though God knows with that response time the crews couldn't have done anything even if they had been armed, with no warning they

Nigel oh Zak look can you find Nigel for me, sounds like, I said, this is Alex, sounds like a madhouse in Central can you

hold it, oh, okay, here

send Reynolds those coordinates pronto I want

Nigel, glad I found you look I've been monitoring all the insuit Maydays and several of them are going spotty on me it's not a relay problem I'm sure of that or pretty sure anyway and

nope there's nothing from the satellite, no interference so that can't be causing it

*Alex Alex this is Nigel here I've cross-checked
and there's no other explanation how long until the
rescue team*

 *hour twenty-seven minutes more Central says
hell can't they*

 *I'm sorry, I, look we just lost one of the insuits,
I thought you'd, I called cause it's the 2.39 gigahertz one Nigel, it's just clean gone.*

The white caked skin was dead and dry, leached of color.
Nigel reached out and rubbed it tentatively. He felt light-
headed and vague, the residue of many hours. Her right
eyelid was closed. Her left had been burned away. The left
side of her face was waxy and hardening. In the enameled
impersonal phosphor light he traced a trembling finger across
the familiar lines, the weathered fretworks and canyons, and
marveled that the wrinkles flowed smoothly into the firming
new flesh without a sign of the transition.

"They'll have the . . . eyelid . . . back on in an hour . . . they
said," Nikka mumbled. The shiny skin was still tight and her
lips were swollen, purple. She had trouble with pronunciation.

"Quiet."

"I'm still not . . . taking orders . . . Nigel."

He stared at her, unable to think of anything to say.

"You . . . were right."

"No, I was simply cautious."

The bright yellow medmon continued to nuzzle her left
side, pausing to manufacture more skin and then nuzzling
again, patient and doglike.

"When my suit intervened and . . . shut down circulation
. . . on my left arm I thought . . ."

"I know."

"I still don't see . . . how . . ."

"It chilled you down by venting gases at the right ports.
Tricky. That was the only way out."

"I . . . didn't think suits could . . ."

"They can't, not without a processor linking into a good
metabolic control program. When your suit stopped broadcasting, we calculated it was probably trying to conserve its
power, use its reserves on insuit medical. So Alex focused the
big dish for transmission, and I called up the needed programs. Alex stepped up his power level and managed to

overrule your suit. He interrogated it, got it to relinquish control and patch through to us. The shipboard programs told your confused little suit-mind how to shut you down, put you on the back burner."

"You make it sound . . . very . . . lighthearted."

His patient-visiting facade vanished instantly.

"You always were a . . . terrible actor."

"Yes, dreadful." He should have known he could not keep the strain and fatigue out of his face.

"I was sure I was dying out there, Nigel."

"So was I."

"I wanted to call out to you . . ."

"I know." There wasn't anything to say, so he held her right hand. It had a soft and worn and kneaded texture. He watched her face as passing storms of emotion swept across it silently, revealed in slight shiftings of expression in the swollen, discolored, patchy flesh.

Through a small window nearby he could see the other survivors lying on white slabs, being operated on by teams of smocked figures. Three were being readied for Sleepslots; their damage was too extensive and deep for *Lancer's* capability. They would be stored in a silent, dreamy nothingness until the return to Earth.

"Has . . . has anything more come out of that . . ."

"No. It looks dead as ever. The other satellite shows no signs of activity, either. Mysterious."

She studied him. "Unconvincing."

"Ummmm?"

"You're piecing this together . . . aren't you?"

"Having a go, yes."

"You don't think the EMs . . . put up those . . . things . . ."

"No. But I have only intuitions. I should never have let bloody cretinous Carlotta—"

"I . . . know." She squeezed his hand and attempted a smile. "We both . . . Carlotta and I . . . reacted . . . to something . . . I don't know, your way of putting it . . . so . . ."

"Undiplomatic."

"Direct, at least." Her dark eyes focused on the glowing ceiling. The medmon altered pitch in its constant labor and she moved uncomfortably. "You . . . you aren't the same now, Nigel. Your . . . I always sensed an equilibrium . . . in you. Now . . ."

"Yes." He looked at her and remembered the long nights together, when they had first met, lying in a cramped bunk buried beneath the Moon, Nikka patient and analytical, while he carried on, ragged and rusty-eyed, pressing against what appeared to be the problem and failing to see into it for what it was, to clutch it to him. The forward tilt in his life sent him down strange routes, kept shaping and reshaping him. In those distant days there had been no equilibrium, not even the dynamic equilibrium like walking, which was a process of falling forward and catching yourself just in time. Not even that was possible when the world showed itself as a riddle and twisted away, manifesting its greased-pig persona which was only another face, but one which had to be answered, that kneaded and molded him as part of the riddle itself, pressing—

"You're going out again . . . aren't you?"

So she sensed it. "Not to the satellites, no."

"The surface." She scowled. The pasty stuff they had used to secure her hair transplant crinkled and a small bubble popped in its surface, leaving a yawning gray crater that quicky filled in. "In person? Or in servo?"

"Servo for me, more's the pity. I'm too much of a tedious tottering wreck to allow on the surface. I'm to be a flunky, really. Daffler gets to make the overtures—he's a comm type. Cool-headed, as well."

"At least they should . . . let you set foot . . ."

"Impossible, I'm afraid. But Ted is finally consenting to a direct contact, so we've won that. It's the only good thing to come out of this satellite farce." Nigel's eyes danced with anticipation. "Plus, I've gotten consent for Daffler to do the overtures in person. Minimum suit."

"Why?"

"So the EMs can see he's a living creature. Not another damned machine."

"I don't understand. Why not send a carefully coded signal down to them?"

"That might be a bit of a dicey proposition, really. Ted and some of his theoreticians brought up an interesting argument against it. The surface team on Satellite A found a web of radiosensitive, metallic stuff all over the rock, woven into it in some fashion. The thing seems extraordinarily sensitive. It can quite easily resolve and monitor the EM transmissions."

"And ours."

"Quite. But it hasn't bothered us, not until we did something out of the ordinary. Apparently our signals, coming from orbit farther out, don't bother the thing. It's—"

"A watcher. Transmissions of that slow chant from the EMs... they're okay. So are ours, since they're coming from far away?" She frowned.

"Yes, Watcher—not a bad name. Point is, what happens if we start returning the EM's hailing signal—that old radio show? How will the Watchers react?"

"So Ted's strategy group thinks... we should hail the EMs from the surface. Where it won't look... unusual."

"That's the theory."

"What do you think?"

Nigel shrugged. "Those things are bloody dangerous. Best to be careful."

"If we only... knew more about them..."

"Ah, but we do. A bit, anyway. The surface team transmitted a spectral analysis of the rock. It was fused in some high-temperature process, about 1.17 million years ago."

"Ummm. Fits with the estimate of the lifetime of their orbits."

"Yes. But about two hundred thousand years older than the maximum limit on their orbit lifetime."

Her eyelids flickered; she was becoming drowsy, the knottings of strain in her face relaxing. Nigel felf a surge of elation himself, a conviction that the crisis was past for her. "I... see. Interesting... but..."

"Exactly. Where were the Watchers for those extra two hundred thousand years?"

Nigel was helping cool down a greenhouse compartment when Carlotta found him. He watched the winter landscape form as the cool air forced a rapid cycle. The condensation of mere moisture, he reflected, was an infinite source of beauty. First frost made her sketches on the panes of the observing station. Curled leaves applauded the winter wind. Fall came, setting forth ice like the best bone china.

"I dropped the ball," Carlotta said. He glanced up at her and she shrugged. "Your self-serve is revoked. I thought I had all the admin programs blocked, but—"

"Ah, well. Cheeky of me, anyway, wanting to slip out from under the microscope."

She put her arm around him. "Think they'll pull you out of servo work?"

"Depends on my next physical." He rubbed his hands together, studying the knuckles. "The joints have been protesting lately."

"Naw, they'll keep on the Grand Old Man."

"Grand Old Crank is more the tune. At staff meetings I keep nattering on about the *Snark* and *Marginis* and machine civilizations in the galaxy. All quite unverifiable, unsubstantial stuff. I . . ." He gathered himself, stopped rubbing his hands, and stood up straight.

"Nigel, you look tired."

"Optical illusion. See here, let me throw some of that Grand Old Sod tonnage around and get you some extra people. I think I know the right lever to use."

"Listen, I am sorry I messed up."

"Carlotta, that wasn't some sort of sly jab. I never thought I'd get away with it for long, anyway."

"If I'd just thought of that one retrieval option, I . . ." She leaned against a bulkhead. *"Madre de Dios."*

"You're the one who needs the help. Extra work for the mission, Nikka's scrape—I'll get you a shift off."

"No, really, I . . ." It was his turn to put an arm around her. "Nonsense. It'll serve other uses, to boot. Just the sort of thing to get Ted's attention. A touch of special influence peddling, quite the way a Grand Ole Schemer would."

"Ummm," she murmured wearily. "So?"

"It'll make me seem a bit more active, stirring up ship politics and all."

"Oh. Listen, I think the medmon won't flag you until after this surface mission, anyway."

He kissed her on the forehead. "Good. Any chance there's a way round that, ah, 'retrieval option' in future?"

She frowned. "Well, if I . . . um, maybe."

"Good. Might need it later. Can you make it look as though we never tried this dodge?"

"Well, if I move fast—Hey, you figuring you might need it again?"

He said lightly, "Could be."

TEN

Nigel moves restlessly on the brow of the hill. He has been told to stay in place, hold his position. The first attempt at contact must be orchestrated with care and each person will cover a piece of this long, sloping valley, but still he has been the quiet, persistent pressure forcing Bob Millard and Ray Landon toward this attempt, and he feels he should make the try himself, he has a sense of these creatures. Now the moment approaches and he is in a fixed spot, ready to flank the converging swarm of EMS and reinforce Daffler's moves, listening to the voices as they report in the EM movements, waiting with the rest. *First chance I get, I'm off*, he had told Nikka this morning, half in jest, but the years of working in teams have blunted somewhat his oblique skepticism, and so he clanks across the hillface, listening, servo'd into this carapace which casts a shadow like an insect on a nearby slate-gray valley wall. A passing mist has cleared the air of sulfur dust. Nigel can hear small animals reviving as the oxy-absorbing dust becomes mud. High clouds let pass a restless flickering of direct Ra light, giving the humped land a glow of sullen rot.

> *I'm leaving cover,* comes from Daffler. *There's a group of them turning their eyes upward. I think they're going to start sending.*

Bob Millard's drawl replies, *Earth just rose above 'at big hill. You figure they're charged up?*

"I guarantee it," Nigel called. "They've been hard by the volcano up there on the ridge."

Working backward from the radio positions of the EMs, folding in the facts of their hunter patterns, the exobiology types have made sense of the EMs' systematic forays out from their crude "villages": excursions for game on the plains, for water in the muddy streams, for the shrubs and lichen they can pull from the ground, but most important, for the upwellings of current that came with the irregular volcanic spurts. They used every source for body mass and energy. When the dust came, scavenging oxygen from the air, they alone had the stored electrical energy to carry on, to continue the hunt for animals now grown sluggish. The rest of the Isis ecology was purely organic, without the semiconductor nervous system. An EM would radiate a focused beam at its prey, and then listen to the side-scattered emission, waiting for the slight shift in the absorption resonance which signaled a hit. Then it would fire its capacitors fully, burning down the prey before it could sense the warming of its tissues.

I've picked out one.
Bob says, *Careful, now. They're singin' up a storm.*

Nigel listens intently to the chromatic layers as they build in the tiers of his radio display. The pauses between the darting blips of noise get shorter, modulating a weave of counterpointing themes, a gathering tempo overriding the booming voices, bringing a swelling percussive urgency. The EMs are tilted back, he can see them now as he moves down the face of the hill. They peer upward and sing in grand unison, calling out as they have been for years with a patient need that somehow comes through the oddly spaced clicks and ringing long notes. Their heads yawn, their legs move, they settle into position. A signal has gone down the valley. In the amber light Nigel sees other EMs stop and tilt and turn, all readying themselves for the soaring song that binds them together. Nigel surges forward, counting them, wanting to be closer to Daffler when he sends the answering pattern they have agreed upon. There are hundreds of EMs in the valley now, coming out from their caves to seek, to hunt, to sing in the clear fine air.

If Isis has a voice it is the wind. Nigel hears its reedy strumming, blowing across his carapace, and the hollow sound seems to blend with the tangled radio pulses until Nigel catches a resonance between them, a dim hint of the EM nature as counterpointing lines merge, oblique intersections of rhythm that come and ebb and volley down through the repeating weave, symphonic, measured, but plunging onward—

Moving down to my right.

—and the mood breaks. Nigel feels it slip through his hands, a trace of a summation he had begun to glimpse now falls away. The EMs apparently cannot hear the roiling winds of this place, anyway, the biomechs say, so the comparison is probably pointless. Nigel shrugs. It is difficult to get the sense of a world when it is necessarily divided up into detail, the facts piled up until, like an Impressionist painting done a dab at a time, the picture emerges—of life enmeshed and triumphant, for to live at all here was a victory in this globe-girdling, silent struggle against Ra's heat engine. The biosphere is linked in subtle ways, they have found: the rate of carbon burial in the wetlands, in the muds of the continental shelves, is precisely what is needed to regulate the concentration of oxygen; nitrogen serves to build pressure to the useful breathing level, and to keep the fine dust aloft; methane regulates the oxygen levels and ventilates the oxygenless muds; the dust suppresses energy levels when it blew, giving the EMs their decisive electrodynamic edge, putting them atop a fragile pyramid.

I've picked out my spot. Range to the customer is—maybe two hundred meters. Daffler sounds sure of himself.

Good, Bob Millard answers. *We copy you beyond its killin' range.*

Close observations have shown that an EM cannot focus and deliver fatal power levels at distances greater than 120 meters. This was of prime importance in designing Daffler's tactics, and his suit. The fabric he wears will reflect above ninety percent of incident radiation at the EM hunter-killer wavelengths. Nigel surges over a field of broken gravel and through a sand lobe, trying to bring Daffler into view. There: he is coming out of a rutted gully, a thin figure in the wan light, kicking up puffs of ruby sand. Nigel can see other servo'd forms at distant spots, dispersed so that the EMs will not be disturbed if they notice something odd about the reflecting disguises the humans use.

Daffler stops, kneels, sets up his apparatus. *Power okay.*

The EM Daffler has selected is a stiff array of folded legs and body, still and waxy in the distance. Nigel suppresses the gathering EM chorus in order to hear Daffler. The EMs are singing out a complex form of darting spikes, coming down hard on a note which forms part of the word *maybe*, still a fragment from that old program from Earth. *May* . . . Daffler taps in his carrier wave; Nigel can hear its hum . . . *beee*

Here goes.

Daffler's reply comes booming in. It starts the antique radio program over from the beginning: *It's Arrr-thur Godfrey time* . . . and the notes roll out from the rutted valley.

Nigel is holding his breath, leaning forward so the pads butt against his shoulders, reminding him of where he is, encapsulated in *Lancer*, and the frozen forms down the amber valley show nothing.

Their chorus pulses on for a beat, two beats, and then there comes from the EMs a curious spiky scattering of notes, a rippling in the higher frequencies which cascades down into their central fugue, spreading noise and confusion through the next word *whhh* . . . until it loses coherence . . . *whhheeerreee* and dissolves in the foam of a thousand random buzzing, clicking jots.

As they have planned, Daffler switches to a new program, now that he has caught the attention of at least some of the aliens. He focuses forward, toward the nearest, and begins the signal. It is a simple code, a few pulses. Beneath it, keeping contact, Daffler sends the continuing program, the long-dead announcer brightly calling out the names of the guests and the background music coming up, piano, light like splashing water.

The nearest EM begins to lower its head. Down the valley the other stickwork shapes are moving, too, the great square heads tipping down from the shrouded red glow above, with its distant beckoning point of radio, alive with the babble of life, and the legs begin to work, tilting them erect as the nearest one suddenly jerks into motion, taking a step, and a new voice pours into the radio spectrum, sharp and clear: a fast chatter of blips that ripple and soar upward in amplitude, obviously something carrying a complex code.

Nigel instinctively starts forward, rocks clattering beneath him as he speeds down the hillside without thinking of the gradient, the hydraulics protesting with a wheezing churn. "It's a framed"—he begins, and a rising tide of anxious clicks stutters across the radio spectrum—"reply," he yells.

Daffler is transmitting his patient tutorial cues beneath the stretched syllables of the program, *thaaattss . . .* It is a simple arithmetic pattern with geometric implications, a form the exologic specialists thought general enough and even obvious.

Clank and suddenly Nigel slews to the left and spins, sensors abruptly canted uphill as he feels the treads and rocker arms lose their grip. Pebbles rattle against him, he slides into the wake of a small avalanche he has started, dust fogs the lenses and he falls, crunches against a boulder, his treads spit gravel, the center axis tilts, and he begins to tip over. He slams on the brake, lets the robot rock backward, and abruptly accelerates, throwing himself to the left as the treads spin, grapples fight for purchase, and the axis comes level. He thuds to a stop *Christ Nigel what're you* suspended a third of the way over the lip of a gully.

In the last two seconds Daffler's geometric hailing signal has spat out another amplitude-modulated spike *ahhll . . .* and a fresh piano note springs into the air, each fragment of time hangs, crystallized. The radio spectrum is a forest of jittering spikes, a pattern Nigel has not seen before, bunching and rebunching, in furious movement like bees swarming around the sober, bell-shaped linewidth that is the envelope of Daffler's steady signal . . . *whheee . . .* Above it the piano note subsides, falling into a bass *uuummmmm* and Nigel sees the EMs have stopped broadcasting their piece of the old program, their energy is now converging and crowding into the shifting, darting turbulence which closes in on Daffler's line.

Nigel peers out at the valley. The EM heads swivel toward Daffler. Their arms flail about, cutting the air in elaborate arcs. They lurch to their feet and the thin spindly legs stamp ritually at the ground, pounding, pounding. Some dart back and forth, heads jerking with anxious energy. Nigel pauses to watch but the soil beneath him crumbles, a shelf cracks and falls away under his forward struts. He clutches at a stone ledge, misses, grasps it, and sags farther over the edge. The gully is rocky and deep. If he falls—

"Daffler!" he sends. "I think they're trying to get a coherent signal together."

Yeah. Good. I'm getting through, at least. Just—

"They must have planned some reply, the same as we. They can triangulate on you so they know you're local, but—"

The ledge slumps and tumbles down the gully. Nigel pushes down on his forward arms, catching at the caked soil to gain an increment of momentum, and thrusts back, motors roaring as a plume of dust gushes from his threads. The steel links catch—slip—catch—and he surges back, scrabbling to safety as Bob's voice repeats *Christ Nigel what the hell is all 'at you're to stay put—*

"They're excited, look at them—"

Yeah give Daffler a minute an' we'll see—

"No, I don't—"

On the spectrum the spikes converge by the hundreds on Daffler's thick line. The EMs are tuning their individual frequencies, flexing interior muscles to adjust the lengths of their metal-laced spines. Their signals sputter with detail, the amplitudes shifting on the carrier waves in complex patterns, spilling into Daffler's line, *caahhnnn* . . . focusing on him, many of them performing the curious jittering back-and-forth dance, agitated in a way never seen before, seized with passion, expending their electric reserves in a spilling torrent, each straining toward Daffler, reaching out with their planned surging stutter.

Nigel senses them trying to see Daffler, to resolve him, to unmuddy the image, but their low frequencies cannot see detail shorter than their wavelengths, cannot pick put the spindly arms and legs which would distinguish Daffler from the native Isis animals, and so a storm of emissions moves to higher frequencies, seeking definition. The EMs are sending their preordained answer and at the same time they try to see Daffler, the bringer of tidings, tilting their heads swiftly, canting themselves at angles, pouring energy into the spectrum—

Daffler cries out.

Jesus—it's—I'm regis—

A sputtering howl comes welling up from the man. He shrieks. Daffler topples, curling up. The parabolic dish beside him crashes over. Daffler writhes, puffs of dust obscure him. The shriek chokes off into a gurgle.

Nigel leaps a narrow ravine and roars down the hillside, scattering stones as the EM spectrum fills with discordant notes and the comm band says *I'm not picking up insult from him—Look I'm moving to flank that nearest bunch of 'em I don't like—His equipment's out—Can't see anything try to move closer—Nigel you make out any movement,* and the EM emissions recede, the spiky jumble dies. Nigel finds a sure path and surges down the slope, toward the pall of fine iron dust that shrouds the area. He approaches.

Daffler's suit had metal framing at the stress points. It is gone now. The dish sags in its mounts. And Daffler... It is like an enormous fowl burned up in a neglected oven, greasy and blistered and seared a blackish brown all over, the whole face burned off, all the hair, even the ears. The stumps of arms and legs are bent at the knees and elbows, clenched rigid in the last moment of life, this ornament of some mother's eye now reduced to a charred mass with wings and shanks sticking out of it.

> *Jesus look*
> *Those bastards didn't give him a chance, just*
> *How long to bring that freezer in we could*
> *Hadn't counted on 'at, I'd give it ten minutes minimum*
> *Cancel, the brain's fried for sure no way we could*
> *Jess burned him down never gave*
> *Fuckin' spiders!*
> *Nigel watch out there these things could*
> *Yeah well they're not gettin' a chance to*
> *Lookit that one 'ere, still pointin' at 'im*
> *I say we break 'em up*
> *Yeah 'at one near you Phillips*
> *I'm on 'im got my grapplers out*

"Wait, we don't know what went on yet, I think they simply—"

Those two Guthridge the legs are the best I'd
Lookit 'im go down, fuckin' spiders cut the
props out from under 'em

Goddammit they got excited, it's a ghastly mistake—"

Holtz, swing round on that one
Chop it down chop it
Lookit 'em can't tell what's hittin' 'em
Filthy goddamn bugs
You got 'im you got 'im look out it doesn't fall
on you.
Jess burned Daffler down like
They're cuttin' they're runnin'
Bastards!—chop ever' one that keeps focused
Yeah never know what these things
Fuckin' spiders don't look so great legs gone do
they
Get 'at one it's still

"—bloody idiots they—"

Cut 'im cut 'im he's
Run 'em, run 'em 'at's right
Shit that gunk jams up the grapplers where you
break the legs watch that
Hey on the left
Fuckin' spiders

ELEVEN

The rock wall of Ted's office was cold to the touch. It had a
low thermal conductivity, but the mass of stone and iron still
allowed the chill beyond to seep into *Lancer*. Years of human
occupation had not warmed the hollowed spaces.

Nigel sat in a low chair, leaning against the wall. Ted

finished his work at the flatscreen, checking the functioning equipment left on the Isis surface. Bob Millard sat in silence on the other side of the room from Nigel. He looked up as Ted dropped his stylus on the desk.

"Well, Nigel," Ted began, "your idea didn't work."

"Perhaps."

"*Perhaps?*" Bob parodied the English accent. "Ah'll say perhaps, yeah. Daffler dead, his rig all melted down—"

"They became excited," Nigel said slowly. "They each tried to send their answering signal. It seemed to be a compressed code."

"Ah wondah what Daffler thought."

"I doubt he had time to think anything," Nigel said.

Ted leaned forward over his desk. "The fact remains that they *attacked* him. Killed him."

"They had expected a response to come from above, from Earth. When they realized Daffler was nearby, they tried to see him. Point is, to see by radar, you have to send. So hundreds of them tried to make him out, and the sum of them— A bad business," he finished lamely.

"Mebee," Bob whispered.

Nigel turned to him. "That's the way it was."

"Yeah? Then why didn't you tell us beforehand? Huh? You were so all-fired hot on this plan, makin' contact, why didn't you figure—"

"Bloody hell, I hadn't counted on everything. Especially on your mob running wild, cutting the EMs down like animals—"

"Wait." Ted held up a palm. "You're both getting carried away. I'll admit the men on the ground got out of line."

"Cut up sixteen a the bastards, scattered the rest— I'd say we saved your neck, Nigel."

"My robot, perhaps. I was servo'd."

"Well, some of us weren't. The men figgered—"

"Okay, okay," Ted said mildly. "My point is that our communication attempt failed."

Nigel raised his eyebrows. "Not at all."

"What do you mean?" Ted asked.

"The answering signal. We have that."

"So what?" Ted said. "Nigel, I don't think you understand the, ah, animosity this incident has stirred up. Daffler had a lot of friends. You—"

"I know. Coming on top of the losses before, this is—
But look, let me work with the Exo-comm team. I suspect we
can find some way of decoding it. Then—"

"Okay, okay. Do what you want. But you're barred from
surface work," Ted said severely. "Understand?"

"Right," Nigel said. "So long as you don't get notions
about going back for another gamble with those satellites,"
He couldn't resist grinding it in. "Just promise me that."

Bob grimaced and said nothing.

The long strings of code were impacted, layered, complex, and yet keyed to a syntax which made the task barely
possible; the EMs had done the difficult work of rendering
their constructions into something resembling human language forms. The patterns emerged like distant signal lamps
seen through an all-consuming cottony fog.

The mathematicians could not be sure where the narra-
tive began or ended, so the pictures and symbols that came
simply remained in a static way, the interrelations suggesting
but not drawing lines of cause and effect.

One picture showed a single perfectly flat and motionless
steel-colored sheet from which distant sticks and black stone
arches leaped, marking perspective with their angular geometry of intersection, fixed and rigid. Something like a road
came from the left and without perceptible slant slipped
abruptly beneath the gray-and-blue surface, like a flat thin
blade sliding obliquely into smooth flesh, guided by a delicate hand.

Nigel watched the picture build on the flatscreen and
then, as more of the code came through, he felt the implied
motion of the water, the sustained layers beneath in which
brown currents carried wriggling, fishlike swarms. The bland
and unhurried surface bore in spots a frothy green scum, sign
of methane-rich outgassings, but otherwise screened the secret speed of the layer a meter down, streaming out from the
distant shoreline and carrying the fat, triple-finned glowlife
which hugged together in swarms for protection in the rust-
rich waters. A sense of swimming, of the soft and sapphire-
tinged swarms beneath, came to Nigel as the picture moved,
and he caught a quiet warm feeling of contentment in this
structure, in this serene plane as ideal as any Euclid ever
dreamed, which stretched to the horizon and teemed with

delicate ripplings of information about the foodlife which was being borne outward on the tidestream below.

The blank disk that squatted overhead, unmoving, was dull red softened by an atmospheric blue, where molecules of water scattered the light. This was Isis, at a seashore unlike any men had found, a beach sliding into a calm sea. When the thick slow viscid ridge of chocolate water formed at the bottom edge of the picture, Nigel knew he was seeing in some nonlinear way the world of the EMs as it had once been, and so the slow appearance of a spindly leg which rose and plunged again into the stream did not surprise him. Arms worked into view, throwing nets. The lines tightened, surging up with a bulging load, and a mass of the softly glowing things appeared, fat and ready. *So this was the EM heaven*, Nigel thought. The contemplative serenity of this place could not be an error of translation. They had shown this because it was some vaulted memory, some touchstone image.

There were others like it. Some were unmistakably art works, and some suggested the passage of vast stretches of time. The astronomers knew that Isis was locked in tidal resonance with the outer gas giant planet, and the ceaseless churn in each world's wind and water tugged Isis outward, closer to the massive, beckoning Jovian-class planet. Keeping careful track of the night sky shown in some of the decoded pictures, they found the apparent diameter of the gas giant and thus the date.

The pictures covered the span of hundreds of thousands of years. And then the images and symbols became mixed, and strange curled ships appeared—schematics, designs, clearly things the aliens had built themselves, to fly in vacuum. Spaceships. Then, abruptly, a picture of a gray-green Isis, and about it a swirling cloud of points like hot crackling cinders, which swelled into asteroids, all systematically descending on the eternal sunward-facing disc.

The long arcs down then blended into a moving view of a flat lake. Plants: saw-edged long stems, electric blue, which grew taller as Nigel watched and then began whipping back, parting as the picture moved forward in the familiar trawl for the swarming sea life below the water, so that sharp spikes thrust at the view like limber knives which cut—it seemed he could feel the shooting pains, the following bleeding moistness— and hampered the harvesting.

And here the mathematicians failed to make coherent the symbols and pictures hammering like hailstones at them, and simply gave them in the order they came: Of an era called the Flux Time, and of a relentless fire-consumed night when the skies were streaked with orange, and of curled profiles that leaped upward into that same night, aimed to destroy or deflect, amid rolling, hammering waves of sound like perpetual cannon-fire off over the flashing horizon. There were hot winds that rushed through black air. And then tangled angular images. And then silence.

He knows he is worn down to a nub of persistence, his muscles cramped from the computer interface booths, and his judgment says to leave Ted Landon's office and rest, calculate, decide how best to report what has come out of the decoding. But in the same moment he knows he cannot do that, the moment must come to a point now, and so, sitting in a calculatedly casual way, nearly lounging, he tells it:

Something came out of interstellar space and perturbed the orbits of the asteroids near Isis. They came down as a slight oddity at first, and then with increasing mass and numbers, and the hammering went on for years. It blasted the surface, destroyed the strange cities of the EMs, threw dust and steam into the Isis air until the wan radiance of Ra was cut to nothing better than Moonlight on Earth. Without photosynthesis the food chains collapsed, destroying the life the EMs knew. They had lived as wading foragers, eating of the food that flowed continually through the rich seashore flatlands. Free of agriculture, they had nonetheless developed a mild technology, and even ships able to reach orbit. They had conducted a short, futile, and puny defense against the infalling rock. In the end the entire subsolar point of Isis was hammered and blasted into a jumbled plain of fresh volcanoes, where the slumbering magma of Isis broke through as the crust itself fractured under the pounding, conjuring up deep tectonic thrashings that forever denied to life the moist birthing point at the warmest spot on the planet, and instead made the Eye.

Nigel pauses and feels the eyes of the others on him in the spaced silence that fills the office. He has been talking swiftly and with fragile momentum, not sure of all the connections but wanting to get it out so the others can work

on it, test the fleeting images which have come to him, the
greased pig, in the light of this they can test and refine and
perhaps even disprove what he thinks he has glimpsed.

Ted says *Seems funny I don't* and a geologist
rushes in with *You know that would match the
dating on the cratering we found, it was planetwide
we do know that* and from Nigel's left comes *Now
that you mention it the age of the satellite surface
was about the same* and softer, farther back in the
crowded, sweaty office *Christ at that scale of time
you can't deduce causality that's absurd* and Nikka
beside him says suddenly, defiantly *Would you mind
giving him a chance to complete his* but he waves
her into silence, it's true that events of a million
years or more ago are dim notions now, fitful spectral
dreams.

So he goes on, and in his mind's eye sees the
quiet calm lives of the stilt-legged creatures who
swayed and stepped among breakers and tide rushes;
seeking the floating ambient glowlife that fed them,
that made possible time around fires at the shore,
and from that brought into being some culture very
distant from the hunter-based and forward-tilting
human imperatives. By the Flux Time they knew
much about themselves, had mastered the coiled
code of DNA and molecular cookery. They survived
the hammering from above and saw their world
wither away, felt the animals and plants dying in the
wan and unforgiving twilight of a dust-shrouded
world, and sensed the coming into being of a new
ecology built on the withered husk of the old. So
their scraps of genetic knowledge were hammered
into instruments for change, solutions titrated, molecules wrenched and reordered, and from themselves they made a new kind of self.

*I dunno, sounds improbable to me, doing a lot
of genetic tinkering on yourself* and *Look the vulca-
nism was increasing, no way they could carry on
without the oxygen-rich air they'd had* and *All that
sulfur pouring outta the volcanoes, might as well* as
the room grows warmer, the scent rises salty and

strong *But that's plain impossible, writing into your own genetic code things like those transistor nerves and the capacitor storage you just can't do that kind of* and softer *Yeah who says?* with *That's old Muriel for ya, anything she doesn't know howta do is a law of nature like God's speed limit* and Nigel sags into his chair, feeling the muscles in his back spasm from the hours of stiff sitting, should have bloody lounges those computer jockeys, math buffs never learned how to live, tangled up in their numbers *It was the only way out maybe* the other exologic types murmuring amongst themselves for they have run their own multifactorial analysis of the EM squirted codes *At least thass an explanation for the lack of other electricity-storing life-forms in the biosphere* and Nigel can see the math division does not quite agree with his explanation, but he shrugs, knowing that this initial smattering of impressions will not converge until more work is done but still the implications *It would imply if I'm not mistaken Dr. Landon that the nominal superconducting "rooms" Bob's group found are in fact artifacts of a million-year-old technology and frankly survival of any superconductor, even two-dimensional, I find incredible over that period of* slowly the sweep of it seeps into them and at first they balk, unable to accept *I mean how could they cling to just one high-tech bit like superconducting sheets and let everything else go jess go* and have not felt yet the humbling sense of what it meant so long ago to change deliberately your own substance to go on living, to harness electrodynamic forces when the chemical pyramid of life failed and could not be revived, because the Eye was always there, the ancestral skies were now smothered with dust and wherever some remnant of technology fought the rust an arcing orange lance would hammer away until they were all dead, the machines broken, snapped, and finally rusted by the altered ecology of sulfur grains and wind-sculpted gnarled plants *But why make it so complete doesn't fit I'd say* and the room dissolves into discussion, Nigel feeling the

points emerge slowly as indeed they did with him
Well radio was the only way to see in that wind-blown crap he presses Nikka's hand, for it was she
who saw the final dark connection *Sure and I guess
the only hope of communicating over interstellar
distances* crying bleak and hungry across the abyss
My God all that just so they could survive a rickety
bagful of working meat, pipes and pouches grown
thick and waxy, soaked with juices, walking on
jointed sticks as they peacefully waded through the
cool shallows, life still hanging on, pulsing, flexing,
bubbling, combusting, and doomed even with their
slowed metabolism to lose their last charge and
decompose into rustrun soils *You know I've been
thinking, using radio in a life-form that way it would
be natural, so to speak, not a product of technology*
and Nigel, seeing they have made the last turn
toward home, puts in a few phrases wearily *Maybe
that's the point the Watchers* a gathering fever of
perception runs through them, a prickly closeness
as each sees a fragment of it *Sure wouldn't regard it
as technology at all, just a quirk of the life-form,
some odd aspect of evolution* and no Watcher
could suspect that even the electromagnetic spectrum, refined over aeons, could give to a life-form
pleasure, nature's sign of approval, *Well Occam's
razor alone would say the Watchers must've been
the cause and now* the Watchers skating endlessly
across a murky ruin of a world *I dunno seems like a
string of* ignoring small hints of life giving rise to
technology again *Still when you think about it*
hoarding energies over the aeons *Damn getting stuffy
in here Nigel you need to get out, rest, let* no *Makes
you wonder if maybe we shouldn't pull our servo'd
vehicles out, or disperse 'em so's they don't attract
attention* no, he shrugs off her concern again *Yeah
'at Watcher gets the idea we're down there an' a
serious civilization or somethin' we're* and Ted says
calmly, to bring it all under control, that of course
the teams will have to look into these ideas, there
will be another meeting tomorrow at 1100 hours
and he expects reports from each division and *Nigel*

let me the room is thick and heavy with their sweat and concentration *Don't try to stand up* but he does and finds the compacted mass of details in his mind does not allow him to move his feet properly, they will not catch his weight as it wishes to rush at the floor in this mild centrifugal gravity *Damn* he curses himself for being so negligent of his body but still there were no clear signs or did he miss them *Hey what's* he crashes down, snapping a wrist and almost welcoming the stabbing pain which follows.

TWELVE

He lay quietly as the machines sniffed and poked at him. Nikka said, "Fatigue, mostly, they think. But your blood chem is off, too."

"Um," Nigel grunted. "Imbalance in the antiaging potions, I suspect. I stayed away from the medmon, once my trick went sour."

"You do look tired. But you got more out of those EM messages than the specialists, so maybe it was worth... What's it doing now?"

"Um? Serving up pills," The medmon pushed a tray toward him, humming.

Nikka asked, "What's the orange one?"

He turned stiffly to see it. "Ah, the orange bugger." Pharmacological peace. He lay with a feed in his nose, diagnostic discs on arms and chest, a thermometer and sampler in his anus, various leads and taps spotted over his belly. "That's my aphrodisiac."

Nikka smiled and the door peeled and Ted Landon came in. Nigel smiled wanly as the three of them went through the customary hospital-visiting remarks. Ted was nervous. To deflect him, Nigel asked about research.

"Oh, we're pretty much sure that idea of yours was right," Ted said. "The EMs must've tinkered with their genes to come up with that semiconductor and electrical storage system."

"By building it into an ecology, they made it look natural? So they could get away with using radio?" Nikka asked.

"Maybe. Something kept the Watchers from attacking them." Ted shrugged. He still seemed distracted.

"They found a loophole. Their radio is natural. The Watchers seem to be hunting down technology. Ergo, natural radio is safe."

"Could be."

"We'll have to study them more to be sure," Nikka said, "But it seems—"

"'Fraid not," Ted stated flatly. "We're moving on."

"*What!*" Nigel spat out.

"Just got a long squirt from Earth. We have a new target star. A long trip."

"Why?"

"Things have changed back there. There's something in the oceans now. New life-forms." Ted looked at them bleakly. "Looks like somebody dumped them there. That's why Earth wants us to push on. Find out what we can from the EMs sure, but explore other systems, too."

Nikka said slowly, "I don't . . ."

"Somebody's seeded our oceans. Using starships."

THIRTEEN

2057 Deep Space

For weeks now, *Lancer* had been filled with the steady muted roar of the boosters. The huge, ornamented stone arced out from the sullen star, away from Isis, preparing for the ramscoop drive to cut in.

"Nigel? Nikka said I'd find you here."

Nigel turned to find Ted Landon entering the view chamber. "Having a last look?"

"Um."

"I haven't seen you around Control lately."

Nigel turned back to look at the distant ruddy disk of Isis. "I'd have been in the way."

"Look, I know you don't go along with the orders from Earthside, but I'm sure I can rely on you to pitch in where your talents are needed, especially—"

"Yes, right, team player and all that." He folded his arms.

"You didn't attend the community talks—didn't think I'd notice, did you?"

"Hadn't thought, actually,"

"Well, I did, and it was too bad your point of view wasn't better represented there."

"Would've made no difference. Earthside calls out, 'Forge on, mates!' and off we go."

Ted allowed a flash of irritation to cross his face. "Okay, I agree those set-tos were pretty much pro forma, but—"

"Listen." Nigel tapped his wrist. A slow but intricate strumming filled the view chamber, seeming to come from the imaging wall itself. "They're sending their art, their history, the lot."

"Well, yes, but in the form of myths and stories and a lot of indecipherable detail that—"

"That could be understood, in time. Particularly if we operated on the surface, where we could develop some visual signs to help break through the misunderstanding."

"We need to see the pattern to all this, Nigel. That means exploring more than one system. Whatever happened here is long past. We need a line on the general picture, other stars—"

"I was willing to stay behind. A small team could—"

"Could starve to death, yeah. There won't be a backup expedition for decades, maybe longer. I can't spare crew."

Nigel gestured. "They've been calling a long time. Now we've made contact, and then like a flash cut it off. Imagine what that will do to them."

"Sure, and imagine what those Watchers could do to us. There's more riding on *Lancer* than I can risk just to—"

"Shore up some scruffy washouts and have nought to show for it?"

"Damn! You're a sore loser, aren't you?"

"Right, now that you mention it. It's a long way to the next stop, and I have to go whether I want to or not."

Ted touched his front teeth together and rubbed them

carefully back and forth, clearly calculating. "I'll put you in charge of our continuing radio link with the EMs."

Nigel sniffed. "A token. I'll take it, but you know full well we'll get damn little through the ramscoop noise."

Ted shrugged. "Them's the breaks."

"The maths types have already determined that we're the first contact the EMs have had. If we break off, even for a while the blow to their—"

"Nigel, the decision's made."

"By an array of experts."

"Essentially, yeah. You got a better way? We can't run *Lancer* as a seat-of-the-pants showboat. Everybody's glad as hell to get away from the Watchers safely."

"Something tells me they're not a significant danger—"

"Changing your tune! Funny, I remember you were the one who warned us not to touch down on that Watcher, and now you're—"

"As I was about to say, not significant unless they're provoked."

"Why? With dozens dead—?"

"A hunch."

"I can't run a ship on hunches," Ted said sourly. "I need you to help process the data feed we're just starting to get from the gravitational lens back Earthside. You can have your hunches on the side."

Nigel smiled. "I'm getting too many votes in the shipwide congress, eh?"

"I'm not worried."

"I'd scarcely want your job anyway."

"There's always a faction that'll follow your line of thinking. If you could bring them around—"

"Around to *what*? I'm not maneuvering against you, Ted."

"If the people you influence don't go along with our general policy, that's divisive."

"Uh-huh. Science is like that. Full of incorrigibles."

"This isn't science, it's leadership we're talking."

"Maybe the best way to lead is to do nothing."

"What in hell's *that* mean?"

"You don't see that Watcher jumping to conclusions."

"I don't see it doing *anything*."

"Quite. Patience is a strategy, too."

"I'm getting full up to here with you, Nigel."

"You're at the end of a long queue. My whole career's been shot through with that sort of thing."

"You're pretty goddamn cavalier about it."

"At my age you have to be."

"Smug, aren't you!"

"You're not getting the message, Ted."

"Which is?"

"Why can't I get on with Americans? Let's put it this way—we're not talking foreign policy, we're talking *alien* policy. Listen to that EM song for a moment."

"Yeah. Indecipherable without computers."

"I doubt that computers alone could turn the trick. I doubt the Watcher did."

"It's had the time."

"Right, but not the hormones, y'see."

"So?"

"So maybe it's not there to decipher at all. Think about the design of such a thing. It has to last millions of years. Sure, it can repair itself within limits—but who fixes the fixers? You can't rely on redundancy alone for insurance. So your strategy becomes molelike. You make your Watcher careful, conservative. Don't waste energy. Don't risk damage of materials."

"Then why not try to knock us all off, once it killed some of us?"

"Beyond repelling boarders, maybe there are more important objectives. Perhaps it had something more to learn."

"Like what?"

"Where we came from? What we intend?"

"Look, there wasn't time for that Watcher to trigger landings on Earth. Elementary—"

"Granted. So something knew before."

"What?"

"Perhaps the *Snark*?"

"You know ISA doesn't accept your interpretation of that."

"Quite."

"This is just a bunch of speculation, Nigel!"

"For once, I agree."

"Not worth undermining my position."

"I believe this is where I came in."

Nigel stood silent, watching the dwindling light of Isis. "Look," Ted said to break off, "I've got to run. Think all this over, huh? Come by for a drink."

He left quickly. Nigel had let the soft swelling notes of the EM fugue fill the room, thinking it would have the same effect on Landon as it did on him, but the tactic had proved pointless. Others did not seem to hear the same plaintive wail in the widely spaced clicks and jarring clatter. The sounds would fade now, as *Lancer* boosted to near light speed. Perhaps he could have learned something from their songs of vast and empty times, the rolling centuries of sameness.

So now *Lancer* scratched a line across the darkness, fleeing the Watcher, which had won. In this strange strategy, Nigel glimpsed, information was worth more than mere bodies. It was in the nature of organic beings, forged by evolution's hand, to survive for the moment. To flee. While the Watcher could track *Lancer* by its fusion flame. And no matter how swiftly *Lancer* flew, communications at light speed would always outrace her.

PART FOUR 2061 EARTH

ONE

The wind had backed into the northeast and was coming up
strong again. Warren watched the sullen clouds moving in.
He shook his head. It was still hard for him to leave his sleep.

It was three days now since he had passed the island. He
had thought much about the thing with Rosa. When his head
was clear he was certain that he had made no mistake. He
had let her do what she wanted and if she had not understood
it was because he could not find a way to tell her. It was the
sea itself which taught and the Skimmers too and you had to
listen. Rosa had listened only to herself and her belly.

On the second day past the island, the air had become
thick and storm came down from the north. He had thought
it was a squall until the deck began to pitch at steep angles
and a piece broke away with a groan. Then he had lashed
himself to the log and tried to pull the plywood sheet down.
He could reach it, but the collar he had made out of his belt
was slippery with rain. He pulled at the cracked leather. He
thought of using the knife to cut the sheet free but then the
belt would be no good. He twisted at the stiff knot and then
the first big wave broke into foam over the deck and he lost
it. The waves came fast then and he could not get to his feet.
When he looked up it was dark overhead and the plywood
was wrenched away from the mast. The wind battered against
the mast and the collar at the top hung free. A big wave
slapped him and when he next saw the sheet it had splintered.
A piece fell to the deck and Warren groped for it and slipped
on the worn planking. A wave carried the piece over the side.
The boards of the deck worked against each other and there
was more splintering among them. Warren held on to the
log. The second collar on the mast broke and the sheet
slammed into the deck near him. He reached for it with one

145

hand and felt something cut into his arm. The deck pitched. The plywood sheet fell backward and then slid and was over the side before he could try to get to it.

The storm lasted through the night. It washed away the shelter and the supplies. He clung to the log, and the lashing around his waist cut into him in the night. Warren let the water wash freely over the cuts, the salt stinging across his back and over his belly, because it would heal faster that way. He tried to sleep. Toward dawn he dozed and woke only when he sensed a shift in the currents. The wind had backed into the northeast. Chop still washed across the deck and a third of the raft had broken away, but the sea was lessening as dawn came on. Warren woke slowly, not wanting to let go of the dreams.

There was nothing left but the mast, some poles he had lashed to the center log and his knife and arrow. From a pole and a meter of twine he made a gaff with the knife. The twine had frayed. It was slow work and the twine slipped in his raw fingers. The bark of the log had cut them in the night and they were soft from the water and the rubbing. The sun rose quickly and a heat came into the air that worked at the cuts in him and made them sweat. He could feel that the night had tired him and he knew he would have to get food to keep his head clear. The Skimmers would come to him again he knew, and if there was a message he would have to understand it.

He made the knife fast to the pole with the twine but it was not strong and he did not want to risk using it unless he had to. A green patch of seaweed came nearby and he hooked it. He meant to use it for bait if he could, but as he shook it out small shrimp fell to the planking. They jumped and kicked like sand fleas, and without thinking Warren pinched off their heads with his fingernails and ate them. The shells and tails crunched in his teeth and filled his mouth with a salty moist tang.

He kept a few for bait even though they were small. The twine was too heavy for a good line but he used it as he had before, in the first days after the *Manamix* went down, when he had tried with some of their food as bait and had never caught anything. He was a sailor but he did not know how to fish. He set three trailing lines and sat to wait, wishing he had the shelter to stop the sun. The current moved well now and

the chop was down. Warren hefted the gaff and hoped for a
Swarmer to come. He thought of them as moving appetites,
senseless alone, but dangerous if enough came at once and
butted the raft.

He bent over and looked steadily at a ripple of water
about twenty meters from the raft. Something moved. Shifting
prisms of green light descended into the dark waters. He
thought about a lure. With Rosa it had been simple, a
movement to draw them in and a quick shot. Warren turned,
looking for something to rig to coax with, and he saw the
trailing line on the left straightened and then the line hissed
and water jumped from it. He reached to take some of the
weight off and play in the line. It snapped. To the right
something leaped from the water. The slim blue form whacked
its tail noisily three times. Another sailed aloft on the other
side of the raft as the first crashed back in a loud white
splash. A third leaped and shone silver-blue in the sun and
another and another and they were jumping to all sides at
once, breaking free of the flat sea, their heads tilted sideways
to see the raft. Warren had never seen Skimmers in schools
and the way they rippled the water with their quick rushes.
They were not like the Swarmers in their grace and the way
they glided in the air for longer than seemed right, until you
looked closely at the two aft tails that beat the water and gave
the look of almost walking.

Warren stood and stared. The acrobatic swivel of the
Skimmers at the peak of their arc was swift and deft, a dash of
zest. Their markings ran downward toward the tail. There
were purplings and then three fine white stripes that fanned
into the aft tails. There was no hole in the gut like the place
where the Swarmers spun out their strands. Warren guessed
the smallest of them was three meters long. Bigger than most
marlin or sharks. Their thin mouths parted at the top of the
arc and sharp narrow teeth showed white against the slick
blue skin.

It was easy to see why his clumsy fishing had never
hooked any big fish. These creatures and the Swarmers had
teeth for a reason. There were many of them in the oceans
now and they had to feed on something.

They leaped and leaped and leaped again. Their forefins
wriggled in flight. The fins separated into bony ridges at their
edge and rippled quickly. Each ridge made a stubby projec-

tion. The rear fins were the same. They smacked the water
powerfully and filled the air with so much spray that he could
see a rainbow in one of the fine white clouds.

Just as suddenly they were gone.

Warren waited for them to return. After a while he
licked his lips and sat down. He began to think of water
without wanting to. He had caught some rain in his mouth
the night before but it was little. When the waves were
washing the deck he had been forced to stop because the salt
water would set him back even though it would have felt
good to drink it along with the rain.

He had to catch a Swarmer. He wondered if the Skimmers drove them away. To catch an ordinary fish would be a
little help, but the ones out here did not give much liquid
even when you squeezed the flesh and anyway he had only
two lines now and the small shrimp for bait. He needed a
Swarmer.

In the afternoon he saw a rippling to the east but it
passed going north. The high, hard glare of the sun weighed
on him. Nothing tugged at his lines. The mast traced an
ellipse in the sky as the waves came. The current ran strong.

A white dab of light caught his eye. it was a blotch on
the flat plane of the sea. It came steadily closer. He squinted.

Canvas. Under it was a blue form tugging at a corner.
Warren hauled it aboard and the alien leaped high, showering
him, the bony head slanted to bring one of the big elliptical
white eyes toward the figure on the deck. The Skimmer
plunged, leaped again, and swam away fast, taking short
leaps.

Warren studied the soggy, bleached canvas. It looked
like a tarp used to cover the gun emplacements on the
Manamix but he could not be sure. There were copper-
rimmed holes along one edge. He used them to hoist up
the mast, lashing it with wire and punching new holes to
fasten the boom. He did not have enough lines to get it right
but the canvas filled with the quickening breeze of late
afternoon.

He watched the bulging canvas and patiently did not
think about his thirst. A splash of spray startled him. A
Skimmer—the same one?—was leaping next to the raft.

He licked his swollen lips and thought for a moment of
fetching the gaff and then put the idea away. He watched the

Skimmer arc and plunge and then speed away. It went a few tens of meters and then leaped high and turned and came back. It splashed him and then left and did the same thing again.

Warren frowned. The Skimmer was heading southwest. It cut a straight line in the shifting waters.

To keep that heading he would need a tiller. He tore up a plank at the raft edge and lashed a pole to it. Fashioning a collar that would seat in the deck was harder. He finally wrapped strips of bark firmly into a hole he had punched with the gaff. They held for a while and he had to keep replacing them. The tiller was weak and he could not turn it quickly for fear of breaking the lashing. It was impossible to perform any serious maneuver like coming about if the wind shifted, but the sunset breeze usually held steady, and anyway he could haul down the canvas if the wind changed too much. He nodded. It would be enough.

He brought the bow around on the path the Skimmer was marking. The current tugged him sideways and he could feel it through the tiller, but the raft steadied and began to make a gurgle where it swept against the drift. The canvas filled.

The clouds were fattening again and he hoped there would not be another storm. The raft was weaker and the boards creaked with the rise and fall of each wave. He would not last an hour if he had to cling to a log in the water.

A heavy fatigue settled in him.

The sea was calming, going flat. He scratched his skin where the salt had caked and stung. He slitted his eyes and looked toward the sunset. Banks of clouds were reflected in the ocean that now at sunset was like a lake. Waves made the image of the clouds into stacked bars of light. Pale cloud, then three washes of blue, then rods of cloud again. The reflection made light seem bony, broken into beams and angles. Square custard wedges floated on the glassy skin. He looked up the empty sky, above the orange ball of sun, and saw a thin streak of white. At first he tried to figure out how this illusion was made, but there was nothing in optics that would give a line of light that jutted upward, rather than lying horizontal. It was no jet or rocket trail. It thickened slightly as it rose up into the dark bowl of the sky.

After describing it to himself this way Warren then knew

what it had to be. The Skyhook. He had forgotten the project, had not heard it mentioned in years. He supposed they were still building it. The strand started far out in orbit and lowered toward the Earth as men added to it. It would be more years before the tip touched the air and began the worst part of the job. If they could lower it through the miles of air and pin it to the ground, the thing would make a kind of elevator. People and machines would ride up it and into orbit and the rockets would not streak the sky anymore. Warren had thought years ago about trying to get a job working on the Skyhook, but he knew only how engines worked and they did not use any of that up there, nothing that needed air to burn. It was a fine thing where it caught the sun like a spider thread. He watched it until it turned red against the black and then faded as the night came on.

TWO

He woke in the morning with the first glow of light. His left arm was crooked around the tiller to hold it even though he had moored it with a wire. The first thing he checked was the heading. It had drifted some and he sat up to correct it and then found that his left arm was cramped. He shook it. It would not loosen so he gave it a few minutes to come right while he unlashed the tiller and brought them around to the right bearing. He was pretty sure he knew the setting even though he could feel that the current had changed. The raft cut across the shallow waves more at this new angle. Foam broke over the deck and the swell was deeper and the planking groaned but he held to it.

The left arm would not uncramp. The cold of the night and sleeping on it had done this. He hoped the warmth later would loosen the muscles though he knew it was probably because his body was not getting enough food or the right food. The arm would just have to come loose on its own. He massaged it. The muscles jumped under his right hand and after a while he could feel a tingling all down the arm although that was probably from rubbing the salt in, he knew.

There was nothing on his lines. He drew in the bait but it had been nibbled away. He kept himself busy gathering seaweed with the gaff and resetting the lines with the weed but he knew it was not much use and he was trying to keep his mind off the thirst. It had been bad since he woke up and was getting worse as the sun rose. He searched for the Skyhook to take his mind off his throat and the raw puffed-up feel in his mouth but he could not see it.

He checked the bearing whenever he remembered it but there was a buzzing in his head that made it hard to tell how much time had passed. He thought about the Swarmers and how much he wanted one. The Skimmers were different but they had left him here now and he was not sure how much longer he could hold the bearing or even remember what the bearing was. The steady hollow slap of the waves against the underside of the raft soothed him and he closed his eyes against the sun.

He did not know how long he slept, but when he woke his face burned and his left arm had come free. He lay there feeling it and noticed a new kind of buzzing. He looked around for an insect—even though he had not seen any for many days—and then cocked his head up and felt the sound coming out of the sky. Miles away a dot drifted across a cloud. The airplane was small and running on props, not jets. Warren got to his feet with effort and waved his arms. He was sure they would see him because there was nothing else in the sea and he would stick out if he could just keep standing. He waved and the plane kept going straight and he thought he could see under it something jumping in the water after its shadow had passed. Then the plane was a speck and he lost the sound of it and he finally stopped waving his arms although it had not really come to him yet that they had not seen him. He sat down heavily. He was panting from the waving and then without noticing it for a while he began crying.

After a time he checked the bearing again, squinting at the sun and judging the current. He sat and watched and did not think.

*   *   *

The splash and thump startled him out of a fever dream.

The Skimmer darted away, plunging into a wave and out the other side with a turning twist of its aft fins.

A cylinder like the others rolled across the deck. He scrambled to catch it. The rolled sheet inside was ragged and uneven.

    WAKTPL OGO SHIMA
                     WSW WSW CIRCLE ALAPMTO GUNJO
    GEHEN WSW WSW
    SCHLECT SCHLECT YOUTH UNSSTOP NONGO
    LUCK LOTS

Now instead of NONGO there was OGO. Did they think this was the opposite? Again WSW and again CIRCLE. Another island? The misspelled SCHLECT, if that was what it was, and repeated. A warning? What point could there be in that when he had not seen a Swarmer in days? If UNS was the German *we*, then UNSSTOP might be *we stop*. The line might mean *bad youth we stop not go*. And it might not. But GEHEN WSW WSW meant *go west southwest* or else everything else made no sense at all, and he had been wrong ever since the island. There was Japanese in it too but he had never crewed on a ship where it was spoken and he didn't know any. SHIMA. He remembered the city, Hiroshima and wondered if *shima* was "town" or "river" or something geographical. He shook his head. The last line made him smile. The Skimmers must have been in contact with something well enough to know a salute at the end was a human gesture. Or was that what they meant? The cold thought struck him that this might be *goodbye*. Or, looking at it another way, that they were telling him he needed lots of luck. He shook his head again.

That night he dreamed about the eyes and blood and fin fluid of the Swarmers, about swimming in it and dousing his head in it and about water that was clear and fresh. When he woke, the sun was already high and hot, the sail billowed west. He got the heading close to what he could remember and then crawled into the shadow of the sail, as he had done the days before.

He had kept his clothes on all the time on the raft and they were rags now. They kept off the sun still but were caked with salt and rubbed in the cuts and stung when he moved. At his neck and on his hands were black patches where the skin had peeled away and then burned again. He had worn a kind of hat he made before from Swarmer skin and bone and it was good shade but it had gone overboard in the storm.

Warren thought about the message but could make no more sense of it. He scratched his beard and found it had a crust of salt in it like hoarfrost. The salt was in his eyebrows too and he leaned over the side facedown in the water and scrubbed it away. He peered downward at the descending blades of green light and the dark shadow of the raft tapering away like a steep pyramid into the shifting murky darkness. He thought he saw something moving down there but he could not be sure.

He was getting weak now. He caught some more seaweed and used it as bait on the lines. The effort left him trembling. He set the heading and sat in the shade.

He woke with a jerk and there was splashing near the raft. Skimmers. They leaped into the noonday glare and beyond them was a brown haze. He blinked and it was an island. The wind had picked up and the canvas pulled full-bellied toward the land.

He sat numb and tired at the tiller and brought the raft in toward the island, running fast before the wind and cutting the waves and sending foam over the deck. There was a lagoon. Surf broke on the coral reefs hooking around the island. The land looked to be about a kilometer across, wooded hills and glaring white beaches. The Skimmers moved off to the left, and Warren saw a pale space in the lagoon that looked like a passage.

He slammed the tiller over full and the raft yawed and bucked against the waves that were coming harder now. The deck groaned and the canvas luffed, but the raft came into the pocket of the pale space and then the waves took it through powerfully and fast. Beyond the crashing of surf on the coral he sailed close to the wind to keep away from the dark blotches in the shallows, and then turned toward shore. The Skimmers were gone now, but he did not notice until the raft tugged on a sandbar and he looked around, judging the distance to the beach. He was weak and it would be stupid to risk anything this close. He stood up with a grunt and jumped heavily on the free side of the raft. It slewed and then broke free of the sandbar and the wind blew it fifty meters more. He got his tools and stood on the raft, hesitating as though leaving it after all this time was hard to imagine. Then he swore at himself and stepped off.

He swam slowly until his feet hit sand and then took slow steps up to the beach, careful to keep his balance, so he did not see the man come out of the palms. Warren pitched forward onto the sand and tried to get up. The sand felt hard and hot against him. He stood again with pains in his legs and the man was standing nearby, Chinese or maybe Filipino. He said something to Warren and Warren asked him a question and they stared at each other. Warren waited for an answer, and when he saw there was not going to be one he held out his right hand, palm up. In the silence they shook hands.

THREE

For a day he was weak and could not walk far. The Chinese brought him cold food in tin cans and coconut milk. They talked at each other but neither one knew a single word the other did and soon they stopped. The Chinese pointed to himself and said "Gijan" or something close to it, so Warren called him that.

It looked as though Gijan had drifted here in a small lifeboat. He wore clothes like gray pajamas and had two cases of canned food.

Warren slept deeply and woke to a distant booming. He stumbled down to the beach, looking around for Gijan. The Chinese was standing waist-deep in the lagoon. He pointed a pistol into the water and fired, making a loud bang but not kicking up much spray. Warren watched as slim white fish floated up, stunned. Gijan picked them from the water and put them in a palm frond he carried. He came ashore smiling and held out one of the fish to Warren. Its eyes bulged.

"Raw?" Warren shook his head. But Gijan had no matches. Warren pointed to the pistol. Gijan took the medium caliber automatic and hefted it and looked at him. "No, I mean, give me a shell." He saw it was pointless, talking. He made a gesture of things coming out of the muzzle and Gijan caught it and fished a cartridge out of his pockets. Gijan took the fish up on the sand as they started flopping in the palm frond, waking up from the stunning.

Warren gathered dry brush and twigs and mixed them and dug a pit for the mixture with his hands. He still had his knife and some wire. He forced open the cartridge with them. He mixed the gunpowder with the wood. He had been watching Gijan the night before and the man was not using fire, just eating out of cans. Warren found some hardwood and rubbed the wire along it quickly while Gijan watched, frowning at first. The fish were dead and gleamed in the sun.

Warren was damned if he was going to eat raw fish now that he was on land. He rubbed the wire harder, bracing the wood between his knees and drawing the wire quickly back and forth. He felt it warming in his hands. When he was sweating and the wire was both burning and biting into his hands, he knelt beside the wood and pressed the searing wire into it. The powder fizzled and sputtered for a moment and then with a rush it caught, the twigs snapped and the fire made its own pale yellow glow in the sun. Gijan smiled.

Warren had felt a dislike of using the gun to get the fish. He thought about it as he and Gijan roasted them on sticks, but the thought went away as he started eating them and the rich crisp flavor burst in his mouth. He ate four of them in a row without stopping to drink some of the coconut milk Gijan had in tin cans. The hunger came on him suddenly, as if he had just remembered food, and it did not go away until he finished six fish and ate half the coconut meat. Then he thought again about using the gun that way but it did not seem so bad.

Gijan tried to describe something, using his hands and drawing pictures in the sand. A ship, sinking. Gijan in a boat. The sun coming into the sky seven times. Then the island. Boat broken up on the coral, but Gijan swimming beside it and getting it to the shore, half sunken.

Warren nodded and drew his own story. He did not show the Swarmers or the Skimmers except at the shipwreck, because he did not know how to tell the man what it was like and also he was not sure how Gijan would like the idea of

eating Swarmer. Warren was not sure why this hesitation
came into his head but he decided to stick with it and not tell
Gijan too much about how he survived.

In the afternoon Warren made a hat for himself and
walked around the island. It was flat most of the way near the
beach with a steep outcropping of brown rock where the
ridgeline of the island ran down into the sea. There were
palms and scrub brush and sea grass and dry stream beds. He
found a big rocky flat space on the southern flank of the island
and squinted at it awhile. Then he went back and brought
Gijan to it and made gestures of picking out some of the pale
rocks and carrying them.

The man caught the idea on the second try. Warren
scratched out SOS in the sand and showed it to him. Gijan
frowned, puzzled. He made his own sign with a stick and
Warren could not understand it. There were four lines like
the outline of a house and a crossbar. Warren thumped the
sand next to the SOS and said "Yes!" and thumped it again.

He was pretty sure SOS was an international symbol but
the other man simply stared at him. The silence got longer.
There was tension in the air. Warren could not understand
where it came from. He did not move. After a moment Gijan
shrugged and went off to collect more of the light-colored
rocks.

They laid them out across the stony clearing, letters fifty
meters tall. Warren suspected the airplane he had seen was
searching for survivors of Gijan's ship, which had gone down
nearby, and not the *Manamix*. It was funny Gijan had not
thought of making a signal but then he did not think of
making a fire either.

The next morning Warren drew pictures of fishing and
found that Gijan had not tried it. Warren guessed the man
was simply waiting to be picked up and was a little afraid of
the big silent island and even more of the empty sea. Gijan's
hands were softer than Warren's and he guessed maybe the
man had been mainly a desk worker. When the canned food
ran out Gijan would have tried fishing but not before. So far
all he had done was climb a few palms and knock down
coconuts. The palms were stunted here though, and there
was not much milk in the coconuts. They would need water.

Warren worked the metal in the leftover cans and made

fishhooks. Gijan saw what he was doing and went away into the north part of the island.

Warren was surveying the lagoon, looking for deep spots near the shore when he found the raft moored in a narrow cove. Gijan must have found it drifting and tied it there. The boards looked worn and weak and the whole thing—cracked tiller, bleached canvas, rusted wire lashings—carried the feel of an old useless wreck. Warren studied it for a while and then turned away.

Gijan found him at a rough shelf of rock that stuck out over the lagoon. Gijan was carrying a box Warren had not seen. He put the box down and gestured to it, smiling slightly, proud. Warren looked inside. There was a tangle of fishing line inside, some hooks, a rod, a diving mask, fins, a manual in Chinese or something like it, a screwdriver, and some odds and ends. Warren looked at the man and wished he knew how to ask a question. The box was the same kind that the canned food was in, so Warren guessed Gijan had brought all this in the boat.

They went down to the beach and Gijan drew some more pictures and that was the story that came out of it. He did not draw anything about hiding the box away but Warren could guess that he had. Gijan must have seen the raft coming and in a hurry, afraid, he would snatch up what he could and hide it. Then when he saw that Warren was no trouble he came out and brought the food. He left the rest behind just to be careful. He was still being careful when he used the pistol to fish. Maybe that was a way to show Warren he had it without making any threats.

Warren smiled broadly and shook his hand and insisted on carrying the box back to their camp. Land crabs skittered away from their feet as they walked, two men with a strange silence between them.

Warren fished in the afternoon. The canned goods would not last long with two of them eating and Warren was more hungry than he could ever remember. His body was waking up after being half dead and it wanted food and water, more water than they could get out of the coconuts. He would have to do something about that. He thought about it while he fished, using worms from the shady parts of the island, and then he saw moving shadows in the lagoon. They were big fish but they twisted on their turns in a way he remembered. He watched and they did not break water but he was sure.

He began to notice the thirst again after he had caught two fish. He left a line with bait and went inland and knocked down three coconuts but they did not yield much of the sweet milk. He took the fish back to camp where Gijan was keeping the fire going. Warren sat and watched him gut the fish, not making a good job of it. He felt the way he had in the first days on the raft. New facts, new problems. This island was just a bigger raft with more to take from but you had to learn the ways first.

Gijan's odd box of equipment had some rubber hose that had sheared off some missing piece of equipment. Warren stared at the collection in the box for a while. He began idly making a cover for one of the large tin cans, fitting pieces of metal together. Crimping them over the lip of the can and around the edge of the hose, he found that they made a pretty fair seal. He made a holder for the can, working patiently. Gijan watched him with interest. Warren sent him to get seawater in a big can. He rigged the hose to pass through a series of smaller cans. With the seawater he filled the big can and sealed the tight cover and put it on the fire. The men watched the water boil and then steam came out of the hose. Gijan saw the idea and put seawater into the small cans. It cooled the hose so that at the end the thin steam faded into a dribble of fresh water.

They smiled at each other and watched the slow drip. By late afternoon they had their first drink. It was brackish but not bad.

Warren used gestures and sketches in the sand to ask Gijan about the assortment of equipment. Had he been on a research vessel? A fast skimship?

Gijan drew the profile of an ordinary freighter, even adding the loading booms. Gijan pointed at Warren, so he drew an outline of the *Manamix*. With pantomime and gestures and imitating sounds they got across their trades. Warren worked with machines and Gijan was some kind of trader. Gijan drew a lopsided map of the Pacific and pointed to a speck not big enough or in the right place to be any island Warren knew about. Gijan sketched in nets and motorboats and Warren guessed they had been using a freighter to try for tuna. It sounded stupid. Until now he had not thought about the islands isolated for years now and how they would get food. You could not support a population by fishing from the shore. Most crops were thin in the sandy soil. So he guessed Gijan's island had armored a freighter and sent it out with nets, desperate. If it was a big enough island they might have an airplane and some fuel left and maybe that was the one he saw.

Gijan showed him the stuff in the box again. It was pretty banged up and salt-rusted, and Warren guessed it had been left years ago when the freighter was still working. In the years when the Swarmers were spreading Warren had a gun like everybody else in the crew, not in his own duffel where somebody might find it but in a locker of spare engine parts. Now that he thought about it, a lifeboat was a better place to stow a weapon, down in with some old gear nobody would want. When you needed a gun you would be on deck already and you could get to it easy.

He looked at Gijan's pinched face and tried to read it, but the man's eyes were blank, just watching with a puzzled frown. It was hard to tell what Gijan meant by some of his drawings and Warren got tired of the whole thing.

They ate coconuts at sundown. The green ones were like jelly inside. Gijan had a way of opening them using a stake wedged into the hard-packed ground. The stake was sharp and Gijan slammed the coconut down on it until the green husk split away. The hard-shelled ones had the tough white meat inside but not much milk. The palms were bent over in the trade winds and were short. Warren counted them up and down the beach and estimated how long the two men would take to strip the island. Less than a month.

Afterward Warren went down to the beach and waded out. A current tugged at his ankles and he followed with his eyes the crinkling of the pale water where a deep current ran. It swept around the island toward the passage in the coral, the basin of the lagoon pouring out into the ocean under the night tide. Combers snarled white against the dark wedge of the coral ring and beyond was the jagged black horizon.

They would have to get fish from the lagoon and lines from shore would not be enough. But that was only one of the reasons to go out again.

In the dim moonlight he went back, past the fire where

Gijan sat watching the hissing distiller and then into the scrub. Uphill Warren found a tree and stripped bark from it. He cut it into chips and mashed them on a rock. He was tired by the time he got a sour-smelling soup going on the fire. Gijan watched. Warren did not feel like trying to tell the man what he was doing.

Warren tended the simmering and fell asleep and woke when Gijan bent over him to taste the can's thick mash. Gijan made a face. Warren roughly yanked the can away, burning his own fingers. He shook his head abruptly and set the can where it would come to a rolling boil. Gijan moved off. Warren ignored him and fell back into sleep.

This night mosquitoes found them. Warren woke and slapped his forehead, and each time in the fading orange firelight his hand was covered by a mass of squashed red-brown. Gijan grunted and complained. Toward morning they trudged back into the scrub and the mosquitoes left them and they curled up on the ground to sleep until the sun came through the canopy of fronds above.

The lines Warren had left overnight were empty. The fishing was bound to be bad when you had no chance to play the line. They had more coconuts for breakfast and Warren checked the cooling mash he had made. It was thick and it stained wood a deep black. He put it aside without thinking much about how he could use it.

In the cool of the morning he repaired the raft. The slow working of the tide had loosened the lashings and some of the boards were rotting. It would do for the lagoon, but as he worked he thought of the Swarmers crawling ashore at the last island. The big things had been slow and clumsy, and with Gijan's pistol the men would have an advantage, but there were only two of them. They could never cover the whole island. If the Swarmers came the raft might be the only escape they had.

He brought the fishing gear aboard and cast off. Gijan saw him and came running down the hard white sand. Warren waved. Gijan was excited and jabbering and his eyes rolled back and forth from Warren to the break in the reef. He pulled out his pistol and waved it in the air. Warren ran up the worn canvas sail and swung the boom around so that the raft peeled away from the passage and made headway along the beach, around the island. When he looked back Gijan was aiming the pistol at him.

Warren frowned. He could not understand the man. After a moment when Gijan saw that he was running steady in the lagoon, the pistol came down. Warren saw the man put the thing back in his pocket and then set to work laying his lines. He kept enough wind in the sail to straighten the pull and move the bait so it would look as though it were swimming.

Maybe he should have drawn a sketch for Gijan. Warren thought about it a moment and then shrugged. An aft line jerked as something hit it, and Warren forgot Gijan and his pistol and played in the catch.

He took four big fish in the morning. One had the striped back and silvery belly of a bonito and the others he did not recognize. He and Gijan ate two and stripped and salted the others, and in the afternoon he went out again. Standing on the raft he could see the shadows of the big fish as they came into the lagoon. A Skimmer darted in the distance and he stayed away from it, afraid it would come for the trailing lines. After a while he remembered that they had never hit his lines in the ocean, so then he did not veer the raft when the Skimmer leaped high nearby, rolling over in that strange way. Gijan was standing on the glaring white beach, Warren noticed, watching. Another leap, splashing foam, and then a tube rattled on the boards of the raft.

> SHIMA STONES CROSSING SAFE YOUTH
> WORLD NEST UNSSPRACHEN SHIGANO YOU SPRACHEN
> YOUTH UM! HIRO SAFE NAGARE CIRCLE UNS SHIO
> WAIT WAIT YOU   LUCK

Warren came ashore with it and Gijan reached for the slick sheet. The man moved suddenly and Warren stepped back, bracing himself. The two stood still for a moment, staring at each other. Gijan's face compressed and intent. Then in a controlled way Gijan relaxed, making a careless gesture with his hands. and helped moor the raft. Warren moved the tube and sheet from one hand to the other and finally, feeling awkward, handed them to Gijan. The man read the words slowly, lips pressed together. "Shima," he said. "Shio. Nagare. Umi." He shook his head and looked at Warren, his lips forming the words again silently.

They drew pictures in the sand. For SHIMA Gijan sketched the island and for UMI the sea around it. In the lagoon he drew wavy lines in the water and said several times, "Nagare." Across the island he drew a line and then made swooping motions of bigness and said, "Hiro."

Warren murmured, "Wide island? Hiro shima?" but aside from blinking Gijan gave no sign that he understood. Warren showed him a rock for STONE and drew the Earth for WORLD, but he was not sure if that was what the words on the sheet meant jammed in with the others. What did blackening in the w of WORLD mean?

The men spoke haltingly to each other over the booming on the reef. The clusters of words would not yield to a sensible plan and even if it had, Warren was not sure he could tell Gijan his part of it, the English smattering of words, or that Gijan could get across to him the foreign ones. He felt in Gijan a restless energy now, an impatience with the crabbed jumble of language. WAIT WAIT YOU and then LUCK. It seemed to Warren he had been waiting a long time now. Even though this message had more English and was clearer, there was no way for the Skimmers to know what language Warren understood, not unless he told them. Frowning over a diagram Gijan was drawing in the floury sand, he realized suddenly why he had made the bark mash last night.

It took hours to write a message on the back of the sheet. A bamboo quill stabbed the surface, but if you held it right it did not puncture. The sour black ink dripped and ran, but by pinning the sheet flat in the sun he got it to dry without a lot of blurring.

SPEAK ENGLISH. WILL YOUTH COME HERE? ARE WE SAFE FROM YOUTH ON ISLAND? SHIMA IS ISLAND IN ENGLISH. WHERE ARE YOU FROM? CAN WE HELP YOU? WE ARE FRIENDLY.   LUCK

Gijan could not understand any of it or at least he gave no sign. Warren took the raft out again at dusk as the wind backed into the north and ebbed into fitful breezes. The sail luffed and he had trouble bringing the raft out of the running lagoon currents and toward the spot where flickering shadows played across the white expanse of a sandbar. A Skimmer leaped and turned as he came near. He held the boom to catch the last gusts of sunset wind, and when the shadows were under the raft he threw the tube into the water. It bobbed and began to drift out toward the passage to the sea as Warren waited, watching the shadows, wondering if they had seen it, knowing he could not now catch the tube with the raft before it reached the reef, and then a quick flurry of motion below churned the pale sand and a form came up, ripping the smooth water as it leaped. The Skimmer flexed in air and hung for an instant, rolling, before it fell with a smack and was gone in an upwash of bright foam. The tube was gone.

That night the mosquitoes came again and drove them into the rocky ground near the center of the island. In the morning their hands were blood-streaked where they had slapped their faces and legs in the night and caught the fat mosquitoes partway through their eating.

In the morning Warren went out again and laid his lines as early as possible. Near the sandbar there were many fish. One of them hit a line, and when Warren pulled it in the thing had deep-set eyes, a small mouth like a parrot's beak, slimy gills, and hard blue scales. He pressed at the flesh and a dent stayed in it for a while, the way it did if you squeezed the legs of a man with leprosy or dropsy. The thing smelled bad as it warmed on the planks so he threw it back, pretty sure it was poisonous. It floated and a Skimmer leaped near it and then took the thing and was gone. Warren could see more Skimmers moving below. They were feeding on the poison fish.

He caught two skipjack tuna and brought them ashore for Gijan to clean. The man was watching him steadily from the beach and Warren did not like it. The thing between him and the Skimmers was his, and he did not want any more of the stupid drawing and hand waving of trying to explain it to Gijan.

He went into the palm grove where the fire crackled and got the diving mask he had seen in Gijan's box. It was made for a smaller head, but with the rubber strap drawn tight he could ride it up against the bridge of his nose and make it fit.

As he came back down to the beach Gijan said something but Warren went on to the raft and cast off, bearing in the southerly wind out toward the sandbar. He grounded the raft on the bar to hold it steady.

He lay on the raft and peered down at the moving shapes. They were at least five fathoms down and they had finished off the poison fish. Seven Skimmers hovered over a dark patch, rippling their forefins where the bony ridges stuck out like thick fingers. Sunlight caught a glint from the thing they were working on and suddenly a gout of gray mist came up from it and broke into bubbles. It was steam.

Warren lay halfway over the side of the raft and watched the regular puffs of steam billow up from the machine. Without thinking of the danger he slipped overboard and dove, swimming hard, pushing as deep as he could despite the tightness and burning in his chest. The Skimmers moved as they saw him and the machine became clearer. It was a pile of junk, pieces of a ship's hull and deck collars and fittings of all sizes. Four batteries were mounted on one side and rust-caked cables led from them into the machine. There were other fragments and bits of worked metal and some of it he was sure was not made by men. Knobs of something yellow grew here and there, and in the wavering, rippling green light there was something about the form and shape of the thing that Warren recognized as right and yet he knew he had never seen anything like it before. There is a logic to a piece of equipment that comes out of the job it has to do and he felt that this machine was well shaped, as his lungs at last burned too much and he fought upward, all thought leaving him as he let the air burst from him and followed the silvery bubbles up toward the shifting, slanting blades of yellow-green sun.

FOUR

In the lagoon the water shaded from pale blue at the beach to emerald in the deep channel where the currents ran with the tides. Beyond the snarling reef the sea was a hard gray.

Warren worked for five days in the slow dark waters near the sandbar. He double-anchored the raft so the deck was steady. That way he could write well on it with the bark mash and then dry the sheets the Skimmers brought up to him.

Their first reply was not much better than the earlier messages, but he printed out in capital letters a simple answer and gradually they learned what he could not follow. Their next message had more English in it and less Japanese and German and fewer of the odd words made up out of parts of languages. There were longer stretches in it, too, more like sentences now than strings of nouns.

The Skimmers did not seem to think of things acting but instead of things just being, so they put down names of objects in long rows as though the things named would react on each other, each making the other clearer and more specific and what the things did would be in the relations between them. It was a hard way to learn to think and Warren was not sure he knew what the impacted knots of words meant most of the time. Sometimes the chains of words said nothing to him. The blue forms below would flick across the bone-white sand in elaborate looping arabesques, turning over and over with their ventral fins flared, in designs that escaped him. When the sun was low at morning or at dusk he could not tell the Skimmers from their shadows, and the gliding long forms merged with their dark echoes on the sand in a kind of slow elliptical dance.

He lay halfway off the raft and watched them, when he was tired from the messages, and peered through the mask, and something in their quick darting glide would come through to him. He would try then to ask a simple question. He wrote it out and dried it and threw it into the lagoon. Sometimes that was enough to cut through the jammed lines of endless nouns they had offered him and he would see a small thought that hung between the words in a space each word allowed but did not define. It was as if the words packed together still left a hole between them and the job was to see the hole instead of the blur around it. He watched the skimming grace they had down in the dusky emerald green but he could not sort it out.

He went ashore at dusk each day. The catch from the

trailing lines was good in the morning and went away in the afternoon. Maybe it had something to do with the Skimmers. The easy morning catch left him most of the day to study the many sheets they brought up to him and to work on his own halting answers.

Gijan stood on the beach most of the day and watched. He did not show the pistol again when Warren went out. He kept the fire and the distiller going and they ate well. Warren brought the finished sheets ashore and kept them in Gijan's box, but he could not tell the man much of what was in them, at first because lines in the sand and gestures were not enough and later because Warren did not know himself how to tell it.

Gijan did not seem to mind not knowing. He tended the fire and knocked down coconuts and split them and gutted the catch and after a while asked nothing more. At times he would leave the beach for hours and Warren guessed he was collecting wood or some of the pungent edible leaves they had at supper.

To Warren the knowing was all there was, and he was glad Gijan would do the work and not bother him. At noon beneath the high hard dazzle of the sky he ate little because he wanted to keep his head clear. At night, though, he filled himself with the hot moist fish and tin-flavored water. He woke to a biting early sun. The mosquitoes still stung but he did not mind it so much now.

On the third day like this, he began to write down for himself a kind of patchwork of what he thought they meant. He knew as soon as he read it over that it was not right. He had never been any good with words. When he was married he did not writer letters to his wife when he shipped out even if he was gone half a year. But this writing was a way of getting it down and he liked the act of scratching out the blunt lines on the backs of the Skimmer sheets.

IN THE LONG TIMES BEFORE, THE EARLY FORMS WENT EASY IN THE WORLD, THEN ROSE UP LEAPING OUT OF THE BOTTOM OF THE WORLD, TO THE LAND, MADE THE TOOLS WE KNEW, STRUCK THE FIRE, MADE THE FIRE-HARDENED SAND WE COULD SEE THROUGH SO THAT WE COULD CUP THE LIGHT. THE CLOUDS OPEN, WE CAN SEE LIGHTS, LEARN THE DOTS ABOVE, WE SEE

LIGHTS WE CANNOT REACH, EVEN THE HIGHEST JUMP-
ER OF US CANNOT TOUCH THE LIGHTS THAT MOVE.
WE CUP THE LIGHT, SCOOP IT UP, AND FIND THE
LIGHTS IN THE SKY ARE SMALL AND HOT, BUT THERE IS
ONE LIGHT THAT WE CUP TO US AND FIND IT IS A
STONE IN THE SKY. WE THINK OTHER LIGHTS ARE
STONES IN SKY THOUGH FAR AWAY; WE SEE NO OTHER
PLACE LIKE THE WORLD. WE SWIM AT THE BOTTOM
OF EVERYTHING—IN THE WORLD, THE PLACE WHERE
STONES WANT TO FALL—BUT THE FALLING FLOW TAKES
THE STONES IN THE SKY, MAKES THEM CIRCLE US,
CIRCLE FOREVER LIKE THE HUNTERS IN THE WORLD
BEFORE THEY CLOSE FOR THE KILLING, SO THE STONES
CANNOT STRIKE US IN THE NEST OF US, THE WORLD
OF THE PEOPLE.

WE THOUGHT THAT OURS WAS THE ONLY WORLD AND
THAT ALL ELSE WAS COLD STONE OR BURNING STONE.
AND AS WE CUPPED THE LIGHT NOT THINKING OF IT,
WE SAW THE COLD STONE IN THE SKY GROW A LIGHT
WHICH WENT ON, THEN OFF, THEN ON, AGAIN AND
AGAIN, MOVING NOW STRANGELY IN THE SKY AND
THEN GROWING MORE STONES, MOVING, STONES FALL-
ING INTO THE WORLD, STONES SMALLER THAN THE
BIG SKY STONE, HITTING KILLING BRINGING BIG ANI-
MALS THAT STINK, EATING EVERY PIECE OF THE WORLD
THAT COMES BEFORE THEM, TAKING SOME OF US IN
THEM, BIG STONES MAKING BIG ANIMALS THAT ARE
NOT ALIVE BUT SWALLOW, KEEPING US IN THEM IN
WATER, SOUR WATER THAT BRINGS PAIN, WE LIVE
THERE, LIGHT COMING FROM LAND THAT IS NOT LAND,
A WORLD THAT IS NOT THE WORLD, NO WAVES, NO
LAND BUT THERE IS THE GLOWING STONE ON ALL
SIDES THAT WE CANNOT CLIMB, NO LAND FOR THE
YOUTH TO CRAWL TO, LONG TIME PASSING, WE SING
OVER AND OVER THE SOON-BIRTHING BUT IT DOES NOT
COME, THE SONG DOES NOT MAKE BIRTHING STIR IN
THIS RED WORLD, THIS SMALL WORLD THAT ONE OF
US CAN CROSS IN THE TIME OF A SINGLE SINGING.

THE YOUTH CHANGE THEIR SONG SLOWLY, THEN MORE
AND THEN MORE, THEIR SONG GOES AWAY FROM US,
THEY SING STRANGELY BUT DO NOT CRAWL. HOT RED
THINGS BUBBLE IN THE SMALL WORLD WHERE WE

LIVE AND THE YOUTH DRINK IT. THE SMOOTH STONE ON ALL SIDES THAT MAKES THIS WORLD GLOWS WITH LIGHT THAT NEVER GROWS AND NEVER DIMS. WE KEEP SOME OF OUR TOOLS AND CAN FEEL THE TIME GOING, MANY SONGS PASS, WE DO NOT LET THE YOUTH SING OR CRAWL BUT THEN THEY DO NOT KNOW US AND SING THEIR OWN NOISE, DRINKING IN THE FOUL CURRENTS OF THE BIG ANIMAL WE INHABIT, THE SMOOTH STONE OOZING LIGHT, ALWAYS RUMBLING, THE CURRENTS NOT RIGHT. WE MOVE THICKLY, LOSE OUR TIDES, THE RED CURRENTS SUCK AND BRING FOOD SWEET AND BITTER, WRONG, THE YOUNG ONES WHO SHOULD CRAWL ON LAND NOW EAT THE FOOD AND CHANGE, LONG TIMES THE WALLS HUMMING AND NO WAVES FOR US TO FLY THROUGH AND SPLASH WHITE.

THEN THE SMOOTH STONE GROWS SLOWLY HOT, CRACKS OPEN, SOME OF US DIE, THE SONG DIMS AMONG US, BITTER BLUE CURRENTS DRIVE US DOWN, MORE OF US FALL FROM THE SONG, LONG COLD SOUNDS STAB US, AND MORE FALL, FROM THE SOUR STREAMS COME NOW WAVES, FRESH STREAMS, WE TASTE, SING WEAKLY, SPEAK, IT IS A WORLD LIKE THE ONE WORLD, THE SMOOTH STONE ON ALL SIDES IS GONE, WE BREAK WATER.

THERE ARE WAVES CUTTING WHITE, SHARP, WE FIND SALT FOODS, LEAP INTO HOT AIRS, WAVES HARD FAST, WE CUP THE LIGHT AND SEE BIG STONE IN SKY, FAR STONES MOVING ACROSS THE MANY STONES, LIKE OUR WORLD BUT NOT OF OUR WORLD. THE SONG IS WEAK, WE SEEK TO CROSS THE WORLD BUT CANNOT, WE KNOW WE WILL LOSE OURSELVES IN THIS WORLD IF OUR SONG IS STRETCHED FARTHER.

BUT THE YOUTH HAVE A STRANGE SONG AND THEY GO OUT. THEY FIND FOOD, THEY FIND BIG ANIMALS IN THE WAVES AND BIGGER ANIMALS THAT CRUSH THE WAVES, THEY STRIKE AT THEM IN THE WAY WE ONCE DID LONG TIMES PAST, THROW THEIR WEBS TO BRING DOWN THE CRUSHERS OF WAVES. THESE CRUSHERS ARE NOT THE BIG ANIMALS WE KNEW IN THE WORLD AND WHEN THE YOUTH DRAG THEM DOWN CLOSER TO THE CENTER THEY ARE NOT RIPE, DO NOT BURST WITH

FRUIT, ARE FIERY TO THE MOUTH, AND KILL SOME
YOUTH WITHOUT RELEASING THE PODS THAT WOULD
DRIVE THE YOUTH TO THE LAND, DRIVE THEM TO THE
AIR TO SUCK, DRIVE THE CHANGE TO MAKE THE YOUTH
INTO THE FORM THAT WOULD BE US. THESE THINGS
THAT FLOAT AND CRUSH THE WAVES WE FEAR AND
FLEE, BUT THE YOUTH EAT OF THEM AND YET DO NOT
GO TO THE LAND TO CRAWL; WE LOSE THE SONG WITH
THEM FOREVER, THEY FLY THE WAVES NO MORE, THEY
TAKE THE BIG ANIMALS THAT WALK ABOVE THE WAVES.
THE YOUTH HAVE BECOME ABLE TO KILL THE BITTER
WAVE-WALKERS, THEY FEAST ON THE THINGS IN THEM.
WE SEE FROM A DISTANCE THAT IT IS YOU THE YOUTH
EAT, EVEN IF YOU ARE SICK AND DEATH CAUSING, YOU
ARE KILLED IN THE SKINS THAT CARRY YOU WALKING
THE WAVES. THE YOUTH DO NOT SING, THEY SPLIT
YOUR SKINS, THEY GROW AND EAT ALL THAT COMES
BEFORE THEM.

NOW YOU ARE GONE LIKE US, NEARLY CHEWED. WE
COME TO HERE, WE DRIVE THE YOUTH AWAY, THE ACT
CHEWS US BUT DOES NOT FINISH US. WE FIND YOU IN
THE SKINS YOU LOVE AND WE CANNOT SING WITH YOU.
WE FIND YOU ONE MAN AND IN ONE YOU CAN SING;
TOGETHER YOU ARE DEAF. YOU ARE THE TWENTY-
FOURTH WE HAVE SUNG WITH ON THE WAVES YOUR
KIND CANNOT HEAR UNLESS YOU ARE ONE AND CAN-
NOT SING TO EACH OTHER. MANY OF THE OTHERS
WHO SUNG WITH US ARE NOW CHEWED BUT WE CAN
KEEP THE YOUTH AWAY FOR A TIME WE GROW WEAK
THE YOUTH RUN WITH SORES AND LEAVE STINK IN THE
CURRENTS FOUL WHERE THEY GO WE SMELL THEM THE
WORLD THAT WAS FALSE WORLD MADE THEM THIS
WAY NOT AS THEY WERE WHEN WE KNEW THEM IN THE
WORLD THAT WAS OURS THEY CANNOT SING BUT KNOW
OF THE PLACES WHERE YOU SING TO EACH OTHER AND
SOME NOW GO THERE WITH THEIR SORES MAY BE
CHEWED BY YOU BUT THERE ARE MANY MANY OF THEM
THEY ACHE NOW FOR THE SKINS-THAT-SINK, BUT THEY
ARE MADNESS THEY ARE COMING AND THEY CHEW YOU
OTHERS LAST

FIVE

Each night after it got too dark for Warren to write in the yellow firelight, they would move inland. The mosquitoes stayed near the beach and there were a lot of other insects, too. Warren listened to fish in the lagoon leaping for the insects and the splashing as the Skimmers took the fish in turn. He could see their phosphorescent wakes in the water.

They smeared themselves with mud to keep off the mosquitoes, but it did not keep off the ticks that dropped from the trees. There was no iodine in Gijan's box of random items.

Putting a drop of iodine on the tick's tail was the best treatment and second best was burning them off. Each morning the men inspected each other and there were always a few black dots where the ticks burrowed in. An ember from the fire pressed against the tick's hindquarters made it let go and then Warren could pull the tick out with his fingernails. He knew that if the head came off in the skin, it would rot and the whole area would become a boil. He noticed that Gijan got few ticks and he wondered if it had anything to do with the Oriental skin.

The next morning Warren got a good catch, and when he brought it in he was sore from the days of work on the raft. After eating the fish he went for more coconuts. The softer fronds were good, too, for rubbing the skin to take away the sting of mosquito bites and to get the salt out. Finding good coconuts was harder now and he worked his way across the island, up the ridgeline and down to a swampy part on the southern side. There were edible leaves there and he chewed some slowly as he made his way back, thinking. He was nearly across a bare stretch of soil when he saw it was the place they had laid out the SOS. The light-colored rocks were there but they were scattered. The SOS was broken up.

Gijan was looking in the storage box when Warren came

back into the camp. "Hey!" he called. Gijan looked at him, calm and steady, and then stood up, taking his time.

Warren pointed back to the south and glared at the man and then bent down and drew the SOS in the sand. He rubbed it out and pointed at Gijan.

Warren had expected the man to give him a blank look or a puzzled expression. Instead, Gijan put a hand in a pocket.

Then Gijan said quite clearly, "It does not matter."

Warren stood absolutely still. Gijan pulled the pistol casually out of his pocket but he did not aim it at anything.

Warren said carefully, "Why?"

"Why deceive you? So that you would go on with your"—he paused—"your good work. You have made remarkable progress."

"The Skimmers."

"Yes."

"And the SOS . . ."

"I did not want anyone to spot the island who should not."

"Who would that be?"

"Several. The Japanese. The Americans. There are reports of Soviet interest."

"So you are—"

"Chinese, of course."

"Of course."

"I would like to know how you wrote that summary. I read the direct messages you got from them, read them many times. I could not see in them very much."

"There's more to it than what they wrote."

"You are sure that you brought all their messages ashore?"

"Sure. I kept them all."

"How do you discover things that are not in the messages?"

"I don't think I can tell you that."

"Cannot? Or will not?"

"Can't."

Gijan became pensive, studying Warren. Finally he said, "I cannot pass judgment on that. Others will have to decide that, others who know more than I do." He paused. "Were you truly in a shipwreck?"

"Yeah."

"Remarkable that you survived. I thought you would die when I saw you first. You are a sailor?"

"Engine man. What're you?"

"Soldier. A kind of soldier."

"Funny kind, seems to me."

"This is not the duty I would have chosen. I sit on this terrible place and try to talk to those things."

"Uh-huh. Any luck?"

"Nothing. They do not answer me. The tools I was given do not work. Kinds of flashlights. Sound makers. Things floating in the water. I was told they are drawn to these things."

"What would happen if they did not answer?"

"My job is over then."

"Well, I guess I've put you out of work. We're still going to need something to eat, though." He gestured at the raft and turned toward it and Gijan leveled the pistol.

"You can rest," the man said. "It will not be long."

2060 INTERSTELLAR SPACE BETWEEN RA AND ROSS

ONE

In 2046, earth had launched a series of exploratory probes to the nearby stars. Now they were arriving, sniffing at the myriad mysteries of Epsilon Eridani, Ross 128, 61 Cygni, and other cryptic names that had once been dry catalog symbols and now were luminous targets. The probes transmitted their data both Earthside and to *Lancer*, to save the years of delay in relay. To filter and understand the multichannel flux, Ted Landon set up teams composed of high-flow data analysts, assorted scientists, and anyone with field experience. Nigel drew a slot. To master the lock-in prosessors he had to be sealed off, open only to the steady drumming hail of probe data, focusing on the ebb and surge of sensation from the probes as they glided through stellar systems, plunged into thick atmospheres, and finally jerked forth from their capsules and clanked across the alien lands themselves.

The first automated probe reached Barnard's star and decelerated, passing two small planets. The signals arrived only a few months after *Lancer* left Isis. The Mercury-sized worlds were barren, uninteresting. There seemed to be nothing interesting about the stars, beyond the routine measurements of bow shock waves near the planets, asteroid counts, and sunspot analysis. Halfway across the system, the probe stopped transmitting abruptly. It was never heard from again. The astronomers suspected that, since it was crossing the ecliptic plane of the system at the time, the probe had failed to dodge an asteroid.

*   *   *

Nigel drew time in an isolation capsule, monitoring the incoming stream of data from Epsilon Eridani. The probe glided in, spotting the distant moving glimmers that were planets, sampling the ghostly breeze of the solar wind, mapping the plane of the Eridani ecliptic, sketching in the orbital histories with deft Newtonian strokes. The three people in their cool dark pods, laced with holographic, full-senses data, saw the probe flash by a chunky dim gray patch of light.

Before they could piece together their own impressions, the astrometrical programs aboard the probe scanned the nearby volume, listened for infrared mutter of similar dabs of gray, and found four: an Oort cloud of protocomets, making their slow swoops in shrouds of dust. The spidery probe rushed on, following its own logic. Human receptors piped into the flow of numbers and spectra, making a picture with human implications. Star mass: 0.83 solar. Six planets. Spectral type K2, sunspots visible. Two gas giants; one Mars-size world; the rest, mere rocks. No oceans, no life.

Yeah but the terrestrial type one has an atmosphere, see as they all felt the probe slowing, maneuvering *Sure no oxy though and no disequilibrium gases far as I can* the world was swelling before them *Point taken, but that's mere theory* a smattering of jumbled grays and browns and blacks *Look that's cloud cover all right, the prelim missed it* fields of stone glinting like distant windows of a city reflecting the setting yellow sun *I dunno mica maybe* crumpled mountain ranges, warped valleys *Some signs of tectonics an' I'd say some volcanic action over there by the terminator* windswept and ruined plateaus, gullied and gray *A trifling planet really, thin atmosphere, about 0.32 Earth mass* no spatterings of green near the carving rivers *Look at that readout, CO_2 plus the expected traces* howling storms, blue on the rumpled brown lands, no ears to mark their passage *Whole system's a flop if this is the best* the probe arcing over the planet, pondering to itself the rewards of deploying a surface craft *No*

wait go back to that last image the curve of this
world a shining silver against black *Right the horizon shot* a sliver of gunmetal gray like a fine wire
Funny, planet this small with a ring glowing softly,
but as the probe arcs onward the supposedly straight
line it refuses to fatten, to show a disk *Naw look it
runs straight down to the surface* pinned to the
equator *I'm buggered it's not a Skyhook* the chilly,
answering silence as they stare at the enormous
artifact, its long curve now coming into view, still
hairlike, thin and tapering down to the equator
*Why, why would anybody put up a Skyhook in a
barren* nothing moves on the fiber. They can see
that in the successive exposures the probe sends, its
own judgment centering on the thin wedge of gray
against the stars *Mining? Nothin' else worth a damn
down there* the probe backs away now, the view
shifts *Perhaps it wasn't always that way* wheeling
across star fields *You mean some life down there, a
civilization? But there's no trace of* a speck that
grows *Not now, no* the probe curving around the
bleak horizon *On a geological time scale, what
would last?* a swelling round dot *For something to,
well, there's no life at all, what could* the crescent
flawed, eaten *Yeah if the natives put that up they've
been gone awhile, we're talkin' tens of millions of
years easy an' I don't believe* irregular, grays and
blacks, a side smashed as if by a grazing impact,
stress lines in the ancient rock of this world's small
moon *Stands to reason, sure there's some cratering
but not that much and anyway how can you kill a
whole biosphere* yet something flares sudden bright
orange in the shadowed pits of the moon *Hey you
see that* a churning flame *Just like* jetting out, swelling toward the probe *A thing like before, a Watcher*
filling the lenses *Must be two hun'red klicks range,
more even* orange chaos flecked with angry reds
God I hope hands clenched though they all knew
this happened years before, parsecs away *It's reached
us* but the fast-frames seize them as the orange arms
extend and wrap around the disk antennas *Christ if
it burns those we'll* the inboard acoustics register a

rippling shock which comes to the three as a rumble *Losing the low-frequency stuff* a searing, sizzling feel *It'll fry for sure if that hits the equipcomp* plasma ionizing the precisely aligned interferometers *Telemetry's fluttering* lenses which have faced the high vacuum for a decade—fogged, pitted and fractured *Losing pressure in right cryotank* waning heat splashes through the thin seals *Goddamn goddamn look at 'at* the roiling clouds thin, violet jets flare, ionized hydrogen spits UV and fades *Most a the microwave is out* the stars return *Main functions are truncated* the dwindling dot sucks in its own bloodred tongue *It was 'at flyby velocity an' rebound, got it up to over nine klicks a sec* the cryptlike worn surface below blurs and shimmers with distance *Just outran it is all* the probe falls starward, blinded in the black, and numb *I wonder why it left the Skyhook* its engines dead *It? What it?* and returns dutifully to measuring the wisps of solar winds *The it that put the boot in on that wasteland, leaving our Watcher behind* the woman pipes his image into her plex, squints at him *Maybe too much trouble to knock it down* they uncoil, each, from the tie-in labyrinth *After doing that to the surface?* sour, haggard, each trembling *God knows how but* green Control queries flashing unnoticed *That's an assumption sure Okay maybe having an elevator handy* Nigel's head bowed, his hand rumpling gray hair absently *For what? Work on the surface?* cool enamel glow *Or bring up raw materials, how do I know?* rapping at the hatches of each, the external team worried *It's been there a bloody long time, to make repairs I'd venture, remember the gouge, passing junk, you have to expect that, so it mends itself* sweaty and close, then the hatch pops *Well could be but why take a shot at us* untangling the electronic spaghetti *When the one back at Isis simply let* Lancer *go you mean? Um, perhaps, perhaps this one felt it had nothing more to learn? Um.*

TWO

Nigel wondered how, in as carefully managed a society as this, "lurkey" had become the accepted slang for lousy turkey.

He worked on the lurkey itself. It was a huge, sweaty mass, aslosh in nutrients. It grew so quickly that a team had to cut slices, using servo arms, so the meat didn't outrun its chem supplies. Pseudolife, with all genetic checks on excess deftly edited out. Malthus, exponentiated.

When he had the time he used some of his precious store of wood, shaping and planing the boards until they had a satin finish. Sawdust exuded its sweet weight into the impersonal ship's air. He scavanged some of the forced-growth cellulose stands from the greenhouses, and worked the soft chunks with earnest energy, hammering and planing and using the ripsaw for texture in the speckled grain. There was not much strength in the stuff but it would make furniture. It reminded him that he, too, was three-quarters water, rushing and subsiding according to the hollow knocking in his veins, a hydrostatic being. With a pinch of salt added, to signify his origin.

Every spring when he was a boy, Nigel remembered, he had gone for hikes in the wet meadows. There and in the roadside ditches he would hear a small, shrilling chorus which sounded for all the world like an endlessly repeated, "We're here, we're here, we're here." Frogs, confident little fellows, announcing their occupancy of that particular ecological niche. He suspected that now, to some greater ear than ours, man's expanding bubble of radio babble must make a similar ringing that billowed but a short way into the night. Only when nearby would it be bothersome, when one could pick out one strident voice at a time.

From the heights of the nearby cloaked hills, the frogs blended, not too badly, with all the other ambitious voices that, in croaks and chirrups, were saying the same thing—

We're here, we're here. A bicyclist, intent on his destination, might wheel through the frog chorus, sensing it was there but giving it no attention, not trying to make out the myriad voices. A truly advanced civilization in the galaxy would probably do the same thing to the soft buzz of radio, or to the occasional flyby probe humming, mosquitolike, past its ear.

Others might take a casual slap at such a passing irritant. Or even call for pest control.

Wolf 359 was a dim M8 star with only a tiny nearby volume capable of supporting life. Yet a world orbited there, one remarkably similar to the one around Epsilon Eridani: small, bleak, with a thin wisp of atmosphere. Not ancient, like the skyhook world, but there were signs that once it had been inhabited. No biosphere remained. The small lakes were drying up. The M-class stars are the longest lived of all, and the spectra of Wolf 359 said it was as old as the galaxy. There were aeons enough for life to arise beneath this lukewarm sun.

And time for it to die. The air and land carried traces of the chemical imbalances which are the very minimal definition of life. These signs were slowly ebbing away, but they argued for a biosphere that must have existed within the last few million years.

Around the small planet there were two moons. One was quite sizable, barely bound to its primary. The other was smaller, perhaps a few kilometers across. It had odd markings here and there, markings which might be natural results of meteorite bombardment over time, and then again might not. The probe caught only a fleeting glimpse of it as it arced around the brown and weathered world below, and then went on. It passed by a large gas giant planet on its way out of the system.

God this is really dog work, measuring this and analyzing that, all for the astro types the banded planet coming in from the left *Yeah when you think about it what difference does it make, they're summing the same data base back Earthside* vast and yellow *Keep totting it up, you never know* a sprinkling of light in the plane of rotation *Okay okay God Nigel just 'cause you're team head doesn't mean you can't kid around a* points of brilliance, some white and others ruddy with the reflected

glow of the giant world *Yeah I know her* the probe
swooping in for a boosting rendezvous *Works in
agro I think, bunks over in P4* on a timed flyby of
two moons *Not a looker but I hear* falling powerless
*Ol' Aarons said, Buck teeth? She could eat an apple
through a tennis racket an' the whole crowd they*
sipping of the stellar winds and calibrating particle
energies, plasma density, UV flux *Lavera you're
falling behind* now closing on the first moon *Funny
getting a lot of backscattered light from the rotation
plane an ice disk probably it's pretty cold this far
out* grids deploying, lenses swinging to face the
oncoming pocked and speckled face *Hey I've resolved that so-called ice disk it's not grains at all it's
a long string of stuff, pretty evenly spaced like beads
on a string, pearls really 'cause they're pretty white
an' the radar says they're smooth, no backscatter in
the centimeter wavelengths* deep rutted valleys cast
long shadows at the blue terminator *Lot of little
sources in the plane, but only out from this moon, I
mean there aren't any farther in* a crust of ice
streaked black *Probe's passing close to one of 'em
in few minutes* no craters *First flash looks like some
structure kinda oblong must be an asteroid or maybe a broken-up moon tidal forces maybe pulled it
apart and left all this crap drifting in toward the
primary* a gray dot of light like the others swelling *I
should think not* elongated *Yeah why?* two blobs of
lighter gray separate from the central image *Why
should debris of that type fetch up against this one
moon? Seems some would get by it* the two dollops
now resolving into circles *Damn funny formation*
the angle shifts as the probe moves, coming closer,
focusing, and abruptly a brilliant flare burns in the
field of view *Whazzat so fast* so that the probe stops
down the input, applying polarizers and filters *It's
reflection, reflected light from Wolf 359* until its
motion carries it beyond and the light ebbs and it
can see better the tiny control cabin at the exact
point between the two huge sun sails *Must be using
them to get some push* and behind it the dark mass
of clotted ices and the restraining webbing that fixes

this cargo in place *Launching out from that moon,
you think?* the sails patiently catching the red photons of the distant sun and tilting so that the momentum they impart pushes the dusky ice gently out
from the gas giant *Lavera take a line of sight on
these things, work out their trajectory assuming for
simplicity that something's putting them out at regular intervals from that moon* for decades until the
gravitional tug of the planet is balanced by the pull
of the wan red star *Yeah they're winding out all
right, nice little spiral* distant motes spread in a
broad smooth curve *Only it stops farther out and
they kinda bunch up* as they hesitate and then
empty their small fuel reserves through low-thrust
nozzles, outgassing vapor that has boiled from the
surface of the ices they carry *an' looks like they peel
off an' come back in movin' pretty slow though* this
time moving not in spirals but in long, low-energy
hyperbolic orbits *an' they start spreadin' out pickin'
up speed I guess* plunging down in the grip of the
banded orange-yellow world, past the roiling brown
bands at a higher speed than they have ever known,
correcting their courses under instructions from the
distant ancient parent moon *I'm losin' them after
that, guess they string out gettin' too far away to
pick them up but they're not gravitationally bound
anymore I can tell that* falling free at last toward the
inner world which began it all millions of years
before *I should think with that little thrust the voyage* carrying valuable ice which will intersect the
small planet's orbit and plunge into the wisp of
atmosphere *Right Nigel I make it five, six hunnert
yeʾrs to get into the inner system looks like that
terratype is the target, too, or close to it* so that the
sky begins to glow with a shower of small meteors,
shedding vapor as they fall free *All this just to move
chunks of ice?* the icebergs splitting into showers
that sparkle in the night sky above an arid plain *I
make the rate maybe one a month* the sky warms
*an' at that rate it'd take forty forevers to sock in an
ocean* soft, moist breezes stir beneath a dim but
perpetual sun *Agreed, but that is precisely how long*

they may very well have the icebergs coming to aid
a biosphere which is now long dead but can with
the steady pressure of chemical laws begin again
*What's more, you'll note there were lakes back on
that forlorn little speck* the probe pivots and below a
stark face rushes by *Point is, what's sending them?*
plains cut in rectangular blocks, antlike black forms
moving on designated roads to pick up their loads
of ice and rock and return to a central smudge of
tread-churned brown *Something that can use solar
energy, must be to last this long* vast shining screens,
a sprawl of manufacturing plants, all ice-crusted
*The machines must be able to repair themselves by
the same argument, build new ones like themselves
when needed, guide the ones in flight* slow and
steady, chipping at blue-veined mountains, loading
electromagnetic slingshot launchers *Who'd set all
this running? I mean what's the point of* the ice has
wrenched and split under the changing forces which
came as weight was removed and the moon is
cracked, faulted, and pitted as it is eaten *Whatever
or whoever lived back there, on that planet, millions of years ago, and set this in motion* the machines keep on, gnawing and dying and being
replaced *But they're gone Nigel, the biosphere's
wiped* the probe swings by the ice moon and ar-
rows past the gas giant, changing its momentum to
boost outward for the next star hanging a dozen
light-years away *Surely, but those black specks don't
know that* the ramscoop cuts in *So they're running
on? Christ doesn't make sense when whatever finished off a whole goddamn biosphere came through,
I mean why not just knock off these little* rumbling,
the magnetic fields reach out and grasp ions to
flavor the new fusion fire *I'll fancy we can't say, from
this trifling investment of fact but mind, there was a
Watcher back there round that planet* the gas giant
is blurred in its exhaust *Well might have been we
didn't get a good look an' Landon says he doesn't
see that much similarity* leaving *Good enough, but
how's he to explain the other fact?* the dead worlds
far behind, the moon stirring *What fact? I don't*

outward *That there was no Watcher round that moon*

THREE

In 2045 Lancer had paused in its steady one-g acceleration out from Earth, long enough to deploy the largest telescope ever conceived. It was a gossamer-thin array of optical and microwave receivers, flung out like a fishing net. Nigel had worked for days helping to dispatch the sensors in the right order, avoiding the heavy work for fear it would show a spike of strain on his metabolic report.

Men and women cast their net to capture photons; the telescope itself was provided by the distant, white-bright speck of their sun. Space is not flat, like the marble Italian foyers Galileo imagined, where his gliding blocks went on forever in ideal experiments carried out free of friction. The mass of those hypothetical blocks would stretch space itself, warp the obliging flat plane. Mass tugs at light. Forced into a curve, light will focus. The symmetry of three dimensions in turn shaped any sizable mass into a sphere, perfect for a lens. Each star was a huge refractor, a gravitational lens.

Lancer dropped sensor nets, starting three light-days out from Sol. The nets gathered in photons like a spring harvest, compiling sharp images of distant stars, resolving detail a mere ten kilometers across. For each star the focal distance from the sun was different, and so the webs had to tack against the wind of particles blowing out from the sun, using the magnetic fields beyond the planets to trim and guide their long scalloping orbits.

Lancer rumbled and forked a pure, blue-hot plasma arc, and pulled away from the gravitational lens that was its native star, leaving the colossal telescope behind. It would be six years before the first dim images would be finished. Ever since the sun had formed from infalling dust, pictures from worlds hundreds of parsecs away had been forming in the spaces far beyond the planets. Those focused stories, now forever lost, had run their courses on the gigantic hypothetical screen, the imaging plane. Through billions of years, until this moment, there had been no one in the theater to watch them.

Lancer's destination was a mild red dot known in the catalog as Ross 128. It was the sun's twelfth nearest neighbor, an unremarkable M-5 star. Toward the end of the twentieth century some X-ray astronomers had studied it briefly, comparing the hard radiation from it with our Sun's. It was a little more active, but once the solar physicists on a NASA grant had milked it, they forgot it. So did everybody else.

The gravitational lens array showed a full-sized solar system, though: five gas giants plus two Earth-sized worlds. A robot probe had reached Ross 128 about the time *Lancer* went into orbit around Ra. Something had silenced its transmissions as it entered the system.

Lancer was "nearby." It could study a system far better than any flyby could. Earthside thought that the death of the robot probe was worth a follow-up. Maybe it had smacked into a rock. Or maybe something wanted it to look that way.

Earthside's strategy was to accumulate astronomical information, *fast*, and stir it into the pot with data on the Swarmers and Skimmers. This was a compromise reached by the important space-faring nations, totally outside the aging carcass of the United Nations. The Asian faction wanted to push colonization of the nearby stars as soon as possible. That way, humanity would be dispersed. If the Swarmer-Skimmer fleet returned and destroyed humanity's space resources, at least the race would be already spread among the stars, and relatively invulnerable.

The Europeans and Americans backed a pure exploratory program. Behind this was calculated advantage. The Asian economies were doing better at capitalism than the societies that had invented the notion in the first place. The Western economies were broke. If colonization started right away, the stars would belong to the short and slant-eyed.

Lancer was ordered to investigate Ross 128, then return home. But Ra was not finished with them. After a year of acceleration, *Lancer* leveled out at 0.98 light speed. When it damped its fusion plume, the plasma exhaust unfurling behind it dropped in density. The thinner the plasma, the easier radio waves can get through.

At 15:46 hours, June 11, shipboard antennas picked up an intense burst of microwave emission. It came from dead aft and lasted 73 seconds. After that, nothing.

> *No look I can't break it down further like I was telling you the data's all over the board*
>
> *Dispersion in the pulse from all that crap we're throwin' behind us just plain messed up the signal*
>
> *Not from the EMs though that's not their frequency we never got anything from 'em up at ten GHz*
>
> *Okay sure but Ted here wants to know if there's any chance they sent it*
>
> *Who can tell Christ no info in that burst at all*
>
> *Yeah right but lookit the power man—I'd say doesn't look like a solar flare or anything natural*
>
> *Course not, too tight a band, and a little star like Ra can't do much better than hunnert megahertz never make it up to ten gigs and you're right about the power no way it can be those EMs*
>
> *Ted I got the calibration on it and it's a helluva shot of power innat burst doesn't make sense*
>
> *Too much power yeah I mean no artificial source would put out that much it's crazy*
>
> *Right, if you think they're broadcasting in all directions, a spherical pulse, then it would take a bloody avalanche of power to register as much as we're getting*
>
> *Who's 'at on the line*
>
> *Walmsley sounds like, look Nigel, this's just a tech-talk*
>
> *Merely sitting in, don't pay me any mind*
>
> *Must be artificial though the burst's so short*
>
> *This is Ted I'm sure your results are right overall but honestly gentlemen and ladies I don't believe we can reconcile a power level like that from the EMs or anyone else it must be Ra itself some sort of occasional outburst or*
>
> *Nonsense, I say*

Well Nigel I don't see how you can simply brush aside

Interesting isn't it that our exhaust plume distorts the signal enough so that we can't read it? Decidedly convenient

Well sure but that's just an accident of

In a seventy-three-second burst you can pack a lot

If there is information content sure but who says

Ted this is Nigel, if someone were to beam a tight-focused signal along our trajectory it would seem to have a huge power, because we're analyzing it as though the emission was flooding out over all space, rather than being squeezed into a small angle

Well sure I guess but natural emissions from Ra oh I see

So this tells us somebody sent a message our way but pitched at a frequency that would get bloody well swallowed by our own exhaust so we couldn't unscramble it

Well okay, I mean that's an alternate hypothesis

This is Ted give me the visual on that would you?—guess you're right there's no way to decode a mess like that but look Nigel I don't buy that one I mean why would the EMs broadcast at that high frequency they can't with their body structure and anybody who wanted to communicate would use something we could decode at least

Quite so, if they wanted us to

I don't get

We're on a line of sight from Ra remember

You mean if it wasn't targeted for us at all but instead

Right we're on a dead straight line and Ross 128 is another point on that line

Well we'll take that under advisement Nigel thanks for sure yeah thanks

"Well, I, I don't know," Nigel said.
"Come now. You're positively *shy.*" Nikka grinned.

"Dead right." He liked her in this mood, but sometimes she was, well, too much. He *was* shy, and quite properly so. He looked around at the neat rows of improbably tall vegetables. "Rather public for my taste."

Above he could see a distant figure working a wheat field on the other side of the slowly spinning cylinder. Along the axis a fleet of puffy clouds streamed, ships with a single destination. Nikka said, "Let's go into those trees, there."

Obediently he followed. "Won't we embarrass God?"

"God? She tries to encourage this kind of thing."

"Um." Nigel appreciated her cajoling him into this; it was precisely the craziness of it that would draw him out of himself for a while. They entered a stand of birch. Above, fresh clouds dispersed a blue light. The engineers had rigged mirrors and lenses to bring the exhaust flame's fierce luminosity into the life volume, where its glow brought an irridescent warmth to the air.

"Here," Nikka said, and efficiently shucked her coverall. Underfoot, the earth cracked with a swelling of pseudospring, cradled by the microenviron mechanisms into fresh life. The pace of change was forced by fine-tuning at the molecular level. Still, as Nigel lay down he caught from afar the sodden autumnal ripeness of leaves, mingling with a crisp flavor of new shoots in the birches overhead, and underlying it all, a humid dry richness of the summer crops that blossomed across the axis, where harvesttime was soon to come. On tradition-minded Earth, one never walked amid such a cross-current of seasons.

Kneeling, he noted that they both had begun to sweat. He licked the rivulet between her breasts and found it lukewarm, salty. He encircled her, sipped at her, traced whirlpool wisps that left spittle shimmering in her pubic hair. The faintly violet shafts from a man-made sun shifted through branches and fell across lips, lurid as slices of salmon, as he lost himself in her, seeking some deeper taste, the swollen nerves beneath the moss. His hands traced the waist that billowed downward into an hourglass, and to where the flowing body forked. This portal of curls became the crux of her Euclidean theorem, a pivot where all lines must intersect and lemmas could be learned. She seemed to tumble out of the air to him in this trimmed gravity, breathing shallowly, heart tripping. He took her with the simplicity their years allowed. He clutched her wineglass center and cupped her to him. By easing steps he felt her widening sense of him. He closed his eyes. A breeze stirred boughs above them. Distant machines chugged. He opened his eyes as she gripped him and abstractly he studied her eyelids, veined in wriggles of purple, and beneath, a sly smile. A slick pace came upon her and a swirl of laughter welled out. He kissed her shoulder and felt it as round as a moon. Her face snapped sideways and lifted him so that he felt her to be a craft under him, running to its own currents, something vast from the natural darkness, and in that strange gulf he leaped, and leaped again, to join her. "Oh," she said, and then again.

In a while he found he was on his back, solemnly studying the field tenders a kilometer away who labored upside down. She lay sprawled like a broken toy, accepting entirely the shafts like sunlight. Nigel watched a flock of chickens swim down the axis, out for their constitutional, following corn kernels. Here and there small globs fell from them. Dung, descending in straight lines. In his spinning frame the droppings curved in spirals, Newtonian whorls.

"You're looking contented," Nikka murmured.

"This was a bloody good idea."

"Glad you approve. I was going to ask Carlotta to come also, but she has a shift now."

"Just as well. She and I haven't, well, been getting on lately."

"I thought perhaps that was so. . . . Any particular reason?"

"None I can spot. She simply seems skittish."

"She's been very busy, of course"

"Right. I think that, sexually, we're just not on the same wavelength any longer. Sharp and pungent while it lasted, though." He stretched lazily and rolled in the grass. "Who was it who said that simple pleasures are the last refuge of the complex?"

"Oscar Wilde." Carlotta's voice came from behind them. She approached, apparently having missed the earlier talk. Her dark hair swayed as she looked from Nigel to Nikka.

"I never saw this woman before in my life, Officer," Nigel said.

"Likely story. Neighbors asked me to come hose you two down."

"Why not jump in?" Nikka asked.

"Looks like the main event's over. I always thought gentlemen rose when a lady entered the room."

"Me? I'm a wizened old anxiety case. No gentleman, either. Never learned to hunt or ride or insult waiters,"

Nikka said, "I'm sorry, we would have waited, but I thought you'd still be working."

"No problem. Not in the mood." Carlotta said abruptly, "I ducked out when I got copies of these." She waved a handful of photographs. "Batch of results from the gravitational lens. Fresh from the noise-eraser program."

"Ah," Nigel said, wondering why she had rushed over at precisely this moment, when she knew the two of them would be—but no, that was silly. Could Carlotta know them well enough to guess that Nikka would plan a playful seduction here? Well, he thought grudgingly, maybe so. With a bit better timing, she'd have interrupted them. And though they were still ostensibly on intimate terms, he realized Carlotta's arrival would have embarrassed them all. Created more friction. And the net outcome would have been—what? Difficult to tell. He wondered if Carlotta knew what she was doing, or why. In any case, *he* certainly had no idea.

"Planets galore," Carlotta said. "Around Wolf 359, Ross 154, Luyten 789–6, Sigma 2398, Kapteyn's Star—*every*where."

Dim dots near each star. Close-ups revealed rocky spheres, or gas giants, or bleak, Venuslike cloud worlds. "No Earths," Carlotta noted.

"With so many planets around each star," Nikka said, "the odds for favorable life sites somewhere nearby are good."

"So goes the gospel," Nigel said.

Carlotta said, "There's a lot of analysis behind it. Data, too."

"Yes. Perfectly plausible data."

"Come off it," Carlotta said. "You want to explain everything, using a couple of minutes of garbled talk with the *Snark*, none of it verified—"

"Unverified, yes, for want of trying. Ted won't allocate the resources to interpret the EM language. We could learn a hell of a—"

"God, the computer memory needed to hold all that and process it—I did the study, I should know. Using shipboard systems, we wouldn't have space left to store a lunch menu."

Nikka said mildly, "I expect the Earthside teams will—"

"Ha!" Nigel exploded. "They're busy with Swarmer and Skimmer studies. Banging their heads against the same sort of wall that's between us and the dolphins. Pointless!"

"Look," Carlotta said, "Ted worked over my projections real carefully, he conferred with *every*body concerned, it was a *good* decision. They heard you out, they really gave you every consideration. You keep up this cranky griping, everybody'll start believing what Ted said the other. . . ." She stopped.

"Ah, yes. Ted's always hard on people who've left the room."

"And *you* aren't?" Carlotta said sourly.

"Can't stand close-mindedness, is all."

"You're more close-minded than Ted, for gossakes!"

Nikka said firmly, "No, he's not!"

Nigel smiled wanly. "Maybe reality isn't my strong suit."

"Ted has to balance pressures," Carlotta said. "You're respected, that goes without saying, and if you'd just give him some public support—"

Nigel boomed out in a pompous voice, "Speak into the microphone, just say you're happy, Ivan, in spite of some regrettable things you've done, and we'll take care of the publicity."

Carlotta sniffed. "You're missing the point."

"Probably. Been off my feed lately. This rack of bones could use a tune-up."

Nikka said carefully, "Meaning?"

"Look at my last job rating. I'm sure Ted's memorized it."

Nikka said, "You're exaggerating. Ted hasn't got time—"

"No, he's right," Carlotta said. "Ted's probably 'building a file,' as the administrators say."

Nikka said, "But health problems aren't grounds for—"

"If a majority of our esteemed crewmates think it is, then it *is*. period Nigel said. His face sagged with an inward-looking fatigue.

Nikka said softly, "They might put you in the Slots, then?"

"Slotting might bring you back up to specs for a manual job," Carlotta said thoughtfully.

Nigel sighed and shrugged.

"Look." Carlotta leaned forward. "At a minimum, it'll make you live longer."

"And miss most of the voyage to Ross 128."

"Small price," Carlotta said. "I don't think you have to do it, though. You've got *lots* of sentiment behind you. They may not agree with your theories, but the crew remembers all this started 'way back with the *Snark* and *Mare Marginis* and—"

"I've told you before, I *don't* want to win by pinning on my medals and parading round the ship."

"You want to convince them, right?" Carlotta said sharply. "Only they see things different. Well—"

"Stop, you two," Nikka said, lean and lithe and distant on the grass. "Nigel, if you go into the Slots, I'm going with you."

"What!" Carlotta jumped up.

"I could use some repair myself."

"That's not it." Carlotta's voice rose. "You want to stay with him even if he's *asleep!*"

"My medmon index isn't very high, either," Nikka said neutrally.

"You'd leave me behind just to—"

"Bloody hell, must you forever think in terms of yourself?" Nigel jerked his head irritably. "We wouldn't be slotted for more than a few years at most."

"A few—! But *us*, our—"

"I know," Nikka said soothingly. "I've thought of that, and I'm sorry, but I must stay in good physical condition. It's different when you're old. Nigel, when he comes out, I won't be very much use to him if I'm run down and—"

"You—both of you—leave me—"

Nigel nodded. "I have to. If Nikka follows—well, that's her affair. We each still have some freedom, y'know."

"But I'll be alone."

"It can't be helped," Nikka said firmly. "I'm going with him."

That was all she would ever say about the matter.

ONE

Nigel spun slowly in the Sleepslot. It was not true sleep, but rather a drifting, aimless dreaming. He felt faint tugs and ripples as the fluids moved him—massaging leathery muscles, caring for soft wrinkled tissues, ensuring a regular flow of blood and oxygen. The fluids kept his metabolic level a fraction above the shutoff point that would bring on death.

It was like an achingly labored swimming, clutched in currents one could only dimly sense. He rested in the wetness, free of the labor of breath, lungs filled with a spongy stuff that fed healing fluids and sparkling oxygen directly into him. His skin shed a snow of flakes and grime, a torrent of impurity. Inside, cellular police searched for renegades.

Dying, it had turned out, was often merely an inept response to the universe.

The simplest way for the body to defend itself against invaders was by making antibodies. If that failed, evolution had forged a deeper response. It made killer lymphocytes, white cells that attached themselves to the invaders and made a template of them. They excreted specific, short-range toxins, varying the poison until it destroyed the invader. Long after the battle, the lymphocytes carried the template of this intruder, to recognize and kill on sight any returning enemy.

But this immune response can err. That was why eating meat was dangerous. Unless the meat was well cooked, some raw portion would inevitably get into the body cavity, through holes in membranes. The lymphocytes then developed a killing response to animal protein, since it was a nonhuman cell.

The problem was that animal protein is very similar to human protein. As the lymphocytes drifted through the rivers of blood, finding and killing invaders, they sometimes changed. Radiation or heat could damage them. If the random changes made the animal-protein template resemble human protein, the lymphocytes could become confused. They would attack the body's own cells. Cellular suicide. Cancer.

With age the body developed more and more templates. The chances of a catastrophic error increased. To combat this, the body tried to develop so-called suppressor lymphocytes, which could control the killers and stop them from multiplying. Often this failed.

No matter how many technical fixes could be arranged for heart troubles or organ failures, this irreducible knot of a problem remained. It was rooted in the very nature of the body's age-old defenses.

Evolution did not care if a preventive measure ran amok, once childbearing age passed. In fact, all the better. It was a simple way to clear the stage, once the actors had played their parts.

The medicine of the twenty-first century was preoccupied with runaway immune response, with bodies that had become strangers to themselves.

Nigel dimly felt fluids slosh within him, seeking lymphocytes gone awry. Outside, the grasshopper world clacked on, *Lancer* edged close to light speed, and he thought of the cold world an intelligent machine must know: brittle, arid, a labyrinth of logic and careful design, stale space and geometric rigidities. Quite unlike the milky world that nurtured him here, smoothing the skin now crinkled like old butcher paper.

This treatment would stretch his life-span, free oxygen to swarm through parts of his brain that now ebbed. But it meant years of nothingness, blunted by drugs, telescoped down to a mere self-perceived few days. Years subtracted from the pace of events.

It was deeper than sleep, that great eraser. Like any new technology, it eased you through life, insulated you for a time from a brutal fact, and left you with a disquieting vision: that nature engraved mortality on its children by making them attack themselves.

TWO

2066

Carlotta led them into the huge cavern where nothing was real. "This is it," she said excited. "Surprised?"

"Moderately," Nigel said, though he wasn't sure what moderation was any longer. Five days out of the Sleepslots, and he still carried the wispy, dislocated air of not quite being fully present. An expected side effect, to be sure, but what he had seen around the ship had enhanced the effect. "Ted and the rest actually approved this?"

Carlotta shrugged. "We aren't getting much advice from Earth. There were signs of real morale problems, and the psych types thought— Look, Earthside predicted some fast sociocultural rates shipboard, fax?"

"In five years?" Nikka asked quietly.

"Can you fashion things change just for, you know, change itself? But look, you'll get the mix. Come on."

They followed her. A couple took a tumble slide through purple ice crystals above. A hollow gong; the fine crystals dissolved into a rain of acrid fire. People passed by, rippling, and Nigel saw they had faces that shifted like holograms. Carlotta polarized herself into fundamentals and blended instantly with the dank, humid jungle that was forming around them. They sat at a table. A panther snarled. Nigel saw cat eyes gleaming beneath the folds of a wet elephant ear leaf.

"Shows what a pack of smart lads can do when they've nothing to distract 'em," Nigel said. Carlotta reappeared, wearing a pair of enhanced gloves. She casually lifted the table and the gloves glowed amber. "I was scanning the Earthside briefs," he began, "and they—"

"Amazing, isn't it? That they can't find out anything. Makes you wonder," Carlotta said.

Nigel nodded. The ocean invasion dominated the reports, but there were many political ramifications. There had been the customary Western tut-tutting over the latest purges in the Socialist African Union. Steam was leaking, with a shrill howl, from the New Marxism, which was getting encrusted with the same old blemishes—flagging zeal, increasingly brutal suppression of dissent, no economic miracles. Astonishingly, even the French intellectuals had abandoned them. A century or more of theory, from Fascism through worn-out Marx to PseudoCap, was finally yielding to the sociometric savants, surrendering the Grand Era of sweeping Theory to the comforting rule of Number.

"I gather from the summaries that you've found no life sites, then?" Nigel asked.

"Not yet. Hundreds of planets, either on the grav-lens or by probe, and—nothing."

"Um." He glanced at Nikka. "Think I'll take a walk."

"I'll order drinks for us. Nikka, there's a lot to catch up on, and..."

Nigel passed through private iridescent clouds of yellow and pink and ruby. He became a flitting intruder in a stone courtyard; then a sandy beach; a star cluster; a swirling, tangled struggle between bronze, winged demons; a nineteenth-century office. He met a grinning panda bear with a tennis racket and waved away the animal's whispered proposition. Someone offered him a drink; he slid it into his wrist and felt its tang.

When he returned, three mugs of dark, odoriferous beer sat on the table. At the edge of their cloud sphere, a shabby trio played trumpet, bass, and drums. The air now held the flat, oily memory of yesterday's fried food. The bartender held his post at a crude oak bar and glowered at them. Behind him, taped to a cloudy mirror, a stained sign read: WE RESERVE THE RIGHT TO REFUSE SERVICE TO ANYONE.

"Do you suppose they mean us?" Nigel asked, trying to go along with matters.

"I thought you'd like an old Earth locale. Look, I can update it if you—" She tapped her wrist and a 3-D sprang into life at Nikka's elbow. The bar faded. A fat man was admiring a pile of eggs, delicately scrambled with cream sauce. He began ingesting them, sucking them up through a straw. Nigel looked closer and saw the man himself was made of garlicked spinach, oiled strands of tagliatelli, and his trousers were of pâté.

"Gluttony chic?" he asked, and turned to Nikka. "M'love, you've been out of the Slots for two months—how long does it take to get used to this?"

"The point is," Nikka explained slowly, "to not get accustomed. It's *supposed* to add endless variety."

"This was Earth's idea, too?"

"Shipboard and Earthside worked it out together. There's a new theory of variance-interaction—"

"Spare me. This looks like a bloody amusement park." Carlotta frowned and reached up to tune her hair from black to white. Nigel glanced around. Cloud spheres hung everywhere in the great gallery. Carlotta got up to greet a passing couple. She stood to one side, clutching one elbow, aloft on some new platform sandals like a frail, hoofed animal. Women standing that way seemed to feel more poised, but he reflected that to him it looked just the reverse.

In the crowds Nigel saw men with hair grown all down their backs and in swirling spirals around their bodies; women with patchy skin pigment that shifted as he watched; men with breasts; women without hair.

He shook his head. Carlotta introduced a couple and Nigel nodded, barely remembering them. There was some conversation he could not follow and they left. "Uh...I didn't quite catch...?"

"That was Alex and David," Carlotta said.

"But...Alex..."

"Well, he's had the Change, of course."

Changed *sex*?"

"Just as an experiment. It's completely reversible. About six months in the Slots, rearranging body mass and growing new glands and so on."

"But Alex...was such..."

"Look," Carlotta said, "he had a lot of personality facets he'd suppressed. That was clear, wasn't it, from the stiff kind of way he went around?"

"I thought he was simply disciplined, well organized."

"Look, a lot of engineers seem that way, but if you pry them open, take a look at the guts—"

"Doesn't seem possible, somehow, I..." Confused, Nigel came halfway out of his seat, intending to go after Alex and . . . *And what?* he thought. *Ask him how in God's name he could come to do such a thing?* Nigel stopped himself. It was a deeply personal matter, after all. He shouldn't barge into what was undoubtedly a difficult time for Alex. He sat back down.

"You look a little rocky," Carlotta said sympathetically. He nodded mutely. Moments passed. Discordant music filtered in from other zones. The air became flavored with ozone and perfume. Nikka and Carlotta began to talk about crew members who were in new jobs, had new lovers, or otherwise had done something in the last five years worth chewing over. To Nigel this conversation sounded much like a catching-up over lukewarm gossip such as one might hear in any large office building. The ordinariness of it struck him. Who would have guessed that a starship plowing across the light-years would come to resemble, in its human dimension, any other bureaucratic barge? He let most of the detail slip by him and thus was brought up short when Nikka casually remarked that she had moved into Carlotta's small cabin. She had lived there since she came out of Slotsleep, two months before.

"Then you've done no work on getting our apartment back into order?" he asked.

Nikka pursed her lips. "There's been so much to see, to understand—*Lancer* is much more exciting now, Nigel, since all these changes."

"Indeed," he said wryly.

"And, I don't know why, but Carlotta and I have had so much fun together. Of course, I was sad that we were not slated to come out of the Slots at the same time. But it did give me a chance to adjust to, to all this." She waved a hand at the chasm.

Carlotta smiled winningly. "And it's been great to have you back." She squeezed Nikka's hand. "Both of you."

"I still can't see why *Lancer* should need to have such, such . . ." Nigel let his voice trickle away. Carlotta went into a psychosocial explanation, in part the bounty of the last two decades of work Earthside, which had caught up to *Lancer*. He listened attentively, all the while wondering if his British background made it impossible for him to appreciate fully these rapid-fire swervings of the social matrix. His past was not merely a learned liking for afternoon tea, cold baths, cricket, a certain level of domestic discomfort, and the occasional patrician accent. There were currents in society that ran deeper and, he felt instinctively, could not be so casually deflected by a bit of dewy-eyed technology. You need not be a master of the Snow-called two cultures to see that.

More couples stopped at their table, recognized them, and shook hands warmly. Nigel could remember most of their names; their odd clothes or hair or altered faces seemed not so important after he'd heard the customary didja-have-a-good-sleep, how's-tricks-with-Nikka, say-let's-have-y'all-ovah-foah-dinner-real-soon style of conversation. They were people he still knew pretty well. Displaced in time a bit, yes, and caught up in a novelty-first social air he could not comprehend, quite. In time, no doubt . . .

And yet, and yet—

Many more of them now worked in Interactive Mode, computer-linked to the vast machines that churned in *Lancer*'s bowels. They maintained the fusion fire aft, repaired the life-support apparatus, sensed the flow of water and gas that kept the biosphere regulated. Over the years this had changed them. They talked as though they were always listening for a distant voice, half-heard, that murmured just beyond the hearing of the moment. They rubbed the big raw sockets at hip and elbow and shoulder, where the constellations of motor nerves gathered. They thought differently, talked little, seemed to lean on each word as though it should have more significance than it possibly—to Nigel—could. He discovered that when they wished to learn something, they exchanged cerebral templates with someone who knew the material. The technique had been transmitted from Earth three years before. A techno-summary package came in over the radio link each four months, now, to bring up to parallel specs with Earth.

Nigel smiled and laughed and filed it all away for future pondering. The chasm vibrated with clashing holo-audio fantasies, competing gaudy beams of light, raw scents in the breeze. Nikka and Carlotta mingled with the increasing crowd. Bob Millarc came by, an unaltered face Nigel was glad to see. Whatever he might think of Bob's handling of the Isis exploration, the man's easy hospitality was welcome. They both made passing jokes about the fads around them and then Bob put in casually, "Been lookin' over your medmon specs jess t'day. Pretty good."

"Um. They spruced up my detoxifying mix, cleaned out the ol' bloodstream. Seems to've helped the muscles and ligaments and so on." Nigel kept his voice light, airy.

"Your motor response is back up. Surprisin'. You lookin' to do manual work again?"

A suitable pause. "Would like to, yes."

"Got a job down the drive throat. Scrapin' off the accumulated crud, freein' up the fluxlife." He raised an eyebrow.

Nigel nodded. "I'm on." This still moment passed, and the party swept on around them.

Later, Nigel said pensively, "Must say, I hadn't expected that."

"A manual job?" Carlotta nodded. "I told Ted you wanted to get your hands dirty again. There's plenty of scutwork to go around. Older this ship gets, more it takes. Ted must've put it through the Work Council."

"Without my asking, even?"

"Look, it's been *years* since you two were picking at each other. Ted's bighearted."

Nigel nodded to himself, trying to come to terms with the erased years. Time had blurred and softened everything. He had to remember that these were different people and he could not carry over the old emotions. "Anachronistic thinking," he muttered.

"Yeah. Fresh start, Nigel. You did real well in the Slots—you look great."

"I hope I can handle the work."

"Sure, you can. Bob wouldn't sign you on if the med reports weren't okay."

Nigel nodded again. Fresh start. He felt a vivid surge of joy. "So bring me up to date. What else is new?"

THREE

Procyon was a gleaming white F5 star with an insignificant dull binary companion. The flyby ship tallied the planets and tasted the stellar wind, before plunging close to the only interesting Earth-sized world. It was mottled and cloud-speckled. An ocean wrapped the planet from pole to pole, there was no land. The vast sea showed odd chemical emission lines. The probe checked and rechecked and, in a cybernetic storm of confusion, relayed the answer: This world was awash in oil. Had the reserves in the rock been pressed out onto the surface? Or did organic chemicals in the air condense this way? It was low-quality crude, brackish and high in sulfur. It ran in tides and twisted into funnels beneath furious storms. Evaporation of water ran the weather cycle, but oil was the important surface fluid.

Nothing lived in that sea.

No stony sphere orbited the world.

But battered, worn craft circled it. The probe raced by one and glimpsed a tin-colored, boxy thing. It had solar sails, partly unfurled. None of the grimy ships gave the slightest sign that they had noticed the passing intruder.

There were thousands of them in orbit. A few descended to the surface as the probe watched. A few fought up from launch pads floating on the sea. When these finished their arc up, they deployed immense, tear-shaped bags. They assumed long-lived orbits and their engines' orange plumes ebbed into nothing.

Parking orbits. From the rate of launch it was simple to estimate how long the thousands of craft had been accumulating: several centuries. Their cargo was clearly oil; the probe resolved spidery pumping stations afloat below.

The convoy was waiting, perhaps until each ship was filled. But where would they go? There was nothing else in the Procyon system except gas giant planets and dead moons. How long would it take them to reach any further destination?

Nigel lies mute and blind and pinned in his couch and for a moment feels nothing but the numb silence. It collects in him, blotting out the dim rub of the snouts which cling like lampreys to his nerves and muscles, amplifying every movement, a pressing embrace, and—

—*spang*—

—he slips free of the mooring cables, a rush of sight-sound-taste-touch washes over him, so strong and sudden a welter of senses that he jerks with the impact. He is servo'd to a thing like an eel that swims and flips and dives into a howling dance of protons. His body lies three hundred meters away, safely behind slabs of rock. But the eel is his, the eel is *him*. It shudders and jerks and twists, skating across sleek strands of magnetic plains. To Nigel, it is like swimming.

The torrent gusts around him and he feels its pinprick breath—autumn leaves that burn. In a blinding orange glare Nigel swoops, feeling his power over the servo'd robot grow as he gets the feel of it. The shiny craft is wrapped in a cocoon of looping magnetic fields that turn the protons away, sending them gyrating in a mad gavotte, so the heavy particles cannot crunch and flare against the slick baked skin.

Nigel flexes the skin, supple and strong, and slips through the magnetic turbulence ahead. He feels the magnetic lines of force stretch like rubber bands. He banks and accelerates.

Streams of protons play upon him. They make glancing collisions with each other but do not react. The repulsion between them is too great, and so this plasma cannot make them burn, cannot thrust them together with enough violence. Slapping together mere nude protons is like trying to burn wet wood. Something more is needed or else the ship's throat will fail to harvest the simple hydrogen atoms, fail to kindle it into energy.

There— In the howling storm Nigel sees the blue dots that are the keys, the catalyst: carbon nuclei, hovering like sea gulls in an updraft.

Split-image phosphors gleam, marking his way. He swims in the streaming blue-white glow, through a murky storm of fusing ions. He watches plumes of carbon nuclei striking the swarms of protons, wedding them to form the heavier nitrogen nuclei. The torrent swirls and screams at Nigel's skin and in his sensors he sees and feels and tastes the lumpy, sluggish nitrogen as it finds a fresh incoming proton and with the fleshy smack of fusion the two stick, they hold, they wobble like raindrops—falling together—merging—ballooning into a new nucleus, heavier still: oxygen.

But the green pinpoints of oxygen are unstable. These fragile forms split instantly. Jets of new particles spew through the surrounding glow—neutrinos, ruddy photons of light, and slower, darker, there come the heavy daughters of the marriage: a swollen, burnt-gold cloud. A wobbling, heavier isotope of nitrogen.

Onward the process flies. Each nucleus collides millions of times with the others in a fleck-shot swirl like glowing snowflakes. All in the space of a heartbeat. Flakes ride the magnetic field lines. Gamma rays flare and sputter among the blundering motes like fitful fireflies. Nuclear fire lights the long roaring corridor that is the ship's main drive.

Nigel swims, the white-hot sparks breaking over him like foam. Ahead he sees the violet points of nitrogen and hears them crack into carbon plus an alpha particle. So in the end the long cascade gives forth the carbon that catalyzed it, carbon that will begin again its life in the whistling blizzard of protons coming in from the forward maw of the ship.

With the help of the carbon, an interstellar hydrogen atom has built itself up from mere proton to, finally, an alpha particle—a stable clump of two neutrons and two protons. The alpha particle is the point of it all. It flees from the blurring storm, carrying the energy that fusion affords. The ruby-rich interstellar gas is now wedded, proton to proton, with carbon as the matchmaker.

Nigel feels a rising electric field pluck at him. He moves to shed his excess charge. To carry a cloak of electrons here is fatal. Upstream lies the chewing gullet of the ramscoop, where incoming protons are sucked in, their kinetic power stolen from them by the electric fields. There the particles are slowed, brought to rest inside the ship, their streaming energy stored in capacitors.

A cyclone shrieks behind him. Nigel swims sideways toward the walls of the combustion chamber. The nuclear burn that flares around him is never pure, cannot be pure because the junk of the cosmos pours through here, like barley meal laced with grains of granite. The incoming atomic rain spatters constantly over the fluxlife walls, killing the organic superconductor strands there. Nigel pushes against the rubbery magnetic fields and swoops along the mottled yellow-blue crust of the walls. In the flickering lightning glow of infrared and ultraviolet he sees the scaly muck that deadens the magnetic fields and slows the nuclear burn in the throat. He flexes, wriggles, and turns the eellike form. This brings the electron beam gun around at millimeter range.

He fires. A brittle crackling leaps out onto the scaly wall. The tongue bites and gouges. Flakes bubble up like tar, blacken, and finally roast off. The rushing proton stream washes the flakes away, revealing the gunmetal blue beneath. Now the exposed superconducting threads can begin their own slow pruning of themselves, life casting out its dead.

Their long organic chain molecules can feed and grow anew. As Nigel cuts and turns and carves he watches the spindly fibers coil loose and drift in eddies. Finally they spin away into the erasing proton storm. The dead fibers sputter and flash where the incoming protons strike them and then with a rumble in his acoustic pickup coils he sees them swept away.

Something tugs at him. Ahead lies the puckered scoop where energetic alpha particles shoot by. They dart like luminous jade wasps. The scoop sucks them in. Inside they will be collected, drained of energy, inducing megawatts of power for the ship. The ship will drink their last drop of momentum and leave them behind, a wake of broken atoms.

Suddenly he spins to the left—*Jesus, how can*—he thinks— and the scoop fields lash him. A megavolt per meter of churning electrical vortex snatches at him. Huge, quick, relentless, it clutches at his shiny surfaces. The scoop opening is a plunging, howling mouth. Jets of glowing atoms whirl by him, mocking. The walls near him counter his motion by increasing their magnetic fields. Lines of force stretch and bunch.

How did this—is all he has time to think before a searing spot blooms nearby. His presence so near the scoop has upset the combination rates there. If the reaction gets out of control it can burn through the chamber vessel, through the asteroid rock beyond, and spike with acrid fire into the ship, toward the life dome.

A brassy roar. The scoop sucks at his heels. Ions run white-hot. A warning knot strikes him. Tangled magnetic ropes grope for him, clotting around the shiny skin.

Panic squeezes his throat. Desperately he fires his electron beam gun against the wall, hoping it will give him a push, a fresh vector—

Not enough. Orange ions blossom and rage and swell around him—another death.

"Pretty bad," Ted Landon said. Nigel tried to focus. Therapy devices nuzzled and stroked him like mechanical lovers. He could make out Ted's scowl, and he said in the direction of the blurred image, "What . . . I tried to . . . get back to mooring . . ."

"You didn't make it."

Nigel lay back and let feelings seep into consciousness. His body felt worn and numb. "The . . ."

"Destroyed, lost. Tracer shows it hit the wall. Thing is, you got a big retrofeed shock to your central nervous system when it blew."

"I can't . . . body doesn't feel the same."

"It won't, for a while. So say the medics, anyway. Thing is, we never had this exact injury before. The other guys got out of those surges. You should've been able to get away from it. Nothing special about that surge."

"It . . . got by me, I suppose. I won't let it happen . . ."

"I'm afraid this takes you permanently off manual tasks, Nigel. No way I can let you stay on the roster."

He could think of nothing to say, and in any case he could hardly sort out the confusion of distorted impulses his senses brought him. He gazed out the exop door. People were clustered around, listening as a medic talked in a low whisper. He felt tears tricklng down his face. He had lost something, some inner equilibrium; his body was not the same tuned instrument he had come to take so easily. A wracking sob came from him. He searched among the people and in the back, a point of calming rest in the bunched faces, he found Nikka. She smiled.

FOUR

Nigel's recovery was slow. It was a long time before he could work again in the fields, harvesting, grunting with the effort and trying not to show it. But he liked the work and kept at it. It reminded him of moments in his past when, intent on some worrisome task, he would by chance press a finger to his wrist and feel, like a sudden reminder, the patient throb of his pulse, a steady note that lifted him out of fretful details.

But his internal confusion did not go away. He was enough of a mechanistic thinker to see that sudden jolts to the entire body could act on the mind in unknown ways. The glacial steadiness and resolve he had had since *Marginis* was now faltering, leaving him with strange, drifting anxieties.

About his own mental states he had never had any

theories. He had refused to endorse mystical savants back Earthside. That lot had quite neatly done a job on Alexandria, thank you. More to the point, he could not speak for anyone else. Things happened to you and you learned from them whether you knew it or not, but a pretense of a common interior landscape which could be described, a bloody touring book of the soul—that was a lie. No flat formulas could capture the human interior. Kafka, that gnarled spirit, was right: Life is defined by the closed spaces of the self.

That was why he had all along declined to become a savant figure himself, interpreter of the long-dead aliens of the *Marginis* wreck. He would have lost himself that way, when the whole point was to remain a man, to stay in the gritty world and experience it directly, avoiding abstractions. He knew that this made him appear increasingly isolated, cranky, out of step with the younger crew. But he did little to temper this, and used what pull he could when Nikka drew an assignment working on *Lancer*'s skin, to repair the ramscoop fields. Ted Landon made the quite reasonable point that he could not run a ship according to the loves of the crew. Nigel retorted that with the frequency of sex changes in the crew, it was bloody difficult to tell who was inclined to do what, and to whom. It came to him, then, why Ted smiled benignly on all the self-alteration that was so fashionable in *Lancer*.

"He's got the game down, clean and simple," Nigel said to Carlotta one evening. "People cloning new tissues, people socketed into machines more and more to up efficiency—so's they can have more time off for their pursuits, preoccupation. My God! In a fad-driven society like *Lancer*, Ted looks reassuringly steady. Marvelous, ol' Ted—let him keep a hand on the helm while we go off and console ourselves for the long voyage."

Carlotta shook her head. "Makes no sense. The directives on involution therapy—that's the term, don't wrinkle your nose—came from Earthside. Ted had nothing to do with—"

"Nonsense. Look at that thing you're drinking. Carbonated cherry frappé, seething along with microicebergs of orange floating in it. Where'd the resources for that come from?"

She stirred the silky drink. "Chem section, I guess."

"Fine old Ted could stop such diversions if he wanted,

never mind Earth. No, he's in favor of a holiday air, a regression into—"

"Regression! Look, you may think—"

"Yes, I do. Surely we needn't go into it?"

"It's hard for me to see how you can deny a person a right to, a chance to . . . to find new definitions of themselves."

"I'm simply trying to understand friend Ted. I'm aware that sex change became common Earthside as a method of helping adolescents with their sexual adjustments. And that the pursuit of variety has made it much the fashion back there. But here—"

"I think it's pretty great of Ted and the others to allow use of ship's resources for it. That certainly shows him in a, a fair-minded light."

"Or alternatively, in an engagingly frank and surprisingly open-minded light. It's always one light or another with him, you'll find."

"You're just being cynical."

"Um. 'Cynical' is a term invented by optimists to describe realists."

"You're impossible."

"Um. Usually."

A month passed without his particularly noticing it. One evening when Carlotta came by he muttered a greeting and went back to watching a three-dimensional, color-factored Fourier picture of the EMs signals. They still remained danmed nearly opaque to him. He was getting a hint of some earlier history, of their brief flirtation with spaceships and astronomy. There was something like poetry here, a suggestion of a fractured time, glimmers of the beings who had mustered the strength to remake themselves.

"How do you think we should vote on this case coming up?" Nikka asked.

—fragmented sprockets in the signal there— "Uh, what?"

"This woman who stole all those shipcredits."

"How?"

"False indexing, of course."

"What do you say, Carlotta?"

"She's guilty as sin."

"Um. Always wondered what that meant. What's sin supposed to be guilty *of*?"

—made one wonder if the pre-EM culture had ever gotten out of its own solar system, these images here, could mean outward-stretching limbs or tracers to other stars or a whacking great blowoff of dandelion seed for that matter—

"Take it from me, she did it."

"Um. So the tribunal said."

"The whole crew has to decide what to do about her, though," Nikka said.

—crew's rattled more than they know with this continual stream of bad news from Earth, Swarmers everywhere, even the chemicals don't seem to work on them, and meanwhile the work goes on in orbit above the blighted oceans, a building the starships, using self-programmed machines to do the scutwork, mankind getting ready to burst out like dandelion seeds among the stars, a runaway effect—

Carlotta said, "I think she should be stored away in the Slots."

"That's no punishment," Nikka said.

"Course it is," Nigel mumbled. "She'll wake up Earthside, discredited, having accomplished nothing."

—an unstoppable exodus now, at just the right moment—

"*I* think she should be ostracized," Carlotta put in.

"A collective solution?" Nikka pursed her lips. "I wonder . . ."

—which might just be what leaving the ancient *Mare Marginis* wreck was meant to accomplish, a vault of the ages lying there in lunar pumice, and the *Snark* had "accidentally" activated it, ol' boojum renegade *Snark*, too long gone from its masters, traitor to the lathe that bore it, knew there were only decades left to us once it had relayed what it found, knew something was up the sleeve of its Lords of Antiquity and gave us a slim chance of getting round it, if we could only understand—

They were having a fight.

Nigel realized this slowly. It began with Carlotta saying, "You know, it's been weeks since I've been over here," just casually in the flow of conversation. But Nikka took something in it wrong and sat up stiffly in the couch and replied, "What do you mean?"

"Well, only that I haven't seen very much of you two, that's all."

"We've been busy."

Carlotta was not going to be put off with a bland generality. "You two don't have me over the way we once did."

"Well, *you* don't have us over at all."

"My apartment is crowded and, you know, yours is so much better."

Nigel spoke up. "True enough."

"One of my roomos has rotated, Doris, and this Lydia, the new one, isn't cooperative at all. I think that's why she was put in with us by the Block Council. She needs some socializing after her blowup with some lover, I don't know who, but—"

"Carlotta, that's not what you wanted to talk about," Nikka said with an edge in her voice.

"It wasn't?"

"You've been coming up to me at work, leaving messages—plucking at my sleeve, nagging me for attention."

"Well, I *need* it."

Nigel said, "Don't we all."

"I don't think you understand."

Nikka observed, "The one who doesn't understand is over there."

Nigel raised his head. He had just finished the damned dishes and felt he deserved a moment's break. Apparently it was not to be. "What?"

"Well, at least he's said something germane," Nikka said.

Nigel murmured, "Sorry. Fresh out of gossip."

"Gossip? Not gossip! I want you to *say* something, not sit there and pore over those goddamn transcripts."

"Not transcripts. Logs. Of—"

"Yes, yes, Alex dutifully points our deployed antennas backward each day, so you can get your ration of EM gabble-gabble. But that doesn't mean you have to ignore me."

> Stiffly: "I didn't realize I was."
> Carlotta: "Look, of course you are."
> Defensively: "I work hard. My concentration isn't that good anymore. Things slip by me. I—"
> Carlotta: "You're not responding."
> Nigel: "What is this, groupthink?"
> Nikka: "If this is a threesome we have to *talk*."
> Nigel: "Of course. But I'm explaining—"

Carlotta: "How you've been neglecting the relationship."

Nigel: "That's how you see it?"

Nikka: "Unfortunately, yes."

Nigel: "It's harder to keep three balls in the air than two."

Carlotta: "That's a cliché. What's that *mean*?"

Nigel: "I'm dead pushed and fagged, that's what."

Nikka: "No, it's deeper than that."

Nigel: "To borrow a phrase, what's that bloody *mean*?"

Nikka: "It means I don't like being treated like an old shoe."

Carlotta: "You're aren't tuned in here."

Nikka: "Three-way relationships are hard, but each member must give as much of themselves as—"

Nigel: "Sounds like a flamin' sociology textbook."

Carlotta: "Empathize."

Nigel: "I am. I really am."

Nikka: "You sit around, reading the astrophysical updates, but I never hear you as an ordinary man anymore."

Nigel: "There's the possibility that I'm not."

Carlotta: "Don't go all stiff on us again."

Nigel: "Am I imagining this, or have we gone from Carlotta to me?'

Carlotta: "Maybe it's the same problem."

Nikka: "No, it's *not*. We all help each other. But Nigel has been burrowing into these neuro-anthropological matrix studies of his and, and shutting the world out."

Nigel: "Admittedly."

Carlotta: "Not so fast, *My* feeling is that you two are revolving around each other so much that I can't get in edgewise."

Nikka: "I admit that I've been concerned with him. Perhaps less easy to, to reach, for you. But he is getting more distant from me. And from you."

Carlotta: "Sometimes I think it's just a tactic."

Nigel: "Winning through withdrawal?"

Carlotta: "Not exactly, but—"

Nigel: "Then what? I'm a renegade, I've admitted that. And I sop up great gouts of time plugging away at my obsessions. But they're *my* obsessions. Haven't I buggering well earned the right to—"

Nikka: "Not in this relationship, you haven't. You've got to participate."

Carlotta: "Look, I think you ought to consider what you're doing with, or doing *to* Nikka. She isn't the same person now that she was when we left Earthside. She doesn't respond to people, to me, the way she did then and I think it's—"

Nikka turned to Carlotta. "Why don't you just do what you *want*? What you really feel, instead of echoing and reacting to *us*, to *me*, to—"

Nigel said slowly, "Yes, I should think—"

"And *you*—!" Nikka cried. "We're supposed to tiptoe softly around you while you're muttering deep thoughts about who knows what!"

Carlotta began, "Look—"

Nikka whirled to her. "We each have to have our own lives. Don't you see that? Three-sided things are harder. They only work if one pair is no more important than the other."

Carlotta said, "But you and Nigel are more important than you and me, or Nigel and me."

Nigel: "Give it time." Though he didn't really feel that way.

Nikka sighed. She said quietly to Carlotta, "Do what you *really* want. That's the answer. It's the only way you'll be happy."

Nigel nodded, a bit dazed. The storm of the two women had washed over him suddenly and he was not sure what it meant. "And I, in turn, shall try not to withdraw so much," he said formally. He was damned if he could see how, though.

He was doing therapy when Bob came by, sweating from running.

"Still gettin' inna box, uh?" Bob asked. He thumped the gray metal. "This's the neurotiming one?"

"Right." Nigel grimaced. "Not my favorite. Sends prickly

feelings up your nerves, like chilled mice running toward your heart."

Bob shuddered. "Me, I stay away from this stuff."

"Do, yes."

"Ever' time I have to come in for some med work I feel like I'm puttin' my balls in a grinder. Somethin' goes wrong—poof!"

"No choices left for me. Afraid I won't be working for you again. In fact, I was surprised when you let me onto the throat-scraping team."

Bob leaned against the massive cabinet and mopped sweat from his face, grimacing. "Wasn't me. Ted overrode my judgment. Wish I haddna let him."

"Not your fault. My medical was good, after all."

"Marginal. Just marginal."

"Oh."

"Thing was, I rejected you right off. Ted came and leaned on me—*really* leaned. Called in some obligations, had Sanchez over in Medical sweet-talk me. The works. I finally caved in."

"Ah."

"Wish I haddna."

It was, of course, the sort of thing you could never be sure of. Still, from Ted's point of view, the calculation was simple enough: How could Ted lose? If Nigel did well in the job, things would have gone on as before. When he failed, instead, his long recovery reduced his political effectiveness.

Or was this paranoia? Hard to tell. He decided to keep his thoughts to himself. After all, there was always the possibility that this was merely an opening move.

Carlotta said, "I still don't buy it," and sipped at her drink. It was another fizzing orange thing, filling the air with a tingling sweetness.

Nigel persisted. "Machines can evolve, just as animals do."

"Look—those things we've found, orbiting god-awful messed-up worlds. Sure, they're automated artifacts. But intelligent? Self-reproducing, okay. The time needed to make a really smart entity is—"

"Enormous. Granted. We haven't dated most of those worlds—can't, with just one flyby. They could be billions of years older than Earth."

There was the rub. It was difficult to think of what the galaxy might be like if organically derived intelligence was a mere passing glimmer, if machine evolution dominated in the long run. The ruins *Lancer* and the probes were finding seemed to say that even societies which had colonized other worlds could still be vulnerable to species suicide. Complex systems in orbit would have the best chance to live. A war would be a powerful selection pressure for survival among machines which had, in whatever weak form, a desire for survival. Given time . . .

That was the point. Events on a galactic scale were slow, majestic. That fact had been written into the structure of the universe, from the beginning. In order for galaxies to form at all, the expansion energy of the Big Bang had to be just the right amount. To make stars coalesce from dust clouds, certain physical constants had to be the correct size. Otherwise, ordinary hydrogen would not be so widespread, and stellar evolution would be quite different. If nuclear forces were slightly weaker than they are, no complex chemical elements would be possible. Planets would be dull places, without a variety of elements to cook into life.

The size of stars, and their distances from each other, were not arbitrary. If they were not thinly spread, collisions between them would have soon disrupted the planetary systems orbiting them. The size of the galaxy was set, among other things, by the strength of gravity. The fact that gravity was relatively weak, compared to electromagnetism and other forces, allowed the galaxy to have a hundred billion stars in it. This same weakness let living entities evolve which were bigger than microbes, without being crushed by their planet's gravity. That meant they could be big enough, and complex enough, to dream of voyaging to the distant dots of light in a black sky.

Those organic dreamers were doomed to a poignant end. Evolution worked remorselessly in a cycle of birth, begetting, and death. Each life-form had to make room for its children, or else the weight of the past would bear down on any mutation, smothering change. So death was written into the genetic code. Evolution's judicial indifference selected for death as well as life.

The coming of intelligent entities meant the birth of tragedy, the dawning realization of personal finiteness. Given the distance of habitable planets from a star, deducing the surface temperature, factoring in the physical constants that predicated chemistry—it was not hard to work out the approximate lifetime that evolution would ordain for human-sized intelligent life: a century or so. Which meant there was barely time to look around, understand, and work for a few frantic decades, before the darkness closed in. At best, an intelligent organism could make its mark in one or two areas of thought. It came and vanished in a flicker. Through its lifetime the night sky would not appear to move at all. The galaxy seemed frozen, unchanging.

Unmoving stars, distant targets. The organic beings, knowing of their own coming deaths, could still dream of going there. Yet on their voyages they were subject to the speed limit set by light. If light's velocity had been higher, allowing rapid flight between stars, there would have been a huge price to pay. Nuclear forces would be different; the stars' slow percolating of the heavy elements would not work. The long march upward that led to human-sized creatures would never have gotten started.

So it all knitted together: To arise naturally out of this universe meant a sure knowledge of impending death. That foreshortened all perspectives, forcing a creature to think on short time scales—times so truncated that a journey between stars was a life-devouring odyssey.

"—doesn't explain the Swarmers, doesn't account for the EMs adequately," Carlotta was saying. "Your explanation has too many holes. Too many unjustified assumptions."

"He hasn't had help with a detailed analysis, remember that," Nikka put in.

"No," Nigel said, "Carlotta's right. It needs work. Conceptual work."

He sat back while the women discussed the latest grav-lens images, his mind still wandering. He watched Carlotta's quick, deft movements. She spent a lot of time on her dress, making artful concoctions from the skimpy supplies available. He was losing touch with her. She saw more of Nikka than of him, and knew a lot of the crewmen who were multisocketed now. Those people spent not only their working hours but their recreation as well, plugged in, taking part in—what was the phrase?—"computer-assisted socialization." Meanwhile, Theory Section was producing no new hypotheses, nothing beyond a bland compiling of data. As the light-years piled up, the crew was turning inward, away from the awful emptiness that lay beyond *Lancer*'s stone buffers. Few went outside anymore, to gaze upon the relativistically Dopplered rainbow unaided. Weeks went by without his hearing even a mention of Earthside in casual conversation. In the face of immensity, something ingrained in humans made them reduce matters to the local, the present, the specific.

Admittedly, Lancer was packed with ambitious, intelligent folk. Given the years in flight, social diversions had undoubtedly been on from the start. But this... No, something rang wrong. Something beyond his curmudgeon's distrust. Ted Landon and the rest could tune down this sort of thing if they desired. But a crew distracted was a crew easily misled, easily manipulated. And from such a muddle, a strong leader often eventually emerged when a crisis finally came.

He watched Carlotta stirring the orange ice shards in her noisy drink. He thought of Magellan, voyaging with thin hopes and not enough oranges to stave off scurvy. And of the *Titantic*, which sailed with absolute certainty and oranges galore.

"—wouldn't they?" Carlotta was asking him a question.

"I don't catch the drift," he said to cover his daydreaming.

"I mean, what's going to force them to evolve higher intelligence?"

"Self-replicating machines can forage for raw materials anywhere. Lord knows they work better in space than we do—we're hopeless, messy sods. But resources always run out. That will ensure competition."

"It takes so *long* to exhaust a whole solar system," Nikka said.

"Um. Yes. Hard for us to think on that time scale, isn't it? Perhaps a reasonably bright machine needn't wait around for evolution to do its work, though. It can augment its intelligence by adding on units, remember. Manufacturing, then delegating tasks to its new subsystems. Boosts the thinking speed, which is at least a step in the right direction. Simpler than willing yourself to have more brain cells, which is what *we'd* have to do."

"Look, I'm the computer hack here," Carlotta said. "I say artificial intelligence isn't that easy. Earthside's huge machines are sharp, sure, but it's not just a question of adding more capacity."

"Granted. But we're talking about million of years of evolution here—perhaps billions."

"That's a big, glossy generalization you're making," Carlotta said.

"So it is. I suppose I ought to think matters through better."

"Listen," Carlotta pressed him, "this is *science*. You've got to make a prediction if you want people to listen."

"Right. Here it is. A Watcher will appear around every world where technology is *possible*. Or where it once was and might come again. They're cops, you see. But they only police spots where technology might come from a naturally arising species. An organic one."

Carlotta frowned. "Let's see . . . That fits—"

Nigel broke in eagerly, "The robots which were shuttling ice at Wolf 359, for example. No Watcher there, because those patient little fellows are an early form of a machine society. Give 'em a few million years of exposure to cosmic rays, a shortage of materials—they'll evolve. Become a member of the club."

"Club?" Nikka asked.

"A network of ancient machine civilizations. They sent the Watchers."

"I still don't understand why the concentration on machines versus us," Nikka said.

"Partly I'm relying on what the *Snark* said, and events afterward."

"Well, Nigel," Carlotta said diplomatically, "most people think you were, you know, off the deep end back then. . . ."

"I never claimed to be a conservative Republican. But there's good reason to believe machines left over from a nuclear Armageddon won't be friendly as lap dogs."

"Why?"

"They started off with a genocide. One we caused. They'll remember that."

He wrote up his theory and duly gave a seminar for ExoBio and Theory sections. It was politely received.

The Watcher around Epsilon Eridani, he said, was there to be certain that no organic form arose again (or returned

from nearby stars—there might be colonies). Something—the
Watcher?—had destroyed the native organic civilization. It
had incinerated the planet in such a way that the Skyhook
remained.

Why leave the Skyhook? Most likely, because the Watcher
wanted an economical way to send expeditions to the surface,
where remnants could be sought out and exterminated.

He reviewed the observations of the oil haulers of Procyon.
At highest magnification the machines looked well-designed,
sprouting antennas and hatches. Nigel deduced that they
were perhaps a bit further advanced beyond the Wolf 359 ice
luggers. Still carrying out mechanical tasks, but not running
on instructions left over from a long-dead society. Instead,
they seemed to be integrated into some interstellar economic
scheme. An ocean of oil was a great boon, of course—but not
merely for making energy. Anything that could cross between
stars would not be hobbled by a chemical-energy economy.
They might well need plentiful lubricants, though.

Isis was harder to explain. The EMs had engineered
themselves to use radio as their basic sense. Was this to
deceive the two Watchers into considering them a protomachine
society?

That would imply a certain rigidity and literal-mindedness
in those Watchers. Maybe they were old, decaying? Or else
biding their time, studying the EMs. The fact that one
Watcher attacked any attempt to inspect it tended to support
the second point of view.

Nigel used all the data he could muster. He compared
spectra and diagnostics of the various Watchers, estimated
their ages (all gave billion-year upper bounds), and correlated
as many variables as he could plausibly justify. There was no
clean way to show a common origin for the Watchers. On the
other hand, he pointed out, there was no reason to believe
the Watchers had been constructed at the same place or
time.

His theory did not muster much support. He had not
expected it to.

The prevailing notion in Theory Section was the simplest—
Occam's razor triumphant. All these worlds, Theory said,
were the husks of war-obliterated cultures. They proved that
intelligent life was plentiful but suicidal. The Watchers were
simply a common form of weapon, reinvented again and again

in separately evolving societies. Battle stations. By the time a race developed one, it was close to annihilation.

As for Isis—the specifics of the great war that doomed that world were now mired in the EM legends. And legends were notoriously unreliable sources of hard facts. The EMs had modified their own bodies to survive, pure and simple, in the ruin they had made.

Neither side could explain the Swarmers and Skimmers. Nigel stood before the audience and countered arguments as best he could. He had a vague sense that the Skimmers and the EMs were somehow similar, but knew enough not to venture such an idea without an underpinning of hard explanation.

Someone from ExoBio pointed out that the Swarmers at least demonstrated the prevalence of violence and warfare in other life-forms. There was applause after this remark. Nigel stood silent, not knowing how to counter it.

He saw the polite, well-concealed disbelief in their faces and accepted it. He merely hammered home again his prediction: Whatever they found ahead at Ross 128, if a world could possibly bring forth organic life—or had—it would have a circling Watcher. Walmsley's Rule, someone called it.

His point made, he sat down to moderate applause. The seminar turned on to other topics in astrophysics and biology. No one, he noted, brought up the obvious exception to Walmsley's Rule: Earth.

FIVE

Nigel stayed in their apartment much of the time. Nikka was quite fit, and did a variety of jobs around the ship. He participated in seminars and helped with assembly nets, all done over the apartment flatscreen. He liked the isolation and peace, but in fact it was forced on him by the need to tie into the blood filter four times daily. He and Nikka had put the rig together using gear from ship's surplus; medical engineering was as easy as auto repair, most of it modular and plug-in. Still, they were tinkering with his life; Nikka checked the flow patterns every day. Of course, bypassing the medmons was a violation of shipregs, but that didn't cause them any fretting.

He regularly tapped into the ExoBio seminars, mostly to use the interactive data bases and 3-D choice-theory-outcome representations. These last were visualizations of the overall consequences of any theory of extraterrestrial life, tracing the many strands of planetary evolution, biology, and socioeconomics. Earthside's spotty flow of news on the Swarmers and Skimmers had to be folded into what *Lancer* and the independent probes found. There were competing schools of thought, led by specialist analysts among the crew. Nigel seldom met these savants. They existed for him as disembodied constellations of theory in the seminar representations, ways of organizing the data. Their command of interconnections was formidable. They could relate the structure of the *Marginis* wreck to the swim patterns of the Swarmers, fold it into a theory of universal languages, and come up with (a) an estimate of the probability that most galactic lifeforms still lived exclusively in oceans, (b) a best-choice scheme for achieving radio contact through use of gigawatt-level radio beacons; (c) a recalculated optimum-search strategy for probes to stars within a hundred light-years. Nigel recalled Mark Twain's remark that the wonder of science was how vast a return of speculation you got for such a trifling investment of fact.

The snag was that you had to have some initial premise to fit it all together. Shipboard, the running consensus was that all earlier alien contacts—the *Snark* craft that Nigel spoke to briefly, and the *Marginis* wreck—had been feelers. Something, probably the Swarmers and Skimmers themselves, had probed Earth for a long time, sizing up its suitability as a biosphere. The conventional wisdom of the past, that no species would bother to invade another world, seemed no longer true. *Lancer* had found that most planets were blasted relics. It would be far easier to adapt to an existing biosphere like Earth, than to start at zero with a smashed, barren planet. So the Swarmers had probably been bioengineering themselves to adapt to Earth's oceans, ever since they discovered it in the expedition that left the *Marginis* wreck.

The theory even explained Walmsley's Rule. The Swarmers—or the civilization they represented, the technology that built the starships they came in—made the Watchers, to keep track of other possible life sites, other developing societies. Some Watchers survived the final war that scraped some worlds free of life; others didn't. Man was coming late upon the galactic stage; he should expect to find some props from earlier acts—most of them tragedies. Thus went the conventional wisdom, new edition.

Nigel's point of view was duly heard, discussed, footnoted in later work—and then the stream of theories and models and self-consistency checks flowed on around it, a consensus river skirting an island. He did not know enough about analysis to integrate his model with the wealth of data. He thought it probable that the *Marginis* wreck had died while destroying Earth's Watcher. Over half a million years after its crash, the crumpled eggshell vessel had demonstrated powerful weapons—which was how Moon Operations found it. At full capability, the wreck could have blown apart whole asteroids—and Nigel suspected that was precisely what it was designed to do. Many of the worlds they'd seen by probe—and Isis, too—had been pulverized by bombardment. It was the cheapest way to damage a planetary surface. in terms of energy invested. So the *Marginis* wreck had laid there as man evolved up from apes. The wreck could detect and smash any large asteroid falling toward the biosphere. But its strength ebbed. It had stood up to battering attacks, only to fade slowly as time wore it down.

Now humanity could defend itself against asteroids or even worse weapons. *As long*, Nigel thought to himself, *as we can* recognize *them as weapons.*

SIX

Luyten 789–6 had only one world, circling near one of the two small suns, and it was devoured by fire.

As the probe swung near it, the spectral traces and

photometry showed a pall of smoke and sheets of flame. The planet was Earth-sized, comfortably warm, 80 percent ocean. Above the seas the oxygen content of the air was 25.4 percent, and over the continents, 23.7 percent.

It did not take much analysis to see what had happened. Warm surface temperatures made sea life abundant. Microorganisms there exhaled large amounts of oxygen. On Earth the same process ran, too, but oxygen was only 21 percent of the air.

The probability of forest fire nearly doubles with each 1 percent rise in oxygen. On the sole world of Luyten 789–6, the sea life poured oxygen into the forever burning tropical forests. Even Arctic tundra ignited. In the planet's winter season plants grew despite the cold, driven by the high chemical reaction rates, and by processes in the soil. With summer came worldwide fires.

On Earth, methane belched up from mud ponds soaks oxygen from the air, keeping a stable balance. Somehow that mechanism had failed here. There was evidence from the chem sampling that this world was older than Earth; the grow-and-burn cycle had been running for billions of years. No animal life moved on the land; none could survive the fires. Yet a Watcher circled the world—impassive, scarred, and ancient.

"Carlotta!"

She turned. Nigel walked faster with obvious effort and caught up at a Y in the corridors. "Time for some talk?"

She grinned. "Sure. I've been wanting to bring something up myself. Just haven't had an opportunity."

They made their way to a viewpod that looked out on the base of the ship's axis. Here the centrifugal gravity was low. Nigel's face showed relief at the lessened strain. Beyond, they could see a globe of water ejected at the axis. People swam in it as it wobbled and flowed along the axis in free fall. They had thin rubber bands fixed to their ankles, in case they broke the surface tension and fell outward. Few did; they were adept fish, showering droplets and laughter.

"I miss that," Nigel mused. "Haven't done it for years."

"Well, soon you'll be able to again and we can—"

"No. I've been putting off my medical, but I can tell matters aren't improving."

"Chem?"

"Right. Radicals in the blood, so the body leaps to my defense"—a wry shrug—"and overcompensates."

"Cancer."

"That's the homey name for it, yes. I've been doing a lot of blood filtering on my own—don't look so shocked, it's a simple trick, really—but I can't get past the medmon sniffer anymore."

'Some therapy—'

He shook his head. "I know what Medical and Ted will say. I'm too much a bloody precious relic to risk. They'll pop me into a Sleepslot until we're Earthside."

"Look, landfall at Ross is nearly a year away. I'm sure they'd let you last through that."

"Um. Risk me dying from inadequate treatment? Unlikely."

"You're valuable to us, too. Didn't Luyten 789–6 prove Walmsley's Rule?"

"The first law of management is: Cover your ass. This shall ye honor before all else. Ted doesn't want to haul me back to Earth a corpse."

"You don't want that either. There's nothing you can do except take the luck you're handed. Look, you know time in the Slots isn't so bad, I'm going in myself for four months, next Friday."

"What for?"

"I . . . A tune-up, sort of. I . . . We all three should talk about it, I guess . . ." She paused and then went on briskly. "You have no choice."

"I've ducked by Medical before."

She saw what he meant. "Uh-oh . . ."

"Right." He grinned. "You took me out, put me on self-serve, remember, years ago? Do it again. Please."

"I . . . You know I care for you, I still do, even if we aren't . . . together now . . . but . . ."

"Please."

"Do you really care that much about making landfall?"

"Yes. Yes, I do." He surged up from his hammock chair and winced at sudden pain. He had not yet acquired all the habits of the elderly, the perception of unbalanced forces acting through fragile, brittle axes, in ankles, knees, elbows, spine. Carlotta studied him and sighed.

"Monitoring systems are better now," she said. "The

programs and data bases trigger decision algorithms fairly high up in the sentience pyramid. I would have to..."

He hung on her next words. She bit her lip. "Look, I'm not saying it'll work. I can get close, but—"

"I appreciate that, luv. But close counts only in horse-shoes and hand grenades. I need to get out from under them for *sure*. Something they can't trace."

She sighed. "The things you ask for. Jesus, I didn't know you were this bad off. Thought you were skimming a fra-poff, sure, but real *cancer*—Lord, that's supposed to be *fix*able."

He blinked wearily. "The older the body, the more rickety the immune response gets. That's what all the aging diseases are, I suppose. Inappropriate response. The easiest way to kill a living thing is to get it to do most of the damage to itself. Merely add the right outside irritant..." His voice trailed off. Silently Carlotta rose to embrace him.

"Y'know, you said once that intelligence is the ability to learn from other people's mistakes." Carlotta studied him gravely. "You sure as hell aren't. Why not pack it in, eh?"

He smiled defiantly. "I paid my admission. I want to see how the movie ends."

SEVEN

He went for long walks through *Lancer*, seeing little of it. Instead, he tried to recall Earth, to forget the rumors of influence peddling and maneuverings on shipboard that might, finally, decide his fate. He remembered the last place he had gone before boarding *Lancer:* Venice. Nikka was visiting her family so he was left alone, ambling down gray flagstone streets with no footpaths. Men charged along them, pushing barrows and shouting. *"Le gambe!"*—which Nigel dutifully looked up in his dictionary and found meant "Legs!" a rather abrupt warning. It reminded him of the American "Heads up!" which was used when the appropriate response was precisely the opposite.

He let himself be tugged by crowds into Saint Mark's

Square, amid their chatter and dark round eyes. At the height of Venetian power the square had been named Il Broglio, intrigue, because from 10:00 A.M. to noon only the nobles were allowed to meet there and hatch their plots. He thought of Ted and Bob, bland names which hid riddles.

He went inside the vast, hollow spaces of the basilica. From the high bulbous domes gold saints stared down at the masses of working, breathing carbon chemistry below. He climbed. The upper walkways brought these spiritual heroes closer, revealing them to be made of chips of blue and rose and white, a millimeter deep.

The rising spaces reminded him of the small cylinder worlds, just big enough to make a man feel dwarfed. Architects had been trying for that effect for millennia. He remembered that originally the pyramids outside Alexandria—*she was lying sprawled, unconscious, the life draining*—he cut off the thought.

The basilica walls were encrusted with Constantinople sculptures and Holy Land jewels. Booty of the Crusades. The desire for huge surroundings seemed to run in parallel with the lust for vast voyages, for causes, and for stacks of stone to remember them by. *Look, see what I did!* Future schoolchildren would goggle, to be sure—and then bow their reverent heads back to their ice creams.

Outside, waves slapped against the quay, playful, throwing spray in his eyes to remind him of how big they had been farther out where the ocean was still deep and blue. He wondered, *What drew such crowds to this place?* Then, seeing the marble standing luminous before the sea, it was suddenly clear. Here men had come, fleeing barbarism. Once they had tamed the sea and traded on it, they built stone statements, denying that the outcome was ever in doubt. These mobs knew that he saw, and preferred the cool stone, tight streets, and arched bridges that asserted the rule of geometry over the waves. These carved boxes of marble should, must, *would*, outlast the sea's random rub.

On Ascension Day the Doge, the Venetian ruler, would sail out from the city in his gilded state galley, to throw a ring overboard, symbolizing the wedding of Venice to the waters. But in the end the marriage was not valid, because it lacked the consent of the bride. Venice clung to its carved rock and waned.

*   *   *

He still did as much manual work as he could, but the jobs seemed harder and the weakness came on him earlier in the day. He did analysis and routine jobs of maintenance, to keep busy and justify his presence, if only to himself. His digestion got worse. His muscles were always sore in the mornings and he felt a general unsteadiness. The worsening was blissfully gradual. He saw, ruefully, that he had reacted to it as most do. First you blame minor illnesses rather than age, and claim that pretty soon you will be up and about and back to tending the crops. He made this observation to Nikka many times and finally, afterward, she would become silent, and he would spend a restless night. He was going to the stars, but evolution's need for mortality reached him even here.

Slowly he gathered, from slight elevations of eyelashes and side glances of friends, that his birthdays were not seen now as accomplishments, but as postponements. He looked for some weariness with life, with the doing of things, that would make the end less fearsome.

Surprisingly, perhaps gladly, he couldn't find any.

Nigel looked from the prelim photos of Ross 128. "Pretty blurred," he said to Nikka.

They're from the gravitational telescope. Years old, of course—they're working fast as they can, but the light-travel delay—"

"Right." He studied the hazy blobs. "Some Jovians, two terrestrials. Not bad." Because *Lancer* had boosted to 0.98 light speed, these images were only a few months older than the first ones they had received, years ago, back at Isis. "Carlotta's working on reprocessing this stuff, isn't she? When will we get better—"

"She's in the Slots."

"What? I didn't—How long?"

"Two weeks now."

Nigel was startled. He hadn't even noticed her absence. And he disliked abrupt changes like this, friends suddenly disappearing. "When do they uncork her?"

"Six months, I think."

"We'll be nearly at landfall then!"

Nikka looked up from her workpad. "Slots are R and R.

She'll come out refreshed, able to relieve somebody who's been hustling to get ready for Ross."

"Ummm." He frowned. "Seems reasonable...but...I don't like it." He shook his head and went back to mulling over the prints. But he could not concentrate.

EIGHT

Warning gongs rang throughout *Lancer*. Nigel crossed his legs and ignored them. The ship was striking a dense dust cloud, and the ramscoop would either work or not, nothing he could do would matter. He slid a stick into the spine of a book and opened it. The stick overfilled the book, so he thumbed for the second projection and started reading on page 287. *And then Tom he talked along and talked along, and says, le's all three slide out of here one of these nights and get an outfit, and go for howling adventures amongst the Injuns, over in the territory, for a couple of weeks or two; and I says, all right, that suits me, but I ain't got no money for to buy the outfit, and I reckon I couldn't get none from home—*

"Nigel!" his comm cried. He tapped his fingernail in answer. "Cut into shipspeak—fast." It was Nikka, gone before he could reply. He punched into his flatscreen and overvocal and listened.

> drive tube's holding okay, max'ed on momentum transport
> betcher butt we're gonna sail right through no prob
> what's the sci package picking up I'm gettin' funny
> it's dropped clear of our wake now pickin' up samples
> lookit that absorption line there, big fat one sittin' at 2200 angstroms thick as your thumb
> absorption cross section about 4 tim 10_{-17} cm_2 yeah

I got the culprit right here, the sampler's got a slide on now, looks like silicate grains only that's no silicon line

average size right aroun' 10^{-5} cm I make it

Christ 'at stuff is peptides clear as a bell see those linkages

long chain stuff too all over the outer surface of those grains things are coated with it like an oil slick or somethin'

I don't get it we're seein' amino acids in there too

those're supposed to be dust particles what's that stuff doing sticking to

look at that structure like a wall, long chains and the rest it's a cell barrier got to be

doesn't make sense

only use for a cell wall is to keep out your enemies

out here that means ultraviolet, UV'd blow those peptide chains to hell except for that li'l membrane there, bet it's got silicon in it to block the UV

so peptides can stay inside the cell wall an' link up an' reproduce 'at's the only thing logical I can make out

living stuff in clouds I don't look it's cold as a hoor's tit out there what's the thermodynamic driver for life

lots of IR around that's how you saw that absorption line, same line that comes in most carbon complexes

see there in the middle that's a silicate, the original piece of dust this cell started out on I bet

an' two of 'em stickin' together right there look the chains are migratin' to the cell wall that's it that's it

my Gawd the density of 'em in here the ramscoop is nearly chokin' on 'em and the fluxlife is gettin' barnacles of this goop all over we're gonna have to clean up this mess

mess hell it's reproducing cells man in these big clouds, there's more mass in these clouds than

in the goddamn stars for sure, look at all the dark
patches in the night sky for sure it means there's this
peptide chem happenin' everywhere...

Nigel watched the list of molecules and free radicals stack up: ethanol, cyanoacetylene, carbon monoxide, ammonia, methane, water—and realized that as far as the universe was concerned, this was where chemistry occurred. The planets were negligible. Driven by starlight, here the twisting coils had time to find their mates and build even more complexity. These molecular clouds were the compost heaps where the stars formed. They also swept through solar systems, littering the planets with sticky, hungry cells.

In the tenor of the crew voices he heard a strain of excitement. They had seen dozens of dead worlds and now had stumbled blindly into a caldron of life. The molecular clouds were the most massive objects in the galaxy, and they had been brewing longer than the stars. *Lancer* surged and burned a hole through this one, leaving fiery remnants. Ahead, glimmering dimly through the smoky fog of chemistry, was the wan glow of Ross 128.

PART SEVEN 2061 EARTH

ONE

In midafternoon six delta-planes came in low, made a pass and arced up, one at a time, to land in V-mode. They came down in the rocky area to the south, and a few minutes after the shrieking engines shut down three squads of fast, lean-looking infantry came double-timing onto the beach.

Warren watched them from the shade where he sat within clear view of Gijan. The man had made him carry the radio and power supply from its concealment in the scrub and onto the beach, where he could talk down the planes. Gijan shouted at the men and they backed away from the beach where the Skimmers might see them. A squad took Warren and marched him south, saying nothing. At the landing site, men and forklifts were unloading and building and no one looked at him twice. The squad took him to a small building set down on rocky soil and locked him inside.

It was light durablock construction, three meters square with three windows with heavy wire mesh over them. There was a squat wooden chair, a thin sleeping pad on the floor, and a fifty-watt glow plate in the ceiling that did not work. Warren tasted the water in a gallon jug and found it tepid and metallic. There was a bucket to use as a toilet.

He could not see much through the windows but the clang and rumble of unloading went on. Darkness came. A motor started up nearby and he tried to tell if it was going or coming until he realized it was turning over at a steady rpm. He touched the wall switch and the soft glow above came on, so he guessed the generator had started. In the dim light everything in the room stood out bleak and cold.

Later a muscular soldier came with a tin plate of vegetable stew. Warren ate it slowly, tasting the boiled onions and carrots and spinach and tomatoes, holding back his sudden

appetite so that he got each taste separately. He licked the
pan clean and drank some water. Rather than sit and think
fruitlessly he lay down and slept.

At dawn the same guard came again with more of the
stew, cold this time. Warren had not finished it when the
guard came back and took it away and yanked him to his feet.
The soldier quick-marched him across a compound in the
pale morning light. Warren memorized the sizes and distances of the buildings as well as he could. The guard took
him to the biggest building in the compound, a prefab that
was camouflage-speckled for the jungle. The front room was
an office with Gijan sitting in one of the four flimsy chairs and
a tall man, Chinese or Japanese, standing beside a plywood
desk.

"You know Underofficer Gijan? Good. Sit." The tall man
moved quickly to offer Warren a chair. He turned and sat
behind the desk and Warren watched him. Each motion of
the man had a kind of sliding quality to it, as though he was
keeping his body centered and balanced at all times to take a
new angle of defense or attack if needed.

"Please relax," the man said. Warren noticed that he was
sitting on the edge of the chair. He settled back in it, using
the moment to locate the guard in a far corner to his right, an
unreachable two meters away.

"What is your name?"

"Warren."

"You have only one name?" the man asked, smiling.

"Your men didn't introduce themselves either. I didn't
think I had to be formal."

"I am sure you understand the circumstances, Warren.
In any case, my name is Tseng Wong. Since we are using
only single names, call me Tseng." His words came out
separately, like smooth round objects forming in the still air.

"I can see that conditions have been hard on you."

"Not so bad."

Tseng pursed his lips. "The evidence given by your
little"—he searched for the word—"spasm in the face, is
enough to show me—"

"What spasm?"

"Perhaps you do not notice it any longer. The left side, a
tightening in the eyes and the mouth."

"I don't have anything like that."

Tseng looked at Gijan, just a quick glance, and then back at Warren. There was something in it Warren did not like and he found himself focusing his attention on his own face, waiting to see if there was anything wrong with it he had not noticed. Maybe he—

"Well, we shall let it pass. A casual remark, that is all. I did not come to criticize you but to, first, ask for your help, and second, to get you off this terrible island."

"You coulda got me off here days ago. Gijan had the radio."

"His task came first. You are fascinated by the same problem, are you, Warren?"

"Seems to me my big problem is you people."

"I believe your long exposure out here has distorted your judgment, Warren. I also believe you overestimate your ability to survive for long on this island. With Underofficer Gijan the two of you did well enough, but in the long run I—" Tseng stopped when he saw the slight upward turn of Warren's mouth that was clearly a look of disdain.

"I saw that case of rations Gijan had stashed back in the brush," Warren said. "None of you know nothing about living out here."

Tseng stood up, tall and straight, and leaned against the back wall of the office. It gave him a more casual look but put him so that Warren had to look up to talk to him.

"I will do you the courtesy of speaking frankly. My government—and several others, we believe—has suspected for some time that there are two distinct populations among the aliens. One—the Swarmers—is capable of mass actions, almost instinctive actions, which are quite effective against ships. The others, the Skimmers, are far more intelligent. They are also verbal. Yet they did not respond to our research vessels. They ignored attempts to communicate."

Warren said, "You still have ships?"

For the first time Gijan spoke. "No. I was on one of the last that went down. They got us off with helicopters, and then—"

"No need to go into that," Tseng cut him off smoothly.

"It was the Swarmers who sank you. Not Skimmers," Warren said. It was not a question.

"Skimmer intelligence was really only an hypothesis," Tseng said, "until we had reports that they had sought out

single men or women. Usually people adrift, though sometimes even at the shore."

"Safer for them," Warren said.

"Apparently. They avoid the Swarmers. They avoid ships.
Isolated contact is all that is left to them. It was really quite
stupid of us not to have thought of that earlier."

"Yeah."

Tseng smiled slightly. "Everything is of course clearer
in, as you say, the rearview mirror."

"Uh-huh."

"It seems they learned the bits of German and Japanese
and English from different individual encounters. The words
were passed among the Skimmers so that each new contact
had more available vocabulary."

"But they didn't know the words were from different
languages," Gijan added.

"Maybe they only got one," Warren said.

"So we gather," Tseng said. "I have read your, ah, summary. Yours is the most advanced contact so far."

"A lot of it doesn't make much sense," Warren said. He
knew Tseng was drawing him into the conversation, but it did
not matter. Tseng would have to give away information to get
some.

"The earlier contacts confirm part of your summary."

"Uh-huh."

"They said that Swarmers can go ashore."

"Uh-huh."

"How do you know that?"

"It's in the stuff I wrote. The stuff Gijan stole."

Gijan said sharply, "You showed it to me."

Warren looked at him without expression and Gijan
stared back and after a moment looked away.

"Let us not bother with that. We are all working on the
same problem, after all."

"Okay," Warren said. He had managed to get the talk
away from how he knew about the Swarmers going on the
land. Tseng was good at talking, a lot better than Warren, so
he would have to keep the man away from some things. He
volunteered, "I guess going up on the shore is part of their,
uh, evolution."

"You mean their development?"

"They said something, the last day I saw them, about a

deathlight. A deathlight coming on the land and only the Swarmers could live through it."

"Light from their star?"

"Guess so. It comes sometimes and that's why the Skimmers don't go up onto the land."

Tseng stood and began pacing against the back wall. Warren wondered if he knew that Swarmers had already gone inland on an island near here. Tseng gave no sign of it and said out of his concentration, "That agrees with the earlier survivors' reports. We think that means their star is irregular. It flares in the UV. The Swarmers have simple nervous systems, smaller brains. They can survive a high UV flux."

"For about two of their planet's years, the Skimmers said," Warren murmured. "But you're wrong—the Swarmers aren't dumb."

"They have heads of mostly bone."

"That's for killing the big animals, the ones that float on the surface of their sea. Something like whales, I guess. Maybe they stay at the top to use the UV or something."

"The Swarmers ram them, throw those webs over them? Sink them?"

"Yeah. Just what they did to our ships."

"Target confusion. They think ships are animals."

"The Swarmers, they drag the floaters under, eat some kind of pods inside 'em. That's what triggers their going up on the land."

"If we could find a way to prevent their confusing our ships with—"

Gijan said, "But they are going to the land now. They are in the next mode."

"Uh-huh." Warren studied the two men, tried to guess if they knew anything he could use. "Look, what're they doing when they get ashore?"

Tseng looked at him sharply. "What do the Skimmers say?"

"Far as I can tell, the Swarmers aren't dumb, not once they get on land. They make the machines and stuff for the Skimmers. They're really the same kind of animal. They grow hands and feet and the Skimmers have some way to tell them—singing—how to build stuff, make batteries, tools, that stuff."

Tseng stared at Warren for a long moment. "A break in the evolutionary ladder? Life trying to get out of the oceans, but turned back by the solar flares?" Tseng leaned forward and rested his knuckles on the gray plywood. He had a strange weight and force about him. And a desperate need.

Warren said, "Maybe it started out with the Swarmers crawling up on the beaches to lay eggs or something. Good odds they'd be back in the water before a flare came. Then the Skimmers invented tools and saw they needed things on the land, needed to make fire or something. So they got the Swarmers, the younger form of their species, to help. Maybe—"

"The high UV speeded up their evolutionary rate. Perhaps the Swarmers became more intelligent, in their last phase, on land, where the intelligence would be useful in making the tools. Um, yes."

Tseng gave Gijan an intense glance. "Possible. But I think there is more than that. These creatures are here for some purpose beyond this charming little piece of natural history we have been told. Or sold."

Tseng turned back to Warren. "We have our partially successful procedures of communication, as you have probably guessed. I have been ordered to carry out systematic methods of approach." He was brisk and sure, as though he had digested Warren's information and found a way to classify it. "Yours will be among them. But it is an idiosyncratic technique and I doubt we could teach it to our field men. Underofficer Gijan, for example." The contempt in his voice for Gijan was obvious. "Meanwhile, I will call upon you for help if we need it, Warren."

"Uh-huh."

He took a map of the ocean from his desk drawer and flipped it across to Warren. "I trust this will be of help in writing your report."

"Report?"

"An account of your interactions with the aliens. I must file it with my superior. I am sure it will be in your own interests to make it as accurate as possible." He made a smile without any emotion behind it. "If you can fix the point where your ship went down, we might even be able to find some other survivors."

Warren could see there was nothing in this last promise. He thought and then said, "Mr. Wong, I wondered if I could, you know, rest a little. And when the guard there brings me my food, I'd like a long time to eat it. My stomach, being out on the ocean so long, it can't take your food unless I kind of take it easy."

"Of course, of course." Tseng smiled with genuine emotion this time. Warren could see that he was glad to be dispensing favors and that the act made Tseng sure he had judged the situation and had it right.

"Sure do appreciate that, Mr. Wong," he said, getting the right tone into the words so that the man would classify him and file him away and forget him.

TWO

He worked for two days on the report. The guard gave him a pad of paper and a short stubby little pen and Tseng told him to write it in English. Warren smiled at that. They thought any seaman had to speak a couple of languages, but he had never had any trouble getting around with one and a few words picked up from others. You learned more from watching people than from listening to all their talk anyway.

He had never been any good at writing and a lot of the things about the Skimmers he could not get down. He worked on the writing in his cell, listening all the time for the sound of new motors or big things moving. It was hard to tell anything about what the teams were doing. He was glad he could rest in the shadows of the cell and think, eating the food they brought him as quickly as he could while still getting the taste of it.

The same chinless guard he had from the first came once a day to take him down to the shore. Warren carried the waste bucket. The guard would not let him take the time to bury the waste and instead made him throw it into the surf. The guard stayed back in the sea-grape bushes while Warren went down to the lagoon. The man was probably under orders not to show himself on the beach, Warren guessed. On the windward side of the island there was a lot of dry grass and some gullies. Dried-up stream beds ran down into little half-moon beaches and Warren could see the teams had moored catboats and other small craft there. Some of the troops had pitched tents far back in the gullies but most of them were empty. The guard marched him back that way. On one of the sandy crescents Warren's raft was beached, dragged up above the tide line but not weighted down or moored.

Coming back on the second day some sooty terns were hanging in the wind, calling with long low cries. Some were nested in the rocks up at the windward and others in the grass of the lee. The terns would fall off the wind and swoop down over the heads of the men gathering eggs out of the rocky nests. The birds cawed and dipped down through the wind but the men did not look up.

The next morning the chinless soldier came too soon after the breakfast tin and Warren had to straighten his sleeping pad in a hurry. The guard never came into the shadowy cell because of the smell from the bucket which Warren kept next to the door. The man had discovered that Warren knew no Chinese and so instead of giving orders he shoved Warren in whatever direction he wanted. This time they went north.

Tseng was surveying a work team at a point halfway up the ridge at the middle of the island. He nodded to Warren and signaled that the guard should remain nearby. "Your report?"

"Nearly done with it."

"Good. I will translate it myself. Be sure it is legible."

"I printed it out."

"Just as do the Skimmers."

"Yeah."

"We duplicated your methods, you know, and dropped several messages into the lagoon." He pointed to a spot north of the pass through the reef. From here on the ridge the moving shadows were plain against the sand. The soft green of the lagoon was like a ring and beyond it was the hard blue that went to the horizon. "No reply."

"How'd you deliver them?"

"Three men, two armed for safety. After so many incidents they are afraid to go out unprotected."

"They go in that?" Warren pointed to a skiff beached below them.

"Yes. I'm going to supplement their work with a set of acoustics. They should be—Yes, here we are." A buzz came from the south and a motorboat came up the lagoon leaving a white wake. It cut in among the shoals and sandbars and a big reel on the back of it was spinning in the sun, throwing quick darts of yellow into Warren's eyes.

"We will have a complete acoustic bed. A very promising method."

"You make sense out of that?"

Tseng shaded his eyes against the glare and turned to smile at Warren. "Their high-frequency 'songs' are their basic method of communication. We already have much experience with the dolphins. We can converse freely with them. Only on simpleminded subjects, of course. Much of what we know about Swarmer and Skimmers movements comes from the dolphins."

Warren said sharply, "Look, why fool with that stuff. Let me go out and I'll ask them what you want."

Tseng nodded. "Eventually I might. But you must understand that the Skimmers have reasons of their own for not telling you everything that is important."

"Such as?"

"Here." Tseng snapped his fingers at an aide standing nearby. The soldier brought over a document pouch. Tseng took out a set of photographs and handed them to Warren. The top one was a color shot of a woman's stomach and breasts. There were small bumps on them, white mounds on the tan skin. One lump was in her swollen left nipple.

Warren went on to the next, and the next. The lumps got bigger and whiter. "They are quite painful," Tseng said distantly. "Some kind of larva burrows into a sweat-sore and in a day this begins. The larva is biggest near the skin, armed with sharp yellow spines. The worm turns as it feeds. Spines grate against the nerves. The victim feels sudden, deep pain. Within another day the victim is hysterical and tries to claw the larva out. These are small larvae. There are reports of larger ones."

In one photograph the open sores were bleeding and dripping a white pus. "Like a tick," Warren said. "Burn it out. Use iodine. Or cover it with tape so it can't get air."

Tseng sighed. "Any such attack and the larva releases something, we are unsure what, into the victim's bloodstream. It paralyzes the victim so he cannot treat himself further."

"Well, if you—"

"The larva apparently does not breathe. It takes oxygen directly from the host. If anything dislodges the spines, once they are hooked in, the larva releases the paralyzer and something else, something that carries a kind of egg so that other larvae can grow elsewhere. All this in minutes."

Warren shook his head. "Never heard of any tick or bug like that."

"They come from the Swarmers. When they are ashore."

Warren watched the motorboat methodically crisscrossing the lagoon, the reel spinning. He shook his head. "Something to do with their mating? Don't know. Doesn't make sense. The Skimmers—"

"They said nothing about it. Interesting, eh?"

"Maybe they don't know."

"It seems unlikely."

"So you're listening for what?"

"Contact between the Skimmers and the Swarmers. Some knowledge of how they interact."

"Can't you treat this bug, get rid of it?"

"Possibly. The European medical centers are at work now. But there are other diseases. They are spreading rapidly from contact points near Ning-po and Macao."

"Maybe you can block them off."

"The things are everywhere. They come ashore and the larvae are carried by the birds, by animals—somehow. That is why we burn our reserves of fuel to come this far."

"To the islands?"

"Only in isolation do they make contract. The reported incidents are from the Pacific basin. That is why there are Japanese aircraft near here, Soviet, American—you are an American, aren't you?"

"No."

"Oh? Somehow I thought—but never mind. The other powers are desperate. They do not know what is happening and they envy our lead in information. You will notice the installation to the south?"

Tseng gestured. Warren saw at the rocky tip of the island a fan of slender shapes knifing up at the sky. "Anti-air missiles. We would not want anyone else to exploit this opportunity."

"Uh-huh."

The motorboat droned, working its way up the eas ern shore. Warren studied the island, noticing where the tents were pitched and where the men moved in work teams and where the scrub jungle cut off visibility.

"If you're smart you won't use a motor in the lagoon."

"The men will not go out without some way of returning quickly. I understand their fear. I have seen—"

An aide approached, lugging a case. He spoke quickly in Chinese. As Tseng answered, Warren watched the motorboat cross near the sandbar. Beneath it shadows darted, swift black shapes in the watery green light.

"The boats found something unusual," Tseng said, gesturing to the aide to open the case. "They washed up on the reef."

Inside, still wet, were three white, rhombohedral blocks. Warren crouched and touched one. It was lightweight and pearly, the corners unevenly turned.

"Packing material, I suppose," Tseng said.

"Funny manufacture," Warren said. "Irregular. No forming creases on them."

"From your own shipwreck, perhaps? No matter. I have no more time for you today, Mr. Warren. Or would you prefer being addressed by your military rank?"

"I don't have any."

'So you say." Tseng nodded to the nearby guard. "Goodbye."

That night he felt a dark hammering thing above him that wove and wove, its shadow a rippling of sunlight. The thing swam badly, moving in straight lines without flexing itself, firm and unnatural, and it dropped metal that settled on him, heavy and foul. The steady dead rasp from above cut and burned. A harsh buzzing jarred him, coming into his teeth with a slicing pain, and he turned on his side. Then he rose out and away, somewhere up high above what he now saw was a motor. He sensed the fuel line backfilled and felt the sluggish rumble as they blew the lines out and heard the plugs not running right either.

Sudden thoughts came— That was it: nothing ran right. Humans were great talkers but down here, lofting in the salty murk, he could see them above, at the shoreline and in the ratcheting boats, working their mouths and yet without effect, stiff and distant, their jaws pointlessly working, humans in uniform—but *uniform* meant to be the same, and how could anyone want that?—the words falling dead in the void between them. In Tokyo he had never learned a word of Japanese, and here Gijan had played a mute without Warren's minding, and now the Chinese were trying to talk to Skimmers—who wanted something they couldn't say, either—and each life-form had its own private language.

He turned over again and felt his wife sleeping against him, warm and moist, and then on top of him the way she liked. She pressed down too like the falling, spreading metal that the hammering machine laid in the lagoon, leaden, dark and descending. She rolled easily on him, heavy and yet soft, and her hair lay on his face silky and in his eyes. Moving in shadows, her face was intersecting planes, lean and white, and he took her hair in his mouth and tasted it. The salt and musk were like her sex below. He touched the canted planes of her and remembered that she had fallen away from him when more than anything he had wanted her weight. And her hair swinging across his face and the taste of it. Years ago now, she had done away with all that and was now a man. The softness now was slabs of muscle and the organs—squinting at her on the beach in the distance, he had not been able to tell, it was just a dark patch, the organs were in the end a detail, but the act of changing had made the final huge difference. He had wanted her weight. And her hair swinging across him and the taste of it.

When he woke the pad was damp with sweat. He felt in the blackness for the table turned over on its side to conceal the far wall, and this reassuring flat plane of wood gave him back the present so he did not have to think about the past. But he remembered the rasping from above and the falling cold metal and knew how much they hated what was happening to them out in the lagoon.

She came again and lay on him as he felt the towering weight of water above him, wondered what it was like to live in a layered element with a boundary above you, a place to go and stare out rose up leaping out of the bottom of the World with shapes moving in the thin stuff above the water, clouds, hovering facts that meant there were at least two elements in the world, the first recognition of material you could handle made the tools we knew that in time could be used the clouds open, we can see lights, all the time struggling to reach up onto the land, where things were dry always and more science was possible, made the fire-hardened sand and you looked still upward, saw and studied stars, as we cupped the light and so knew the distant origin of stones falling into the World. They had been scooped up into false World—a ship?—and carried away. To survive a many-year voyage inside an automatic machine required strong social organization, when the animals that are not alive but swallow— some kind of robot hunter?—took them far from their home seas and in the long years began to change them, upsetting their mating and birthing times, sour water, changing the newborn, their song goes away from us, killing many, until finally there were fresh streams and they swam weakly into a new ocean, alien like our World but not out World, their youth spreading out and behaving strangely, attacking ships, when they should be taking part in an ancient genetically ordained hunt of large surface animals. In their home oceans the hunt triggered the going-to-land, but on Earth a grotesque version of it ran on, driving ships from the sea, and the youth now were afflicted with sores, while their elders, the Skimmers, tried to make sense of their chaos and despair. They had cleared the area near this island we drive the youth away, the act chews us but does not finish us but now it was up to humans, not humans in ships we find you in the skins you love we cannot sing to you but on this island and perhaps the Skimmers would speak only with humans who were alone your kind cannot hear unless you are one but the Skimmers were fading, they could not protect the island forever they may be chewed by you but there are many many of them and Warren knew their despair at the motorboats in the lagoon, a sign to the Skimmers that the blind, dumb kind of humans had returned, men who would not know enough, who could not stop the Swarmers from attacking they ache now for the skins-that-sink any more than they had before they are madness they are coming and they chew you others last.

He rolled over and over, smacking against the wall, and woke up. He reached for his wife but she was gone. He had the new thoughts, he understood more, yes—but in the chill before dawn he drew himself up into a tight little ball, seeking sleep again, for in the dream he had been happier than he could remember ever being.

Before dawn his cell rattled and a booming rolled down from the sky. He woke and looked out the windows through the heavy wire mesh. High up in the black, luminous things tumbled and exploded into auras of blue and crimson and then gutted into nothing. Distant hollow boomings came long after the lights were gone and then the sounds faded into the crashing on the reef.

In the morning the chinless soldier came again and took the tin dish that Warren had rubbed clean. The soldier did not like his job and he cuffed Warren twice to show him where to walk. First they went to the beach with the waste bucket, which had more in it now because Warren's body no longer absorbed almost everything he was fed. From the beach he watched the small motor ketches and cats that stayed near the shore while they laid something into the water, dropping boxes off the stern where they would lie on the bottom and, Warren was sure, report on the passing sounds and movements.

The guard took him north and inland, just out of view of the reef. Tseng was there with a crowd and they were all watching the green water from far back among the trees.

"See them?" Tseng said to Warren when he had worked his way through the group of men and women. Warren looked out past the brilliant white sand that stung the eyes and saw silver-blue forms leaping.

"What's— Why are they doing that?" he asked.

"We are returning their acoustic signals to them. As a kind of test."

"Not smart."

"Oh?" Tseng turned with interest. "Why?"

"I can't really tell you but—"

"It is a technique of progression. We play their songs back to them, appropriately modulated. We see how they react. The dolphins eventually did well with this approach."

"These aren't dolphins."

"So. Yes." Tseng seemed to lose interest in the splashing forms in the lagoon. He turned, hands placed neatly behind his back, and led Warren through the group of advisers around them. "But you must admit they are giving a kind of response."

Warren swore. "Would you talk to somebody if they kept poking you in the eye?"

"Not a good analogy."

"Yeah?"

"Still . . ." Tseng slowed, peering out through the brush and palm trees at the glistening water. "You are the only one who got the material about how they came here. Getting scooped up and going on a long voyage and then being dumped into the ocean—you got that. I had not heard it before."

"Uh. Huh."

"It does make a certain kind of sense. Fish like that—they might make printed messages, yes. They have shown they can put together our own wreckage and make a kind of electrostatic printing press—underwater, even. But to build a rocket? A ship that goes between stars? No."

"Somebody brought them."

"I am beginning to believe that. But why? To spread these diseases?"

"I dunno. Let me go out and—"

"Later, when we are more sure. Yes, then. But tomorrow we have more tests."

"Have you counted the number of them out there?"

"No. They are hard to keep track of. I—"

"There are a lot less of 'em now. I can see. You know what happens when you drive them away?"

"Warren, you will get your turn." Tseng put a restraining hand on his sleeve. "I know you have had a hard time here and on that raft, but believe me, we are able to—"

Gijan approached, carrying some pieces of paper. He rattled off something in Chinese and Tseng nodded. "I am afraid we are being interrupted once more. Those incidents last night—you saw them?—have involved us, a research party, in—Well, the Americans have been humiliated again. Their missiles we knocked down with ease."

"You're sure that stuff was theirs?"

"They are the ones complaining—isn't the conclusion obvious? I believe they and perhaps, too, their lackeys, the Japanese, have discovered how much progress we are making. They would very much like to turn the Swarmers and

their larva to their own nationalistic advantage. These messages"
—he waved the pack of them—"are more diplomatic notices.
The Japanese have given my government an ultimatum of
sorts. Ha! Imagine them—!" He snorted derisively.

"Think they have forces near here?" Warren asked.

"Improbable. Other powers, however . . ." He eyed Warren. "One of our men is missing."

"Oh?"

"We gather he sneaked off to go fishing last night. On
the beach—no one is stupid enough to go out on the water
alone, not even a trooper. He did not return."

"Huh. The Skimmers usually go out beyond the reef at
sundown. Shouldn't be anything in the lagoon at night.
Fishing's lousy then, anyway."

"A trooper would not know that. He perhaps thought to
get fresh meat. Understandable." Tseng frowned for a moment and then said formally, "I am sure even you understand
that this is part of a larger game. China does not, of course,
wish to use the Swarmers against other powers. Even if we
knew how to do so."

"I don't know anything about that."

"But I thought you were American."

"I don't think I said."

"I see. I think it is time to have Underofficer Gijan take
you back to your little room, then."

PART EIGHT NEAR ROSS 128

ONE

Nigel made his slow way along a rocky corridor. He preferred the low-g sections of the ship, where a stumble could be turned into a slight imbalance, rather than a resounding, bone-splintering crash. Crew members passed him easily, since he moved with deliberate caution. He recognized few of them now. He had spent most of the voyage from Isis working by himself, and the faces he saw no longer called up automatic names and associations. But one did catch his attention and he slowed, reached out—

"Nigel," the man said, "I didn't want it to come like this. I need a few weeks more of, of getting used to—"

Then it struck him. The similarities were too close, and yet—

"Carlotta!"

"Honestly, I was going to leave a letter for you and Nikka, but at the last minute, somehow I couldn't get it down right and—"

"You've, you've..." Carlotta had the same wiry build, but the softening curves were gone, replaced by slabs of muscle. The face was more chunky, but beneath the changes he had instantly seen the same bone structure. The muscles still gave the same slightly askew smile, the backward tilt to the head when she spoke.

"Let's get away from here. I can see you— Well, we need to talk." Her voice was a deeper version of the familiar Californian accent.

He followed her, confused and inarticulate. They sat in a bower overlooking Lurkey's brimming yellow vat. Carlotta spoke simply, slowly, detailing her reasons. He could not follow much of what she meant. When she began to speak of Nikka it became clearer to him.

243

"There is a thing between men and women," Carlotta said. "Not deeper, maybe, but certainly different from the relationship of women to each other, no matter how hard you try to make it—" She stopped. "I'm not getting through, am I?"

"I . . . You seem to be saying, indirectly, that you've done this because of Nikka? That you're my rival, now?"

"Bad choice of words. But if you want it that way, then, yes. I always was."

"But you and me, we slept together—"

"So did Nikka and I."

"You understood . . . I mean, I knew, that was all right."

"Yes. But—"

"I've got nothing against it. Look, Ted Landon's been sleeping with some guy in BioEngineering for years, and it never undermined his position. Nobody gives a damn anymore."

"You're saying that's okay, but what I've just done—"

"That's different."

"I knew you wouldn't—"

"How could you expect me to—"

"Wait. Just wait, Nigel. Look, on a long expedition like this, what's the point of being a woman? Having kids takes too much time, and anyway shipboard population shouldn't be increased beyond—"

"Theoretical reasons."

"Okay. I want to be in charge of, of a relationship. Not just helpful and supportive. And I wanted to *try* it. See what being a man—"

"Ummmm."

"That damned 'ummmm' of yours! Sitting back, judging—a very male noise, Nigel. Well, *I* want to make that noise, too." He made a sound halfway between a murmur and a grunt.

Nigel smiled slightly. "Carlotta, there's more to—"

"Carlos."

Something in the tone of the word made Nigel stiffen. "If you're going to come between Nikka and me, I—"

"I wasn't between you before?"

"Not this way, not—"

"Not as a 'rival,' as you so charmingly put it?"

"You're twisting what I say."

"Not as much as you think, what you *really* think."

Nigel said coldly, "That remains—"

"Notice how much of a confrontation this has turned into? Two men, not giving an inch."

"Why should I give—"

"You don't have to. I'm not changing everything. We'll still have a loose triangle. My relationship with Nikka will be different, but there's no reason—"

"No. I don't like it."

"I want to, to face the world with a new persona. Try out this heavy, bulky body. You have no idea how it *is*." Carlos rolled his thick shoulder muscles experimentally.

Despite himself, Nigel asked, "How different... is it?"

Carlos smiled in a friendly way. "Very."

Carlos began to see Nikka, but never in Nigel's company. Nikka found Carlos attractive, and Nigel could find no reason why he should object to her using the privileges they had always accorded each other. Their relationship had never been completely binding, after all. But the theoretical perspective did nothing to alter his deeply smoldering feelings of anger and, yes, envy. Carlos was younger and more vibrant, that was part of his appeal. He easily slipped into the fast pace of preparations for exploring the Ross system. Nigel spent time on the analysis net, but if anything it made him more withdrawn.

He spoke with Nikka about it. To her the facts were plain and, in the light of medicosurgery, unexceptional. Freedom to alter one's sex was as basic as any other right. Nigel could accept this theoretically, but he came to an abrupt halt at the specific case of Carlos. There was something to the entire issue that set his teeth on edge, something beyond simple rivalry, and yet he could not get a sure grip on it. When he spoke his throat seemed to get tight, his voice dry and scratchy.

It was confusing to him, particularly since no one else, even Nikka, appeared to take the emergence of Carlos a more than a passing, mildly interesting bit of gossip. It cropped up in conversation among their friends for a week or so, and then vanished in the general hubbub about Ross 128.

TWO

It's a pretty faint little bugger, we can hardly make out any of its planets in the optical

Well down in the infrared I'm picking up plenty from the two terrestrial-sized planets looks like a high albedo on both of 'em

Wish we had a decent-sized star to reconnoiter this damn one's small as Ra an' got a lotta flares on it give a look at 'at corona big splotches all over it

Bound to be variable, all the small stars are, so according to theory those terrestrials'll have big swings in the weather

Doesn't look good for a stable biosphere on those

Outer planets all 'bout Saturn-sized lotsa moons and two rings, some asteroids between those two, looks like it's a pretty standard pattern

Why the Isis Watcher would beam a signal to this dead place I dunno maybe a mistake, huh Nigel?

Wait until the returns are in

Got an image here yeah give a look that first terrestrial's got no atmosphere, high albedo, must be bare rock

You got those IRs on the second yet I know there's a malf in that sensor but we been waitin' damn long time

Comin' in now looks like mebbe 178 degrees kelvin, pretty cold, but we expected that with a pip-squeak sun to warm it, I sure don't pick up much else

Some carbon dioxide, little ammonia—maybe a lot of ice an' snow

Bring the right scope down some, that reflectivity

it's jumpin' all over when I put it on tight beam, must mean there's plenty of reflectin' surfaces, ice fields I bet

No sign of bioactivity in that atmosphere dull as dishwater

The grav-lens told us it looked jolly crappy, no surprise there

Goddamn all this way an' nothin' but junk

We knew all along with an M star like this it was rather like expecting roses in a jam jar to look for a biosphere

Cold as a hoor's tit an' we're years from anythin' interestin' even if we had the juice to get there

Ted we haven't lost all our thrust we could boost back up, just swing through the Ross system and head on out

I like 'at we could pick up couple months on gettin' back up to near-light speed 'stead of wallowin' round in this icebox

Better hurry up on it if we're gonna do it got a critical transition comin' up in the reaction engines Ted

Bloody hell we're not done with recon yet

Betcher butt there won't be nothin' to see

Nothing alive that's for sure

Scrub it I say

We need a vote 'a the whole ship to do 'at

Na, rule is section leaders can decide in a pinch an' this sure as hell is one

Janet send in a formal request from ExoBio if it's your judgment that there're no life sites here

Alex you're in the net still—aren't you?—Alex? —he isn't repped in

So skip him there's no time

No I can't make a decision—with Section leaders' consent of course—until I've heard from Alex

The big radio dishes aren't fully deployed yet I don't see

Ted this is Alex—sorry, we had a resolution problem on aft antenna but I've got the outer part of the Ross system mapped now, the big gas giants and there's something there with a lot of metal in it

Step up the gain I need more detail

Ted this is Nigel it's just not on to cancel this early

Christ don't listen to him this is ExoBio Ted look he's just tryin' to stretch out the encounter time to prove out this theory of his that nobody believes anyway an' this's the last hurrah anyway for him I say we boost soon's Alex

Yeah we can pick up rest of the data on the flyout

We got a good fraction of the minimum already

I don't give a sweet shit about minimum performance we're facing years of voyage Christ what's a few more months

Spend the time in Slots Nigel do you good

Give it a rest, eh? Ted, I appeal to you, don't

Gentlemen we got maybe ten minutes to decide, tops, or I got to shut the drive down

Christ Alex can you see anymore?

I'm getting some kind of metal on one of the gas giant moons that's all I can say right now looks like very bright in the radio reflectivity but that's all I can say

Section leaders this is Ted I'm reviewing ExoBio's request you people got any further input shoot it in now

Y'know it's a good idea to keep the reaction goin' just in case I mean the biggest malf probability is in the start-up phase

Yeah keep that in mind Ted we got risk every time we shut down

Look—damn!—we can't make a balls-up of this because of some sodding engineering constraint

Quiet Nigel—look, any more input before I

Yeah shut up the old crock and get us out of this pisshole

Seems to me it's pretty clear we seen plenty systems like this already from the probes

The grav-lens told us most of this already, point is to look closer—

Okay this is Ted after reviewing the systems board I can see the logic of picking up some time on our outbound

Alex is there any new

Throw in the towel Nigel for Chrissake

Hey I've lost the reflection

What's 'at?

No radio reflection at all from that moon now, just gone out

Check for detuning of the antenna Alex that's pro'bly it

No I'm still bringing in good radio images of the gas giant, no degrading of the system—I'd say the thing's just plain gone

Musta been a ghost image jest forget it

No possibility of that, I had it dead for sure, big as your mouth 'n' twice as wide, even got a spectrum 'fore it vanished

How fast is that moon spining Alex?

Lessee, nothin' much—no, too slow, it's tide-locked, that can't explain it

Then it was something in orbit around the Moon, that's the only way it could go out that fast. It simply fell below the horizon from our angle of view

Possible I guess but

Possible hell you think of something else

Well ah I

Ted you've got to let us have a look at whatever that was

Hell he does! We don' have to do anything unless a majority

No time for that

Damn—look, this is Ted—I'm asking for a quick vote

Don't give bugger all for a vote this is a scientific issue man not a

Alex here look I think he's got you there Ted our mandate is to study not just survey and could be the thing did drop out of sight which makes it a damned funny configuration in its own right, never mind if it's an artifact or not

Listen, we skip this radio blip, we can pick up

months, *not have to worry about the drive start-up
routine*

*Yeah, who wants to be the one goes in there
an' scrapes the throat walls while rest you guys are
playin' astronomer*

*Quiet look this is Ted and I—well, the direc-
tives don't leave me much choice*

Damn

We've got to take a look at that site

Alex this turns out to be a screw-up I'm gonna

*And I want a rendezvous orbit near that gas
giant*

Bang on that's it

Yeah

THREE

Rain had brought out the scents of the gardens—loquats,
crisp grains, roots, fresh-turned earth, blending and subduing
them. Nigel paused in his creaking labors and looked toward
the nose of the ship, where the life sphere tapered into a bare
point. It was like peering into the underside of a silagree of
stone, an inverted spire spun by some huge spider.

He stretched to ease his back muscles. *Ah.* He could
barely manage an hour of this labor now. He told Nikka it was
for the appearance of the thing, to defuse comments about his
general incompetence at things physical, to derail a close
inspection of his medical situation. But in fact he liked this
turning of the soil, this $6CO_2 + 6H_2O$, in turn giving
forth starchy $C_6H_{12}O_6$ + oxygen to burn anew, onboard as it
is in heaven. With the drive off there was no ready ultraviolet for the engineers to step down into the optical region,
so they had gone back to using phosphors strung along
the zero-g axis. These luminous ropes gave off a harsh glare
he found unpleasant, but the plants grew well; a leaf is
indifferent to where it gets its photons.

Lancer was taking a long loop through the Ross 128

system, coming around to rendezvous with the gas giant and its interesting moon. He preferred to pass the time away from the clatter of the Operating Net.

He bent back to plucking tomatoes free of their vines. To his mind the prime virtue of artificial biospheres was the lack of weeds, for otherwise it'd be a sore job to—

"I could hear the grunting from a hundred meters away," Ted Landon said.

Nigel straightened as quickly as he could without wincing, and smiled. "Like to work up a sweat."

"The fellas missed you on the net this morning."

"Figured you could do without my mumbling."

"Latest scans on that moon came in."

"Really?"

"Standard gas giant satellite. Funny purple coloring, some ice tectonics making ridges. Heavily cratered, too."

"Like Ganymede." He did not mention that he'd tapped into the map subroutines and gotten the drift direct, some hours before the net did.

"Yeah, looks that way. You were right about the asteroid orbiting it, though."

Nigel kept harvesting tomatoes. Ted squatted and pulled a few ripe ones. "Big durosteel hull on one side of it," he said casually.

"A Watcher, then."

"Looks like it. Kind of gives the fork to Walmsley's Rule."

"Ummm. A Watcher, yet not a prayer that this moon was ever a life site?"

"Going to lower your stock on the net. First clear case we get to check your rule, it fails."

"Glad I wasn't on the net, then."

"Yeah."

"Rather like being at a posh reception and finding you've caught your cock in your zip."

Ted laughed.

"It's a case worth studying, though, eh?"

Ted straightened and studied a tomato reflectively. "That's not what I came about." He looked soberly at Nigel.

"Oh?" Nigel stood up, too, glad that they had at last gotten through the opening moves.

"Carlos tells me you're taking this thing of his pretty hard."

"Perhaps for Americans it's easier. Priests of high tech, no matter where it leads, and all that."

"Think you're overdoing it, maybe?"

"Possibly." It was always best to leave some area of uncertainty, for later compromise once the man had made his point.

"You're not the first ever faced this, y'know."

"True."

"Think I'd like to see you try some of the therapy environments. We got some fresh ones on tightbeam from Earthside, just last year."

"Well," Nigel said brightly, "that seems quite possible."

"Not just possible," Ted said quietly, putting weight on each word. "You know I don't like to do more than make suggestions, but the numerical sociometric people say this kind of thing can get out of hand."

"I scarcely think—"

"I've cleared a spot for you." Ted smiled broadly. "Can't have our number one citizen waiting, huh?"

Nigel made himself smile, too. "Quite so."

Ted clapped him on the back. "C'mon, have a drink."

"I should finish up—"

"Forget it. You've already put in your hour."

Nigel smiled wryly. So Ted kept track of that, too. "Quite so."

Nigel allowed himself to be sealed into the sum-sense pod. He had tried to argue them out of the medical sensors and transducers, but the attendants cited his age as cause for taking precautions. Therapy sessions were confidential, he knew, so after thinking it over he decided the medical data would do him no harm. They merely wanted to ensure that he did not suffer overstimulation.

He felt himself floating, free of sensation. This would take only a few hours, and then he could be back working. He felt the splice-ins activate, tapping directly into the sensory zones of his cerebrum. He fell—faster, faster, into something far below—

—Sitting. Sitting in a wicker chair. A sluggishness filled him. Added weight, a paunch at his middle, clothes tight. An itch on the right thigh. Gradually the room filled in, emerging from a fog.

Glazed glass walls, tiles, a ceramic clatter as waiters removed plates from nearby tables. Pale yellow light. Garlic butter taste in his mouth. A slick, imitation-elegant tablecloth under his left palm. Background murmur of conversation. Humidity adding weight to each breath he took. A woman across the table, attractive, talking (he suddenly realized) to him—

"We're not *doing* anything," Helen said.

"We've seen a lot," her husband murmured defensively.

"The Berkeley ruins, the Monument of Bones, the arroyos," she said. "Then we have dinner and go to bed. That's all. And the bed part is no great attraction, is it?"

"Just last night we went to Casa Sigma—"

"If you weren't with *me* you'd find some, you know, places."

Robert had to admit this was true. He pretended to concentrate on draining the last of his drink and studied her expression through slitted eyes. She had made her hair blue and rather longer than usual today and the soft moonlight gave it a lush cast. He did not like it very much. She had tuned her skin to a fashionable pallor for the evening, but here in sun-baked California it was unconvincing because one knew it had to be artificial. On the other hand, perhaps that was largely immaterial these days. The thin lines of irritation around her mouth set the tone of her whole expression. There seemed to be little she could do about that. An hour after a facial tuning they returned, as deep as before.

"Before we came on this trip you said we would take a spice bath."

"Not here, Helen. It's illegal. Wait until Japan."

"There must be, well, *places* here."

"Filthy ones, yes. The Americans would stare at us. Especially at you. They don't take women to them here. The Americans are rigid. It's comic, I know, but—"

"You're the rigid one."

He played his hole card. "Those spots are full of insects. The Americans don't mind them."

She blinked. "If I was alone in as exotic a place as this you can be sure I'd go to all sorts of these spots."

"The motorbike dances . . ."

She scoffed. "Clumsy. Those are for tourists."

He began to notice his anger. He had spent a good deal of money to bring her along on this business trip. He had left her behind so often before. Lately his conscience had begun to bother him about it. Decades before, their marriage had been the central fact in his life, a fulfillment. Those feelings had ebbed away. He had gotten caught up in the raw competitive world of men. And he had relished that sense of rasping conflict, of heady victories after strenuous effort.

Still, he felt a duty to her. But traveling with a woman you don't love was proving worse than living with her.

He finished his drink and slammed the glass down on the marble tabletop. "My," she said archly.

He stood up. His chair scraped harshly and a waiter, startled, came quickly. Robert waved the man away. "All right," he said loudly. "I'll find something. Your kind of *place*." He spat out the last word.

Robert left the ornamented hotel and walked down Ashby. He was feeling warm from the meal or from the anger and he moved quickly. He did not noticed the thin man who came up alongside him and said in an oily way, "Something?"

Robert stopped. "I've got my own woman," was all he could immediately think to say.

"An appetizer, then?"

"What?"

"A boy?"

Strong, confusing emotions swept through him. He pushed the man aside and made a rough, incoherent noise.

He walked away swiftly, his steps bringing a harsh slap from the damp paving stones. He went two blocks without seeing the neon jumble around him or noting the sleazy shops.

Someone tapped him on the shoulder. He turned and saw the same gaunt man, this time standing at a safe distance. There was a look of bland, wise confidence on the man's face.

"Senso?" he asked.

Robert paused and was surprised to find he had no anger left. The walking had leached it from him.

"How much?"

With the taxi and the thin man as guide it came to over a thousand yen. Robert knew the man had hiked the price over the usual street value, from the look on his face, but that did not matter. This would provide a simple way to stop Helen's prattle about "places" and it might even be enjoyable. Better than the real thing had been for quite a long while, at least. He turned back to fetch Helen.

The three of them took a route north into Richmond, over a slimy canal crusted with salt from the deadlands to the north. The taxi wheezed through twisting streets and stopped outside a sprawling bungalow with dim orange lights outside. "Perfectly ghastly," Robert muttered to himself, but Helen did not reply.

They went up creaking wooden stairs and beneath a punctured solar heating panel that had slid halfway off the roof. "Is this a commercial one?" Helen asked and reached for his arm.

"Of course not," he said stiffly, pulling away from her. "It's illegal here."

They clumped across linoleum floors and through two empty rooms. The guide slipped a key into a doorplate and a wall swung free. This let them into a red-lit room with two glossy, molded chairs perched among a tangle of electronics. A bored-looking attendant stood up from a couch where he had been watching a 3-D. He helped the two of them into the chairs. The equipment looked reasonably new. It had the comfortable cerebral lead-ins Robert had seen in the European advertisements. His opinion of the place rose. Helen made a fuss about getting the attachments settled at her neck and wrists and then quieted down for the first run.

The first was a warm-up, an erotic hors d'oeuvre. A middle-aged man met a younger woman in a restaurant. After a few perfunctory bits of social back-and-forth, they went to her apartment. The senso consisted of extensive foreplay and some fantasizing, though the graphic parts were convincing and strong. He felt the languid satin rub of the woman's skin, the delicious pull of young muscles, the musky smell, a red lust building in the young man. Robert liked the piece overall, though the woman's hairdo reminded him of someone he knew and that rather spoiled the associations for him. He guessed that their guide had picked this particular one because the man rather resembled himself, and using a younger woman would cater to the self-images of both parties. He smiled at the calculation.

When it was over he found himself panting slightly and said, "Adequate," as though he were experienced at this.

"And that's all? Not very—"

"No, no, the entrée comes next."

It started. The scene was an old-fashioned street at dusk. A man approached a woman waiting for a bus. The woman wore rather pretty clothes and a head ornament, three decades out of date, which shadowed her face. There was little conversation. Much was conveyed by the man's swagger, the woman's jutting hip, a sultry exchange of glances. In the wan traces of sunset their faces were shrouded and a streetlamp caught only suggestive nuances of their expressions, setting a tone of gathering erotic energy.

She responded to a tilt of his head and a murmured invitation. Robert enjoyed this sultry, casual courting, liked the feel of a slim, muscled body. The man had a fine-honed tension running through him, that tightness and pressure which ebbs with age.

They walked a short distance to his apartment. It was atmospheric and suited to the swarthy, intimidating manner of the man. He undressed first, revealing a barrel chest and bushy, black body hair. The arrangement of the lighting cast the woman in a mysterious way as she reclined. There was a hovering excitement in her manner.

The man looked in a full-length mirror nearby. This was to establish identification with the character, but seeing the face full on brought a sudden jolt of recognition to Robert. The hooded look of the man, that frayed lounge in the corner, a familiar French watercolor near the mirror—

The man began some foreplay between the woman's legs and the humid feel of the bed came through to Robert as he struggled with memories.

My. The thought from Susan, overriding the senso input, startled him. The man was having his effect.

Too raw for me, he thought strongly, hoping to get through the rush of sensation that he could feel between them. *I'd like to break it off.*

The man moved adroitly with practiced skill. Yes, Robert thought to himself, it was skill, technique. Mere technique. At the time he had thought it was a passion as full and new as the woman's. He had not allowed for the fact that the barrel-chested man was six years older than she, and far more sophisticated.

No. I want to stay. Concentrate. It might help you, she finished dryly.

I really think—

No. If you break off the thing stops, doesn't it? And I want to go on.

Robert knew he could rip the connections away, end this now. He reached for the leads, seized one, and stopped. Something in him wanted this to happen. Old memories stirred.

The man embraced the languid woman and his hands moved expertly over her. The woman—a girl, really—rolled to the side at his command. Her movements had a fresh quality to them despite the artificial situation. To fix Helen's role identification, she looked at herself in the mirror.

He felt Helen's quick flash of surprise.

It's—she's—you!

Was me. Over thirty years ago. The girl stroked the dark, muscular body and Robert caught the tremor of excitement that leaped in Manuel, the man.

But I—you never told me—all these—

I met you long after.

The face, your face—even with the age, and the changes, I can see it is you.

I changed as little as possible. Redistributed body weight, altered hormones—

All this time—

Yes.

You could have told me—

No. My, my change had to be complete. No looking back.

Then that's why you couldn't have children. And I thought—

Yes.

My God, I don't think I can—

But the surge of emotion that came into her cut off the words. Robert felt the same tidal rhythm grasp him and did not fight against it. The heat and harsh cries of decades before seized them both. It went on for unendurably long moments bringing him to a fevered, shuttering, simulated climax.

In the silence afterward the images dwindled, the tingling sensations drained away. They were left, two people in the glossy chairs, the cables dangling from them.

They said nothing as Robert paid off the man and got into the taxi for the hotel.

"It's revolting," Helen said. "To learn this way..."

"The practice is common now."

"Not among the people we know, not—" She stopped.

"I had to conceal it. I moved away afterward, to Chile, where no one knew I had the Change."

"What, what was your name?"

"Susan."

"I see," she said stiffly.

What did she expect, he thought bitterly. That I changed Roberta to Robert, like some cheap joke?

"So you were the sort of woman who makes things like that senso."

"For him, yes, I was."

"He was repulsive."

"He was hypnotic. I see that now."

"He must have been, to make you do degrading things like—"

"Is it more degrading to do them, or to need their help?"

Her face tightened and he regretted saying it. She said bitterly, "*I'm* not the one who needs help, remember. And no wonder—you're not really what everyone's thought, are you?"

He ignored her tone. "I've done well enough. You had no complaints at the beginning, as I remember."

She sat silently. The taxi whistled through dimly lit streets. "You've betrayed me."

"It all happened long before I met you."

"If I'd known you were so, so unbalanced as—"

"It was a decision I made. I had to."

"For what? That man must have—"

"He—" Robert stopped himself. "I loved him."

"What became of him, then?"

"He went away. Left me."

"I'm not surprised. Any woman who would—" She shuddered, and conflicting emotions flickered across her face.

The taxi drew up to the hotel. Beggars came limping out of the shadows, calling. Robert brushed them away. The two walked to their room without a word. Their footsteps echoed hollowly in the old tile corridors. Inside, he took off his coat and noticed that his heart was pounding.

She turned to him decisively. "I want to, to know what it was like. Why you—"

He cut her off with, "The process was crude then. Manuel had left me. I thought then that he had fallen out of love with me, but looking back, feeling that tonight—"

"Yes?"

"I don't know. Maybe he had just gotten tired of me."

"But something made you. . ."

"Yes. It's all gotten so distant now, I can't be sure of what I felt. It's as though there's a fog between me and that senso."

"You didn't recognize it until . . . ?"

"No, I didn't. I went through two years of drugs, depression, therapy, tap-ins. I forgot so much. The strains on my body—"

"I still don't—maybe that man, he was so oily, he must have done things to you, to make you want to change—"

Robert shook his head. He turned abruptly and went into the bathroom. He stayed there a long time, taking a shower and letting the hot water wash away the evening and turn his skin pink. He looked down at himself and thought of what the years had done to the muscles and skin. This body felt heavy, bulky, and oddly like a machine. He wondered what it would have been like if that dimly remembered girl had not . . .

When he returned to the bedroom the lights were out. He went to the bed slowly, uncertain, and heard the crisp rustle of sheets.

"Come here," she said.

She reached for him. "You . . . you have been a good man to me." A tentative touch. "I suppose I can't . . . blame you for a past you had . . . erased, even before we . . ."

He kissed her. She murmured, "You were weaker then, you know. I thought it was just being young, inexperienced. But you got strong, in the years afterward. I was surprised, I remember."

He saw where she was headed and said, "Because of you."

And it was true. She was starting to realize that it was she, and the glorious first years of their marriage, that had made him truly into a man. And this realization was pulling her free of her confused swirl of emotions.

She tried the things she had done so many times before. To his surprise there was some response. The deep feelings of the senso had perhaps reached into him and found some reservoir.

A moist heat grew rapidly in her and he went along, making the old moves he knew would do the job. She quickened further. Some part of him kept up a lukewarm interest, enough to make the performance convincing. She gasped, and gasped again. Something in tonight had made her swirl of emotions condense into this act, some titillation had come out of the senso and the shock. Now she responded to him as if he were some exotic thing.

Robert suddenly remembered Manuel. *God, I hope he's dead now.* It would be better if the possibility of him was gone from life forever. The therapy had smothered and blotted out Manuel. The therapists had been very sure that was for the best.

Helen moved energetically under him, trying to provoke a passion he could no longer feel. *Christ*, he thought. He felt a new empathy for her, for what help she would find in this.

Suddenly he sensed himself above the tangled bodies that labored in the bed. He saw the passion from a high but not disparaging perspective, a double vision of himself. It was like the multiple layers of sensation one had in the senso, the sense of being several people at once. But stranger, and deeper.

He saw that the simple event of coupling was surrounded with an aura, a different halo of associations for each sex. An act of essential self-definition. It truly was difficult to express how profound the difference was.

A surge came in him and he thought again of Manuel. That bright, trusting girl back there—she had wanted Manuel so badly. And when he left, the only way to hold on to him was to try, in a strange way, to flee from herself, and become what she wanted to hold.

Helen groaned and clutched at him, as if for shelter in this private storm, and gave an abrupt, piercing cry. He stroked her and wept and for the first time in many years he saw truly again, in Helen and in that girl of long ago, the other side of a wide mute river he could never cross again.

FOUR

Nigel shivered. The drama had been intense, close, more intimate than anything artificial he had ever experienced.

They had obviously selected a drama tuned to his age, his sex—and then pulled the rug from under him, jolted his expectations.

He wasn't that rather tired, dulled man, and yet, yet—there was something . . . Even the man's dialogue was slightly British, like one who had lived abroad for decades, just as Nigel had. Yes, it was a damned finely tuned bit of business. And not at all amusing.

But amusement was not the aim. With a blurring sense of movement everything shifted, melted, reformed—

And he was the gaunt little man, spotting his mark on the dingy Berkeley street. Nigel felt himself swept along as he approached the heavyset, distracted figure and said, "Something?"

From there the drama proceeded as before, giving Nigel a rather distant view of the events, letting emotions seep away—

Another swirling, blurred transition. Nigel became Helen.

"We're not *doing* anything," he said, and felt the rising waspish irritation. He knew what was coming and yet the emotions that came through from the fictional Helen moved him. Events carried him forward. Robert simmered in his tight-faced anger, the senso started, Helen's shock lanced through him—

And he saw that it was like his own, with Carlos. But worse. It bit deeply. There was betrayal with it, a hollow feeling of the ground opening under Helen. She had struggled to see her own past clearly. Everything she had felt, each day, now meant something different. This taciturn stranger next to her in the slick chair knew everything about her but had been hiding himself—*herself*—every day of their lives. Helen had stroked him, receive him into herself, accepted and savored his maleness, all without a thought—

Helen struggled bleakly, trying to find a hold. She would have to begin again, learn to accept Robert as something both more and less than she had ever thought, make herself—

Nigel tore himself away from the churn of emotions. He thumbed ESCAPE and the tangled world dropped away.

They peeled the pod back and crisp light flooded in. He wriggled out. The attendants smiled professionally. He ignored their warm, well-modulated voices, their polite questions. He wrapped himself snugly in a blue terry-cloth robe and started toward the dressing room.

"Wait! Your consultation—"

"Not having any."

"It's part of the—"

"Not mandatory, is it?"

"No, but we—"

"Thought so. I don't have to talk to you sods and I frigging well don't intend to."

"It will go on the record," the woman said as a warning.

"Dear me. Pity."

"Isn't it a little obvious to be so hostile to analysis?"

Nigel hesitated, knowing he should be civil to this person, even if he was shaken. He teetered on the brink, feeling the weight of her expectations, how the society of the ship would evaluate this, and in the long gliding moment felt a sureness come into himself that had been there before, but that he had lost years before. "Fuck off," he said precisely.

"How did it go?" Nikka asked.

He lay back, letting their jury-rigged machine minister to him. It burbled and sucked and the pumps rattled, but it worked. He had actually come to feel a certain affection for the damned thing. "Hated it."

She sighed. "That will not put you further into the good graces of—"

"I know, I know."

"You saw the maps of that moon? Craters everywhere. They're calling it Pocks. No official name yet."

"Appropriate. Think you can wangle some surface duty?"

"What surface duty?" She sat up. "The net hasn't even discussed—"

"I found a system interface into the engine section. They're lower than they thought on plain old deuterium inventory. Before we ignite the drive again, they'll need to store up some."

"From the moon, uh, Pocks."

"Right."

FIVE

Look man Pocks is riddled jess same as Europa
an' Callisto an' the resta the Jovian moons, dozens
like this, seen one you seen 'em all

Some interestin' ice flows see there that es-
caprment methane ice maybe

Might as well send down some scientific personnel with the mining crew

Could take some deep borings, even find a
vent for access to deeper, get a good metal abundance
measurement, make the ExoGeo boys Earthside happy

Trouble is the ice is all carbon dioxide, methane, ammonia, not much water

We'd do better to send down that submersible gear

What're you sayin' use that subsurface stuff

Sure it works on Ganymede we brought it
along for just exactly this kind of case

That ice skin is, what, fifteen klicks thick

There's cracks and vents we already spotted
them on recon

Sure, work your way down those, subs will
take that pressure easy remember the gravity's less
than a fifth g

Penetrate the ice surface Christ

I dunno strip mining is safer and you can lift off
if anything goes wrong

Sure but it takes three times the work crew and
you have to hunt around for veins of water

Yeah the submarines are better, they can scoop
up lots, and it's pure water, no impurities from
meteorites

Ted I'll recommend that if you want somethin'
official

I have no problem with that no need to be so

formal Bob we'll be sending a pretty big team I want that deuterium out fast

No reason to wait aroun' with that Watcher close by

If I might butt in I must say I still don't like mining Pocks with that Watcher in range, bloody risky

No easy alternative as we decided yesterday, where've you been Nigel, there's no other moon here that has the right topography—rest of 'em are rocks

Whole system's bone-dry must have all the light elements locked up in the gas giants

Pocks is a typical snowball moon, fraction over two thousand klicks radius, ninety percent slush inside with an ice crust

Lot like Ganymede only more craters lot of crustal movement too

Nigel you been out of the loop to long shoot him the recap on that probe we sent to the Watcher

What! You poked your nose into—

Don't get all fluffed up now look at it this way we were testing Walmsley's Rule, giving it a last chance

It failed too you'll notice

Lookit the robot probe walked all over the Watcher, banged on the hull, took a sample—nothing special, gamma-hardened alloy—tried radio and IR and

Found bunch of old sensors and stuff on the surface dead as can be

Burrowed inside maybe twenty meters all the circuits inactive, no acoustic pattern, no sign of anything working

Funny equipment pretty simpleminded circuits looked to me all crapped out it's old as hell too

Still that doesn't mean you sods didn't awaken something—

Nigel this is Ted, we've got work to do here and you can get all this on recap I'd advise you drop off the net and come back when you

Sounds to me like he's pissed his Rule didn't work out

Not that's not it at all, I merely meant

Well hell Walmsley first place we try it your theory isn't worth a fart that moon's never had any life on it lookit those surveys no bioproducts on the surface no atmosphere just lots of ice and rock that's been pounded for billions of years

So that Watcher's not waiting for life there hell the thing probably ran out of gas explorin' this system an' went dead looks like a kinda crude low-velocity ship burning its own rock for reaction mass

Yeah a ham-fisted piece of tech you ask me

Take forever to get to the next star

Well if you've got sodding forever—

Face it Walmsley the Watchers aren't all the same they're leftover weapons or explorers no reason to think they're related to each other

Stuff in orbit lasts long time is all

There's to much evidence to ignore, my damned Rule aside—

No Nigel this is Ted now I'd like you to drop out of the net take a rest maybe look over the recon stuff file a report with us later if you want to say your piece but we can't be squabbling over theory when we have to do a big minimax calculation on the mining operation

I'll say

Very well Ted I'll do that but

Good now I want a touchdown to begin excavations within forty-eight hours Sheila get those submersibles in the surface landers I want backup crews all down the line too

Good-bye you lot

SIX

He had never meant for him and Nikka and Carlotta to choose up and play Nuclear Family, but the old times between them had called up a blood-rush swelling, as each slid over the others' love-slicked skin, gasping at the dazzling slides of fingers, seeking the sag of aging muscles without judgment, yielding to the jut of bone. He dimly recalled how furious it had been between them. Then came the cooling, time leaching away the weight of each other. Now the past ambitions unspoken surfaced, and Carlotta was smothered in apparatus.

Nigel gingerly unhooked himself from the machine. He sealed the cap on his leg vein input. The memories surfaced often now. He had regained a good deal of his old mental equilibrium, enough to permit the old hurts and joys to resurface. Whatever in him had learned to repress was now itself in retreat.

Nikka moved to help him up but he waved her away. "I'm feeling a lot better. Stronger."

"I'd still like you to rest more. You've been working in the gardens too much."

"No, just barely enough. I'm beginning to think this whole blood imbalance thing, the buildup of ruddy rogue cells and that rot—quite literally, rot—it's all been due to something from that injury in the damned fluxlife-cleaning job." He stretched, enjoying the delicious pop of his joints.

Nikka smiled tolerantly. As she opened her mouth to speak he saw in an instant her fatigue, pushed back beyond notice, silted up inside her by the currents of despair she must have suffered in these years of watching him slowly go dull and listless. The fretwork of lines near her eyes had deepened and turned downward. Her laugh was blunted now, seldom heard, weighted.

"Things are going to be better now," he said impulsively. "I'm sure I've beaten it."

"Yes," she said, and put her arms around him. "Yes."

He saw that she did not believe. She thought his words meant no more than the compulsive optimism of a man who knew deeply that he would die. "No, I want you to see it . . . see better. I *am* getting—"

A knock at the door. They went into the living room, closing the bedroom door to hide the medical machines. Nigel opened the door. He kept his face blank when he saw it was Carlos and Ted Landon. Carlos had been coming by regularly, but Nigel had decided it was best for the moment to be neither friendly nor hostile. Simple distance might be the best.

Carlos was nervous, sweating. He said abruptly, "Nigel, I told you it wouldn't last, that medmon dodge. While I was in the Slots a systems inventory turned up a glitch, where I'd covered for you. They just now unraveled it and—"

"I thought it was a good idea to bring along Carlos, so he could explain," Ted broke in smoothly. "He didn't rat on you." Nigel shrugged.

"I don't blame Carlos for this at all," Ted said with heavy seriousness. "He's been under pressure, as we all know. I do blame *you*, though." He tapped Nigel's chest. "You're going in for a full check. Now."

Nigel shrugged again. "Fair enough." He glanced at Nikka and saw she was thinking the same: With his blood newly filtered, he might pass.

Carlos said, "I'm sorry, but it had to . . ."

Nigel felt a surge of sympathy for the man. He patted Carlos tentatively on the shoulder. "Never mind. Forget all this old stuff, from before you went to the Slots." He wanted to suggest that it would be best to make a whole new life, forgetting himself and Nikka, but he saw that would be the wrong note to sound so soon.

He was naked, so Ted saw nothing unusual about his retiring to pull on some clothes. In the bathroom he drank a solution of antioxidants and other control agents, to mask the clear signature effects of the blood processing. When he returned Carlos was out of his mood and was explaining to Nikka that he had successfully applied for a job on the ground team on Pocks.

"Grunt work, sure, but it'll get me down on a planet again." He shifted heavily, still unused to the feel of the bulk of muscle, but eager to use it. Nikka seemed pleased. Nigel marveled at how she covered her anxiety so well. If they treated this all very matter-of-factly, and the tests weren't too probing, they might just bring it off.

"Come on," he said mildly, "I've got work to do. Bring on your needles."

Ted walked with him to the medical center. There was going to be a shipwide meeting later that day, over the net. Ted was distracted. He grudgingly gave up the information that the latest transmission from Earth was full of news. The gravitational telescope had surveyed two more planetary systems. Each had a terrestrial-sized world, and around each a Watcher orbited. That brought the count to nineteen terrestrial-type worlds discovered, fourteen with Watchers, out of thirty-seven star systems.

"Life turns up everywhere, I guess," Ted said. "But it commits suicide just as fast."

"Ummmm."

"They've got their hands full back there, with the ocean thing. Everything happens at once. They're not processing the planetary data fast, 'cause this Swarmer stuff is—"

"What stuff?"

"I'll announce it today. They're coming ashore. Killing people, somehow."

Nigel nodded, silent.

They put him into a kind of fuzzy sleepstate for the tests. He ignored them and focused on Ted's news. It was important to understand this event, there was a clue buried somewhere. But the sleep dragged him down.

SEVEN

When he woke up he was dead.

Utter blackness, total silence. Nothing.

No smells. There should be the clean, efficient scent of a medical center.

No background rustle of steps. No drone of air conditioning, no distant murmur of conversations, no jangle of a telephone.

He could not feel any press of his own weight. No cold table or starched sheets rubbed his skin.

They had disconnected all his external nerves.

He felt a rush of fear. Loss of senses. To do that required finding the major nerves as they wound up through the spine. Then a medical tech had to splice them out of the tangled knot at the back of the neck. Delicate work.

They were preparing him for the Sleepslots. Shutting him down this far meant he was going into semipermanent storage. Which meant he had failed the medmon exam, and badly.

But they never slotted you without telling you. Even critically ill people got to say good-bye, finish up details, prepare themselves if at all possible.

Which meant Ted had lied. The smooth, casual manner, bringing Carlos along to deflect Nigel's attention onto the other man—yes, that was his style. Avoid confrontation, then act decisively. With Walmsley's Rule disproved, his medical deception uncovered . . . a good time to swat Nigel's gadfly, bothersome buzzing.

The medmon had probably turned up some incriminating information, but that was certainly not enough to slot him without warning. No, it had to be a pretext—one he could contest only years later, Earthside.

He fought the rising confusion in his mind. He had to explore this, think.

Was he fully dead? He waited, letting his fear wash away.

Concentrate. Think of quietness, stillness . . .

Yes. *There.*

He felt a weak, regular thump that might be his heart.

Behind that, as though far away, came a slow, faint fluttering of lungs.

That was all. The body's internal nerves were thinly spread, he knew. They gave only vague, blunt senses. But there was enough to tell him that the basic functions were still plodding on.

There was a dim pressure that might be his bladder. He could pick up nothing specific from legs or arms.

He tried to move his head. Nothing. No feedback.

Open an eye? Only blackness.

Legs—he tried both, hoping that only the sensations were gone. He might be able to detect a leg moving by the change in pressure somewhere in his body.

No response. But if he could sense his bladder, he should have gotten something back from the shifting weight of a leg.

That meant his lower motor control was shut off.

Panic rose in him. It was a cold, brittle sensation. Normally this strong an emotion would bring deeper breathing, a heavier heartbeat, flexing muscles, a tingling urgency. He felt none of that. There was only a swirl of conflicting thoughts, a jittery forking in his mind like summer lightning. This was what it was like to be an analytical thing, a machine, a moving matrix of calculation, without chemical or glandular ties.

They weren't finished, or else he'd never have come awake again. Some technician had screwed up. Shut off a nerve center somewhere, using pinpoint interrupters, perhaps pinching one filament too many.

They worked at the big junction between brain and spinal cord, down at the base of the skull. It was like a big cable back there, and the techs found their way by feedback analysis. It was easy to get the microscopic nerve fibers mixed up. If the tech was working fast, looking forward to coffee break, he could reactivate the conscious cerebral functions and not notice it on the scope until later.

He had to do something.

The strange, cold panic seized him again. Adrenaline, left over from some earlier, deep physiological response? He was afraid now, but there was no answering chemical symphony of the body. His gland subsystems were shut down.

There was no way to tell how rapidly time passed. He counted heartbeats, but his pulse rate depended on so many factors—

Okay, then—how long did he have? He knew it took hours to shut down a nervous system, damp the lymphatic zones, leach the blood of residues. Hours. And the technicians would leave a lot of the job on automatic.

He noticed a faint background sensation of chill. It seemed to spread as he paid attention to it, filling his body, bringing a pleasant, mild quiet...a drifting...a slow slide toward sleep...

Deep within him, something said *no*.

He willed himself to think in the blackness and the creeping cold. The technicians always left a pathway to the outside, so if something went wrong the patient could signal. It was a precaution to take care of situations like this.

Eyebrows? He tried them, fled nothing.

Mouth? The same.

He made himself think of the steps necessary to form a

word. Constrict the throat. Force air out at a faster rate. Move the tongue and lips.

Nothing. No faint hum echoing in his sinus cavities to tell him that muscles worked, that breath strummed his vocal cords

The easiest slotting method was to simply shut down a whole section of the body. That must be what was happening. Right. His head was out, legs out. Feet gone, too. And genitals, he thought wryly, weren't under conscious control even at the best of times.

Arms, then. He tried the left. No answering shift of internal pressures. But how big would the effect be? He might be waving his hand straight up in the air, and never know it.

Try the right. Again, no way to tell if . . .

No, wait. A diffuse sense of something . . .

Try to remember which muscles to move. He had gone through life with instant feedback from every fiber, anchoring him in his body, every gesture suggesting the next. Now he had to analyze precisely.

How did he make his arm rise? Muscles contracted to pull on one side of the arm and shoulder. Others relaxed to let the arm swing. He tried it.

Was there an answering weight? Faint, too faint. Maybe his imagination.

The right arm could be jutting up, and he wouldn't know it. The attendants would see it, though, and patch into him, ask what was going on . . . unless they weren't around. Unless they had gone off for coffee, leaving the sagging old body to stage down gradually into long-term stasis, with the medmon checking to be sure nothing failed in the ancient carcass . . .

Suppose the arm worked. Even if somebody saw it, was that what he wanted? If they turned his head back on, what would he do? Demand his rights? Ted had undoubtedly disposed of that issue by now. The attendants were certainly under orders to slide him into a slot, no matter what he said. *For his own good, y'know.*

Despairing, he stopped his concentration, willed the muscles to go suddenly slack.

And was rewarded with an answering *thump*.

It had hit the table. It bloody well *worked*.

He waited. Nothing came to him in the blackness. No attendant came tapping in to correct the mistake.

He was probably alone. Where?

Not already in a slot, or else he wouldn't be able to think clearly. On a medmon slab, then.

He tried to remember the arrangement. The access terminals were on both sides, mirroring the body. So maybe, if it stretched, the right hand could reach half the input switchings.

He concentrated and brought the arm up again. The hand probably worked; it would've been too much trouble to disconnect it while the arm stayed live. Remembering carefully, he lowered the arm, rotating it—

A thump. Someone approaching? No, too close. The arm had fallen.

Balance was going to be hard. He practiced rotating the arm without raising it. No way to know if he was successful, but some moves seemed correct, familiar, while others did not. He worked without feedback, trying to summon up the exact sensation of turning the arm. Dipping it to the side, over the edge. Working the fingers.

He stopped. If he hit the wrong control he could turn off the arm. Without external nerves, there was no way to tell if he was doing the right thing.

Pure gamble. If he had been able to, Nigel would have shrugged. What the hell.

He stabbed with straightened fingers. Nothing.

He fumbled and somehow knew through dull patterns that his fingers were striking the side of the slab. The knowledge came from below, some kind of holistic sensation from the thin nerve nets deep inside him. The body could not be wholly cut up into pieces; information spread, and the mute kidneys and liver and intestines knew in some dim way what went on outside.

A wan answering pressure told him that his fingers had closed on something, were squeezing it. he made the fingers turn.

Nothing happened. Not a knob, then. A button?

He stabbed down. In his sinus cavities he felt slight jolts. He must be smacking the slab hard, to do that. With no feedback there was no way to judge force. He stabbed; a jolt. Again. *Again*—

A cold tremor ran up his right calf. Pain flooded in. His leg was in spasm. It jerked on the slab, striking the medmon. The sudden rush of sensations startled him. In the heady surge he could hardly tell pain from pleasure.

The leg banged on the slab like a crazed animal. His autonomic system was trying to maintain body temperature by muscle spasms, sucking the energy out of the sugar left in the tissues. A standard reaction; that was one reason why he was shut down.

But he had activated a neural web, that was the point. He stabbed blindly with his fingers again.

A welling coldness in his midsection. Again.

More cold, now in the right foot. Again.

A prickly sensation on his lips, on his cheeks. But not full senses; he could not feel his chest or arms. He started to press another button and then stopped, thinking.

So far he had been lucky. He was opening the sensory nets. Most of his right side was transmitting external data. His leg was jerking less now as he brought it under control.

But if he hit the shutdown button for his right arm next, he was finished. He would lie there helpless until the technicians came back.

Nigel worked the arm back onto the slab. He made it shift awkwardly across his chest. His motor control must extend into his upper chest and shoulders to let him do this, but without any input from there he did not know how much he could make work.

He willed the muscles to lurch to the left. A strange impression of tilting came into him. A tension somewhere. Muscles straining, locked, clenched and reaching, a stretching — More —

A warm hardness on his cheek. His nose pressed against it but he had no sense of smell. The slab top. He had rolled himself partway over.

He felt a gathering, diffuse weariness. The arm muscles were broadcasting to the surrounding body their agony, fed by the buildup of exhausted sugar-bearing molecules.

No time to rest. The muscles would just have to keep working. He willed the arm to reach over the left side of the slab. He could feel nothing, but now he could make no fatal mistake.

He punched down at random, searching. A spike of pain

shot through his left side. Behind it came biting cold. Slabs of muscle began shaking violently, sending rippling pain through his left side.

He stabbed down with fingers again. Light poured in on him. He had hit the optical nerve net. A gaudy, rich redness. He realized his eyes were still closed. He opened them. Yellow flooded in. He closed them against the glare and punched down again.

The crisp, chill hospital smell. Another stab.

Sound washed over him. A mechanical clanking, a distant buzz, the whir of air circulators. No voices.

He squinted. He was lying on a white slab, staring up at fluorescent lights. Now that he could see, he got back the rest of his nets quickly.

He reached up toward his neck—and his hand went the other way. He stopped it, moved the fingers tentatively. His arm was coming from above his head, reaching down . . . but that was impossible. He moved the other arm. It came into his vision the same way, from above.

Something was wrong with him. He closed his eyes. What could make . . . ?

He rolled over partway and looked around the medmon bay. The sign on the door leaped out at him. It was upside down. He reached out, clutched the edge of the slab. It was upside down, too.

That was it. When the eye took light and cast it on the retina, ordinary optics inverted the image. The retinal nerves filtered that signal and set it upright for the brain.

So the med tech had screwed that up, too. The retinal nerves weren't working right. That might be easy to fix, just move a fine-point fiber junction a fraction of a millimeter. But Nigel couldn't, didn't know how. He would have to manage.

Nigel began to fumble with the thicket of leads that snaked over his body. It was easier if he didn't look at what he was doing. He had to carefully disconnect the tap-ins at nerve nexus points. The big knot of them at the nape of his neck was hard to detach. It jerked free.

He felt a hot, diffuse pain from the region, spreading up into his skull. The nerves were exposed, sending scattershot impressions through the area, provoking spasms in the muscles.

He rolled over and studied the work table next to the slab. It was a jumble of connectors, microelectronics, and coils of nearly invisible wires. There was a patch that looked the right shape. He reached out for it and missed. His brain saw his arm moving up and corrected, always in the wrong direction.

It took three tries before he could override his own coordination. He snagged the patch and nearly dropped it. Carefully he brought it to his head. The floppy oval of wires fitted over the gaping hole at the back of his neck. He fiddled with it until it slid—*snick*—into place. The pain tapered off.

He sat up. Spasms shot through him. He gasped. Pain blossomed with every move. But he felt fully awake and deeply angry. He was in a deserted medical bay.

He studied the liquid-optical readouts on his medical monitor. The program profile was mostly numbers. He couldn't tilt his head far enough over to read the upside-down numbers. He worked on reading them directly. After a moment it wasn't so hard. The winking digital program profile told him that his shutdown was scheduled to take another fifty-seven minutes.

He got to his feet, shaky and light-headed. It was good to have his own chemistry back. He was tempted to rest for a moment and let the endless river of sensations wash over him. Even this sterile room of barren white light was lurid, packed with details, smells, sensations. He had never loved life so much.

But he wasn't safe. Coffee breaks didn't last forever. He would have to find his clothes, get out—

He started for a side door. The first few steps taught him to keep his head tilted down, toward his feet. He had to move his eyes the opposite way, though, to shift his vision. He bumped into the medmon and nearly fell over a desk. After a moment he could navigate around things. He went carefully, feeling each twinge of lancing pain as his left side protested. His right arm ached and trembled from spasm.

He reached the door, opened it slightly, peered through. The equipment beyond was hard to recognize upside down. Clothes on pegs jutted straight up. Chairs clung to the ceiling. He fought down a sense of vertigo. His eyes were telling his brain that he was standing on the ceiling, and somewhere inside him alarm systems clamored to be heard.

There were open drawers of surgical instruments, a washup station, electronics gear. A prep room. He eased through.

He found his clothes hanging in a locker, defying gravity.

It was easier to put them on if he closed his eyes, going by feel alone. Too bad he couldn't walk that way.

EIGHT

Crisp, cycled air cut in his throat. Down the bright claustrocorridors he went, brushing by the few who passed in this narrow side passage, their faces flashing before him. He reached an obscure storage vault and slipped inside, feeling strangely exhilarated. He tapped his fingernail and tweaked a nodule by his ear. Shipcomm:

> *suggest that in light of the news Earthside I go through these minor items of collective business quickly*

His thumbnail, knowing he had come on line late, flashed an outline of the shipwide congress Ted had called. A flashing red dot showed they were still among the first Items of Business.

> *matter of Nigel Walmsley, the facts of which are given in your update. He has shown an attitude in the past which I can only characterize as non-communal. He weasled by several regs during his ground duty at Isis. He has been nonconstructive in the analysis net. All these are disagreeable features of a man I know many of us revere for his early role in the discovery of the Marginis wreck. However it has come to my attention—the facts are laid out and witnessed in your summaries—that he has been sys-tematically deceiving the medical teams about his declining health. He did this from a misguided sense*

Nigel studied the summary, including a detailed analysis of his reaction to the analysis net, to Carlos, to suggestions that he give up his jobs. Quite factual. He returned to the corridor and began to walk, listening, watching the faces that passed.

steady buildup of sociopathic responses, well documented by the therapists

Men and women slid by. They were selected for their compatability, their ease with each other, for who else could endure the long compression between the stars? No sun hung here behind a veiled sky, no sudden rains or dark storms stirred the spirit. Only the slow steady strum of canned breezes, ripples of pressure, a programmed replication of distant Earth. They shared these mild rhythms, smooth faces free of madmen and Mozart, no leaping soaring flying dying. They turned away from the silent steady abyss outside, the long pressing silence that enclosed them, the emptiness that defined their place.

in the midst of studying this constellation of acommunal responses, many of them no doubt the product of his physical deterioration, the therapists also detected the medical deception

So Ted had conned him into the therapy, knowing it would help build a file on him, suspecting it would turn up a glitch in the medical profile. Quite clever.

and as many of you know he has held on in hopes of proving his personal and rather eccentric model of the situation humanity faces

Nigel walked as quickly as he could toward the big bowl auditorium where the bulk of *Lancer*'s crew would be assembled. He would confront Ted there, have it out.

but that hope has vanished and it would be a kindness for him to not let him wither out here, getting mean and withdrawing even more from the fellowship of his

Quite shrewd of Ted to slip it in before a big discussion of Earthside news, when everyone was champing at the bit to hear.

so though the medical situation is not really bad I still recommend

He hurried. Ahead two ship's officers leaned against a bulkhead. Nigel slowed. They might not know anything, but then again— He veered down a roundabout route. And hurried.

he be put into the Sleepslots until we make Earthside. I'm sure it would be more poetic if he died out here but simple humanity

He was getting close. There would be discussion and that would give him time.

so I throw it open to discussion before we take up the Earthside

He was within sight of the auditorium doors when three women from the senior crew saw him.

his absence from this gathering of his fellows speaks volumes about his attitudes and, yes, I think his own shame at his childish deception he has

The women started toward him. He backed away and walked rapidly toward a drop tube.

well it appears no one wishes to counter my recommendation and therefore

Nikka! Why hadn't she said anything argued—

pass on to the fresh news of a Swarmer offensive against all mainlands and indications of their concerted biological campaign

Whatever she thought of him, surely the thing with Carlos could not have made her go along with this. Nigel refused to think otherwise. He fell three decks at maximum speed in the drop tube. He came out next to a work gang carrying a thruster housing and fell in behind them unnoticed. When the women came out of the tube he was bent over, pretending to adjust the magnetic sled's balance. He ducked into a prep-up room and waited. Then he doubled back on his trail. The women were gone.

as well as, we are told, continuing provocative allegations about cooperation—yes, I know this is hard to believe—between the Chinese and some elements of the Swarmers

He sent a query to their flat, but it answered that no one was home. He kept moving. If she was not at the meeting, then— Of course.

and since the newest information on this biological transformation of the enemy may tie into or provide a clue about their planetary origins, I think we should move immediately to review this data in the light of

He approached the medical complex quietly, carefully. he found Nikka arguing with an administrator. He waited until she looked around in exasperation, caught her eye, and signaled for silence. She said nothing until they were out of sight of the big med center archway.

"I came to get you! What took you so long? Ted has called a—"

"I know." He explained in rapid, clipped sentences, feeling a sure anger come welling up. "And there's no point in barging in there now. That lot won't give me a hearing."

"You've *got* to."

"Ted hasn't the power of a captain, but the consensus is clearly with him. And consensus, luv, is everything."

"In a free discussion—"

"Right you are. But getting it free, there's the rub. Ol' Ted's been quite pissed at me for some time, I gather. He's a very smart man."

"He is unprincipled, short—"

"Has it occurred to you that all I'm resisting is a soft ride home?"

"It's more than that. This is, well, your *life*."

"Was."

"It still can be."

"Hard to see how to beat him." He took her head in his hands and kissed her on the forehead with a wan, distant affection. He felt strange energies building in him, a resolve he had thought lost.

"We can go home, refuse to let them in. Request time on the group net to discuss your case."

"There's plenty of evidence for Ted's position."

"Empty facts."

He sagged against a bulkhead. Under pressure he had been dealing adequately with the inverted vision, but the strain was beginning to tell. Turning his head rapidly brought on nausea. Upside down, people's expressions were alarming, grotesque, usually impossible to decipher.

"Y'know, I *am* rather a bastard. Surely it's not escaped your notice."

Nikka grinned and looked determined. "They don't—"

"Wait." Nigel held up a palm. "Listen. Shipcomm."

—I've just been handed an emergency signal from Earthside. I'll read it: "Nuclear weapons were used today in a military confrontation off the coast of China. The combatants are China, the USSR and USA, as well as smaller fleet forces of Japan and Brazil. Damage is unknown. Satellite recons shows the engagement is continuing and spreading, with apparently all major forces engaged. Cause is unknown. May have been triggered by attempt to inhibit Swarmer landings on seacoasts. Will advise shortly on possible implications for space communications net." Well, I don't know what to say—

Nigel smacked his fist against the bulkhead. "That's it."

"Wh-what?"

"They've bitten into the apple. Not much good our information'll do 'em now."

"This, this may be a mistake—"

"No mistake. All quite predictable, I expect. If any of us had been half swift..." He sighed.

"Well..." She blinked, confused. "Let's, let's go home. We can forget about our problems..."

He nodded grimly, putting his arms on her shoulders, peering into her lined, coppery face. "But don't you see? That message is years old! We can't influence events there. We're on our own."

"Well, yes, but..."

"Whatever happens, ol' friend Ted will still carry out his precious policy. So we might as well do as we like, too. Earth's another issue."

"I, I don't know... everything's... so fast."

"Look, it'll be awhile before we learn more from Earth. The big satellite transmitters have got other things to do than beam to us."

"Yes, I suppose..."

"So Ted's going to go on with business. And so should we."

"Let's go *home*."

"Right. For a bit. But there's really only one place left for us now, luv."

NINE

They crouched together in the freight elevator, hemmed in by crates.

"Are you all right? Your eyes?" Nikka asked.

"I think I'm integrating the change. Resting helped."

"I've heard something about that medtech error. It's a common one, easy to make."

Nigel chuckled. "Gratifying to know."

"I don't think I can fix it."

"Not without microsurgery tools, no."

"I remember that the brain adjusts, though. Eventually you'll see upright images."

"How long?"

"A few days."

"Um. I say, it seems that long since I went merrily off with smiling Ted. How long was I gone?"

"Half a day," Nikka said. "They came and told me. I argued with Ted but he was busy. Carlos was there."

"What was his reaction?"

"Sad. He went down to Pocks on the morning shuttle, just after you left. Reporting for his new job. A chance to put his training into action. I think he wants to—"

"Wash his hands of it all. Quite so. There's still you, waiting here, after he's done."

"Nigel, that's not fair."

"Who said I was fair? Carlos is confused, but he's not dumb."

"Can't we forget that? With all that's happening—"

"No, we can't. Might have to use it." He slapped the portable medfilter resting between them. The elevator whine reverberated in the sheet-metal floor. It had taken over an hour for Nikka to strip Nigel's jury-rigged device down to essentials, and then wedge it into a carrying case. Their apartment was no longer a candidate for *House Beautiful*.

He hoped the filter would still work. It was touch and go getting out of the apartment, too—Ted hadn't put guards on their door, but Nigel was sure someone would lay hand on him if he showed his face in public.

"You're going to have to keep the dockmen busy while I get this on," he said.

She nodded. "Our chances aren't good."

"So what? Haven't any choices left. Ted will nab us in hours if we stay."

The elevator groaned to a stop in near-zero gravity. The door lurched open, revealing the aft ship's lock. No one in view.

"I'll nip across," Nigel said. He slipped into the darkness of the shuttle's hold. Nikka drew a deep breath and went in search of the crew.

Pocks was gunmetal gray. Long white filaments stretched across it, rays of debris from ancient meteors. Crusts of rock blotched the dirty purple ice fields.

Nigel could feel the chill through his servo'd suit. He moved carefully across the crumpled plain. Nikka pointed to the spherical submarine berthed at the edge of an orange-green lake. "That's where the log says Carlos is on duty."

Nigel picked up the pace. Between them they carried the portable medfilter.

They began to puff with the effort. Boots crunched on the purple ice. Nigel stepped up his opticals to see what the surface looked like unaugmented. It was barren, lit by an angry red dot. High up he caught the gliding gray smudge of the Watcher. The *Lancer* analysis net had stopped calling the moonlet by that name, but he refused to. Was there a shifting glimmer where the weak sun struck the ancient hull? He blinked. Perhaps a facet catching the light. Or more probably, he reminded himself, a trick of his eyes. He was catching, seeing better, but there were still illusions, distortions.

They were five hundred meters from the descent craft. As yet no one had tried to stop them. There had been questioning looks from the shuttle crew, but Nikka had made up some apparently plausible story. They had counted on the fact that aboard *Lancer* there were no security measures, any more than there were guards on an ordinary naval vessel. But once Landon and that lot worked out where they must have gone—

"Hey!" Nigel stopped dead still, startled by the shout. He turned. No one behind them. It came from a figure trotting toward them from the submersible. His helmet overlay winked a color-coded ID: Carlos.

"What's this about you coming down? Nigel shouldn't be out—"

"Explain inside," Nikka said roughly, and pushed Carlos back toward the submersible. "Quick!"

Nigel panted hard beneath the black sky. It was difficult going and something about it satisfied him. He did not ask Carlos to help.

Bubbles bulged and popped on the lake and then it went glassy and smooth again beneath the ember glow of Ross 128. Near the lake a sulfurous yellow muck sucked at their boots. "Outflow," Carlos said. "Like a tidal flat, only worse. The lake's all liquid ammonia, but every few days it belches. Potassium salts, sulfur, have to wash it off at the lock—"

Nikka waved him to be silent. She glanced behind them;

no one following. Nigel felt secure; she looked as though she could handle anyone.

It took over ten minutes to shuck their suits and get to the cranny where Carlos slept. He turned on them, blocking the doorway, and said, "Now let's hear it. After I got your message I checked the shuttle manifest. You two weren't on it."

"Last-minute holiday," Nigel said. "Simply caught the first thing out of town."

Nikka smiled tolerantly. "You can tell when things are desperate," she said. "He always makes a joke."

"That's what jokes are for," Nigel said, stretching out on Carlos' bunk. He rested while Nikka sketched in the jumble of events. He enjoyed hearing it all played back from another perspective. It was particularly pleasant to relax utterly and let someone else take charge, as Nikka had been doing ever since they nonchalantly walked aboard the shuttle. She had done marvelously well at persuading the pilot. However this might come out—and he had few delusions on that score—it was delicious to be moving and acting again. The worst part of age was the feeling of helplessness, of being disengaged from life. The middle-aged treated the old with the same serenely contemptuous condescension they used for children. That unthinking attitude was what lay behind Ted's actions.

"You're stupid," Carlos said bluntly. "*Stupid*. Whatever you think Landon was doing, you're building a great case for him by—"

"Shove off that, eh? If we'd stayed on *Lancer* we'd be swimming in a slot by now." Nigel stretched lazily, though he did not feel tired.

"*You*, maybe. Not her."

"We're together," Nikka said simply.

"Not necessarily," Carlos said carefully.

"I would protest Nigel going into the Slots. If I failed to get him revived, I would follow. So that we will lose no time together."

"I don't think you mean that," Carlos said. "You still have work to do here. And you and I, we need each other too, you have to—"

"We'll get bugger-all done if we recycle our stale statements while the clock runs," Nigel said forcefully. "I need shelter, Carlos. That's the nub of it. Either you give it to me or you don't."

Nigel watched conflicting emotions in the man's face. He'd done the classic male-challenge thing, of course—interrupt Carlos, and abruptly shift the subject, to boot. Not wise, generally. But Carlos was a deeply conflicted person, uncertain how to respond to those signals. This was precisely what Nigel had hoped: that the deeply embedded responses of each sex would get tangled, and in his confusion Carlos would yield. Nigel recalled Blake's notion of the ideal human: Male and female somehow blended in the same body, anima and animus united, entwined. He wished the poet could be here to see the result. Dreams were best when not made concrete.

Carlos dodged. "I can't do anything. In a few minutes somebody'll—"

"I've filed a formal complaint. Put it into shipcomm from our apartment. That *has* to be heard—even Ted can't block that."

"By the rules," Nikka added, "it must go on open net for twelve hours. He requested a mandatory vote, so people can't ignore it."

Carlos nodded. "Then you have nothing to worry about."

"Don't be thick. If Ted can pop me back in the soup before the vote's resolved, nobody'll take the small risk of reviving me unnecessarily. Possession's nine-tenths of the game here."

Nikka asked thoughtfully, "You truly think he would?"

"More's the fool he, if he doesn't. Ted sees me as a kernel for opposition forces. Why not eliminate me? This expedition's turning out stale as old beer. He wants something dramatic to pin his name on, is my guess."

Carlos frowned. "Like what?"

"It may've occurred to him that *Lancer*'s a damn ferocious weapon."

"How?" Carlos seemed to be regaining his equilibrium. He stood up, clearly feeling his heft and strength in comparison with these other two. "Look, you're sounding more and more—"

Carlos! They with you?

The voice came over general audio, filling the small cabin. "Well, it didn't take them long," Nikka said.

"He's got you," Carlos said.

"Depends," Nigel said. "Everybody's fretting about Earthside, granted—that gives him freedom of maneuver with us. No one'll give a frap if we—"

Carlos! Then, fainter, Where in hell is he? I thought you saw him go in there with the two of them.

"I've got to answer him," Carlos said.

Nigel nodded. He went to a spot mike and tuned it in. "We hear you."

Nigel? Just what the hell you think you're—

"Fairly obvious, I should think."

Don't give me that arched-eyebrow shit. You left medical without a release, you ignored the directive approved by shipwide congress, then you—

"Please, no boring list of sins."

The council orders you to march over to HQ there and—

Give it a rest," Nigel said sourly.

You sneaky bastard! You slipped by once but damned if we'll let you take up any more of our time now, when—

"Stop playing to the gallery, can't you?"

Stop playing! Yeah, that's what we're going to do. I've got men all around that submersible. They're coming in after you unless you pop that hatch and walk out. You're just a sick old man, and we don't want to be rough. But this is a crisis. You've got three minutes.

Nigel switched off his personal transmitter. "Sounds earnest."

"Damn right he is," Carlos said. "Let's go. There's no way out."

Nigel said hurriedly, "Course there is. Take us down."

"Into the *vent*?"

"Right. You're set to do a bit of snagging soon anyway—the Task Schedule says so."

"My, my copilot's not on board."

"We won't be down long," Nikka said reasonably. "Those ones outside will back off fast when you rev up."

"But I . . ." Carlos looked from one to the other.

Nigel waited, knowing this was the crucial moment. The plan he'd worked out on the way down hung on what Carlos would do. Nigel was not above using the man's devotion to Nikka, either. Carlotta had worked her way into this strange triangle and then changed the vectors abruptly. So be it; each coin had two faces.

"I need time to think. Nikka, do you really want this?" The man bent down, earnestly peering into her eyes.

"There isn't time for that," Nigel said rapidly.

"Look, this is a pretty serious violation of regs. You might—"

"Decide," Nikka said. "We've had troubles, but we three are still together. Or are we?" Nigel's heart swelled at the clear, even-tempered way she said it. Perhaps her perception of Carlos was coming around to his. A bit late, but . . .

Carlos straightened. "Okay. Look, I can say I had good personal reasons. And I do. We have things between us, things I haven't been able to . . ." His words trickled away. Then he said grimly, "Damned if I'm going to let Ted muscle me around, either."

Nikka embraced Carlos. Nigel put a hand on his shoulder. Carlos said gruffly, "Prob'ly get us killed, I bet."

PART NINE 2061 EARTH

ONE

The guard took Warren down the center of the island, along a path worn smooth in the last few days by the troops. They passed a dozen technicians working on acoustic equipment and playing back the high-pitched squeals of Skimmer song. The troops were making entries on computer screens and chattering to each other, breaking down the problem into bits that could be cross-referenced and reassembled to make patterns that people could understand. It would have to be good because they wanted to eavesdrop. But the way the Skimmers talked to the Swarmers might not be anything like the songs the Skimmers sung among themselves.

It made no sense that the Skimmers had much control over the Swarmers, Warren thought to himself as he marched down the dirt path. No sense at all. Something had brought them all to Earth and given the Swarmers some disease and the answer lay in thinking about that fact, not playing stupid games with machines in the water.

The troops were spread out more now, he saw. There were nests of high-caliber cannon strung out along the ridge and down near the beaches men were digging in where they could set up a cross fire over the natural clearings.

The men and women he passed were talking among themselves now, not silent and efficient the way they had been at first. They looked at him with suspicion. He guessed the missile attack in the night had made them nervous and even the hot work of clearing fields of fire in the heavy humidity did not take it out of them.

Coming down the rocky ridgeline Warren slipped on a stone and fell. The guard laughed in a kind of high, fast way and kicked him to get him to hurry. Warren went on and saw ahead one of the bushes with leaves he knew he could eat

289

and when he went by it he pulled some off and started to stuff them into his pockets for later. The guard shouted and hit him in the back with the butt of his rifle and Warren went down suddenly, banging his knee on a big tree root. The guard kicked him in the ribs and Warren saw the man was jumpy and bored at the same time. That was dangerous. He carefully got up and moved along the path, limping from the dull pain spreading in his knee. The guard pushed him into his cell and kicked him again. Warren fell and laid there, not moving, waiting, and the guard finally grunted and slammed the door.

Noon came and went and he got no food. He ate the leaves. They were a poor trade for the stiffness in his knee. He listened to the shouted orders and sounds of work and it seemed to him the camp was restless, the sounds moving one way and then the other. He did not blame the Chinese for the way they treated him. The great powers all acted the same, independent of what they said their politics was, and it was easier to think of them as big machines that do what they were designed to do rather than as bunches of people.

Night came. Warren had gotten used to not thinking about food when he was on the raft and he was just as glad the guard did not bring any. Eventually the squat chinless soldier would come all the way into the cell and look behind the table which was overturned and would see the dirt mounds. Warren lay on the rocky ground that was the floor and listened to the snarling surf on the reef. He wondered if he would dream of his wife again. It was a good dream because it took away all the pain they both had caused and left only her smells and taste. But when he dozed off he was in the deep place where clanking came from above, a metallic sound that blended with the dull buzzing he had heard all that afternoon from the motorboat in the lagoon, the sounds washing together until he realized they were the same, but the loud clanking one was the way the Skimmers heard it. It was hard to think with the ringing hammering sound in his head and he tried to swim up and break water to get away from it. The clanking went on and then was a roar, louder, and he woke up suddenly and felt the sides of the cell tremble with the sound. Two quick crashes came down out of the sky and then sudden blue light.

Warren looked out through the mesh on the windows

and saw men running. There was no moon but in the starlight he could see they were carrying rifles. A sudden rattling came from the north and west. More crashes and then answering fire from up on the ridge.

He listened as it got louder and then used the flickering light from the windows to find the map Tseng had given him. He pulled back the sleeping pad to expose the hole he had dug and without hesitation crawled in. He knew the feel of it well and in the complete dark found the stone at the end he used. He had estimated that there was only a foot of dirt left above. Using the pan to scrape away the last few feet of dirt had left him with a feel for how strong the earth was above, but when he hit it with the stone it did not give. There was not much room to swing and three more solid hits did not even shake loose clods of it. Warren was sweating in the closeness of the tunnel and the dirt stuck to his face as he chipped away at the hard soil over him. It was hard-packed and filled with rocks that struck him in the face and rolled onto his chest. His arm started to ache and then tire out but he did not stop. He switched the stone to his left hand and felt a softness give above and then was hitting nothing. The stone broke the crust and he could see stars.

He studied the area carefully. A soldier ran by carrying a tripod for an automatic rifle. The sharp crackling fire still came from north and west.

There was a spark of light high up and Warren snapped his head away to keep his night vision. Then the glare was gone and a hollow roar rolled over the camp. Mortars, not far away. He struggled up out of the tunnel and ran for the trees nearby. Halfway there his knee folded under him and he cursed it silently as he went down. It was worse than he had thought and lying on the hard cell floor had made it go stiff. He got up and limped to the trees, each moment feeling a spot between his shoulder blades where the slug would come if any of the running men in the camp behind him saw the shadow making its painful way. The slug did not come but a flare went up as he reached the clump of bushes. He threw himself into them and rolled over so he could see the clearing. The flare had taken away most of his night vision. He waited for it to come back and smelled the wind. There was something heavy and musky in it. It was the easterly trade, blowing steady, which meant the tide was getting ready to shift and it was past midnight. Coming from the east the wind should not have picked up the smell of the firefight, so the musky smell was something else. Warren knew the taste but could not remember what it was and what it might mean about the tide. He squinted, moving back into the bush, and saw a man in the camp coming straight toward him.

The figure stopped at the door of Warren's cell. He fumbled at the door and a banging of automatic weapons fire came from the other side of camp. The man jumped back and yelled to someone and then went back to trying to unlock the door. Warren glanced into the distance where sudden flashes lit the camp in pale orange light. The firing got heavier and when he looked back at the cell there were two men there and the first one was opening the door. Warren crawled out of the dry bushes, moving when a burst of machine-gun fire covered any sound he might make. He got to a thin stand of trees and turned. A flare went up, burning yellow. It was the chinless soldier. He had the door open and Gijan was coming out, waving a hand, pointing north. They shouted at each other for a moment. Warren edged back farther into the trees. He was about fifty meters away now and could see each man unshoulder the slim rifles they carried. They held them at the ready. Gijan pointed again and the two men separated, moving apart about thirty meters. They were going to search. They turned and walked into the brush. Gijan came straight at Warren.

It would be easy to give himself up now. Wait for a flare and come forward with his hands held high. He had counted on getting farther away than this before anyone came after him. Now in the dark and with the fighting going there was a good chance they were jumpy and would shoot him if they saw some movement. But as he thought this Warren moved back, sinking into the shadows. He had faced worse than this on the raft. He limped away, going by feel in the shadows.

He reached a line of palms and moved along them toward the north. He was still about five hundred meters from the beach but there was a big clearing in the way so he angled in toward the ridge. Muffled thuds from the west told him that the Chinese were using mortars against whoever was coming in on the beaches. Five spaced screeches cut through the deep sounds of distant battle.

Warren guessed the Japanese or the Americans had decided to take the island and try to speak to the Skimmers themselves. Maybe they would try their own machines and codes. They might know about him though. The Chinese wanted to keep him or else Gijan would not have come with the soldier. Warren stumbled and slammed his knee into a tree. He paused, panting and trying to see if the men were within sight. With a moment to think he saw that Gijan might want to kill him to keep him out of the hands of the others. He could not be sure that giving himself up was safe anymore.

The five shrill notes came again and he recognized them as an emergency signal, blown on a whistle. They were from close by. Gijan was calling for help. With the Chinese fighting other troops on the other side of the island, Gijan might not get a quick answer. But help would come and then they would box him in.

Warren turned toward the beach. He moved as fast as he could without making a lot of noise. His knee went out from under him again, and as he got up he realized he was not going to give them much trouble. They had him bracketed already, they had good knees, and help was coming. He could not outrun them. The only chance he had was to circle around and ambush one of them, ambush an armed, well-trained man using his bare hands. Then get away before the other one found out.

He picked up a rock and put it in his pocket. It banged against his leg with each step. A rustling came from behind him and he hurried and stumbled at the edge of a gully.

A shout. He jumped down into the gully. As he landed there was a sharp crack and something zipped by overhead. It chunked into a tree on the other bank. Warren knew there was no point in going back now.

He trotted down the deepening water-carved wash. It was too narrow for two men. He tired to think how Gijan would figure it. The smartest thing was to wait for the other troops and then comb the area.

But Warren might reach the beach by then. Better to send one man down the gully and another through the trees, to cut him off.

Warren went what felt like a hundred meters before he stopped to listen. A *crack* of a twig snapping came from far back in the blackness. To the left? He could not be sure. The

gully was rocky and it slowed him down. There were some
good places to hide in the shadows and then try to hit the
following man as he came by. Better than in the scrub above,
anyway. But by then the other man would have gotten
between him and the beach.

A pebble rattled faintly behind him. He stopped. The
hard clay of the gully was three meters high here and steep.
He found some thick roots sticking out and carefully pulled
himself up. He stuck his head above the edge and looked
around. Nothing moving. He crawled over the lip and a rock
came loose under his foot. He lunged and caught it. A
stabbing pain came in his knee, and he bit his tongue to keep
from making a noise.

The scrub was thicker here. He rolled into a stand of
trees, keeping down and out of the starlight. Twigs snagged at
his clothes.

There was an even chance the man would come on this
side of the gully. If he didn't Warren could slip off to the
north. But Gijan had probably guessed where he was headed
and he would not have much of a lead when he reached the
beach. On the open sand he would be exposed, easy to pick
off.

Warren crawled into the dark patches under the trees
and waited, rubbing his leg. The wind smelled bad here,
damp and heavy. He wondered if the tide had changed.

He leaned his head on his hands to rest and felt a muscle
jump in his face. It startled him. He could not feel it unless
he put his hand to it. So Tseng had been right and he did
have a spasm without knowing it. Warren frowned. He did
not know what to think about that. It was a fact he would
have to understand. For now, though, he put the thought
away from him and watched the darkness.

He pulled the rock out of his pocket and hefted it and a
pale form moved in the trees forty meters inland. It was a
short soldier, the chinless one. Warren crouched low to
follow. The pain that shot through his knee reminded him of
how the chinless man had kicked him but the memory did
not make him feel anything about what he was going to do.
He moved forward.

In the dry brush he kept as quiet as he could. The dull
claps and crashes that came over the ridge were muffled now,
just when he needed them to be loud. Under the trees it was

quieter and he was surprised to hear the rasping of the soldier breathing. The man moved slowly, rifle at the ready, the weapon looking big in the starlight. The man kept in the starlight and watched the shadows. That was smart.

The breathing got louder. Warren moved, favoring his knee. He would have to jump up fast and take the soldier from behind.

The figure came closer. Suddenly Warren saw that the man wore a helmet. To use the rock now he would have to hit him in the face. That made the odds a lot worse. But he would have to try. The man stopped, turned, looked around. Warren froze and waited. The head turned away and Warren eased forward, closing, the pain shooting in his knee. The leg would try to give way when he came up for the rush. He would watch for that and force it to hold. The air was still and heavy under the trees and the smell was worse, something from the beach. The soldier was the only visible movement.

In the quilted pattern of shadows and light it was hard to follow the silhouette. Warren put his hand out and gathered his feet under him and felt something wet and slick ahead and suddenly knew that the slow rasping laboring breath did not come from the chinless soldier but from something between them.

He felt the ground, brought his hand up to his face and smelled the strong reek he had tasted on the wind. Ahead in the faint light that fell between two palms he saw the long form struggling, pulling itself forward on blunt legs. It sucked in the air with each step. It was thick and heavy and the skin was a gunmetal gray, pocked with inch-wide round holes. Warren felt a whirring in the air and something brushed against his face, lingered, and was gone. Another whirring followed, so quiet he could barely hear it

The stubby fin-legs of the Swarmer went mechanically forward and back, dragging its bloated body. In the starlight he could see the glistening where fluid seeped from the moist holes. THE YOUNG RUN WITH SORES. Another small whirring sound came and he saw from one of the dark openings a thing as big as a finger spring out, slick with moisture, and spread its wings. It beat against the thick and reeking air and then lifted its heavy body, coming free of its hole, wings fluttering. It lifted into the air and hovered, seeking. It darted away, missing Warren, passing on into the night. He did not move.

The Swarmer pulled itself forward. Its dry, rattling gasps caught the attention of the soldier. The man turned, took a step. The Swarmer gathered itself and sprang.

It reached the man's leg and the massive head turned to take the calf between its jaws. It seized and twisted and Warren heard the sharp intake of breath before the soldier went down. He screamed and the Swarmer turned itself and rolled over the man. The long blunt head came up and nuzzled down into the belly of the man and the sharp, shrill scream cut off suddenly.

Warren stood, the smell stronger now, and watched the two forms struggle on the open sand. The man pawed for his rifle where it had fallen and the thick leg of the Swarmer pinned his arm. They rolled to the side. The thing wallowed on him, covering him with a slick sheen, cutting off the low moans he made. Warren ran toward them and picked up the rifle. He backed away, thumbing off the safety. The man went limp and the air rushed out of him as the alien settled into place. Its head turned toward Warren and held there for a moment and then it turned back and dipped down to the belly of the man. It began feeding.

Gijan had heard the screams and would be here soon. There was no point in shooting the Swarmer and giving Gijan a sound to follow. Warren turned and limped away from the licking and chewing sounds.

He walked silently through brush, hobbling. The rifle had a bayonet on the muzzle. If a Swarmer came at him he would use that instead of firing. He stayed in the open, watching the shadows.

Abruptly from behind him came a loud hammering of automatic fire. Warren dodged to the side and then realized that no rounds were thumping into the trees near him. It was Gijan, killing the Swarmer a hundred meters or more away.

Warren was sure the Chinese did not know the Swarmers were crawling ashore or else they would have come after him in a group. Now Gijan would be shaken and uncertain. But in a few minutes he would recover and know what he had to do. Gijan would run to the beach, moving faster than Warren could, and try to cut him off.

Warren heard a light humming. He looked up between the trees where the sound came and could see nothing against the stars.

THE WORLD THAT WAS FALSE WORLD MADE THEM
THIS WAY NOT AS THEY WERE WHEN WE KNEW THEM
IN THE WORLD THAT WAS OURS THEY CANNOT SING
BUT KNOW OF THE PLACES WHERE YOU SING TO EACH
OTHER AND SOME NOW GO THERE WITH THEIR SORES
THEY MAY BE CHEWED BY YOU BUT THERE ARE MANY
MANY

Something smacked into his throat.

It was wet and it attached itself with a sudden clenching
thrust like a ball of needles. Warren snatched at it. He
stopped an inch short of grabbing at the thing when he
caught the musty sea stench full in his nostrils. The moist
lump dripped something down his neck.

He brought the rifle up quickly and pointed the bayonet
at his throat and jabbed, aiming by instinct in the dark. He
felt the tip go into the thing and he turned the blade so it
scraped, pulling the wet centimeter-long larva out. It came
away before the spines had sunk in. Blood seeped out and
trickled down his neck.

He sopped it up with his sleeve and held the bayonet up
in the starlight. The larva was white as a maggot and twisted
feebly on the blade. One wing fluttered. The other was gone.
The skin of it peeled back some more and the wing fell off.
He stuck the blade into the sand to clean it and stepped on
the thing that moved in spasms on the ground. Something
still stuck on his neck. He scraped it off. The other wing was
on the blade and some thin dark needles. He wiped them on
the sand and with a sudden rushing rear slammed his heel
down on them again and again.

He was breathing hard by the time he reached the
beach. The fear had gone away when he had concentrated on
staying away from the shadows, not thinking about what could
be in them. The stabbing pain in his knee helped. He
listened for the deep rasping and the humming and tasted the
wind for their smell.

He hobbled out from the last line of palms and onto the
white glow of the beach beneath the stars. He could see
maybe fifty meters and there were no dark forms struggling
up from the water. To the north he could hear faint shouts.
That did not bother him because he did not have far to go.

He stumbled toward the shouts, ignoring the quick, rippling flashes of yellow light from a mortar barrage and the long *crump* that came after them. There were motorboats moored in the shallows with the big reels in the stern, but no one in them. He took an oar out of one.

He came around the last horn of a crescent beach and saw ahead the dark blotch of the raft far up on the sand. He threw his rifle aboard and began dragging the raft toward the water. Big combers boomed on the reef.

He got it into the shallows and rolled aboard without looking back. He pushed off with the oar and kept pushing until he felt the current catch him. Speed, now. Speed.

The tide had just turned. It was slow but it would pick up in a few minutes and take him toward the pass in the reef. When he was sure of that he sat down and felt for the rifle. Sitting, he would be harder to see and he could steady the rifle against his good knee. His throat had nearly stopped bleeding but his shirt was heavy with blood. He wondered if the flying things would smell it and find him. The Skimmers had never said anything about the things like maggots with wings and he was sure now it was because they did not know about them. There was no reason the Swarmers would have evolved a thing like that to help them live on the land. And with the Skimmers driven from the lagoon by the men there was nothing to keep the Swarmers from bringing the things ashore.

He saw something move on the land and he lay down on the raft and Gijan came out onto the sand, running. Gijan stopped and looked straight out at Warren and then turned and ran north.

Warren picked up his rifle. Gijan was carrying his weapon at the ready. Was the man trying to cut him off but keep him alive? Then he should have run south, toward the motorboats. But there might be boats to the north, too. Maybe Gijan had heard the shouts in that direction and was running for help.

Warren thumbed off the safety on his rifle and put it on automatic fire. He would know what to do if Gijan would tell him by some action what the man intended to do. If he could just shout to the man, ask him— But maybe Gijan had not seen him after all. And the man might lie even if he answered.

Warren knew he could not trust words from Gijan or even silence from him; they were all the same.

Suddenly the running figure dropped his rifle and slapped at his neck and then fell heavily on the sand. He twisted and brought both hands to his neck and struggled for a moment. Then he brought something out from his neck and threw it into the water and made a sound of fear. Gijan lurched up and staggered. He still clutched his neck with one hand but turned and looked for his weapon. He seemed dazed. His head came up and his gaze swept past Warren and then came back again. Gijan had seen the raft for sure this time.

Warren wished he could read the man's face. Gijan hesitated only a moment. Then he picked up his weapon and turned to the north. He took some steps and Warren relaxed and then there as something about the way Gijan moved his arm. Warren aimed quickly, with no pause for conscious thought, and Gijan was bringing the rifle around. It made a bright yellow flash, firing on automatic, as Gijan swept the muzzle, fanning, and Warren fired a burst. It took Gijan high in the shoulder and then in the chest, spinning him. The flashes stopped coming from Gijan's rifle and Warren was startled by the loud chatter of his weapon but kept it on the toppling figure, rolling him over and over until he was a loose bunch of rags and blood.

Warren slowly put down the rifle, panting. He had not thought at all about killing Gijan but had just done it, not stopping for the instant of balancing the equation and seeing if it had to be that way, and that was what had saved him. If Gijan had gotten off another few rounds it would have been enough.

He peered shoreward again. Voices, near. There was some sea still running against the ebb but now the tide was taking hold and carrying him out. The pass was a dark patch in the snarling white of the combers.

He had to get away fast now because the men to the north would be coming toward the gunfire. Hoisting the sail would just give them a target. He had to wait for the slow steady draw to take him through.

Something thumped against the bottom of the raft. It came again. Warren stood and cradled the rifle. The boards worked against each other as they came into the chop near the pass. A big dark thing broke water and rolled hugely.

Eyes looked at him and legs that had grown from fins kicked against the current. The Swarmer turned and wallowed in the wash from the passage and then sank, the great head turning toward shore. The lagoon swallowed it.

Warren used the oar to turn the raft free of the rocks. The surf broke to each side and the deep bands of current sucked the raft through with a sudden rush. Behind him Warren heard a cry, lonely and harsh and full of surprise. The warring rumbled beyond the ridge and was lost in the crashing of the waves running hard before an east wind, and he went out into the dark ocean, the raft rising fast and plunging as it came into the full sea swell.

A sharp crack. A motorboat was coming fast behind. Warren lay flat on the raft and groped for his rifle. Another shot whispered overhead.

They would get him out here for sure. He aimed at the place where the pilot would be but in the fast chop he knew he would miss. There came a short, stuttering bark of automatic weapons fire. He heard the shots go by, not close. They did not have to be accurate though if they had enough ammunition.

The raft slewed port and the boat turned to follow. Warren crawled to the edge of the raft, ready to slip overboard when they got too close. It would be better than getting cut down, even with the Swarmers in the water.

The boat whined and bounced on the swell, bearing down. He lifted the rifle to take aim and knew the odds were damn long against him. He saw a muzzle flash and the deck spat splinters at him where the shots hit.

Warren squeezed carefully and narrowed his eyes to frame the target and saw something leap suddenly across the bow of the boat. It was big and another followed, landing in front of the pilot and wriggling back over the windshield in one motion. It crashed into the men there. Shouts. A blue-white shape flicked a man overboard and knocked another sprawling. The boat veered to starboard. From this angle Warren could see the pilot, holding to the wheel and crouched to avoid the flicking tail of the Skimmer. The boat bucked and slewed in the chop and its engine roared.

A hammering of the automatic weapon. The Skimmer jumped and slashed at the man with its tail. Warren leaped up and rocked against the swell to improve his aim. He got off two quick shots at the man. The figure staggered and the Skimmer struck him solidly and he pitched over the side. The pilot glanced back and saw he was alone. The Skimmer stopped thrashing and went still. Warren did not give the man time to think. He fired at the dark splotch at the wheel until it was gone. The boat throttled into silence. Nothing moved.

Distant shouts came from shore but no sounds of another boat. The boat drifted away. Warren though of the Skimmer who lay dead in it. He tried to reach the boat, but the currents separated them farther. In moments it was gone in the darkness and the island itself faded into a mere looming shadow on the sea.

TWO

At noon the next day three big fighter-bombers split the sky with their roaring and passed over to the south. After that craft streaked across the sky for hours, high and soundless.

He had rounded the island in the dark and put up his worn sail and then run before the wind to get distance. He had the map from Tseng. The fishing lines were still on the raft with their hooks. The rifle had no rounds left in its clip but with the bayonet it made a good gaff.

He had a strike at dawn from a small tuna. It got away as he hauled it in. He hoped there would be more now that the Swarmers were going to land and not taking them.

He got a small fish at noon and another near sunset. He slept most of the day, beneath a pale and heatless wafer disk of a sun. Welts and broken blisters made it hard to lie on his back.

In the night there was a sudden distant glare of orange reflected off clouds near the horizon. It eased into a glow as the color seeped out of it and then it was gone. Afterward a rolling hammer blow of sound came. There were more bursts of light, fainter.

High up, silvery specks coasted smoothly across the

dark. One by one they vanished in bright firefly sparks—
yellow, hard blue. Satellite warfare. Soon they were gone.

At dawn he woke and searched the sky to find the thin
silver thread that reached up into the dark bowl overhead.

Now it curled about itself. Warren looked down the sky
toward the dawn, shielding his eyes, and found another pale
streak far below, where nothing should be.

The Skyhook was broken. Part of it was turning upward
while the other fell. Somebody had blown it in two.

For long moments he watched the faint band come
down. Finally he lost it in the glare as the sun rose. There
had been men and women working on the lower tip of the
Skyhook, engineers, and he tried to imagine what it was to
fall hopeless that far and that long and then burn quick and
high in the air like a shooting star.

His knee had swollen up and he could not stand so he
lay in the sail's shadow. The wound in his neck throbbed and
had a crusted blue scab. He didn't touch it.

A fever came and he sweated, delirious. He saw his wife
walking toward him across the sloping waves, called out to
her with a caked tongue. Then he was in the lagoon, floating
lazily, staring up at the cascading sunbeams that played on
him while a motor's *rrrrrr* purred in his ear.

There was nothing to fear, he saw. A little time swimming like this in the bright water and then some rest and a
cool drink, with ice cubes in it, and food, hot crisp toast,
butter running on it, and steak well marbled with fat and
then corned beef hash with the potatoes well browned, and
iced tea, plenty of tea, pitchers of it, drinking it in the shade.

Then the sweating passed and he rested. A school of fish
passed and he got one, gutted and skinned it and ate it whole
inside a minute. A little while later he got another and could
start to think.

He would ask the Skimmers about the larvae, he thought,
but probably it would be no use. He was sure they were not
natural to the Swarmers.

He remembered the sheets he had written on long ago,
the tangled thoughts. The Skimmers hated the machines that
had intruded into their home waters. They had learned about
them in the long years of voyaging, moved and fed and poked
at by things that hummed and jerked and yet had no true life.
Not like life that arose from nothing at all, flowering wher-

ever chemicals met and sunlight boomed through a blanket of gas.

Their hate had brought them through a long journey. So when they saw the simple, noisy ships of men they hated those, too.

The machines would have known that. Planned that. Easy. So easy.

He fished more but caught nothing.

That night there were more orange flashes to the west.

Then, in the hours before dawn, things moved in the sky. Shapes glided through the black, catching the sunlight as they came out of Earth's shadow.

They were close in, moving fast, their orbits repeating in less than an hour. Huge, irregular, their surfaces grainy and blotched. For Warren to be able to see the features on them they had to be far bigger than the ships that had brought the Swarmers and Skimmers. Asteroid-sized.

No defenses rose to meet the shapes. There were no military satellites left. No high-energy lasers. No particle-beam weapons. None of the apparatus that had kept the nuclear peace between humans for half a century.

The ships absorbed the sunlight and gave back a strange glowing gray. As Warren watched they began to split. Chunks broke away and fell, separating again and again as they streaked across the sky.

With dawn the light came back into the sky. The ocean was discolored around the raft. Nearby the water was pale, with a border, more than a hundred meters away, where the water got dark blue again.

There was something under him. It didn't move.

Warren stayed silent, peering down.

A machine? From the gray ships?

But it did nothing.

He probed down with a stick. No resistance. The chop was low and after a while he could tell the raft was not moving any, not following the steady pressure of waves.

The thing below was holding him in place.

He had to risk it. He leaned quickly over the side and put his head under. A line ran from the middle of the raft, down to something white. Something solid. Amber phosphorescence rippled through it.

He watched it for an hour and it did not move, did not rise closer or drift off.

No fish ventured near. If he stayed here like this he would starve.

The rifle was useless but he took the knife. He dove in and swam down rapidly. He felt less vulnerable below the surface.

Refraction misled the eye. It was deeper than he thought, bigger, and he nearly failed to reach it.

His lungs already burned. Patterns raced across the faces of pearly walls. Twisting, he looked through them and saw floors and levels beyond. Nothing moved inside.

There was a hole lower down and he swam toward it, throat constricting. He had to get a look at the underside, some glimpse of the engine or driving screw or whatever moved it. As he turned under the sharp edge of the hole he flexed upward, peering toward a refracting edge of light, and his face broke through into air.

He gasped. It was a stale pocket, trapped between levels. He floated for a moment, trying to make structure out of the fuzzy images around him, confused by the liquid interplay of water and light. Translucent walls blended silvery wads of air with rippling shafts of green sunlight.

There was nothing mechanical. He swam past quilted, blurred boundaries. the surfaces were smooth, with a resisting softness when he pressed. Some were curved, others flat. He found a ledge and crawled up onto it.

He rested, surrounded by a play of filtered jade light. The white stuff that made the walls was, he saw, assembled nearly seamlessly from the kind of blocks that had washed up on the island, that Tseng had showed him. The ledge was narrow and bumpy. Crawling along it took him to a low wall he could climb. Beyond lay a flat floor, pitted by random holes nearly a meter wide. Beyond that, more.

He explored the labyrinth for a long time, cautiously, slipping in the slick, narrow corridors. There seemed no scheme to it, only twisting passageways and small rooms. About a third of the whole structure held trapped air. Water-filled tubes intersected irregular rooms in a kind of curvilinear logic.

He worked his way up, following the shafts of shadow that descended through milky walls, There—equipment, carelessly dumped into piles, soaked. Wreckage from ships—twisted superstructure, jumbles of electronics, valves and pipes and cables. An entire combustion assembly. There was a whole radio rig, compact, sealed against water, intact with emergency battery. A good ship's set, with high-frequency bands.

The debris was unsorted, scattered around a long room which had more of the round openings in the floor. No sign of how it got here.

He worked on the radio for a while. Some hookup wire was missing but he scavenged some from nearby and got it up and running. It would be heavy, but maybe he could take it up to the raft. He peered at the thick cable lancing up to the raft.

Green fingers of sunlight came down obliquely now; dusk. He found a hole in the floor that weaved for ten meters and then gave onto the outer wall of the structure. He panted for two minutes, filling his blood with oxygen, and then slipped through, working his way down a wide tube and then out, into open water. Once he was free the tightness in his chest vanished and he opened his mouth and let the air rush out. As he rose, the ocean's pressure eased and more air filled him, a seeming unending fountain of it, fat bubbles wobbling upward toward the raft.

The swell lapped at creaking boards. Fish jumped and the horizon was a clean line. The sea was gathering itself again after the long time of the Swarmers, blossoming, the schools returning. He could live here now.

He got his fishing lines and the rifle and then dove in, carrying them down, entering the structure again. As the light ebbed, schools of fish gathered in the sheltered openings and tube. He trailed his lines down to them and got three.

Darkness came swiftly. He lay on the floor. There was enough air in the labyrinth to last for the night, and plenty of time to think tomorrow. He dozed fitfully, and in the night his thoughts were ragged.

There had been no more flashes over the horizon. So one part of it was finished, he thought. To set one kind of life against another. To upset the precarious balance and give humans what they thought at first was a simple fight with something from the sea.

The men had done what they always did in groups and somehow the thing had gotten away from them. And they had killed the Skyhook, too.

All without knowing that somewhere something wanted life to cancel other life and for each form to pull the other down. Clearing the way for the gray ships that now hurled themselves into the sea, far from the futile battles raging on the continents.

Something was moving beyond the walls.

He woke instantly, muscles stiff, and searched the pearly shafts of light nearby. Air and water bled into each other, catching the cool gleam of dawn, fooling the eye—

There. Quick, darting movements. Skimmers.

They entered through the tubes of water, swimming close to his room. And somehow these Skimmers knew about the time before, knew the difficult slow progress, knew the patience it demanded.

It took hours to understand and more still to get the words right. They had brought something they probably thought would serve as writing implements. The crude pen barely made scratches on the oily, crinkled pages they gave him. He wrote and they replied and he tried to see through the packed strings of words.

THE GRAY THINGS FLOAT FAR DOWN. THEY MINE THE SEA THEIR FACTORIES CLANK WE CAN HEAR THEM. THEIR SOUNDS TRAPPED IN THE PLANES OF WATER COME LONG DISTANCES. THEY MAKE MORE COPIES OF THEMSELVES. THE SWARMERS ARE GONE TO LAND THE GRAY THINGS THINK THEY ARE SAFE.

Warren knew he was a hard man, uninterested in talk, never easy with fellow crew members, comfortable only with his wife, and that for a mere few years, before the gray shield had descended between them. There was an emptiness inside him he knew that too without feeling shame or loss, not a lack but a blank space—a vacancy that made him hear the wind whisper and the slosh of waves and, because of the vacancy, to truly listen, not thinking of them as background to man's incessant mad talk, but as a separate song, the breathing of the planet. So he had an ear for the Skimmers and things

meant and shown but not said. He made it into words
because he was irreducibly human and the writing of it was a
way of fixing it, a mere human impulse against the rub of
time, to pin things with words. And the vacancy had saved
him, years of interior silence had made a quietness that was
solid now, stonelike.

> THEY THINK THEY ARE SAFE. THEY THINK THERE
> IS ONLY US, TRAPPED IN THIS NEW WORLD. WE BRING
> YOU TOOLS. WE KNOW THE WATERS. GRAY MACHINES
> MOVE NOW DO NOT SENSE CANNOT KNOW. CANNOT
> TASTE THE WATERS.

That afternoon the Skimmers carried more shipwreck
debris in, hauling it awkwardly in rope cradles they had
made, whole teams sharing the weight. He picked among it,
sorting and thinking. Later they brought him a skipjack to
eat.

He was tinkering with an antenna, making one from
cables, when the light abruptly faded. As he peered upward a
long shadow drifted against his raft. The underside was a
jumble of planking and timbers.

It held to his raft and Warren wondered wildly if it could
be from the gray ships, something made to float and find
survivors. He crouched down among the motors and parts,
staring upward, unable to see any Swarmers.

Something struck the water and fanned into a cascade of
bubbles. It twisted and flailed and suddenly Warren saw it
was a woman, swimming around the big shape, inspecting it
from below. She tugged at something, found it firm, and went
on. She glanced down, stopped stroking and hung there,
staring. He had the sense that she was looking through the
milky blocks of light and could see him. Just before she ran
out of air she made a gesture, a brief, choppy signal—and
darted upward, air rushing from her.

People. Other men and women who had learned to live
on the sea. Remnants.

Now a Skimmer came lazily into view, then more, and
Warren saw they had led these people on their large raft, led
them here.

Bringing together a ragtag bunch of survivors and aliens

without hands, adrift in an ocean already infested by the gray machines.

They would have little to work with. Wrecks. Salvage. Maybe some ships fleeing from the mainland, where the death was still spreading. But they could fashion things.

He was pretty sure that if he spread an antenna across the raft the radio could reach the deep orbit space stations, get word to them, if anyone still lived.

He would have to build a parabolic antenna, to broadcast in a narrow cone, with no side-lobes. If he kept the transmissions short the only chance of being detected was if one of their orbital craft passed through the cone.

Even if not, there must be more humans on the sea. They would have to be careful to avoid detection.

The gray things would wait until the fighting was over on land. Then they would move. They would have to come up, ready to take the solid ground. But they would have to cross the remaining ocean first, and now it was a sea with Skimmers in it and men upon it, life that had fought and lost and endured and fought again and went on silently, peering forward and by instinct seeking other life, still waiting when the gray things began to move again—life still powerful and still asking as life always does, and still dangerous and still coming.

He finished the skipjack, waiting. Presently the silvery sky overhead broke into jewels and the woman splashed through the bubbles, stroking downward powerfully. She circled, studying. Even this deep he felt the slow roll of waves that made the structure creak.

He rose. She caught sight of him and waved. Suddenly excited he threw his hands into the air, waving madly. Shouting. Though he knew she could not hear him yet.

PART TEN POCKS

ONE

Downward, into an ocean of night. The submersible was a bright, gaudy Christmas ball with spangles of running lights. It cast a wan glow on the massive shelves of carbon dioxide ice that walled the vent. Motors whirred. In the tight cabin the air chilled and pressure climbed.

Lancer's recon analysis had located dozens of warm spots on the surface. They were cracks in the ice layers, where warming currents below had worked their way up the fracture faults of the ice continents. The mountain ranges of ice and rock moved and shifted in gravid tectonics, breaking and folding and splintering.

This moon was bigger than Ganymede. Below its icy skin, a huge volume of slush and liquid circulated. At the center, a core of rock and metal became hotter as the radioactive elements decayed. Earth itself gained most of its internal heart from decay of radium and uranium. Here the heat from below sought an exit, working at the thin spherical cap of ice, seeping upward, finding an opening here, a weakness there, and at last breaking onto the surface in short-lived victory.

When the flow came strongly, escaping liquids built volcanoes. From their crown and flanks steam rose incessantly. They created lake-speckled plains when the currents ebbed. The ground crews had chosen a quiet upwelling, so they did not have to fight strong turbulence when the submersible descended, searching.

The vent widened as they plunged. Chunks of ice drifted by in the amber spotlights. They dropped several kilometers through solutions of ammonia, carbon dioxide slush, methane crystals, and twinkling specks of debris. The moon's spin stirred the grains of rock, keeping a fine suspension hanging like a shimmering curtain before the working lights.

They reached a zone of reasonably pure water. Carlos deployed a huge sac and ran nose into the current. It billowed and filled—strong, though only one molecule thick. Carlos showed Nikka how to attach floaters to the tail of the sac while he ran the board. He found a strong updraft. When he called out, she released the floaters and the sac self-sealed. Guided by the floaters, it rose up the vent. It would bob to the surface of the lake, be snagged ashore, and a mass spectrometer would separate out the rare deuterium. *Lancer's* fusion motors could burn the deuterium, as backup to the reactions that ran in the ramscoop drive.

"Rather a lot registering on the impurity detectors," Nigel observed.

"Whole zoo of stuff out there," Carlos muttered. He had been quiet since their descent. His face knotted with conflicting thoughts and he kept his attention fixed on the complex half-moon control pit.

"What's it look like?" Nikka had come forward after freeing the floaters manually.

"Chicken soup, actually. Or the Ross 128 equivalent," Nigel said from the wall bunk where he lay.

Carlos said, "Science Section's coming down in a few days, take deep samples."

"Interesting. Heavy molecular stuff. Free radicals, too."

"This water's too cold to make free radicals spontaneously," Nikka remarked. "No energy source."

"Indeed." Nigel frowned. "You'd imagine—"

Carlos. Want to talk to those passengers of yours.

"That's the fifth time he's called," Carlos said.

Nigel yawned. "Poor fellow. Ask if there's news."

"Ted, this situation is really out of hand and I just want to do what's—"

I know that. Hitting you all of a sudden like that, really mixing up your loyalties—I know, Carlos.

*   *   *

Nigel whispered, "Sounds quite judicious and forgiving. Man for all ages, is Ted."

Nikka smiled and shushed him.

"Marvelous actor. I never appreciated that till now."

Carlos had said little the last hour. The release of talking to a third party opened him up. He could not hide his own confusion and uncertainty, but this came through as reluctance to own up to his actions; or so Landon would interpret, Nigel guessed. Landon listened and conferred with the director of Pocks Operations. The surface crews were angry at the violation of regs and the possible danger—principally to the equipment; it was good to remember what was replaceable—in case Carlos got into a jam. But if he stayed away from the vent walls it made sense to let him go ahead, locating streams of pure water and filling the teardrop sacs. Landon conferred some more and then provisionally approved Carlos staying down. If anything changed, or Nigel's condition deteriorated, however—

"I've got a filter with me," Nigel put in.

Was wondering when I'd hear from the king-pin. I must say this is right in line with your whole career. Under pressure you crack.

There was a gentlemanly iciness in Landon's voice. They were, of course, both speaking for the recorded benefit of any future review board.

"Undergo a phase transition, is more the way I'd put it. Or tempering. Marvelous process, that. Lessens brittleness. Reduces internal stresses."

Well, we'll wait out the time for your mandatory vote. Don't think the consensus isn't going to factor in this escapade.

"I came with him, Ted," Nikka said. "Do you want to shut me up, too?"

"Don't commit yourself," Carlos broke in. "Ted, I hope you can see that she's in a very excited state and not really—"

I follow. Well, I could have done without this slice of shit you put on my plate, Nigel. Things are jittery back here as it is, with the Earthside news. We're waiting for an update now and I may have to replan everything if—

"What's the news?" Nikka asked.

Getting a spotty carrier wave. More thermonu- clear strikes, looks like. Satellite warfare seems to have gone just the way everyone predicted—complete cancellation. Reports of alien craft in orbit, too. Some are landing in the oceans.

"My God," Nikka said softly.

Yeah. And Nigel picks this moment to pull one of his—

"Bit cavalier about causality, aren't you?" Nigel said sharply. "You already had warning signals about the Earthside situation—it's been brewing for a week. So you thought you'd slot me away while everyone's distracted. No accident it's all happening at once. Only it's not going as you'd planned, is it?"

Paranoid, Nigel, real paranoid.

"We'll see. If I've any friends up there who'll vote for me—"

After this? Don't bet on it.

Nigel grimaced in irritation. "No point in this talk. Carlos, what's that on the sonar? Big structure in the left quadrant."

"Signing off," Carlos barked. The job took precedence over all else. He banked to port in a downstream.

"That was to get him off the air," Nigel said gently. "Needn't shy away from everything."

"If we hit one a those bergs—"

"Doesn't mean we must stand off by kilometers. Might as well get in a bit of exploring while we're waiting for the hangman."

"Nikka, want to deploy a bag? Getting good percentages here."

She moved back to the manuals. The floater frames and sacs were neatly arranged in the big bay that comprised most of the ship's volume. She worked the big controls at the mouth of the bay. "Free!" An answering *thump* and *whoosh*.

Carlos nodded. Nigel moved forward to the copilot's couch and lay in it, studying the board. A prickly sensation running through him. Carlos bent over the crescent array of controls, involved. The man had shown typical male responses during the talk with Landon. It was often that way when the conversation involved mostly men; each was bursting with something to say, waiting for the other to finish, for his own precious chance to impose his own pattern. Nigel had done that often enough to recognize the mode. But what was new to him was in fact that recognition. He had spent his life pressing forward, maneuvering the talk the way he wanted it to go. Focusing, always focusing. There were other ways to work, less wearing paths. He had learned those slowly, gradually. The fact that Carlos was showing recognizable signs meant that the man was working out for himself some sense of identity. Good. But it promised problems in the hours to come.

"Ready to tie it off?" Carlos called.

"Sealant deployed. One, two, *mark*." Nikka came forward, brushing her hands on her crimson jumper.

"Mind dropping a bit to the northwest?" Nigel said mildly.

"What for? Current's vectoring to the high quadrant."

"Some optical spectrum from over there."

"Huh. Okay."

Into the murk. They fell in blackness, the obliging whine of the motors making a high keening background wail they scarcely noticed. The dark clasped them and removed all sense of direction save the press of Pocks's muted gravity. They sought a glimmer, but in the shifting currents the craft could not hold to the course.

It was one of the fine ironies of history, Nigel thought, that this craft was in the end the result of classic, constricted warfare. Submarines had become the carriers of thermonuclear death nearly a century before. The major powers built involuted vessels which could withstand vast pressures, seek any enemy, survive, and track in utter blackness. When the

Jovian moons were explored, it was natural to use such technology to penetrate the ice crust, sniff the seas below. The marriage of war and science continued, despite occasional domestic spats. So *Lancer* had carried a team of submersibles, in case open oceans were rare on planets, and they had to penetrate a moon.

He squinted at the blank blackness before them. He knew with a dead finality that this was as far as he was going to get. He had stalled for time but now he was tiring. A few hours, a meaningless gesture of defiance—and then a sad, sour return.

Sod that, he thought suddenly. *I'm not going.*

There were some things a man wouldn't do.

TWO

They searched for hours. They ate, argued, took samples, deployed sacs, and sent them rising to the vent, tugged by racks of floaters.

They spoke fitfully, without making any clear progress. Nigel had been in a deeply conflicted three-way before, and recognized some old patterns. It occurred to him that he sought these complex emotional geometries because they removed some of the pressure of demand from him, allowed him to dream and laze about, focused on his own inner states. Not a wholly welcome revelation. But coming at the tether of a life, it at least implied that he could accept this truth, too, for it was clearly too late now. Then he laughed at himself—provoking a quizzical glance from Nikka, who probably suspected why—for this also was a conveniently intellectual way of escaping the pressure of change. Self-knowledge that arrives too late loses its momentum. He laughed again.

"I'm getting a lot more of that molecular stuff," Carlos said gruffly.

"Deeper, then," Nigel said. "Sniff it out."

"Dammit, I don't take orders!"

"I was suggesting—"

"You're always just 'suggesting' and 'advising,' aren't you?"

"You're quite right. I'll say nothing."

Carlos hesitated, still fuming. With Nigel having given way so easily, he was left with nothing more to say. He busied himself with the control board and after a while began following the direction indicated by the chem sensors. It was, after all, the obvious thing to do.

Slowly, so that at first they were unsure whether they saw it or imagined it, a faint blur of green formed in the dark. The instruments had picked it up, but only the eye gave form and substance to the mottled glow.

Abruptly, green shifted to burnt orange. Something came at them out of the blankness. It was long and spindly. Disjointed parts flexed and turned as it swept silently by. Trailing strands wove in the turbulent passing. Then it was gone.

"What the—"

"Exactly the question."

Nikka said softly, "Self-luminous."

"Yes. Feeding off the free radicals, I'll wager."

"No eyes."

"No reason to evolve them here."

"What do you figure—"

"Over that way."

A dim glow. The craft gave off a high-pitched *ping* and *crack* as they descended.

"What's that?"

"Can't make it out."

"Must be far away. No resolution."

"If it's that bright—"

"Right. Bloody luminous."

"Not one of the things we just saw."

"No. Bigger. A lot bigger."

It grew. Yellow bars of light moved in the suspended wash of particles. The craft bucked and turned against sudden currents.

"It's moving."

"A pattern. Look, see, it repeats."

"Revolving."

"Yeah. Spins around in 'bout two minutes."

The thing swelled. It was huge and pitted with fire. Brownish gold and orange swept across its face. From each

bright flare point burst a cascade of bubbles, each working
with its own inner fire.

"Damn thing's more'n a click across."

"Yes. See those big bags attached?"

"Balloons."

"To keep it afloat?"

"Must. Spectrometer says that's rock there. Hot."

"The free radicals."

"Dead right."

"They come from that?"

"Big fat energy source."

"Samplers out?"

"Yeah, got it. Lots of energetic molecular stuff."

"Food."

"For . . ."

The three humans shifted uneasily in their couches.
Their spotlights ebbed away in the silted darkness. They
watched the thing that spun slowly in the black and pulsed
irregularly, throwing out gouts of orange and burnished green
and gold and red, showers of hot bubbles. They strained
forward, trying to see farther.

"Lot of radioactivity."

"Figures."

"I'm . . . getting kind of nervous."

"Yeah. You feel it, Nigel?"

"What?"

"Like . . . something's out there"

"Moving."

"Beyond our lights? . . . Yes."

"We're in the updraft from it now. Getting a lot more
Geiger."

"Dangerous?"

"No. The gammas can't get through our skin."

"Blowoff from that thing."

"Suppose so. That big rock . . ."

"Right. A crude nuclear reactor."

"Duct chemicals through it, they get bombarded—"

"—you get excited molecular forms."

"What's the source of organic molecules?"

"Below here? Something's got to supply them."

"Right. Tending the fire."

"Why put it near a vent?"

"Why move to Florida? Warmer."

"No, wait, that's the wrong way round. The vent, the vent is here—"

"*Because* of this."

"The whole thing's artificial."

"The volcanoes, the lakes, they're made by things like *this*?"

"Walmsley's Rule."

"In spades. Warm currents, food—"

"And an opening to the surface."

Carlos said, "To do what? I mean . . ."

"I don't know," Nigel said.

"Why are we whispering?" Nikka asked.

Nigel shouted, "Maybe they can hear!"

"Jesus!" Carlos said.

"Then again, maybe not." Nigel settled back in his couch. "They've overheard our motors long before this, if they do. And they must, come to think of it. Acoustics are the fish's eye."

Nikka said, "That thing that went by us was luminous."

"So?" Carlos said.

"There must be a reason for that. To find prey."

Nigel murmured, "Or lure it."

Carlos said, "I wonder if I should douse our running lights."

"It might well be a good idea," Nikka said.

He snapped off several switches. The control crescent cast angular shadows in the cabin.

Nigel said softly, "Should call *Lancer*, let them know."

Carlos did. Before he could explain, Ted Landon came on the line. "We've got a solid majority vote on your petition, Nigel. Sorry 'bout that."

Nigel shook himself from his dreamy state. "What . . . oh, yes. So?"

"You've lost. C'mon out."

Nigel sighed. Ted was in quite a jovial mood. "Tell him, Carlos."

Talk continued, but he knew what would come next. He felt a fatigue seeping into him but with it came an old certainty. Ted was a stickler for the rules, especially those rubber-stamped by the consensus mandate of the beloved bloody people.

Carlos spoke with assurance, putting down the facts in steady fashion, orderly and authoritative. He would be more difficult to deal with, the more he clarified his own idea of himself.

Nigel got up and moved casually to the rear of the ship.

"Nature calls," he said to Nikka. He could not risk a parting wink.

THREE

Their suits were racked in smooth-swiveling braces. He swung one out in an arc until it clipped onto the self-suiting platform. He backed into its enfolding grip. He jackknifed forward to get his arms into the sleeves and then worked his head through the neck ring. It enveloped him, an action that to Nigel always carried the quality of shaking hands with a corpse. He straightened and the rack zipped him up the chest. Helmet locks snapped and clicked home. The suit had full thermal insulation and heavy heaters, weighing on him like a blanket.

He shambled into the equipment bay, an ankle protesting the added bulk. A hexagonal frame was resting in the launch pod. It held the six floaters for the next sac. Nigel detached the leaders to the sac so that the frame stood alone. He took the two central floaters out and climbed into the vacant space.

The balance would be wrong. He looked around for something massive. His eye stopped on the medfilter, set down and forgotten hours ago.

Why not? Infernal thing, reminder of countless hours spent in its clutches. This was the last act, but still the thing could perhaps keep him alert, fight off the nausea if it returned. And he needed ballast. He fetched it and clamped it to the midsection of the frame, moving as quickly as he could.

Very well. Time to go.

He turned the manual controls and leaned back. A

conveyor carried the frame into the lock. He found a way to clip his suit belt to the frame. Nigel punched in instructions for his suit as the lock sealed behind him. Air fled, pressure dropped, he braced himself—

The outer lock irised open. *Whoomp.* The frame shot off the platform. Air broke into a gush of bubbles and the roar carried him out, tumbling. The floaters popped free and began to swell. He spun, weightless, the fulcrum of vectoring forces as his suit creaked and his ears popped and a shower of bubbles rose around him like a flock of bright birds. Then the dark descended.

He came upright and saw the ship below, glistening. The floaters bobbed and sucked him upward. He had not thought through the balance of buoyancy and now saw he was too light.

What the—Must be a misfire Nikka go back there check the

He was rushing away from the glimmering ball of light. Farther below the smoldering fires of the stony reactor reddened the water. From this perspective they were remarkably similar pieces of technology.

Bags are free? How'd that happen must've been

Nikka answered, *No I think wait*

Ted says we should back away from this don't worry about the equipment might be a pressure malf anyway we should get clear fast let ExoBio get in on this

He was rising too quickly. The frame would scoot all the way to the ice skin with so little weight to drag. Nigel suddenly realized that his suit could take extreme pressures, but could not adjust quickly to rapid changes in depth. If he kept rising—

Carlos where is he I can't

*　　*　　*

Nigel's ears popped. He stared upward at the floaters, swelling as they rose. Darkness cloaked him now as the ship fell away below. He did not dare show a light this close but he would need it to free one of the floaters. Now he could scarcely make out the bulk of them.

You mean you think he

The suit was bulky and awkward in the water and he had to search for the tabs on his left arm. He uncapped the spike and raised the arm. The third button should be—

A bright blue line sliced the water. He fanned it, leaving behind curling wisps of steam. The laser cutter boiled away a thin column and found a floater. The bag crinkled, turned brown—

Broke. Air gushed out. Nigel fired again, at the opposite floater. The beam churned the water soundlessly. It ate a thin, straight path, ghostly blue, haloed by steam. If the power ran out before—

That's crazy! Mierda seca, the old bastard'll
That suit can take it but listen to me damn it
turn on the spots we can trace him

The second floater burst. The beam leaped across the inside of it and punched a hole through the top. Nigel felt himself falling and then the frame slowed, still dropping. Equilibrium.

I'll call Ted he'll
Later. See anything? There might be a suit light.
Try the tracer.
Something wrong no pickup I can see
He can't be beyond range this soon
Look for yourself his code shows nonoperational.
He doctored it before he left must be

Floating, in an absence of space and light and weight. It was like the time on the slab, disconnected from the wearing of the world. Being in the high dark emptiness of space was much like the blank absorbing blackness here. His movements were sluggish, blunted by the unseen waters. No sound. When his boots struck the piping there came not a ringing but a muffled thud. He hung loosely to the frame and waited for something to come.

> *Look Ted's on the line says he's too busy to worry about this old fart there's news from Earthside looks bad new assembly starting in a few minutes*
> *They can't leave him out there call the teams on the surface get some more subs down here and*
> *Nikka, this is Ted. Admittedly Nigel was right about one thing looks like—I mean his Walmsley's Rule and all that. That must be a Watcher and Operations tells me it's showing signs of life now, probably in response to our ground teams so*
> *Then send down some submersibles damn it*
> *Look there's too many things happening at once Nikka I don't have time to hunt for that bastard right now let him stew*
> *He did it to stall for time don't you see that*
> *Stupid move just makes us more pissed up here Ted I appeal to*
> *He's acting like a horse's ass over nothing. I'm through with all this shit of his! Maybe he thought he'd get some sympathy support this way, but it won't cut up here, I can tell you that in spades*

He sensed the running current taking him farther away from them. This was the farthest he had ever been, the natural tether. It was better to do it this way, in pursuit.

> *I'm pulling you people out soon as I can and if he's gone he's just gone that's it*
> *It will take hours*
> *Okay you can search for a while the assembly starts in ten minutes anyway but I warn you—look, if he's patched in still he can hear this. Nigel, this is it man, the last*

He ignored the barking voice. Something more immediate disturbed him.

Rippling currents. He ignited a small helmet phosphor.

The bars of the frame leaped into being around him, yellow and stark.

Nothing nearby. A tug, a fresh direction—

Something glimmered. It grew. A ball of ruddy clouds. Swelling toward him, coming fast—

Things moved inside. Specks in the clouds. Drifting dots. He tried to judge size but without perspective—

The color. A smoldering red, dying embers—

He held onto the pipes of the frame as the cage jiggled and surged sideways. Where had he seen—?

The specks did not drift aimlessly. The clouds were in fact hillsides and the dots walked on them, slowly, amid swirls of dust. They were large, stately, with four smoothly articulating legs—

EMs.

But not the huge-headed beasts he knew. These were slim, tall, graceful in their grave pacing.

Not EMs, not without the radio-dish heads and the awkward carapace that housed the reworked guts.

These were what the EMs had been before.

Before the asteroid rain crushed their biosphere. Before they had to remake themselves into something the Watchers would pass as perhaps machinelike.

They were inside a vast ball, fully five kilometers across. Inside were hills, streams, dusty clouds, high forests of blue and brown. It reminded him of those childhood toys which, shaken, show a winter scene with descending snow. Only here the liquid was outside, and within moved a trapped world of air and growth. The sphere's shell glowed, casting ruddy light inward. Above it, dark masses. Ballast? Stabilizers?

It began to dwindle. The currents were sweeping him past, taking him away. He fired his laser beam over his head, making a blue arc. One of the tall moving figures seemed to pause, to look outward.

Had they seen him? Did they know what had happened to their race back on the home world? Deformed, beaten down but still going on—

Of course they knew something. They must be the remnants of an earlier age, a time when their world sent out ships and explored the nearby stars. They had taken shelter inside this moon.

So close! He knew their descendants, could tell them

that the home world hung on still. If he could make a sign, some gesture across the abyss—

The red world shrank rapidly. He waved once, forlornly, and rested heavily against the medfilter. The chance had slipped by him.

He closed his eyes and let time pass. The image of the tall, grave creatures faded slowly.

FOUR

Something moved.

He jerked awake. Nigel shook himself and wondered how long he had been asleep. The suit warmed him, made him comfortable even in this cold murk. He had been trying to fit the pieces together...

> *See anything of him?*
> *No. Damn all, how could he get so far so fast?*

He wondered why they could not pick him up on long-range sonar. Surely he could not have drifted that far away, not with them following the same currents he did.

> *Look at this video image from Earthside. One of those things in orbit, looks hell of a lot like a Watcher.*

If he was close enough to pick up their general craft transmissions, they *had* to see him. Unless something was behind him, so they couldn't pick up his image against it.

Movement again.

He clicked on a helmet phosphor. The sharp outline and colors of the floater frame leaped out at him. The medfilter, shiny aluminum pipes, floaters billowing above him...

Something beyond. Something in the shadows.

A huge wall coming at him out of the blackness.

Gray pores. Speckled bands of red and purple.

A vast oval opening in the wall of flesh, rimmed with ridges of cartilage.

It brushed against the frame. Suckers in its side clasped the support rods. Slick brown tendrils curled about the metal.

Tasting? Whatever, the motion stopped. Nigel waited. He shook the frame. The grip tightened.

It didn't seem to want to eat him. Was it studying him somehow? Best to wait and see.

He heard nothing from Carlos and Nikka. The bulk of this thing must be blocking them.

Time ticked by. He felt the old weakness slide into him, the sign of his body going awry again. Sudden activity, without rest, had thrown his chemistry out of balance. He surveyed the huge creature that gripped the frame, and wondered if it knew he was here. Or what kind of thing he might be.

Weakly:

> How we going to find him in this?
> Lot of floating junk. Follow the currents, keep away from that big stuff.

He had known they had to be out here, hanging away from the strange intruding craft that spewed fumes and whined and bucked against the currents instead of following them.

The gamble was that they would not have a history of intrusions like that, that the Watcher had not sent down craft that cracked the ice and searched out life wherever it could be found, that the Watcher would wait in its rigid orbit and peer downward and know that as long as life kept inside its shell of ice it was harmless. The Watchers were patient and abiding and knew more of life than men, knew that it could arise wherever energy passed through a chemical environment and drove the processes that made a mockery of entropy, building up order.

This was the secret that Pocks had to teach: that at a moon's core, nuclear isotopes collected and sputtered and delivered up their warmth to an ocean of elemental matter, and that was enough.

Eventually molecules would snag other links and make a

crude copy, driven in this inward ocean to grow, clustered around the mock sun at the core of the world, amid crushing pressures and stinging dark, without lightning to hasten the brew or streaming baths of light from the sky, but merely and simply from the silent churn of nuclear decay, the way life springs from a heap of moist humus in a forgotten back corner, making use of energy from below in an ocean capped by ice, thermal cells mixing the chemicals which sought each other in their passion—at first plants innocent of photosynthesis, and then predators and prey who basked in the rich streams of life that were born amid the continual upwelling of free radicals. Sulfur compounds, like those bubbling from the volcanic vents in Earth's oceans, could metabolize this brawling jungle with restless energy.

The nature of life here was to be always rejected, forced up by the thermals, into the upper blackness, pushed away from the molecular fire, a biosphere doomed to seek the searing dark. When the core ebbed, the long radioactive half-lives done, there came cutting competition, a narrowing event like the ancient drought in Africa that had sharpened the wits of primates. As the crimson corefires damped, at first life must have merely fought for places near the bubbling fires, but in time some being saw that the heat could be clasped, moved, used to push—upward through the weightless rigid black, against the ice, and into it, and then beyond—scavenging the crusty rocks that held radioactives, seeking in the hostile vacuum and searing cold.

There must have been a time when they struggled to understand their ice surface, perhaps managed to discover electricity and begin to tinker with radio, a time when the pre-EMs came, when the races met. A first, tenuous contact. But those first sputters announced their presence in a swelling bubble moving at light speed.

So there appeared above in the brilliant night a gray thing ancient and knowing, which hurled down rock and pitted the icelands and drove the creatures back, forced them retreating through the vent into the inward sea, where now with crude tools they kept watch, their brute sciences used to cup some rock from the core and buoy it, to make the upwellings and warm spots in the crust that would keep the vents wide, allow a shred of possibility that these huge things needed and would not let slip from them.

So the impasse came, with the slow tick of time running against these blind things, against the pre-EMs who had fled downward with them. For a while they would be safe from the passive Watcher. Ten kilometers of ice could stop any thermonuclear blast, absorb the slamming punch of an asteroid, withstand the furious bursting of its sun going nova—which the machine civilizations had used before in Aquila; Nigel knew that from the *Marginis* records, though the conventional astronomers had another explanation—and so the Watcher waited.

Impasse. They remained, enduring and yet trapped, sealed into their bleak sea with the certainty that the stone above would win in the end. Without the freedom to crawl out, to learn the Newtonian web of laws that governed life in freedom from water but enslaved to gravity, they could not hope to match and destroy the Watcher.

So in their songs there had to be tales of a brave and foolish time when gallant ones had sought the vacuum, been pounded and destroyed, and so dragged back down to make their tales and rage against the thing that waited at the top of the long vents. Yet the fact that they kept the vents open, tending them like fires that must never go out, meant that the tales still lived and the harsh judgment of history had not bowed them down, not driven them finally back to the core, where they would cluster about the embers and die.

> *Okay keep looking but I tell you he's gone.*
> *Stay at this depth, Carlos, I'm not leaving—*
> *Okay okay, but I want to hear the report.*
> *Shut up—hey—no light in the cabin!—I can't*
> see with—
> *I just want to—*
> *Shut up*

He felt a slackness in his legs. Every movement took enormous energy. He reached over, got a grip on the medfilter. It looked okay. The plug-ins—

He swore. The canister of interfaces was gone. The hoses where it clamped to the side were open, bare. Hitting this creature had ripped it away.

So he was finished. Within an hour the buildup of

residue in his blood would lead from nausea to spasms and then into a merciful coma. Without a receiving system, some fine-webbed fiber to accept the sludge that the medfilter leached from him, the device would not work.

Nigel sighed. Betrayed in the end by a malf. No philosophical lesson here, unless it was the eternal one: We die from entropy.

He peered down. No sign of the ship. He would call them now. If they could find him in time, all well and good. It had been a temporary gesture, irrational at best, an attempt, he now saw, to make some fleeting contact with the life he knew must lurk in the shadows beyond the lights. He smiled at his own folly. So—

Something made him turn to the mottled, pitted hide beside him. It stretched away, filling half of space, mute as stone waiting for the chisel. He frowned.

> *Jesus you hear that* Madre Dios *a war*

If there was the right kind of fiber under the skin . . .

> *Ninety percent destruction a full nuclear exchange all four major powers Jesus*
> *Where's the message from then*
> *Orbital stations they're still alive but they say there's no way they can continue transmission for long the power requirements are too much now but Jesus*

Nigel hung, letting the news wash over him, and for a long time could not think. Humanity driven to its knees. And by its own hand.

Talk flooded through him, from the submersible and then a full comm from the *Lancer* meeting. He listened and yet the weight of it could not fully come to bear. His instinctive defenses blunted the news, the details, the train of numbers and blasted cities and death counts, of nations erased and lands turned to cinder.

Slowly he began to move again. He blocked the stream of talk. He drew back into himself and made his hands do what he knew they had to do, despite the chaos of emotions that ran through him.

Unclamp the medfilter. Cut some piping from the frame sharpen the pipe to a point, using the laser cutter.

Attach the tubing. Issue start-up commands.

Even at these pressures and in this chill, the system came up to full mode. He hooked it into the med inputs in his suit. A simple vein tap was enough for now.

The wall of flesh glistened beneath his working phosphors. It writhed with soft bands of pale crimson and purple. Intricate patterns, arabesques of line and big, mottled patches. So he had been wrong: In this ocean that was a world lived something that could see such patterns, or else they would not have evolved. Perhaps the swift self-luminous thing they saw earlier? There had to be a vast, complex ecology here, schools of fishlike things to feed on, a pyramid of life. The submersible had probably frightened them away.

He realized he was theorizing, delaying. The knowing of it released him from the storm of emotion he was repressing and he gave himself over to it.

He drove the point of the pipe full into the mass of flesh. The movement cast a shadow, lunging and enormous across the plain.

It went halfway. Nigel pushed hard and buried it farther. He felt no response, no tremor, no sign of pain. Moving sluggishly, he completed the hookup. Turned on the pumps. Relaxed into a dazed and empty state, a strange pulse flowing in him.

FIVE

Inert. Drifting. Disconnected from glands and the singing of blood. Awake but not fully aware.

This was how it might be for the Watchers, and the machine labyrinths that had made them. Patient and calculating, in principle like life in their analytic function and in the laws of evolution that acted equally on silicon-germanium as it did on DNA, yet they were not fully in the world as life was, they had not risen from the crusted bonds of molecular law, did not thrive in the universe of essences—as the Snark had put it, groping for a human term to tell what it felt lay forever beyond its cybernetic grasp—and thus feared and hated the organic things that had given birth to them and died in turn.

Or perhaps the words *hate* and *fear* could not penetrate the cool world where thought did not stir hormones to love or flee or fight, where analysis reigned and built with bricks of syllogism a world that knew the hard hand of competition but not the organic wholeness that came out of an enduring mortality.

Yet the Watchers had things in common with organic life. A loyalty to their kind.

They had destroyed utterly the world around Wolf 359, and patrolled it still. But they did not oversee the dutiful robots who chipped bergs from the outer ice moons and sent them spiraling in, to crash on what was once their home world. A Watcher circled that world, to guard against any organic form that might arise when the vapor and liquid brought sunward finally collected into ponds and seas.

It would have been simpler to destroy those robots too, leaving all barren and without hope. The Watcher allowed those simple servants to continue, knowing they would some-day err in their self-replication as they repaired themselves, and in that moment begin machine evolution anew.

So the machines wanted their own diversity to spill over and bring fresh forms to the galaxy—all the while guarding against a new biosphere, which the patient, loyal robots labored to make—so that machine societies would not be static and thus in the end vulnerable no matter how strong now.

They needed the many functions, echoing life—the oil carriers who voyaged to some distant metropolis, the Snarks to explore and report and dream in their long exile, the Watchers who hammered worlds again and again with asteroids.

Yet they must know of the chemical feast within the giant molecular clouds that *Lancer* had brushed by. Know that every world would be seeded perpetually by the swelling massive clouds. Know, then, that the conflict would go on for eternity; there was no victory but only bitter war.

If the machines crushed life where they could, why had humanity arisen at all? Something must have guarded them.

The Watchers kept sentinel for signs of spacegoing life, signaling to each other as the one at Isis had sent a microwave burst past *Lancer*, to Ross 128. The *Marginis* wreck was evidence that Earth's Watcher had been destroyed by someone, a race now gone a million years.

The pre-EMs? The race that remade itself at Isis?

The thought came suddenly. Perhaps. So much was lost in time...

Whoever had come to that ancient Earth had left fluxlife, a sure sign that the *Marginis* wreck carried organic beings, for only they would use a thing that reproduced itself with a molecular genetic code. And fluxlife was the sign and the gift: an opening to the stars.

The pulsing in him was becoming a song and the harmonics of it called up the long weary wail of the EMs, in a timeless weave that blended this huge blind creature into the same slow, ponderous hymn of life in the galaxy, weighed and hammered down yet still with an abiding hope, a need, a calling.

He felt his mind clearing.

He checked his medcomp. It was good, no trace of the runaway reactions. He gingerly detached from the silent solid mass. Pulled out the sharpened pipe.

The tendrils holding the frame jerked away in a spasm of rejection. The frame shuddered and came free.

The medmon tumbled out of the pipe brace. Nigel twisted around and snatched, gasping. Caught it.

He grabbed for the frame, too, and pain shot through his arm. He held.

Stretched between two charging horses, he thought wildly. The frame wrenched sideways. His joints popped. *Can't take much of this*. By the dim suit lamp he saw the slowly turning struts. Limp bags trailed it. Most of the floaters were crushed.

Falling. Above, the vast bulk faded in the dimming amber light and yet it was so large that it did not seem to grow smaller as the distance increased. He could not see the sides of it.

Nigel fought for a hold with his boots. The frame tumbled. Currents plucked at him, trying to snatch away the medfilter, to loosen his hand on the pipe.

He fought—and then realized he did not need the frame

any longer. It was falling too, floaters useless. He simply let go. Darkness swallowed the skeletal shape.

His final security was gone. He was falling in absolute hard black, clutching his faintly ludicrous filter, invisible currents swirling and gurgling.

He came back from the blurred pain in his arms, to hear the ragged lines of argument from *Lancer*'s consensus meeting.

> *Swarmers had something to do with it everything to do with it of course don't be a fool*
> *But there's no evidence not clear evidence anyway*
> *Plain as the nose on your face they were the advance party*
> *Yeah these ships in orbit now they look like the ones the Swarmers came in just look at the*
> *All mixed in together*

Nikka's voice broke in, *Nigel! Nigel! Time is—* "Yes, I hear."

> *You had your reasons I'm sure but too much is happening, I'm frightened, I don't want you out there when—*

"Of course. I . . . I'm sorry. I was shagged out, dead bushed, and this seemed the only way to finally . . . I haven't been on a planetary surface, I've had no chance to ever really, to . . . I . . ." His voice trailed away as he felt the old block, the inability to communicate deep recesses that lay beyond language.

> *Turn on your tracer. It works, doesn't it?*

"Done, I'm falling," he added mildly.

> *How did—*

"A boring long tale."

> *We're coming. You're picking up the* Lancer *comm? I piped it through on open circuit.*

*   *   *

"Yes. Dead awful." He could think of nothing more to say. The full weight of it would come on him later, he knew. The mind did what it must to survive.

> I've got you fixed a few klicks away but you're moving fast nothing nearby
> Jesus we'll have to catch him how can we

Nigel relaxed, spread-eagling himself to offer the most flow resistance. His ears popped. Suit adjustment.

> It's impossible, we don't have that kind of maneuvering ability
> Shut up, he'll hear you, Carlos
> But it—look, we can get there but Madre Dios it'll take ten minutes minimum and we'll be moving too fast.

Knobbed joints grumbling with pain, muscles whining, heart thumping dumbly in the converging dark.
"Get—get under me. Then . . . deploy . . . a sac."
Gliding in the soft night. Coasting. What was coming depended on relaxation, reaching out with the senses. He could not tighten up or the frail ol muscles would tire before they were needed. He had to let go.

SIX

Decades ago, after Alexandria's death, Mr. Ichino had said to him, *I wish you the strength to let go.*
He needed that now. Until he saw the submersible and knew which direction to bank toward, there was nothing productive he could do. Either they would snag him in time, or else he would fall farther in this cold murk, into higher

pressures, and his suit would fail. He would squash like a grape.

From the *Lancer* meeting came

> *Obviously those goddamn Swarmers started it*
>
> *Yeah the Trojan horse*
>
> *Dunno how the nukes got going but when those Swarmers started coming ashore what was China supposed to do, matter of survival if what they say about the Americans is true*
>
> *Was true you mean—North America's gone, incinerated*
>
> *Those high-burst bombs, just one'll ignite a continent*
>
> *Asian mainland took less nukes, looks like Swarmers are getting pasted good there thank God*
>
> *Merde je ne*
>
> *Those flying things—ugly, you see 'em, horrible— an' that on-site report says the Swarmers don' re- produce usin' the flyin' thing at all they're some kind of add-on*
>
> *Damn Swarmers musta planned it from 'way back an' bioengineered themselves*
>
> *Point is it's all linked—the Watchers an' those gray ships an' the Swarmers—all in it together*

He felt the waters rushing by, gurgling and whispering to him. He was without weight and form and felt himself spreading ever wider, as if his legs and arms were detached, a flag filling. Words and sentences and garbled bits came from *Lancer* and the submersible, but they seemed hollow and distant and finally irrelevant.

He wondered if the huge creatures perceived him, a falling mote, and puzzled over the brilliant bubble that swam to meet him.

> *Damfino how it all works but it's plain as the nose on your face*
>
> *Goddamn Ted we got to do somethin'*
>
> *Latest says the deepspace net is sending in fragmentation loads, blow them up ten thousand*

klicks out and try to knock out some of their ships in orbit

    Might get some of the small stuff but those big ones

He saw a faint luminous thread of orange to the left, turning and twisting and darting away, and felt at the same moment a long booming note that tolled through the water like a distant bell. It reminded him of the EMs and their song, and as he lazily plunged toward the heart of this ocean world he saw suddenly how this tied together with the Swarmers, all forms of life victimized and beaten down because in the end the machines could not stop life, could not smother it, could not eliminate forever the endlessly burgeoning forms which competed with the machines for resources and space, and so in the end they enlisted some forms of life to stop their worst competitors, the budding technologies.

The machines had known of Earth for a long time, they had fought some titanic battle there millions of years ago and lost—the *Marginis* wreck was the only mute remaining testament of that—and in the losing had become fearful of simply blasting it with asteroids or doing anything else which could perhaps be blocked by the *Marginis* wreck or by humans themselves. If they tried bombardment, as they did with Isis, and the humans captured some of their vessels, deciphered where their centers of power were, then the same crushing warfare might reach across the stars and find them in their lairs, unleash the terrible marriage of mind and instinct—which the machines did not have—and destroy all that the patient and implacable cybernetic beings had built up.

No, it was much easier to use organic forms against each other, to divert their attention, to strike at the weak spot all beings who grew out of chemistry had and which was both biological and social in form, and went by many names: cancer, overreactive immune systems, inappropriate response.

There was the key. Far easier to make humans destroy themselves and Swarmers as well. Far easier to feed on the deep and primordial antagonisms all organic forms felt for the outsider, the intruder, the alien.

*   *   *

Goddamnit I say we got to learn something about these things not just shy away from them

What we learn will help Earthside they've got the same kind over 'em right now

Years ago yeah remember the light travel time we're talking about a crisis that happened nine years back

Doesn't change the fact that we're the only ones know much about these things an' here right here we have a chance to see what it can take

Light. A faint smudge of phosphors. Growing.

Nigel we've got the sac deployed below and with the mouth open

He banked left, sensing the currents, hearing a faint strum like a song of deep bass. His ears popped again. Suit pressure too high, overloaded. Pocks had light gravity, so pressure built only a tenth as fast as on Earth, but now he felt his suit creak. Monitor bulbs below his chin flashed angry red.

He's dropping too fast, we're too far away
Cut the speed damn it he needs a stationary
No got to get closer

"Hold your course!"

A ball of yellow and blue and amber. He thought of himself as a wing, turning and riding in the streams. He tried to catch the turn at the right moment, altering his vector to bring himself down at a steeper angle, then using the medfilter pack to cant himself to the right again—now down, now to the side, the bright ball growing and the big floodlights poking fingers through the silted murk. He grunted with the strain of keeping himself rigid, a hydrofoil. His pulse quickened. He was coming in at a good angle now and ahead he saw the filmy wisp of the sac, its mouth yawning, unexploded floaters weighing down its tail.

*   *   *

I've got you on the optical 'scope. How are you doing?

"Rilly trif."

Drop the pack Nigel you'll have a better chance of making it without that thing

"I think...I'll need it..." he panted.

Swooping. Flying. A grain in the deep clotted darkness, insect flying into the harsh glare of the bulb.

The mouth swallowed him.

SEVEN

Nigel woke as they docked.

Sleep had helped. His vision was nearly right now; quick turns of his head brought only momentary confusion.

Nikka had gotten him to a bunk and he had waved aside all talk. There was more to come, he could sense that in the scattershot babble over the comm lines. So in the long journey floating up through the vent, he had slept. Now he lay resting and listened to the *Lancer* line.

Goddamnit we've got to move

Yeah no telling what that thing will do to us if we try to leave after this

Hell yes that Watcher's got word from Earth sure as we have

Look at it, things moving on its surface again

Just lights looks like to me

Bob you want to send some servo'd squad down there have a look

Naw can't you get it straight this is no time for half measures

Ted! I say we shouldn't try anything so dangerous, I mean the Watcher around Isis let us go

*Lissen to him crawlin' on his belly about how
the damn thing might let us go if we're good boys
don't make trouble Jesus*

There was no point in trying to intervene in the hubbub
aboard *Lancer*. His stock was at an all-time low, even though
Walmsley's Rule had turned out true.

They left the submersible and crossed the bleak purple
ice. Carlos rattled on about the *Lancer* concensus, the rage,
the horror, but the words went by Nigel without stirring him.

He leaned on Nikka for support as they shuffled away
from the lake, boots crunching on ice. A fine-grained fatigue
laced through him, bringing a giddy clarity.

His suit had burnished marks where the big creature had
apparently tried to hold onto him. He had never noticed.

Near the fissures something a curious pale gray covered
the ice. It stretched across the plain in long fingers. In places
it seemed to seek the full sunlight glare from Ross.

"What's that?" Nigel gestured.

"Some kind of plant that can grow in vacuum, I'd guess,"
Nikka said.

Nigel paused to look at the stuff. It was crusty on top.
He thumped it with a fist. It clenched. "Grips the ice, looks
like," he said. "Marvelous."

This thin remnant cheered him. Life had crawled out
onto even this blasted, hostile place. Life simply kept on.
Blindly, yes, but undefeated.

"Looks a bit like algae," he said, squatting. "See how it
holds onto the ice?" He tried to pry up the edge. With
considerable effort he managed to lift an inch-thick slab the
size of his fist. The ice under it was pitted. It oozed a filmy
liquid. When he let go the pancakelike algae flopped back
down onto the ice.

"Come on," Nikka said, ever the efficient, careful worker.
"Let's get to shelter."

"Comin', luv," Nigel said in a parody of a British accent.

He felt oddly elated. Emotional currents moved in him.

He watched the crews laboring on the plain, beneath a
black sky. For an instant he tried to see them as the Watcher
would: Bags of ropy guts, skin shiny with grease, food stuck
between their teeth, scaly with constantly decaying cells that
fell from them as they walked, moving garbage, yellow fat

caught between brittle white bones, stringy muscles clenching
and stretching to move a cage of calcium rods around, oozing
and stinking and—

He shook himself. The machine cultures had been in the
galaxy a long time, since the first inhabited world committed
nuclear suicide. They were an accidental fact of the universe,
arising from the inappropriate response of the organic beings.
But that did not mean they would reign supreme, that their
vision was any more true than his own oblique perspective.

>*Earth needs all the information it can get*
>*With nine years' time delay?*
>*You heard that message they picked up from
>the Pacific. People out there afloat, workin' with the
>Skimmers, talkin' to 'em, waitin' for those gray
>amphibious things to come up to the surface after
>they landed—*
>*He's right, we got to get information, figure out
>what's goin' on, how these Watchers work, send it
>Earthside to help them.*
>*Damn right Ted we got to*
>*Now listen, I'm as brassed off as any of you at
>all this delay but believe me I want us to have a full
>consensus here*
>*What the hell you saying?*
>*You don't act, Ted, we can replace you fast,
>real fast—*
>*Plenty of people can step right in, take over*
>*Sure, listen, it could be that Watcher hasn't
>gotten the whole story from Earthside yet, from
>those gray ships, they must be pretty damn busy*
>*That Watcher's old, slow*
>*We hit it now maybe take it by surprise—*
>*Enough of your waffling Ted*
>*Yeah you got the sense of the meeting*
>*You do something and fast or we vote you out,
>Ted*
>*Simple as that*
>*I understand your concern and if you'll merely
>let me think*
>*I'm calling the question Mr. Chairman*
>*No wait let me ask—Bob?*

Uh, yes, Ted?
Are we cleared?
All revved.
*All right then I'm ordering Propulsion to bring
the ramscoop up to ignition*
That's great!
*I take it I have the approval of you all? And
does anybody have anything further to add?*
All primed Ted
Team here is ready

Nigel shook himself. Ted has used the consensus for so
long, and now it was using him.

"Don't you think we should get inside?" Nikka asked.

"That air bubble won't be any protection. Quite the
reverse, if you shed your helmet."

Carlos called, "Look! They're turning *Lancer*." Then,
plaintively; "They're not going to evacuate first."

"The Watcher is active. It might skrag our shuttle,"
Nigel said, looking at Carlos.

The man was making an effort to be more authoritative
now, speaking more deeply and using more abrupt phrases.
Still, it was unconvincing. *Inappropriate response.* Yes, that
was the nub of it, the wrong answer to one of the inherent
troubles of organic life. The machines had no need of sex;
they could reproduce through a template And they could
alter themselves at will, a form of voluntary evolution.

Organic beings were forever split into the efficient yet
isolating bonds of two sexes, two views of the world, two
dynamics that only partially overlapped, two beings who
desired the other but could never wholly *be* the other, no
matter how surgery or simulations promised a fleeting false
liberation from the problem of forever being who you truly
were, separate and unlike and yearning in the darkness you
made for yourself.

Overhead in the hard night, *Lancer* moved.

It turned on its axis and brought the exhaust of the
ramscoop to bear on the Watcher. Men and women stood on
the barren plain and watched the silvery dot that was their
home. *Lancer* pulsed with fresh energy. The magnetic fields
gathered, driven by the awakened fluxlife.

"Hope they burn the damn thing to a cinder," Carlos said fiercely.

"Nigel, I don't like this," Nikka whispered.

Nigel said laconically, "Listen. They're calling it an 'exploratory attack.'"

"It's revenge," Nikka said.

"Don't be such a coward," Carlos said roughly. "It's about time somebody *did* something."

Nigel's eyebrows arched like iron-gray caterpillars. "Indeed. But not this."

Crusted orange lights moved on the Watcher. Blue bands crisscrossed it. A halo of darting burnt-yellow specks appeared around *Lancer* as the drive engaged. The ramscoop required a mix of deuterium and other isotopes to begin the fire.

Carlos began, "I bet it's never seen a fusion drive before, or it'd be more—" and the sky exploded.

A gout of flame curled out of *Lancer*'s exhaust. The fusion start-up belched ionized plasma in a roaring streak that slammed into the Watcher.

"Jesus!" Carlos cried. "That'll fry it for sure."

Soundless, the stream poured forth, spattering streamers of blue and gold and crimson on the Watcher's gray stone and tarnished metal.

"This is mere show," Nigel said. Arcing plasma lit the plain around them, throwing grotesque shadows. "The high-energy gamma rays are doing the real damage."

"How long can it . . . ?" Nikka said.

"*Lancer* can keep this up for hours, but—ah, see, it's altering orbit from the reaction already."

"Damn thing'll be fried good by—"

Movement from the Watcher.

A thin spout of crisp orange flame shot forward, spanning the distance to *Lancer* so quickly it appeared instantly as a bar of light between the two. It wrapped around the flux lines of the magnetic throat and exhaust, licking and eating at the ship, curling down the long magnetic tunnels, spewing into the drive tubes, burning everywhere, gnawing at the delicate electronics and fluxlife and humans inside.

Lancer's drive sputtered. Died. The Watcher's orange flame went on and one in a deepening, deadening silence, cutting and searing and boiling.

A low moan came over the group comm line. Nigel stood rigid, his chest locked, seeking a purchase on this.

We should have called it Pox, he thought. He looked around at the blind craters: blinkless sockets.

Above, a spot on the Watcher exploded in a shower of crimson and violet. Silent smoke and debris spread a gray fog. "Something in the gamma-ray beam touched off a delayed reaction," Nigel murmured.

—and he felt himself again, after so many years, living in a place absolutely blank and waiting for each moment to write upon it, time like water pouring through, the quality that the *Marginis* aliens had tried to bring to humans and that Nigel had gotten a fragment of—they had come bearing enlightenment, the one wedding to the world that the machines lacked, sought, and knew only as a sucking vacancy.

Nigel saw in an instant, as the flame from the Watcher cooled, that he had lost it years ago—become tied to events by ropes of care which sank him, tugging him below the waves—and now had found it again, falling down there in that great perpetual night beneath his feet, found it by finally letting go. He stood empty now, his past pilfered from him, free of the baggage of age and death and having to be Walmsley's Fool, free again to measure each moment by what it was, *le's all slide out of here one of these nights*

> *Casualties! God so many of them look at those indicators*
> *What happened what went wrong*

endless clashing cross talk, human or Skimmer or EM, all welling up from the depths, the rattling chatter of minds forever cut off from integrating with each other but seeking, talking, yammering hammering on

> *Total electrical failure onboard looks like*
> *Where're the Life Support Indices I get damn little*

He sucked in a gulp of air, and realized he had been holding his breath.

He thought of the beasts below. There was a natural alliance possible, they knew the piercing of mortality, felt the immemorial sweep carrying forward *and go for howling adventures amongst the Injuns.*

amid the rush and ruination

over in the territory but they were all out in the territory now, the country of the strange—but linked to Earth and Skimmer and the mute, huge, blood-rich things below by cycles of talk and sign and inevitable death

> *Watcher's damaged sir but still active I'm getting counts from it*
> *damn we didn't get it*
> *Weak signal from* Lancer, *nothing on shipcomm at all*
> *Lots of casualties, it got most of 'em in the hall*
> *Ted? What about Ted*
> *Nothing*

Ted had never been a captain and had never had a ship.

> *The drive's out! Blew it out! We got no way home—*

The voices rang on, thin with panic.

He had been here before, in the land of the seemingly defeated. But they had not.

He remembered the radio clamor that carried the EMs through their blasted red world; remembered the booming songs he had heard in the ocean below his feet; remembered the cramped message received from Earth only hours ago, about one man, Warren, and his scribbled words from the Skimmers; remembered how humanity seemed to him one unending sea of talk—unthinking, automatic, like breathing.

All the myriad voices, *and I says all right, that suits me.* He could hear them all—EM, Skimmer, human—from Pocks, no need to voyage back to Earth, and the incessant mad organic talk would go on.

Nikka whispered, "So many . . . gone . . ."

"Yes."

"Now we're . . . we're like the Skimmers. Far from home and no way back."

Carlos began to sob. He collapsed onto the gritty purple

ice. He pounded at it with a fist. "We're alone!" he cried out. "We'll die here."

There was a long silence on the stark bare plain. Then: "Probably," Nigel said. And for some reason, he smiled.

EIGHT

He waited for the Watcher to emerge.

Nigel's heart still tripped with skittering excitement. Something in him recalled days long ago, when he had boosted up above Earth's filmy air in transatmospheric craft. There had been the same steady tug of acceleration as the sluggish plane skated up into the thin reaches of atmosphere. Then the rocket part of the hybrid would thunder into life, ramming him at the hard blue-black sky. He had gone up that way on his first deep space mission, to the gas-cloaked asteroid Icarus. But that small world had turned out to be a ruined spaceship, and so had launched him on a long career of flinty risk, of unastronautlike disobedience.

Now his heart recalled those days. It thumped agreeable, happy to be riding a torch up into weightlessness. He felt the pressure of acceleration dwindle. He floated with the sudden buoyancy that for an aging man spelled returning youth. His idiot heart wanted conflict, exploration, zest, the fierce emptiness, and the black velocities.

He glided above Pocks, bound with parabolic grace toward the Watcher.

You all right? Nikka called on comm. He turned and waved at her. They rode on makeshift braces, twelve people crammed into the shuttle space meant for five. Carlos was wedged into a cranny halfway between them, his eyes studying the viewscreen anxiously.

Now was the moment. They had boosted off from Pocks and now would come within view of the Watcher within seconds. If it saw them, they were dead.

Nigel peered ahead. Using override command, he called for a closeup of the Watcher as soon as its outline nudged above the tightly curved horizon of Pocks. Then he searched for the missile they had launched against the Watcher. It was their only hope.

There. A dim blob of gray hung against the unyielding black of space.

If they had sent anything metallic against the Watcher it would have quickly sensed it. Metals were the language and substrate of machines. Their textures and electromagnetic glints were as natural to the Watcher as skin and smell were to humans.

And there lay a vulnerability. Or so Nigel guessed. And bet his life upon.

They had spent days gathering the odd, pale gray algae that lived in utter vacuum. Evolution's persistence had somehow forced waterborne life up, out of the fissures in the ice. There it had adapted to a cold, airless world. It had learned to suck sustenance from ice. The top surface of the lichen was a hard, silicon-rich armor against the piercing ultraviolet of Pocks's star, Ross. Its underside transferred Ross's heat, minutely melting the ice and brewing a slow-kindled photosynthesis. The slimy stiff took a tenacious grip on whatever it found.

It could survive for a while in vacuum without clinging to ice. It could withstand the boost into orbit.

Better, it had no metal innards, was transparent to radar.

So the small band of isolated humans had cobbled together some thrusters and made a kind of balloon filled with algae. They had to do this while the Watcher was on the other side of Pocks, so that their activity did not catch the Watcher's interest.

Nigel had spent long hours scooping up the muck. It clung to its forlorn ice and rock. He had grunted with effort, yanking it free. And been reminded of gardening in far off Pasadena, of the whole warm brush of life that perfumed Earth's air. The work had put him right again. His limp went away. His pulse steadied. He felt ten years younger—no, twenty.

Then they launched.

Slimeball's coming up on the Watcher, someone sent.

Nigel braced himself, then relaxed and felt foolish.

On the screen the gray dab coasted toward the curved horizon, a few minutes ahead of them in orbit. And in a moment, as if in answer to the life-filled balloon, the silhouette of the Watcher would poke above the smooth roundness of Pocks.

Seconds were crucial. The Watcher would see them soon. They were defenseless against it. But first...

Tock. Their charge detonated on the leading edge of the balloon. The sound of the balloon splitting came to Nigel over the comm. A faint, still sound.

Go, slimeball!

Ahead of them the gray mass spread outward. An organic shotgun blast into—

The roughened hull of the Watcher loomed above Pocks. Gray groping fingers reached out toward it... touched... and swarmed over the leading surface, smothering the Watcher in a sucking, hungry tide.

Made it!

Dead on!

Eat it, slimeball!

Nigel smiled. He felt strength flooding into him from some buried resource.

It is pleasant enough to be abstractly right. He had had quite enough of that during the years on *Lancer*, thank you. It was far finer to act and win. He had advanced the algae idea to the others, half expecting them to shrug it off. He was sure that despite all, they would still rather have had Ted leading them. Good old savvy Ted. But they were desperate. The notion had stuck.

Just as the algae itself now stuck and crawled and slithered over the eyes and ears of the Watcher. Eating at the delicate sensors. Blinding them.

So that as the humans in their frail craft glided close, no bolt answered them.

Nikka sent, *I'd hate to have some of that ice-eating fuzz on me*.

"All life's an ally," Nigel murmured. Not all life's responses were inappropriate.

He was already readying himself for the battle.

The Watcher was a labyrinth. It wasn't easy to get in, even with the external sensors covered by the thirsty algae. They had to burn it away from the hull to find a way in.

After they had forced an entrance at a bulky lock, the

party of twelve found themselves floating through winding spaghetti corridors. Some necked down to scarcely a hand's width. Others swelled until an elephant could have wallowed through.

A strange humming fled through the lacquered walls. Skittering tones shot through the electromagnetic spectrum. Nigel followed Carlos down a tube that seemed to drop away into infinity. Red panels spattered random glows on bulkheads and complex equipment. Nigel tried to see a pattern to the illumination, but most of it seemed to be wasted on bare, plain metal and stone.

The Watcher was half an asteroid, just as the ancient Icarus craft had been. Into the carbon and raw metal of a minor planet something had fitted elaborate technology. And whatever ran the Watcher lurked somewhere here. Nigel drew Nikka close and followed Carlos. The silence of the place hung like a warning.

They did not have to wait long.

Things long and snakelike scuttled from holes. Bigger machines, tubular and awkward, jetted down side corridors.

There were impossibly many of them. The humans fired at the approaching machines with a grim desperation. Laser bolts and e-beam cutters lanced forth.

They were almost surprised to see their shots fall sure and hard on the machines. Parts blew away. Electrical arcs flared blue-white, then died. The machines tumbled forward, out of control, and smashed into walls.

There are so many! Carlos called. He had a laser projector in each hand and two power packs strapped to him.

Turn sideways, so you'll be a smaller target, Nikka answered.

Down this way, Nigel called.

They fled the hordes. Nigel rebounded from three walls in quick succession and darted down a narrow tube. Weightlessness gave him back the deft reflexes he had too long missed. As soon as Carlos and Nikka had caught up to him he turned down a side passage. Two slender machines, glossy with glazed ceramic, came at him. He punctured each with a bolt of tightly bound electrons.

Carlos began, *What are—*

Nigel sent a signal back into the passage they had left.

Crimson light burst upon them. A crackling of electromagnetic death ricocheted through their comm lines.

"Implosion devices I cooked up," Nigel said. "Spits out electromagnetic noise. I've been dropping them every hundred meters."

Nikka said, *I see. It will burn out these creatures?*

"Hope so."

It did. The swarms who staffed the Watcher had once been made to defend it against intrusion. But time works its way even with stolid machines. Those which wore out were replaced, but each time the basic instructions were engraved into fresh silicon or ferrite memory, a small probability existed of a mistake. The weight of these errors accumulated, like autumn leaves blown into a chance pocket of a backyard, making improbably dense piles.

So the minions of the Watcher had devolved. They were slow, sluggish, and dumb in just the deadly crafts of battle that life could never afford to neglect. Humanity's penchant for warfare now paid off.

It took hours to work their way through the Watcher. Small machines launched themselves at any moving figure. Some exploded suicidally. Others jumped from ambush. Mines detonated, ripping at legs and lungs.

Nigel played cat and mouse down the dark corridors. He used stealth and tricks and, to his own vast surprise, stayed alive.

More men and women launched from the base on Pocks. They slipped aboard like pirates and joined battle.

In the end the machines retreated. Running, they were even less able. They were blown apart or fried with microwave bursts. Every machine fought to the very end. It was obvious that whatever had designed the Watcher had not thought deeply about the chance that it would be boarded. After all, the vast ship was intended to bombard planets, perhaps even kindle suns to a quickening fire. Hand-to-hand fighting was not its style.

Still, over half of the humanity that entered the Watcher left as corpses. Many more groaned and sweated with deep wounds. Others bit their lips at the pain and swore with ragged, angry pride. The last machines they found, cowering now in dim hiding holes, they smashed with great relish into small, twisted fragments.

*   *   *

Much of the Watcher labyrinth they would never understand. It was a forest of glazed surfaces, nested cables, inexplicable tangles of technology alien to all humanity's avenues of thought.

But they did understand the small ship they found.

It was buried near the center of the vast complex. It had a curious blue-white sheen, as if the metal were fired in some unimaginably hot furnace. Yet it opened easily at a touch of a control panel.

Carlos said, "It's not the same design as the rest of this Watcher. Looks finer, I'd say. The Watcher is solid but crude. This thing..."

Nigel nodded. The craft was a hundred meters long, but still seemed tiny and precious compared with the monstrous Watcher. And its arabesqued surfaces, its feeling of lightness and swift grace, conveyed its function.

"It's a fast ship," Nikka observed, passing a hand over circuits that leapt into amber life.

"I agree," Nigel said. "The Watcher's a blunderbuss. This is a stiletto. Or maybe an arrow."

Carlos touched the hard, dimly alabaster-lit surfaces of it. They stood in what had to be a control room. Screens blossomed into unintelligible displays when they approached. "Robots flew it, I guess," Carlos said. "Must've built the Watcher around this."

"Perhaps." Nigel calculated. They had already found evidence that the Watcher was very old, perhaps as much as a billion years. Radioactive isotope dating techniques were fairly accurate, even for such long durations. If this ship was older, it implied a machine civilization of vast age.

"I wonder if we could use it? Figure out the controls?" Nigel wondered.

Carlos brightened. "Sail it to Earth? My God! Yes!"

"Earth?" Nigel hadn't thought of that.

They were all intensely aware that they were like fishermen swallowed by a whale.

Somewhere in the huge Watcher was the guiding intelligence. Its minions destroyed, it had withdrawn. But it would not give up.

Eventually it would find a way to strike back at the

vermin which had invaded it. The Watcher had time. It could move subtly, deliberately.

The corridors took on a brooding, watchful cast.

No one went anywhere alone.

It took three days to find the core.

A crewman led Nigel to the small, compact room near the geometric center of the Watcher's huge mass.

"Looks like an art gallery, I'd wager," Nigel said after a long moment of surveying the curved walls.

It was a wilderness of tangled curves. Nothing sat flush with the walls. Small, ornate surfaces butted against each other, each rippling with embedded detail. Patterns swam, merged, oozed. A giddy sense of flight swept over Nigel as he watched the endless slide of structure move through the room.

"This is where it thinks?" he asked.

A crewman said at his elbow. "Maybe. Functions seem to lead into here."

"What's that?" A hole gaped, showing raw splintered struts.

"Defense mechanism. Killed Roselyn when she came in. I got it with a scrambler."

Nigel noticed that some of the panels were spattered with drying brown flecks. The Watcher was exacting a price for each of its secrets.

He sighed and pointed. "And that?"

The crewman shrugged.

A pattern came and went, as though it was a huge ocean wreck seen deep beneath the shifting waves.

It was first a line, then an ellipse, and now a circle. Its surface piped and worked with tenuous detail. Somehow the walls seemed to contain it as an embedded image, persistent against the passing shower of lesser facts. Nigel frowned. An unsettling, alien way to display information. If that's what it was.

Again came the sequence. Line, oval, circle, oval, line. Then it struck him. "It's the galaxy."

"What?" Nikka had just arrived. "What *is* all this?"

"Watch." He pointed. "See the broad line of tiny lights? That's the galaxy as it looks from the side. That's the way we see it from Earth, a plane seen edge-on. Now watch." His lined hands carved the air.

The line thickened, winking with a cascade of lights. It swelled into an oval as other data sped across the image, like clouds rushing over the face of a slumbering continent. Fires lit in the oval. Traceries shot through it. It grew into a circle. Strands within it flexed and spilled with light.

Nigel said, "Catch the spiral arms? There. Faint outlines against those bright points."

"Well . . ." she looked doubtful. "Maybe."

"See those blue points?" Dabs of blue light stood out against the other tiny glows. Evidently they were all stars. But . . . "I wonder what those stand for?"

"Other Watchers?" Nikka asked.

"Could be. But think. This is a map of the whole damn galaxy." He said it quietly but it had an effect on the others now crowding into the cramped room. "Seen from every angle. Which means somebody—some*thing*—has done that. Sailed far up above the whole disk and looked down on it. Charted the inlets of gas and dust and old dead suns. Seen it all."

In the silence of the strange room they watched the galaxy spin. It moved with stately slowness. Grave and ghostly movements changed it. Sparks came and vanished. Dim gray presences passed across its face. Lingered. Were gone.

Then a specialist Nigel knew slightly, a wiry astronomer, said, "I think I recognize some of the pattern."

"Where?" Nigel asked.

"See that quadrant? I think it's ours."

A segment of the galaxy did seem to Nigel, now that the astronomer pointed it out, slightly more crowded and luminous than the rest. He frowned as thin mists seemed to spill liquidly through the pie-slice segment. "You recognize stars?"

"In a way," the astronomer said with a certain prim precision. "Not optical stars, no. Pulsars."

"Where?"

"See the deep blue ones?"

"Yes, I was wondering—"

"They're where pulsars should be."

Nigel remembered vaguely that rapidly spinning neutron stars accounted for the pulsar phenomenon. As the compacted cores of these dense stars spun, they released streams of plasma. These luminous swarms flapped like flags as they left the star. They emitted gouts of radio noise. As a star spun, it directed these beams of radio emission outward, like a lighthouse sweeping its lamp across a distant ship. When the beam chanced to intersect the Earth, astronomers saw it, measured its frequency of sweep.

The astronomer went on, "They're so prominent in this map. Far more luminous than they are in reality."

"Perhaps they are important?" Nikka asked.

"Umm." The astronomer frowned. His face was lined with fatigue but the fascination of this place washed away the past. Even amid tragedy, curiosity was an itch that needed scratching. "Could be. As navigation beacons, maybe?"

Nigel thought of his lighthouse analogy. Beeping signals across the blind abyss?

But there were easier ways to find your way among the stars. He pointed again. "Why is there that big blue patch at the center, then?"

The astronomer looked more puzzled. "There aren't any pulsars at the galactic center."

Nikka asked, "What is there? Just stars?"

"Well, it's got a lot of gas, turbulent motions, maybe a black hole. It's the most active region of the whole galaxy, sure, but..."

Nikka asked, "Could it be that the galactic center and pulsars have something in common?"

The astronomer pursed his lips, as if he disliked making such leaps. "Well... there's a lot of plasma."

Nigel asked slowly, "What kind?"

"All kinds," the astronomer said with a touch of condescension. "Hot gas made still hotter. Until the electrons separate from the ions and the whole system becomes electrically active."

Nigel shook his head, not knowing himself where he was headed. You just skated, and went where the ice took you. "Not around pulsars. I remember that much."

The astronomer blinked. In his concentration the weight of the last few days slipped from him and his face smoothed. "Oh. Oh, you're right. Pulsars put out *really* relativistic plasma. The stuff comes whipping off the neutron star surface close to the speed of light."

Nigel wasn't in the mood for a lecture. Still, something tugged at him. "What kind of plasma?"

"There aren't any heavy ions, no protons to speak of. It's all electrons and their antiparticles."

"Positrons," Nigel said.

"Right, positrons. The electrons interact with the positrons in some fashion and make the radio emission. We—"

"And at galactic center?" Nigel persisted.

The astronomer blinked. "Well, yeah . . . There was report a while back. . . . A detection of positrons at the galactic center." His voice caught and then a wondering enthusiasm crept into it. Nigel watched the man's face fill with a wan yet growing delight. "Positrons. If they slow down, meet electrons, the two annihilate. Give off gamma rays. A gamma-ray telescope Earthside, Jacobson's group I think it was, saw the annihilation line."

Nigel felt a slow, gathering certainty. "Those blue dots . . ."

Nikka said softly, "The Watcher keeps track of where positrons appeared naturally in the galaxy."

The fact sank into them. The Watcher's main job was to stamp out organic life, that was clear. But something had told the ancient craft to notice pulsars and the positron plasmas they spewed out into the galaxy. A phenomenon that occurred also at galactic center—but on a hugely larger scale, apparently, judging by the large blue zone at the very hub of the rotating swirl.

The astronomer said, puzzled, "But there can't be so many pulsars at the center of the galaxy . . ."

"Still, there is that blue globe," Nigel said.

Something was happening at galactic center. Something important.

And the machine civilization thought it was vital, perhaps as important as the obliteration of the organic yeast they so hated.

Nigel said softly, with a gathering certainty, "If we are ever to deal with these things, with their Watchers and Snarks and the whole damn mechanical zoo of them . . . we've got to confront them."

Nikka saw what he meant. "But—Earth! We can return now. There is so much to be done."

He shook his head. Looking around the room, with its

myriad sliding sheets of alien thought and strange design, he watched the luminescence play upon the haggard faces.

Faces pursued by a voracious and unyielding intelligence. Faces lined and worn by the silent anxiety they all felt, just being here.

The Watcher would give them no rest. They had to get out. Move on.

But not simply run back home. Earth was no haven. There was no blithe sanctuary now. Not anywhere in the whole swarming galaxy.

"No. We've got the means. That little ship we found. It must be a fast craft. I'll bet it came here and supervised the building of this Watcher."

"Nigel . . ." Nikka began a protest, then stopped.

"That ship still works. It could go back. Back where it came from. Where we must go."

They began to murmur and protest.

A small band of humans, their incessant crosstalk rebounding from the alien surfaces. Nigel smiled.

Their dreams lay Earthward. They would have to be convinced.

le's all slide out of here one of these nights

But he knew he could convince them. The rest of humanity was reeling under war and a vast, brute yoke. If this small knot did not seize this opportunity, humanity would dwell forever in the dimness of ignorance. Victims. Prey.

and go for howling adventures amongst the Injuns

There was no turning back now. Maybe there never had been any possibility of turning away from what lay out here. He had felt it for a long time, since the first vague pricklings of understanding at the sunny, long lost Jet Propulsion Laboratory. Odd, he felt almost nostalgic for the place now.

Now that he knew he would certainly never see it again.

For there was always the opening-out, and it would always win.

over in the territory

He pointed at the somber, revolving disk of countless fevered stars. Unfathomable messages glided across quilted surfaces.

and I says all right, that suits me

"Let's go," he said, and pointed at the galactic center.

ABOUT THE AUTHOR

Gregory Benford is the author of several acclaimed novels, including *Heart of the Comet* (with David Brin), *In the Ocean of Night*, *Against Infinity*, *Artifact*, and *Timescape*, which won the Nebula Award, the British Science Fiction Award, the John W. Campbell Memorial Award, and the Australian Ditmar Award. Dr. Benford, a Woodrow Wilson Fellow, is a professor of physics at the University of California, Irvine. He and his wife live in Laguna Beach. He is presently at work on a new novel, which Bantam Spectra will publish in the fall.

GREGORY BENFORD

GREAT SKY RIVER

Something was after them.

The Family had just come straggling over a razor-backed ridge, beneath a pale jade sky. Killeen's shocks wheezed as his steady lope ate up the downgrade.

The red soil was deeply wrinkled and gullied. Cross-hatching was still sharp in the tractor-tread prints that cut the parched clay. There had been so little rain the prints could well be a century old.

A black-ribbed factory complex sprawled at the base of the slope. Killeen flew over the polished ebony domes, sending navvys scuttling away from his shadow, clacking their rude dumb irritation.

Killeen hardly saw them. He was watching spiky telltales strobe-highlighted on his right retina.

There: a quick jitter of green, pretty far back.

It came and went, but always in a new place.

There, again. Far behind.

Not directly following them, either. Not a typical Marauder maneuver. Smart.

He blinked, got the alternative display. The Family was a ragged spread of blue dabs on his topo map. He was pleased to see they kept a pretty fair lopsided triangle. Cermo-the-Slow was dragging ass behind, as always.

Killeen saw himself, an amber winking dot at the apex. Point man. Target.

He grimaced. This was his first time ever as point, and here came some damn puzzle. He'd tried to beg off when Cap'n Fanny ordered him to the front. There were others better experienced—Ledroff, Jocelyn, Cermo. He'd much rather have stayed back. Fanny kept giving him extra jobs like this, and while he'd do whatever she said without protest, this had made him jittery from the start.

Fanny knew more than anybody, could see through Marauder tricks. She should be up here. But she kept pushing him.

Now this. He dropped from the air, eyes slitted.

Killeen came down on a pocked polyalum slab, the old kind that mechs had used for some long-forgotten purpose. Packing fluff blew in the warm wind, making dirty gray drifts against his cushioned crustcarbon boots. Mechmess littered the ground, so common he did not notice it.

"Got a pointer behind," Killeen sent to Fanny.

—Snout?— she answered.

"Nossir noway," Killeen answered quickly to cover his nerves. "Think I'd sing out if was that same old Snout, been tagging us for days?"

—What is, then?—

"Dunno. Looks big, then small."

Killeen did not understand how his retinal area scan worked, had only a vague idea about radar pulses. He did know things weren't supposed to look large on one pass and small the next, though. Habit told you more than analysis.

—'Quipment's bust?—

"I dunno. Flashes okay," Killeen said reluctantly. Was Fanny joshing him? He didn't know which he liked less, something that could come up on them this way, or his gear gone flatline on him.

Fanny sighed. She was a nearly invisible speck to his right rear, wiry and quick. Killeen could hear her clicking her teeth together, trying to decide, the way she always did.

"Whatsay?" he prodded impatiently. It was up to her. She was Cap'n of the Family and had a long lifetime rich in story and experience, the kind of gut savvy that meant more in dealing with Marauder mechs than anything else.

She had been Cap'n for all the years that Family Bishop had been on the move. She knew the crafts of flight and pursuit, of foraging and stealing, of deception and attack. And through terrible years she had held the Family together.

—Comes closer?—

"Looks. Dodging fast."

Fanny clicked her teeth again. Killeen could see in his mind's eye her wise old eyes crinkling as she judged their positions. Her warm presence suffused his sensorium, bringing a sure, steady calm. She had been Cap'n so long and so well, Killeen could not conceive how the Family had done without her before, when they lived in the Citadel.

—We make the fist, then,—she said with finality.

Killeen was relieved. "Goodsay."

—Sound the call.—

He blinked. "Won't you?"

—You're point. Act like one.—

"But you know more about . . ." Killeen hesitated. He did not like admitting to his own doubts, not with Ledroff and others probably listening in. He liked even less the prospect of leading an attack.

"Look, Ledroff has done this before. Jocelyn, too. I'll drop back and—"

—No. *You.*—

"But I don't—"

—Naysay!— She was abrupt, biting. —Call!—

Killeen wet his lips and steadied himself. He sent over general comm, —Heysay lookleft! Fist!—

Most of the Family were over the ragged ridgeline now. That would provide some shelter from whatever was coming from behind. He watched as they came spilling down the ruddy, gorge-pocked hillsides. They were a slow tumbling fluid, their individual tinny acknowledgments coming as thin insect cries.

Killeen did not consider for a moment that the voices he heard were carried on radio waves, for he had lived all his life in a sensory bath provided by the linking of acoustic and electromagnetic signals. The distinction between them would have demanded more science than he had ever mastered, ever would master. Instead he heard the gathering peppery voices as scattershot ringings, carrying long and remote across the hot still silence of dusty late afternoon. Though each Family member glided in beautiful long arcs, the Family itself seemed to Killeen to hang suspended in the middle distance, so gradual was its progress, like thick dark down-swarming molasses. Gravid and slow they came, this worn and perhaps only remaining remnant of humanity: eagering, homing, tribing.

Killeen caught fragments of talk from Ledroff. —Why'd Cap'n put *him* . . . Damfino why he's up there . . .—

"Cut the chatter!" Killeen called.

—Couldn't find his ass w'both hands . . .—

"I said *quiet!*" he whispered fiercely.

Killeen had heard Ledroff's muttered jibes through the comm before. Until now he had ignored them. No need to provoke a faceoff with the big, self-assured man. But this time Killeen couldn't let it pass. Not when it endangered them.

—Seems me he's jumpin' at spooks,— Ledroff got in, then fell silent.

Killeen wished Cap'n Fanny had come on full comm line and cut off Ledroff. A mere disapproving click of her tongue would have shut him up.

The Family skimmed low, using savvy earned through hard years. Wheeling left, they seeped down among the knobby, domed buildings of the manufacturing complex.

Factory mechs wrenched to a stop as the Family skipped light and fast through their workyards. Then the blocky, awkward-looking machines hunkered down, withdrawing their extensors into marred aluminum shells. Such mechs had no other defense mechanisms, so the Family gave the slope-nosed, turtlelike forms no notice.

Still, the humans had to be fast. They knew if they stayed here long these slow-thinking drudges would send out a call. Lancers would come. Or worse.

Killeen pondered for a moment the possibility that the thing trailing them was a lone Lancer, summoned by a minor pillage the Family had made a few days before. He checked the faint, flickering tracers behind.

No, nothing like a Lancer. Something smaller, certainly. It gave off hardly any image at all. Still . . .

"Yea!" he called. Tapping his right temple twice with a forefinger, he sent his scan topo map to the entire Family. "We're bunching up!"

With muttered irritation they spread out, dissolving their moving beeswarm triangle. They formed the traditional concentric rings, ragged because the Family numbered a mere 278 now. And some of them were achingly slow—gimpy, or old, or wounded from past scrapes and fights and blunders.

Fanny saw the problem and called, —Show the wind our heels!—

The old saying worked. They began to run faster now, a keen unspoken fear at their backs.

He sent the latest topo to Fanny. It showed a muddle of bluewhite tracers behind them.

Fanny sent, —Where's it?—

Killeen admitted, "Dunno. Looks to be some kinda screen."

—Deliberate confusion?—

"Don't think so. But . . ."

—Situation like this, your topo's no good for figurin' size. Go by speed. No 'facturing mech moves quick as a Marauder.—

"This one's slow, then fast."

—Must be a Marauder.—

"Think we should stand 'n' wait for it?"

He felt her assessing regard like a cool wedge in his sensorium.

—What *you* think?—

"Well . . . it might just be reconning us."

—Could be.—

She was giving nothing away. "So'd be best if we keep on, make like we don't see it."

—Long's we can keep track of it, sure.—

Killeen wondered what Fanny meant by that, but he didn't want to ask, not with Ledroff listening. He said guardedly, "It keeps jumpin' round."

—Might be some new mechtech.—

So? he thought. *How do we respond?* He kept his voice flat and assured, though, as he said, "I figure we don't give away that we see it. If it's just checkin' its 'quipment, it'll go away."

—And come back when we're sleepin',— she said flatly.

"So? Our watch'll pick it up. But if we take a shot at it now, when we can't see it so good, maybe it gets away. Next time it comes back with better mechtech. So then we don't pick it up and it skrags us."

Fanny didn't answer for a long moment and Killeen wondered if he had made a fool of himself. She had coached him in the crafts and he always felt inadequate compared with her sure, almost casual grasp of Family lore. She could be a stern Cap'n, a shrewd tactician, firm and fast. And when they had fought or fled, and again gathered around nightfires to tell their tales, she could be warm and grandmotherly. Killeen would do anything to avoid disappointing her. But he had to know *what* to do, and she was giving him no easy answers.

—Yeasay. That's best, long as this's a reg'lar Marauder.—

Killeen felt a burst of pride at her approval. But a note of concern in her voice made him ask, "What if it's not?"

—Then we run. Hard.—

They were out of the foothills now. The Family sprinted across eroded flatlands.

Fanny asked as she panted, —See it yet?—

"Naysay."

—Should've climbed the ridge by now. Don't like this.—

"Think maybe a trap?" Killeen cast about for possibilities as he searched his topo display. Again he wished Jocelyn or even goddamn Ledroff had this job. If an attack came he wanted to be near his son. He scanned ahead and found Toby in the middle of the moving Family formation.

Fanny dropped back, scanning the ridgeline.

Killeen searched again for the elusive pursuer. The topo danced in his eye, speeding ribbons of light.

More cloudy tracers.

To the right came a dim speckling of pale blue.

Killeen realized too late that it would have been better to hold the ridgeline. They were exposed and had lost the enemy. He grunted in frustration and sped forward.

They were partway down the broad valley when he looked right and saw first the overlay winking green and then the far rocky scarp. It was fresh rock, cleaved by some mining mech, its amber faces gouged and grooved.

But the clear bare cut hadn't been there moments before. Killeen was sure of that.

"Bear on my arrow!" he shouted to the whole Family. He cut toward a low hill. "Fanny, you'd—"

Killeen heard a sharp crackling.

He saw Fanny fall. She gave a cry of surprise. Then her voice sharpened, riding an outrushing gasp of startled pain.

He turned and fired at the distant carved hills, where stood half-finished blocks of rhomboid stone.

Back came an answering echo of snapping, crisp circuit death.

A hit. Probably not enough to drop the thing dead, but it would buy some seconds.

He shouted, "Max it!"

With Fanny down, he'd have to get the Family away, fast. Killeen blinked, saw the blue dots of the Family swerve toward broken terrain that provided some shelter. Good.

Killeen dropped to the ground. "Fanny! How you?"

—I . . . auhhhh . . . can't . . .—

"This thing—what *is* it?"

—I . . . haven't seen . . . years . . .—

"What'll we *do*?"

Ledroff tried to cut in on the narrow-cone comm line. Killeen swore and blanked him out.

—Don't . . . believe . . . what you . . . see . . .—

"What's—"

She coughed. Her line went silent.

Fanny knew more than anybody in the Family about the rare, deadly mechs. She'd fought them a long time, back before Killeen was born. But Killeen could tell from her sluggish voice that this thing had clipped her solid, blown some nerves maybe.

No help from the fine, wise old woman, then.

Killeen looked back at the warped, worked shapes of stone on the far hillside. There were contorted planes, surfaces carved for purposes incomprehensible to humans. He thought of them not at all, had long ago learned to look past that which no man could riddle out. Instead he searched for the freshness of the cleavecuts, the telltale signs of autochisel.

Which weren't there.

"Jocelyn!"

The scraped stone surfaces thinned. Shimmered. Killeen had the dizzying sensation of seeing through the naked rock into a suddenly materializing city of ramparts and solid granite walls. It hummed with red energy, swelled as he watched.

"Damnall what's that," he muttered to himself.

The city shimmered, crystal and remote. Plain rock melted to glassy finery.

And then back again to chipped stone.

Jocelyn called, disbelieving, —The whole hillside?—

Killeen grunted. "Mirage that size takes a big mech."

—Or new kind,— Jocelyn said.

She came in from his right, bent low and running with compressors. Behind them the Family fled full bore, their pantings and gaspings coming to Killeen in proportion to their distance. They were a constant background chorus, as though they all watched him, as though all the Family was both running for safety and yet still here, witness to this latest infinitesimal addition to the long losing struggle with the machines. He felt them around him like a silent jury.

Jocelyn called, —You hit somethin'?—

Killeen ducked behind an outcropping of ancient, tortured girders. Their thick spans were blighted with scabs of burnt-red rust. "Think so."

—Solid?—

"Naysay. Sounded like hitting a mech circuit, is all."

—It's still there, then. Hiding.—

No chance to try for Fanny yet. He kept a safe distance from her crumpled form, sure she would by now be a well-found target point.

—I can smell it.— Jocelyn's alto voice, normally so cottonsoft, was stretched thin and high.

He could, too, now that he'd calmed a fraction. A heavy, oily flavor. His inbuilt detectors gave him the smell, rather than encoded parameters; humans remembered scents better than data. But he could not recognize the close, thick flavor. He was sure he had never met it before.

A fevered hollow *whuuung* twisted the air. It came to Killeen as a sound beyond anything ear could capture, a blend of infra-acoustic rumble at his feet and electromagnetic screech, ascending to frequencies high and thin in the roiling breeze.

"It's throwing us blocks," he said. "Musta used a combination on Fanny, but it don' work on us."

—She got old 'quipment,— Jocelyn said.

"It's prob'ly sweeping keys right now," Killeen said, breathing hard and wanting something to do, anything.

—Looking for ours.—

"Yeasay, yeasay," Killeen muttered. He tried to remember. There had been some mech who'd done that, years back. It broadcast something that got into your *self*, worked right on the way you saw. It could make you believe you were looking at the landscape when in fact the picture was edited, leaving out the—

"Mantis," he said suddenly. "Mantis, Fanny called it. She'd seen it a couple times."

The Mantis projected illusions better than any mech ever had. It could call up past pictures and push them into your head so quickly you didn't know what was real. And behind the picture was the Mantis, getting closer, trying to breach you.

—Figure to run?— Jocelyn called. She was a distant speck and already backing off, ready to go.

"Not with a big green spot on my back."

Killeen laughed crazily, which for this instant was easier than thinking, and he had learned to take these things by the instant. Any other thinking was just worry and that slowed you when you needed to be fast.

His problem was the topo and mapping gear, which he alone carried in the Family. He backpacked his on his lower spine.

Legend had it that the topo man was the first to fry. The story was that hunter mechs—Lancers, Stalkers, Rattlers—saw the gear as a bright green dot and homed in on it. They could bounce their low hooting voices off the stuff, get some kind of directional sense from that. And then hoot louder, sending something that invaded the topo man's gear and then slithered into his head.

—What do then?—

"Got to shoot."

He heard Jocelyn's grudging grunt. She didn't like that. For that matter, he didn't either. If this Mantis thing was half as good as Fanny'd said, it could trace your shot and find you before your defenses went up.

But if they didn't kill the Mantis now, it would track them. Hide behind its mirages at night. It could walk up and pry them apart with its own cutters, before they even laid eyes on it.

"Wait. Just 'membered something Fanny said."

—Better 'member fast.—

Fanny's way of teaching was to tell stories. She'd said something about the Calamity, about how in the midst of humanity's worst battle some Bishops had found a way to penetrate the mirages.

He tapped his teeth together carefully, experimentally— one long, one short. That set his vision so the reds came up strong. Blues washed away, leaving a glowing, rumpled land seething into liquid fire. The sky was a blank nothing. Across the far hillside swept crimson tides of temperature as his eyes slid down the spectrum.

—Fanny's hurt. Think we should try for her?—

"Quiet!"

He shook his head violently, staring straight ahead, keeping his eyes fixed on one place. What had Fanny said . . . ? Go to fastflick red, watch out of the corners of your eyes.

Something wavered. Among the sculpted sheets of win- try-gray stone stood something gangly, curved, arabesqued with traceries of luminous worms. The image merged with the rock and then swam up out of it, coming visible only if Killeen jerked his head to the side fast.

The illusion corrected quickly but not perfectly, and for fractions of a second he could see the thing of tubular legs, cowled head, a long knobby body prickly with antennae.

—Gettin' much?—

"Lessee, I—"

Something punched a hole in his eye and went in.

He rolled backward, blinking, trying to feel-follow the ricochet of howling heat that ran in fast jabbing forks through his body.

Molten agony flooded his neural self. It swarmed, spilling and rampaging.

He felt/saw old, remembered faces, pale and wisp-thin. They shot toward him and then away, as though a giant hand were riffling through a deck of cards so that each face loomed sharp and full for only an instant. And with each slipping-by memory there came a flash of chrome-bright hurt.

The Mantis was fishing in his past. Searching, recording. Killeen yelled with rage.

He fought against a grasping touch.

"I—it got in—" and then he felt the pain-darter clasped by a cool quickness in his right leg. He sensed the roving heat-thing sputtering, dying. It was swallowed by some deeply buried, spider-fine trap, fashioned by minds long lost.

Killeen did not consider what had saved him. He understood his own body no more than he understood the mechs. He simply sprang up again, finding himself at the bottom of a crumbling sandy slope which his spasms had taken him down. In his sensorium strobed the afterimage of the pain-darter.

And his directional finder had followed the telltale pulses to their source.

"Jocelyn! I can get a fix," he called.

—Damnfast it, then.—

"It's moving!"

In the glowering ruby twilight the Mantis jerked and clambered toward Fanny's sprawled body. Killeen heard a low bass sawing sound that raised the hair on the back of his neck.

Like yellowed teeth sawing through bone. If it got close to Fanny—

Killeen sighted on the flickering image of the moving Mantis while his left index finger pressed a spot in his chest. In his left eye a sharp purple circle grew, surrounding the volume where the Mantis image oozed in and out. He tapped his right temple and Jocelyn got the fix.

—Wanna frizz it?— she called. She was a small dot across the valley. They would get good triangulation on the Mantis.

"Naysay. Let's blow the bastard."

—Ayesay. Go!—

He fired. Sharp claps in the stillness.

The two old-style charges smacked the mech fore and aft. Legs blew away. Antennae slammed to the ground.

Killeen could see the Mantis's blue-green electric life droop and wink out, all its internals dying as the mainmind tried to stay alive by sacrificing them. But mechanical damage you couldn't fix with a quick reflowing of 'tricity, he remembered grimly.

The mechs were often most vulnerable that way. Killeen liked seeing them blown to pieces, gratifyingly obvious. Which was the real reason he used charges when he could.

He bounded up, running full tilt toward the still-slow-dissolving Mantis. Popping ball-joints let the legs go. Its trunk hit the ground rolling. The mainmind would be in there, trying to save itself.

Killeen approached gingerly, across sandy ground littered with mechwaste jumble. He kicked aside small machine parts, his eyes never leaving the Mantis. Jocelyn came pounding in from the other side.

"Booby trap, could be," he said.

"Dunno. Never saw anythin' this big."

"I'll yeasay that," Killeen murmured, impressed.

All splayed out, the Mantis was longer than ten humans laid end to end. For him the heft and size of things went deadsmooth direct into him. Without thought he sensed whether something weighed too much to carry a day's march, or if it was within range of a given weapon.

Numbers flitted in his left eye, giving the Mantis dimensions and mass. He could not read these ancient squiggles of his ancestors, scarcely registered them. He didn't need to. His inner, deep-bedded chips and subsystems processed all this into direct senses. They came as naturally and unremarkably as did the brush of the warm wind now curling his faded black hair, the low electromagnetic groans of the Mantis dying, the dim irk that told him to pee soon.

"Look," Jocelyn said. This close he heard her through acoustics, her voice a touch jittery now from the exertion and afterfear. "Mainmind's in there." She pointed.

A coppery cowling was trying to dig its way into the soil, and making fast work of it, too. Jocelyn stepped closer and aimed a scrambler at it.

"Use a thumper," Killeen said.

She took out a disc-loaded tube and primed it. The disc went *chunk* as she fired it into the burnished, rivet-ribbed cowling. The carapace rocked from the impact. Steel-blue borers on its underside whined into silence.

"Good," Killeen said. Nearby, two navvys scuttled away. Both had crosshatched patterns on their side panels. He had never seen navvys traveling with a high-order mech. "Hit those two," he said, raising his gun.

"Just navvys—forget 'em."

"Yeasay." He ran to Fanny. He had been following Fanny's long-established rules—secure the mainmind first, then look to the hurt. But as he loped toward the still, sprawled form his heart sank and he regretted losing even a moment.

Fanny lay tangled, head lolling. Her leathery mouth hung awry, showing yellowed gums and teeth sharpened by long hours of filing. Her lined face stared blankly at the sky and her eyes were a bright, glassy white.

"No!" He couldn't move. Beside him, Jocelyn knelt and pressed her palms against Fanny's upper neck.

Killeen could see there was no tremor. He felt an awful, draining emptiness seep into him. He said slowly, "It . . . blitzed her."

"No! That fast?" Jocelyn stared up at him, eyes fevered and wide, wanting him to deny what she could see.

"Mantis . . ." The realization squeezed his throat. "It's damn quick."

"You hit it, though," Jocelyn said.

"Luck. Just luck."

"We've . . . never . . ."

"This one's got some new tricks."

Jocelyn's voice was watery, plaintive. "But Fanny! She could protect herself better'n anybody!"

"Yeasay. Yeasay."

"She knew *every*thing."

"Not this."

In Fanny's half-closed, fear-racked eyes Killeen saw signs which the Family had been spared for months. Around her eyes oozed pale gray pus. A bloodshot bubble formed in the pus as he watched. The bubble popped and let forth a rancid gas.

The Mantis had somehow interrogated Fanny's nerves, her body, her very self—all in moments. Mechs could never before do that swiftly, from a distance. Until now, a Marauder mech had to capture a human for at least several uninterrupted minutes.

That had been a small advantage humanity had over the roving, predator mechs, and if this Mantis was a sign, that thin edge was now lost.

Killeen bent to see. Jocelyn peeled back the hardwebbed

rubbery skinsuit. Fanny's flesh looked as though thousands of tiny needles had poked through it, from inside. Small splotches of blueblack blood had already dried just under the skin.

The Mantis had invaded her, read all. In a single scratching instant it had peeled back the intertwined neuronets that were Fanny and had learned the story of her, the tale each human embeds within herself. The ways she had taken pleasure. How she had felt the sharp stab of pain. When and why she had weathered the myriad defeats that were backrolled behind her, a long undeviating succession of dark and light and swarming dark again, through which she had advanced with stolid and unyielding pace, her steady path cut through the mosaic of worlds and hopes and incessant war.

The Marauder-class mechs sometimes wanted that: not metals or volatiles or supplies of any sort. Nor even the tiny chips of brimming 'lectric craft which mere men often sought and stole from lesser mechs, the navvys and luggos and pickers.

The suredeath. Marauders wanted information, data, the very self. And in questioning each small corner of Fanny the Mantis had sucked and gnawed and erased everything that had made her Fanny.

Killeen cried in confused rage. He sprinted back to the fragmented Mantis and yanked free a leg strut.

Chest heaving, he slammed the arm-length strut into the wreckage, sending parts flying. Ledroff tried to call to him and he bellowed something and then shut down his comm line entirely.

He did not know how long the smashing and shouting lasted. It filled him and then finally emptied him in the same porportion, expending his rage into the limitless air.

When he was done he walked back to Fanny and raised the strut in mute, defeated salute.

This was the worst kind of death. It took from you more than your present life, far more—it stole also the past of once-felt glory and fleeting verve. It drowned life in the choking black syrup of the mechmind. It laid waste by absorbing and denying, leaving no sign that the gone had ever truly been.

Once so chewed and devoured, the mind could never be rescued by the workings of men. If the Mantis had merely killed her, the Family could probably have salvaged some fraction of the true Fanny. From the cooling brain they could have extracted her knowledge, tinted with her personality. She would have been stored in the mind of a Family member, become an Aspect.

The Mantis had left not even that.

The suredeath. Tonight, in the final laying-low of Fanny, there would be no truth to extract from the limp hollowed body which Killeen saw so forlorn and crumpled before him. The Family could carry none of her forward and so it was almost as though she had never walked the unending march that was humanity's lot.

Killeen began to cry without knowing it. He had left the valley with the Family before he noticed the slowburning ache he carried. Only then did he see that this was a way that Fanny still lived, but all the same it was no comfort.

Buy Great Sky River, *on sale in November wherever Bantam Spectra Books are sold.*

**BANTAM
SHOP·AT·HOME
C·A·T·A·L·O·G**

Special Offer
Buy a Bantam Book
for only 50¢.

Now you can have Bantam's catalog filled with hundreds of titles plus take advantage of our unique and exciting bonus book offer. A special offer which gives you the opportunity to purchase a Bantam book for only 50¢. Here's how!

By ordering any five books at the regular price per order, you can also choose any other single book listed (up to a $4.95 value) for just 50¢. Some restrictions do apply, but for further details why not send for Bantam's catalog of titles today!

Just send us your name and address and we will send you a catalog!